The Café
at
Marigold
Marina

BOOKS BY TILLY TENNANT

The Café at Marigold Marina

TILLY TENNANT

Bookouture

Published by Bookouture in 2022

An imprint of Storyfire Ltd.
Carmelite House
50 Victoria Embankment
London EC4Y 0DZ

www.bookouture.com

ISBN: 978-1-80314-249-4
eBook ISBN: 978-1-80314-250-0

CHAPTER ONE

She'd been dreaming of Fergus. She couldn't recall a single moment of it, even though she'd only just woken, but it had to have been about him because her face was wet with tears.

Rolling over, she smoothed her hand over the cold, crisp cotton of the empty pillow at the other side of the bed, then started to cry once more. Was it even worth trying to sleep again? She never usually managed when she'd woken from a dream about him, so why bother now?

Instead, Rosie went to the window. Beneath her feet were thin rugs, just about covering bare, rough floorboards. She shivered, wrapping the blanket she'd taken from the bed around her. Spring was in evidence during the day, when there was blossom on the trees and fresh, citrus sunshine, but at night it was still freezing.

Even the gloom of her bedroom afforded Rosie enough of a view to remind her that this place was a dump. What was she doing here? This had been Fergus's dream, not hers, and yet she'd carried the plan through without him, enduring all manner of hardships to please a man who'd never get to see the finished result – if it was ever finished of course, and that wasn't a totally questionable prospect. For three months she'd been battling to get the cafe ready, and the flat above it habitable, and it felt as if she'd barely scratched the surface. The cafe, at a pinch, would be ready by summer – the flat seemed like it would be a hovel forever.

The plaster on the walls was bare – she and Fergus had steamed off the tattered old wallpaper, as was his way: doing everything in the wrong order as a result of his enthusiasm for all new projects, they'd realised afterwards that there were far more pressing matters than choosing new paper for the bedroom. They had second-hand rugs spread around and furniture that had once belonged to the previous owner, who'd died a good year before Rosie and Fergus had taken the cafe on. Fergus had said it made sense to sell all the lovely furniture they'd had in their previous home back in Tyneside where she'd left parents she loved dearly and so many happy memories of growing up, so they could put the profits into the business for extra capital, and why wouldn't they be happy enough using the old stuff in situ?

'It's shabby chic,' Fergus had said, folding Rosie into his arms as she'd stared around the flat, shell-shocked by the reality of what she was going to have to live with.

'Shabby chic? Most of this stuff is rotten! Why the hell did I let you talk me into selling all our stuff?'

'Look...' Fergus went over to slap a hand on the old teak wardrobe. 'Solid as the day it was built; nothing to worry about. And isn't it lovely? This could be on *Antiques Roadshow* and the valuer would be telling some old dear it was worth enough for her to go on a Caribbean cruise with the profits.'

'Hmm...' Rosie couldn't deny it *was* quite lovely... well, perhaps it would be once they'd scraped the mould from its surface. 'If it's worth that much, perhaps *we* ought to sell it and go on a Caribbean cruise.'

Fergus had grinned. 'You don't mean that.'

'Don't I?'

'You'd hate cruising.'

'How do you know?'

Crossing the room to take her in his arms again, he kissed her lightly. 'Because I know you. You're at sixes and sevens now, because this place is all new and unfamiliar, but in time it will feel like home, I promise.'

'That's the problem – I always fall for your promises...'

With another grin – a wickedly mischievous one this time – he'd lifted her into his arms and thrown her onto the bed.

'Ugh! There are no sheets on this yet!' Rosie had squealed, but she'd been laughing all the same. 'God knows what's on this mattress!'

'I know exactly what's on this mattress,' Fergus replied slyly, unbuttoning his shirt. 'The girl I'm about to shag senseless.'

'Fergus, no!' Rosie giggled, and as Fergus had jumped on top of her, the bed had collapsed with a dull *thunk*.

'Oh my God!' Rosie cried. 'Now look what you've done! We've got no bed!'

'There's enough of one for what I'm about to do,' he'd growled, tearing off her dress...

The memory of that day was enough to set her crying again. Sometimes she felt as if she'd never stop, but she wanted to, because a life spent crying was no sort of life at all. Her gaze went back to the room she now stood in alone, her only company the ghosts of her first few weeks here with Fergus.

There were worrying cracks in the ceiling – more than once, Rosie had gone to sleep imagining the plaster would fall and bury her in her bed; and the electrical fittings – sockets and light switches – looked as if they'd been installed shortly after light bulbs had been invented. Fergus had never denied it would be tough but had always insisted that they'd do it together, a labour of love. Though she'd had her doubts, she'd pushed them aside and put her faith in him, trusted that he had a plan for their future, that he saw the bigger picture even when she couldn't. Wasn't it just like her wayward husband to go and die on her in the middle of it all? Now it was more of a bricks-and-mortar tribute to his memory than anything else.

Rosie had once said this to her mum when questioned on why she was so adamant she was going to continue with the project.

'Hmm,' her mum had replied carefully. 'I understand that to a point, pet, but perhaps you ought to choose a different way to move on. I mean, as far as I can tell, it's not really moving on at all, is it?'

'I don't want to move on – it's too soon,' Rosie had replied. 'I just want something to remember him by.'

'At the risk of annoying you, I'd say a headstone is a far cheaper way to do that, and definitely a lot easier.'

'Mum! A life on the marina was Fergus's dream!'

'*Fergus's* dream... I seem to recall it wasn't so much yours.'

Rosie grimaced, though it was hard to argue the point. 'But it became mine because we did things together. I supported it then and I'm going to continue to support it now, because it's one way I can keep some connection to him.'

'I'm sorry, but it makes no sense to me. If you want to live there, fine – you're a grown woman and we can't stop you. But if you're doing this for Fergus... well, I'm sorry, but it's crazy.'

Rosie had been stung by her mum's views but later, privately, she'd been forced to agree. It probably *was* crazy, and more than once she'd had to ask herself why she'd gone to such lengths to see the project through by herself.

But now, as Rosie opened the curtains to a huge cream moon hanging over a murmuring river, over row upon row of coloured boats, upon banksides lush with reeds and tall grass, upon a pretty wooden boathouse, on the buildings containing her neighbours – the fishing tackle shop and camping supplies, the farm shop, and the barges containing all manner of business, she understood. This was why she was still here, despite the hardship. This was the dream Fergus had wanted for them, and the life he'd want for her now if he could tell her so. She owed it to him to make it work.

CHAPTER TWO

Spring had turned into summer – just about. It had rained for two long weeks, seeing May out with a soggy whimper. The rain by itself was no big deal, but river levels at the marina had risen alarmingly with every day of it. Many of the other residents took it in their stride, pointing out painted lines on walls that marked impossible levels caused by rains in years gone by. Rosie couldn't fathom how anyone could be so calm about it, until Nicole – the owner of Marigold Marina's gift shop – informed her dryly that it was all bluster and in reality they were all shitting themselves.

Whenever Rosie ventured into the town for supplies, people in shops were either commenting on the rain or talking of the upcoming boat parade – subjects that seemed to be interchangeable, one often leading to the other. The forecast didn't look promising, and everyone reckoned the event would either be called off, or the boats would actually be able to sail wherever they wanted due to Stratford-upon-Avon being submerged by the river responsible for giving the town its name.

In the end, however, someone very important was smiling

down on the town of Stratford on the day of the parade, because as Rosie opened her curtains early in the morning, the sun was shining. While she made her porridge, the presenter of the local breakfast radio show cheerfully announced that the forecast was good, before reading out a list of things one could expect to see at the festivities that year, including live music tents, Shakespeare readings in the park, choral flash mobs courtesy of the cathedral choir (Rosie had absolutely no idea how that would work but found the mental image of a load of choristers in their white robes leaping out from behind bushes and singing at people very funny), cider tasting, a hog roast and, of course, the boat parade itself. The day was set to culminate in the illumination of the floating convoy and then fireworks over the river. All in all – so the presenter said – it promised to be a pretty spectacular event.

After she'd been let down by a kitchen fitter at the last minute, Rosie's cafe wasn't quite ready to open and wouldn't be for another few days. But the rest of the work (what she could do herself and what didn't rely on the fitter) was almost done, so she could spare a few hours to go and check out the festivities for herself. The only problem was that none of her neighbours or the friends she'd made at the marina since her arrival had time to go with her, as most of them were looking at one of the busiest days of their year: if they weren't taking their own boats out onto the water, then they were happily mopping up the extra trade the event brought into the marina.

Rosie popped a handful of leftover blueberries into her mouth to empty the tub – she wanted to return it to the nearby farm shop so they could refill it. As she did so, she stared out of the kitchen window, deep in thought. *Do I actually really want to go?* While the parade sounded like a wonderful day out, she'd be surrounded by families and couples having the best time, and – far from cheering her and distracting her from the stress of

getting the cafe ready to open – it might only serve to remind
her that she had no family nearby, and no loved one to share the
day with.

Not only that, but the parade was one of the events that
Fergus had most been looking forward to. He'd watched videos
of it on YouTube and scrolled through photos of previous years
– he'd even planned to hire a boat so they could join in the
parade. 'I'll stand at the bow dressed as Prince Eric and you can
be Ariel,' he'd told her, laughing at the look of horror on her face
at the prospect of not only being on the water, which terrified
her, but also of dressing up. She'd always hated fancy dress – it
made her feel stupid – but Fergus loved it. She'd done it on
occasion to please him when they'd been invited to parties –
even in the bedroom once or twice – but she'd never felt
comfortable enough to enjoy the experience.

Now that he was gone, she'd give anything to share even this
one last thing with him, even if it meant dressing up. She'd dress
as anything, no matter how stupid, to give him this. It was silly
to dwell on it of course, because promising any amount of
stupidity or personal discomfort wasn't going to change a thing.

Fergus was gone.

Turning from the window, Rosie decided: she would go and
do her best to enjoy the parade to honour him, just as she'd
completed the work on Marigold Cafe to honour him. And she
supposed, looking at it like that, her decision was an easy one.
She ought to go and do the thing he couldn't because she was
still alive and so she could, and how could she possibly deserve
the life he hadn't been gifted if she didn't make the most of it? It
was enough to make her wonder if he ought to have been spared
and Rosie despatched in his place, because it was a safe bet to
assume he wouldn't be moping around like this. She sighed.
Would Fergus have felt so cut adrift if he'd lost Rosie, and not
the other way around? Would he have lost sight of the plans

they'd made together, the path they'd laid out for their lives? Would he have flailed around, wondering what to do next, wondering how to carry on? She'd completed the work on the cafe and had made it ready to open, but now that she had, she didn't have a clue what came next.

Opening a cafe was easy – moving on, that was much harder.

Whatever she did with her day, sitting around in her pyjamas wasn't an option – hadn't she only just told herself that someone who didn't live the life they'd been gifted probably didn't deserve it? Rosie took herself to the bedroom to find something to put on.

As she perused the rail of her wardrobe, she could hear laughter and shouting from outside. This side of the flat afforded lovely views of the river – it was one of the points that had sold the place to Fergus. Rosie went to the window now to see what the commotion was and smiled as she noticed a narrowboat sailing past, a skull and crossbones flag hoisted on a pole sticking out from the cabin and the crew of two elderly women and a man dressed as pirates. From her vantage point – a distance, admittedly – none of them looked younger than eighty. They also looked lithe and full of energy and as if they knew their way around a boat very well, laughing and calling to each other in fake pirate accents: 'Hoist anchor, ye scurvy knave!'

'Ye'll be keel-hauled for this!'

'Haul away, landlubber!'

Rosie's smile grew as she watched the boat move down-stream, presumably to join the flotilla gathering closer to town, ready for the parade.

She was just about to turn away when, from the corner of her eye, she noticed another boat following in its wake. This one was covered in flowers – so many that it looked like a floating garden – crewed by four young women who wore diaphanous white gowns and floral crowns. Rosie couldn't help but think about how cold they must be out on the water in such flimsy clothes, and she wasn't sure what characters they were meant to be portraying, but they did look ethereally lovely.

If these were the sights simply passing by her window, how much more excitement awaited at the actual parade? One of the biggest events of the year was waiting for her and, alone or not, she owed it to Fergus at least to try and enjoy it.

A couple of hours later she was mingling with the crowds on the waterfront of Stratford-upon-Avon. They were gathered in the shadow of the RSC, home to many great and historic performances by legends of the stage, where statues of famous characters from the Bard's plays watched the festivities with impassive bronze eyes.

Everything in this town seemed to be about Shakespeare, even when it wasn't. Every pub, every restaurant, every street sign had some connection. And there was his birthplace of course, a rambling but very pretty Tudor house that had a constant stream of visitors queuing to look around it. When Rosie and Fergus had first arrived at Marigold Marina, they'd spent a day searching for his grave – which Fergus was far more interested in because it was less touristy. This had proved to be rather less easy to find, as it was tucked away in a dark corner of a shaded churchyard off the beaten track, and nobody could say for sure if it was the final resting place of the great man or not. Rosie had found it all quite depressing. It seemed unfair to her that someone so great might have such an unremarkable send-off, while Fergus was less bothered. 'Shakespeare doesn't care now where he is!' Fergus had said cheerfully, and Rosie had to admit he had had a point.

There was no shortage of Shakespeare-themed stalls and events today. What would the man himself have made of it? Rosie wondered. Every other person seemed to be wearing a ruff and a fake bald head, or else looking like an extra from some Elizabethan period drama. Would he have been shocked at his continued cultural presence, hundreds of years after his death? Would he have been pleased? Would he have felt like the worshipped icon the world held him up to be? How would it feel to know you were not only your home town's most famous son but the most famous writer who'd ever lived since the founding of the modern world?

It was all a bit mind-boggling and Rosie soon found her brain tied in knots thinking about it, so she decided not to and tried to concentrate on simply soaking up the sights and sounds of the day. She wandered over to watch a group of teens perform the witches' scene from *Macbeth* in a clearing at the opposite side of the river from the theatre, and then wandered back across to see a group of adults perform something from *Much Ado About Nothing*. Then she checked out a jazz quartet playing further along the river before her tummy rumbled and she went to find a stall she'd seen earlier that day serving haloumi fries topped with minted yogurt and pomegranate seeds.

After the haloumi, which was excellent, she was still peckish, so she bought an ice cream, and then she was thirsty so she followed it up with an apple, melon and spinach smoothie from an organic fruit stand. Crowds thronged around her – every accent different and with many different languages too – while above her the sun kept its promise to shine over the proceedings with a friendly warmth.

Rosie was content as she wandered around, sipping her smoothie – but there was a seam of melancholy running through that contentment. She was having a perfectly nice, interesting day, but it shouldn't have been like this. Fergus should have been there with her. Every acting troupe, every musical performance, every stand selling some new food for her to try reminded her of how much he would have loved it all. Fergus would have got a lot more out of the festivities than Rosie too, who was naturally shyer and more of a home bird than him. While she was enjoying the day, she'd have been just as happy pottering around at home, unlike Fergus, who'd lusted after adventure and newness and had embraced anything out of the ordinary as much as she embraced her favourite chair.

After her lunch, Rosie went to sit by the water for a while. There were boats moored up all along the riverside decorated according to various crazy and not-so crazy themes. Amongst them she spotted the flower boat she'd seen earlier; one decorated like the Mystery Machine and containing characters from *Scooby Doo*; the ubiquitous Shakespeare-themed boat; one that had palm trees, sand and a cardboard pyramid on deck with the crew in ancient Egyptian costumes; and one playing 'The Star-Spangled Banner' at a volume loud enough to distort the tune while American flags fluttered from every available beam. A lot of the boats were simply freshly painted and decked in bunting, flowers or lights, and Rosie enjoyed seeing those just as much as the themed ones.

As she sat and gawped at the riot of colour – and sounds – bobbing up and down on the river, a shout from a nearby boat caught her attention. The voice sounded familiar and she looked up to see Popeye and Bluto engaged in a good-natured debate about beer. In their costumes, Rosie could barely tell who it was, but she recognised the voice of Grant, one of her neighbours on Marigold Marina and owner of the boat-hire business. So if Popeye was Grant, it was a safe bet that Bluto was one of his two grown-up sons who helped him run the boat shed.

Rosie had a lot of time for Grant, who'd largely given her space after Fergus's death but had always made it clear when they'd bumped into each other that she could call on him for anything, any time she needed to. She'd liked that he'd respected her privacy and her grieving while still making himself available – to a naturally shy and private person like Rosie, it seemed the perfect balance. She'd never taken him up on his offer of help, but when she'd felt more able to, she'd had many a pleasant conversation with him when she'd been out and about on the marina. And while he'd kept a respectful distance on a personal level, his advice and recommendations for local tradesmen to help with the cafe renovations had proven invaluable.

She rose from her seat and walked over. 'Wow!' she called from the bank. 'Your boat is looking amazing!'

He looked up from a string of bulbs he'd been adjusting and smiled. He was close to sixty but still incredibly toned, muscles showing clearly through his white T-shirt. His head was smooth except for a whisper of stubble where he'd shaved what nature had left behind to match where he'd gone bald elsewhere. He had a great tan too. Rosie often thought men half his age probably envied a physique that must have come from years of working outside day after day, pulling on ropes and scrubbing down boats.

'Rosie! Enjoying the day?'

'I am. And I'm very impressed with your outfit.'

He grinned broadly now, looking slightly sheepish. 'Don't tell anyone, but we've had this theme for the past four years. A bit lazy really. I keep thinking I'll change it but I never seem to have the time to sort a new one before the next parade is upon us.'

'Well, it's great. I don't see why you'd want to change it.'

'You could be right... If it ain't broke, don't fix it, eh?'

Rosie smiled. 'Is that a Shakespeare quote?'

'It ought to be – everything else is. Are you staying for the night-time events?'

'I might stay for an hour or so.'

'You're down here on your own?'

'Afraid so,' Rosie said, her expression a little rueful now. Of course she was on her own – it seemed to be a theme these days.

'If you're still around after the parade come and find us – quite a few of us will be in the Bard's Beard having a pint.' Grant grinned again. 'You're more than welcome to join us.'

'I might do that, thanks,' Rosie replied, though she knew already that she probably wouldn't. She hadn't set foot in a pub and certainly not drunk with a group of people since Fergus's death. For one thing, she didn't have him to hide behind – he'd always taken care of interesting conversation so she could stand back and lap it up without contributing. It wasn't that she didn't enjoy company, but she needed the filter his presence had provided to stop her from saying things for which people would think her stupid. When Fergus was there, she could have a good time just listening to everyone else without worrying about her own contribution. Now it was just her, and the danger was that everyone would see she'd been a fraud all along, with nothing useful, smart or interesting to say.

'Well,' Grant continued cheerfully, 'we're a friendly and easy-going bunch so you'd fit right in. You'll probably know a few of us already from the marina as well so you won't be a complete stranger.'

Rosie was about to reply when Grant's attention was drawn by a woman with two young boys.

'Excuse me,' the woman said, 'I don't suppose we could get a photo with you?'

'With me?' Grant said, looking faintly bemused.

'And the boat of course,' the woman replied. 'We really like it.'

Grant dropped the bulbs into a box and hopped onto the shore. 'I'm glad to hear it. Travelled far for the parade?'

'Coventry,' the woman said, taking out her phone. Grant gestured for her boys to stand next to him and got down on one knee to be at their level. He held his fake pipe to his lips and did a sort of squinty face as she took the photo.

After he got back up, she showed him the screen of her phone. 'That's brilliant! Thanks so much!'

'You're welcome. Hope you enjoy the rest of your day.'

'We will, thanks!' the woman called, her boys waving shyly as they moved along to marvel at another boat. Rosie watched for a moment as they looked for the owner and then asked a lady dressed as a mermaid for a photo of her.

Rosie smiled. 'Oh, that's so adorable.'

Grant turned to her and nodded. 'Almost enough to make me miss the days my lads were that young and still impressed with just about anything. They're all old and jaded these days, and never impressed by anything.'

'Oi!' Bluto shouted from the deck with a grin. 'I heard that!'

Rosie smiled at him as she recognised him as Grant's younger son, though his name escaped her for that moment.

'I'll be impressed when you show me something impressive,' Bluto continued. 'Now, when you've finished with your adoring public, could we please get these lights fixed?'

Grant shot Rosie an apologetic look.

'It's alright.' She laughed lightly. 'I'll let you get on. I only meant to say a quick hello.'

'You could come aboard if you fancy – join the parade.'

'Oh, God, no!' Rosie said, perhaps a little too fervently. But the fact was she had no wish to be upon the water, even with Grant's sturdy vessel and very capable sailing skills. She hadn't told anyone at the marina this – it seemed silly that a woman scared of the water would choose to live next to a river, but it remained a fact. Fergus had always said a bit of aversion therapy was just the thing she needed to cure her fear and had threatened more than once to throw her in, just to show her that she would be able to get back to shore if her life depended on it. He wouldn't have done of course, but it hadn't stopped her being nervous for the first few weeks every time they walked along the towpath together. Now, after settling in to the flat above the cafe, she was happy to admire the water but was no nearer to boarding a boat than she had been before they'd gone to live there. 'I mean,' she added hurriedly, 'I'm happy just to watch – I'd be in the way on board.'

'Suit yourself,' Grant said, leaping back onto the deck with the grace and agility of a man forty years his junior. 'We'll see you later in the pub then?'

'If I have time,' Rosie said carefully. Not only did it seem an overwhelming prospect, but the following day promised to be full with interviews for a new assistant at the cafe, and she needed a clear head if she was going to choose the right person. 'Have a good day on the water.'

'We will,' Grant said, sucking on his pipe and smacking his lips. 'Now... where's me spinach?'

Bluto rolled his eyes and Rosie smiled as she left them to it and made her way back towards the gardens at the RSC, where she'd noticed a steel drum band setting up a little earlier. Even as she walked along, the sounds of their music floated on the breeze towards her, telling her their set had already started, and her smile became a little bit sadder.

Fergus really would have loved all this.

Darkness had fallen. The night-time part of the boat parade had been every bit as magical as Rosie had imagined it would be and she'd lost herself in the spectacle, just another face in the crowd lit by hundreds of lights moving down river. And then the fireworks had started.

They were still exploding in the sky above her as she walked back to the marina – gold, crimson, silver and orange, some showering down like falling stars, some shooting into the sky with a scream before disappearing into the blackness. She could have stayed longer to see the last of them at the river with everyone else, but she'd started to get cold, her feet were aching and she longed for her little flat. Sometimes she was lonely there but, right then, shutting the door behind her and putting the kettle on for a cup of tea seemed very appealing. Not to mention the fact that she still had a lot to do before she could go to bed and she was already tired from her day out in the open air.

'You're the oldest young person I've ever met,' Fergus used to tell her.

She'd laugh and hold her hands up. 'You got me! It's lucky you're the youngest old person I've ever met.'

'Oi, madam!' he'd cry, pretending to be mortally offended. 'I'm only twelve years older than you, not fifty!'

They'd carry on this way, like they'd never made the joke before. And part of Rosie couldn't help but agree that Fergus was probably right. She did have an old head on her, and it was lucky that he was youthful enough for the both of them. *And anyway*, she thought as she walked along, *what* does *it matter now?* Fergus was no longer there to tell her she needed to lighten up, and besides, widows were meant to be old, weren't they? If she had the label, she might as well embrace what came with it.

Arriving at the marina, she noticed that most of the businesses were locked up and in darkness by now. Some of the houseboats had lights in the windows and the paths were lit, but other than that, things were deathly quiet, apart from the muffled sounds of the party still in full swing in town and the fireworks popping overhead. It was then, as she passed Nicole's gift shop, that she noticed a new boat moored close by. A new resident? Perhaps a new business? It looked as if there was cosmetic work to be done to it, though it seemed sound from what Rosie could tell at that distance. It was in darkness, just bobbing serenely on the water.

Wondering vaguely what new neighbour she might be getting, Rosie searched her bag for her door keys. Once she was inside, she barely gave the boat another thought.

Rosie looked down the list of questions again. They seemed a bit formal considering all she really needed the successful candidate to do was take orders, distribute food to the tables and clean up after the customers had left. Still, the recruitment website Rosie had studied so she'd be ready to interview for her new assistant had recommended them, and as Rosie knew next to nothing about choosing the right employee (or even being an employer, for that matter) she'd decided to use them anyway.

The cafe wasn't open for business yet, but that day was close. The works schedule hadn't been far out in the end, which was a small mercy considering what a difficult road it had been. But she'd earmarked the beginning of summer and, sure enough, June had arrived and she was almost ready.

Rosie had raced around that morning putting tablecloths out and flowers into vases despite there being no prospect of customers just yet. As the cafe wasn't ready to open, the only people who would see the inside, apart from herself of course, were the people who were coming to see her about the job. Still, she wanted it to look homely, like the sort of place someone would want to work. She'd made the same effort for her own appearance, picking out her prettiest dress (black, of course – she didn't want to go *too* crazy), hair smoothed down, make-up done. All that effort made her feel as if she didn't look like herself, because it had been so long since she'd made a real effort. But an old boss had once told her that at interview the candidate was weighing up the company as much as the company was assessing the candidate, and Rosie wanted to make a good impression.

She badly needed the right person to come along, not only to help in the cafe, but because she hoped they'd become a friend and companion as well. The people who ran the businesses around her at Marigold Marina, and the many residents who inhabited boats of all kinds moored up and down the banks – they'd all been friendly and welcoming, but Rosie hadn't really connected with anyone. There was Nicole of course, who owned the gift shop, but their friendship was tinged by sadness because they'd become close only through Fergus's death. Sometimes Rosie found spending time with her difficult, even though she liked her very much, because looking at her reminded her of that. As for everyone else, there was a brisk 'Good morning' here, a 'How are you doing?' there, but it was no antidote to the crushing loneliness Rosie was greeted with when she locked the doors at night.

It should have been Fergus waiting for her at the end of a long day, but fate had had other ideas.

'What's for dinner, my little goth girl?' he'd asked one evening, when they'd both finished work on the cafe renovations for the day. Rosie had tired of telling him that she wasn't a goth – at least, not how he meant it. Just because she had a nose stud, liked to wear black and dye her hair different colours... well, she had before they'd got married. He'd let her keep the nose stud in because she'd told him it would heal over if she left it out, and it was only tiny anyway, and he supposed it did look quite cute, but where her hair was concerned, she'd let her natural brown come through because Fergus preferred it. It wasn't until after his death, during a particularly wretched afternoon, that she'd run out to the shop to buy the violet dye that she currently had on, just to give herself something to do, something... anything to take her mind off her misery.

'Wine and crisps – I'm too exhausted for anything else.'

'Now then... we can do better than that, surely?'

'Seriously, I don't think I could even lift a saucepan.'

'Then let's have takeaway.'

'We can't afford it—'

'Sure we can – just this once.'

Rosie had given him a tired smile. 'OK, that sounds good. The usual place?'

'Why not? Saves having to make huge decisions – we all know how bad you are at that. I'll have the sweet and sour, and don't forget the prawn crackers this time, will you? Not only are you the oldest young person I know, you have the memory of an octogenarian as well.'

'Yeah, I know...'

Like the other times, Rosie had got into the car, even though she could barely keep her eyes open, because the place Fergus was so fond of didn't do deliveries and at least by doing so she was doing something useful and making him happy. When she returned with the food, she knew he'd be freshly showered and changed with an open bottle of wine already half gone, but that meant he'd be in a good mood. She'd get the plates and cutlery and take the food into the living room so they could eat on the sofa.

'Come on...' He'd pat the seat next to him. 'Eat up, then you can get showered too, and if you're very lucky, I might let you shag me.'

She always did, because there was no turning Fergus down when he'd got an idea in his head...

There was a light tap at the door. Rosie jumped. If she was this nervous, goodness knew what her candidates felt like. Being assailed by untimely and unwanted memories of her past with Fergus hardly helped either. Hastily stuffing her question sheet inside a folder, she took a deep breath and went to unlock the door.

'Hello.'

Rosie had checked her expected arrivals at least twenty times that morning and knew the exact order of all eight interviewees by heart.

'Letitia, isn't it?'

The woman put out her hand. Rosie knew from her application that she was fifty-seven, with a grown-up family and years of experience in catering. Her manner was brisk but pleasant, her hair steel grey and cut into a sharp bob. Her black trousers and white blouse were so practical and appropriate it was like she'd come prepared in her own uniform, ready to start work on the spot. 'It is. Pleased to meet you. The place looks lovely – at least the approach does. It's about time someone tackled those overgrown gardens.' She looked around appreciatively. 'Did you do it yourself?'

'I did.' Rosie smiled. 'Come in.'

Letitia followed Rosie inside.

'So, you know this bit of the river well?' Rosie asked as she gestured for Letitia to take a seat.

'I walk the dog down here most days.'

'You live close by then?'

'Yes.'

'I suppose it's a handy location for you, work-wise?'

Letitia nodded. 'Do you need my CV?'

'I've got a copy, thank you.'

'Of course you have... I only asked because I have an extra with me and I thought it might help.'

'So, you left your last job because...' Rosie rifled through her papers for the CV they'd just mentioned but couldn't find it. Typical, she chided herself. How is this impressing anyone? Letitia would soon decide Rosie was an idiot and wouldn't want to work for her at all.

'The owner retired and the shop didn't stay open after that,' Letitia said into the gap. 'It was a small business and nobody saw the potential so nobody bought it. You'd have thought with it being in the middle of town and so many tourists... but no. Shame, really, but I suppose there's not much call for fudge these days. It's a bit old-fashioned, I suppose. It's all organic polenta cakes and honey biscuits round here now, isn't it?'

'I suppose people are a bit more health conscious,' Rosie replied doubtfully and resolved to revise the trendier items on her menu just in case anything on it might offend Letitia's tastes. Despite this, Rosie liked Letitia a lot already. She was closer to Rosie's mum's age than to Rosie's, calm and open, friendly, approachable, seemed wise and had local knowledge – they were all big ticks as far as Rosie could tell. She felt that Letitia would be reliable and handy to have around and would keep her head in a crisis; almost a mother figure, if she was being brutally honest, and that wasn't an unwelcome thing.

But then she realised she hadn't even asked any of her proper interview questions yet. She dragged the sheet from her file and held it up to her face. 'OK, Letitia... what made you choose to apply for this job?'

Rosie lowered the sheet for the answer, but Letitia, though she was obviously trying to hide it, gave a vague frown.

'Well, because you're a cafe. I've always worked in catering, my other job went and... you were advertising? I mean, quite honestly I was just applying for anywhere that had work in food within walking distance of my house. I mean, granted, that's not many...'

Rosie nodded. It was hardly an inspired reply but what had she been expecting? It was only a little job at a little cafe after all. It wasn't like she was offering the opportunity of a lifetime on the board of some multinational company. 'Right... thank you. So would you say you're ambitious?'

'Do I need to be? Don't you just want me to dish out sand-wiches and clean up?'

'Well, yes...' Rosie went back to her list. Even as she was

going down it, reading them out loud suddenly had her wondering why she'd thought any of these questions had a point. Still, she was in the thick of it now and she didn't have anything else prepared so she soldiered on. 'Would you say you're a team player?'

'I can get on with my work mates as well as anyone. Are you employing a lot of people then?'

'No, just the one.'

'So it would be you and whoever you take on?'

Rosie nodded.

'Hardly a team,' Letitia commented.

Was that impatience Rosie detected?

'I suppose it is a team of sorts.'

'I suppose,' Letitia agreed doubtfully.

'What about your future,' Rosie asked. 'Where do you see yourself in five years' time?'

'Five years older, five years fatter and five years off the mortgage, with a bit of luck.'

Rosie frowned. She looked at her questions again. Had Letitia considered them pointless and irrelevant? Rosie was definitely beginning to agree. She was hiring a cafe assistant, not Alan Sugar's new apprentice.

Deciding to abandon them after all and wing it, she stuffed the list back into the file. 'You know what? I'll be honest – I've never done this before. I got these ridiculous questions online and I don't think they're really telling me anything.'

'I hate to say it, but I think you're right.' Letitia let out a laugh. 'If you don't mind me also saying, perhaps all you really need to know is whether you can get along with whoever you take on, and that they won't let you down. I'll tell you now – and I can get good references to back me up – I won't let you down. And whether you feel you can get along with me – well, that's up to you, and I can't do much to swing that either way.'

'I suppose it is hard to tell at first meeting,' Rosie agreed.

'I've got an idea – how about I put the kettle on, make us a drink and we have a chat?'

'I find it's the best way to get to know someone,' Letitia said.

Rosie smiled. 'Brilliant. Do you take sugar in your tea?'

The next candidate didn't show, but as she looked again at her CV, Rosie wasn't surprised. Overqualified really, and had probably been offered something better in the interim. Still, it would have been nice to get a quick call. Then came a sweet but awkward seventeen-year-old named Catlin. Rosie had been tempted by her, as she really liked her, but having no other backup, realistically she might prove to be too flimsy a support in times of stress, and there were no guarantees a young girl like that would want to stay too long. Rosie might just get her confident and then have her leave – which would be typical of her rotten luck these days.

There was a guy who seemed a little uptight and also like he'd be making do. Rosie got the impression his ultimate ambition was to be a chef in a proper restaurant and there was no way she'd ever be able to satisfy that for him, so she figured she'd lose him pretty quickly too. Then there were a couple of nondescripts – she felt guilty thinking of them that way but really hadn't gelled with either of them at all.

Rosie had lunch after those and then opened up again for the next candidate, only to find she had another no-show on her hands.

Which just left the last one of the day, Tabitha, who was twenty.

'Hello...' Rosie opened the door to let her in. Bang on time and smiling warmly as Rosie opened the door – it was a good start. She was very well presented: smart but not too try-hard, striking to look at too, with a head of dark curls, a healthy blush

in her cheeks and eyes the colour of sage. Rosie liked her imme-
diately.

'The cafe looks lovely,' Tabitha said as she took Rosie's
offered seat.

'Thank you,' Rosie said. 'Would you like a cup of tea? Or
coffee perhaps?'

'Wow, this is the first interview where I've been offered tea.'
Tabitha smiled. 'That would be lovely. Thanks.'

'Well, I got fed up pretty quickly of all that formality,' Rosie
said getting up. 'So I just decided to chat with everyone I was
seeing today. I think I realised the most important thing I
needed was to feel I'm employing someone I like and trust.
There's no better way to find out who that is than with a bit of
informality, and no better way to get informality than to have a
cuppa together.'

'I feel as if I ought to be making tea for you,' Tabitha said.
'You know, so you can tell if I make a decent one.'

'Well.' Rosie laughed lightly. 'You can if you really want to.'

Tabitha joined Rosie at the counter and looked expectant.
Rosie had been joking, but clearly Tabitha wasn't.

'Right, if you tell me where everything is, I'll make tea for
you.'

'Right... lovely...' Rosie put the caddy, cups, milk and sugar
out in front of her, then leant back against the counter, arms
folded as she watched Tabitha prepare the drinks.

'So you've had a lot of interviews?' Rosie asked her.

'A few. I mean, not loads.'

'What have you been doing up to now?'

'I've been living in Leeds.'

'Wow, that's a way – almost as far from here as my home
town.'

'Where's that?'

'Newcastle,' Rosie replied. 'I know my accent isn't super

strong – if it was my dad interviewing you right now, you wouldn't be able to tell a word he was saying.'

Tabitha smiled politely and Rosie continued: 'Why did you come back to Stratford then, if that's not too personal a question? I take it you're a local? Your accent...'

'Yes, born and bred here, but I moved away to be with a cretin that I called a boyfriend who persuaded me it was a good idea. Then I realised I'd turned into a cretin too. It must have been all that time I spent with him; it had rubbed off.'

Rosie recognised Tabitha's story only too well. Hadn't she herself ended up here on Marigold Marina for exactly the same reasons – because a man had persuaded her?

Rosie recalled the conversation with crystal clarity, though it had taken place over a year before. Fergus had dashed into the garden of their house in Newcastle where Rosie had been pegging out clothes to dry. The day had been blessed with a stiff breeze and bright spells, and she'd let the wash basket get far too full before she'd been able to get to it, meaning Fergus had been complaining that his favourite shirt hadn't been available when he'd wanted to put it on that morning. His sulking had soon given way to excitement, however. He'd retreated into his study with a scowl but now emerged looking manic.

'I think I've found it!'

Rosie batted away a fly as she turned to him. 'Found what?'

'Our adventure! Look...'

Rosie peered at the screen of his phone, trying to shield it from the glare of the sun. Then she looked up at him, trying not to frown. 'You're not serious? That place?'

'What's wrong with it?' He pouted. 'It's perfect.'

'It's a dump!'

'Well of course it's a dump. That's reflected in the price. We're not going to get something already pristine for our budget.'

'Yes, but...' Rosie had paused. 'It's just... it looks like such a lot of work. Can we even afford to take it on? I mean, I know it's cheap, but it will take a lot of cash to get right, so shouldn't we just spend that on something that's almost right to start with?'

'But we get more for our money this way – surely that's obvious. That's why fixer-uppers are so attractive for home owners. Yes, it'll take work, but the trade-off is we get a much bigger property than we would have otherwise been able to afford.'

'Do we really need something that big? Couldn't we just get a little cafe out in a village somewhere near here? Where is this...? It's in Warwickshire! That's miles away! My mum and dad would freak if I told them I was moving so far away. And it's next to a river – and you know me and open water!'

'It wouldn't be an adventure if it wasn't a bit scary, would it?' he'd asked with that silky half-smile that she never could resist.

'I'm not scared... it's just... well, I think it's too much. What would we do with a place this big? I thought it was just going to be a little tea room or something we could run as a couple, but this...'

'Think about it!' he'd replied, his eyes now shining with a manic energy Rosie recognised only too well. He had the bit between his teeth and she had a feeling he had no intentions of letting it go. 'It doesn't have to be just a lame little tea room... We could run it as a cafe by day and a bistro by night.'

'A bistro! We don't know the first thing about proper cooking! I can fry some bacon up but that's about it.'

'We could learn – how hard could it be? They run cookery courses at the college all the time. All it would take is a few of those, some YouTube videos, a few recipe books...'

'Surely if it were that easy there wouldn't be so much fuss about celebrity chefs, would there?'

He waved a dismissive hand. 'That's all hype. Real cooking is no big deal and most people have no idea whether what they're eating is good or not; they'll just believe it is if you're convincing enough. I'm telling you, Rosie, we can do this.' Grabbing her around the waist and pulling her against him, he'd held her gaze. 'We can... you and me – we can do anything if we're together. You wouldn't have to worry your pretty little head about cooking – you could man the office and keep the books and I'd provide the culinary flair. You know it could work.'

'So I'd essentially be doing the job I'm doing now at the council, only for you instead?'

'For us. That's the big difference.'

Rosie had taken the phone from his hand and looked again. Marigold Marina... it had a certain ring to it that she couldn't deny. And though the cafe looked like something from the set of an apocalypse movie, scrolling through additional estate-agent photos showed it sat in a beautiful area. By a river... maybe she could handle that if she kept her distance from the water – after all, she had no need to get up close and personal.

'I'll think about it,' she'd said, knowing full well from the look on his face that she'd already lost the battle, as she'd lost countless battles before.

And here she was now to prove it.

But while her story had ended very differently, the idea of that common experience made her warm to Tabitha even more than she had done already.

'What did the cretin do to get dumped?' she asked.

'Oh, nothing. He was just generally useless. It was going nowhere so I decided to come home. But, of course, it's not that simple, is it? I'd left my college course, an old job, my mum and everything behind to be with him, so I had to start again – you know, new job, place to live, get back on track. I feel like such a selfish cow when I think about it now.'

'Why selfish?'

'I worried my mum to death and she's... well, she isn't the

strongest person. But that's all behind me now. I'm home and she's much better. I can get on with my life again.'

'Does that include restarting your education?'

'I don't know – maybe.'

'So you might go to university? I hope it doesn't sound nosy; I only ask because I'm trying to figure out how I might accommodate that if I were to give you the job.'

'Honestly, I haven't thought that far ahead. Right now I'm starting with the basics.'

Rosie smiled gravely – she knew how that felt. Start with the basics, which in her case were finding the strength to get up every morning, put food in her mouth, speak when spoken to and make sense, to not start sobbing uncontrollably at the sight of couples holding hands, or any man with a passing resemblance to Fergus. Rebuilding a life from Ground Zero. Different circumstances, but she knew only too well how that felt.

It had been a tough decision, but in the end Rosie had gone with Letitia. She'd felt a real kinship with Tabitha, a soul almost mirroring her own, but perhaps that had the potential to become a negative rather than a positive. She needed someone pragmatic, without baggage to match her own, someone who'd keep her on an even keel, and that someone, she'd concluded, was the older, more practical Letitia.

It had been hard phoning the others to give the bad news. Rosie had especially dreaded Tabitha's call. They'd hit it off and she knew Tabitha needed the job; she supposed they all did. Tabitha had been polite of course, and had taken the news better than Rosie had feared, but then she supposed the girl was hardly going to rant over the phone.

So that was that. Marigold Cafe had a team (as much as two people counted as a team) and was ready to go. Rosie only hoped her nerve and strength would hold. *Just make it through the first year*, she told herself, as Fergus had told her.

'If we can make it through the first year, we're home and dry.'

Easy for him to say – he'd never had to test his theory in the end.

Still, make it through the first year and you might just survive.

If only she could believe that were true.

CHAPTER THREE

Rosie had just taken delivery of a stack of laminated menus. She was reading through one to check for mistakes when there was a tap on the door of the cafe. She looked up to see the owner of the marina's gift shop, Nicole, standing outside. Nautical trinkets and Shakespearean tea towels – that's how Nicole herself always described her stock, though she sold a lot more than that. The shelves of Marigold Gifts – housed in a converted boat shed – groaned with pottery, jewellery, hats, T-shirts, scarves, figurines, tote bags, umbrellas, fridge magnets, posters, pens and notepads... and just about anything else you could emblazon with the words 'Souvenir of Stratford-upon-Avon'.

'Hello,' Rosie said as she opened up. 'Long time no see!'

'Sorry... it's been a bit manic lately,' Nicole replied. 'I know I've neglected you a bit, but I thought I'd drop by to wish you luck for tomorrow.'

'Oh, don't worry about that' – Rosie gestured for Nicole to step inside – 'I know you must be busy, and I've been a bit manic too. It's just nice to see you when you can manage. There's no need to apologise.'

'There's every need. I know the last few months have been

tough for you – probably tougher than anyone knows because you never complain. Tomorrow's a big day and I imagine it's going to be quite bittersweet.'

'Yes,' Rosie said heavily. She'd been trying not to think about how it might feel to stand on the floor of the cafe welcoming customers without Fergus at her side. There were times she'd thought this day would never come, and now, to see it arrive without Fergus – the man whose dream it had really been – would be bittersweet indeed. She liked to think he'd be proud of the way she'd seen it through in his name, of what she'd achieved, but she'd never hear it from his lips, and that was hard to bear. 'But I know I have support here – it's what's kept me going. Especially you – you've been a rock.'

'Well,' Nicole said, 'I don't know about that exactly.'

'You have, and it must have been hard when you'd just gone through your break-up with Ralph too, and then, of course, it was you who found—'

'Let's not dwell on that now, eh?' Nicole said cheerily. 'Today's not the day to look backwards – it's a day to look forward to better times.'

'You're right,' Rosie said. 'Can I get you anything while you're here? I was about to make tea.'

Nicole glanced at the box of menus sitting on a nearby table. 'You're busy – I can come by another time.'

'Don't be daft! I'm never too busy for you! You've been so kind since Fergus and I arrived here, and I don't know what I would have done without you after I lost him.'

'Are you sure you have time?'

'Always for you.'

Nicole hesitated. 'OK,' she said finally. 'Maybe a quick cuppa then.'

'Great!'

Nicole cast around the empty cafe. 'Any particular table?'

'Take your pick!' Rosie called as she filled the kettle. There was a hot-water dispenser installed, but it wasn't worth heating for two cups of tea, so Rosie was going old-school for theirs. 'With a bit of luck, it's the last day I'll ever be able to say that!'

Nicole sat down on the nearest chair. 'Let's hope so. I think you've picked a perfect time to open actually.'

'Well I didn't exactly plan it – more of a case of opening when the renovations were done rather than anything else.'

'Then fate is cutting you a break.'

'About time. Why do you say that anyway?'

'Layla and Tom at the farm shop are expanding – didn't you hear?'

'No – I never seem to hear anything,' Rosie said with a brief laugh. 'Must walk round with my ears stuffed with cotton wool. What sort of expansion?'

'They're opening a pick-your-own section for the summer. Strawberries and raspberries and such. Should bring more people this way. Grant says the boating season's hotting up too – promises to be a good year for him. Then there's the new book barge...'

'Wow... look who has all the gossip! Honestly, how do I not know these things?'

'You're not nearly nosy enough.'

'True. The book barge... I saw a new boat after the parade... Is that going to be it?'

'Moored just along from my place?'

'Yes! I wondered what it was for. A book barge sounds good – I think I might use that a lot. If I ever get time to read again once this place gets going, that is. Perhaps I ought to be hoping to have no time to read.'

'You'll have to get their resident Lord Byron to come and read to you while you work.'

Rosie laughed. 'Lord Byron?'

'Hmm, I'll say. The owner's a bit of alright. Kit Malone.'

'You know him?'

'My little sister was at the same school. He was a cute kid, but even back then you could see he'd be an even cuter man... if you know what I mean.'

Rosie poured hot water into two mugs. 'Well, you're happily single now – haven't you fancied seducing him? Should be easy to get to know him if you already have things in common... like, people in common... if you see what I mean.'

'God, no! That would be weird – my little sister's classmate! He's more your age than mine.'

'Fergus was twelve years older than me and that was never a problem. How much older must you be than this guy? Eight, nine years? It's not so bad.'

'Still...' Nicole seemed distracted for a moment, her gaze going to the window.

'Sorry,' Rosie said.

Nicole turned to her. 'For what?'

'I keep bringing Fergus up. I can't help it, but it must be wearing for people.'

'It wasn't that,' Nicole said. She gave Rosie a smile that seemed a little forced. 'I just don't like being reminded that I'm not young and sexy anymore.'

'Of course you're still sexy.' Rosie smiled. 'You have a better figure than I've ever had – legs for days, and you don't have a single grey hair or wrinkle... You certainly make me jealous anyway.'

'I definitely have wrinkles if you look in the right light, and I dye my greys – but thank you. And stop apologising for talking about Fergus. Why would anyone expect you to stop talking about him?'

'I suppose it seems morbid. I mean, it was nine months ago. I suppose people think I ought to be making an effort to move on.'

'Everyone knows you are. Everyone I talk to is impressed with how well you've coped since...'

'Really?'

They were warm words, full of encouragement, but Rosie wasn't convinced they were entirely true. She barely knew most of her neighbours at the marina past a good morning or a brief enquiry about how she was, and there had barely been a more meaningful conversation than that with any of them. They'd expressed their condolences, of course, told her to look them up if she needed anything and all that stuff that people always said when someone had suffered a loss. Nobody had ever said they'd been impressed with how she was coping or anything about being proud of her. Not that she'd expect it. She and Fergus had barely been at the marina a month before he'd died, and the other traders and residents had been welcoming enough, but at the end of the day, people were busy and it took time to forge friendships – longer still when every day was packed from morning till night with work. In the end, the only reason she was such good friends with Nicole was that it had been Nicole who'd found Fergus after his heart attack and had called the ambulance. That had connected the women in a way nothing else could have. It had been a sad and tragic beginning – not the usual starting place for a friendship.

She gave a bleak smile. 'I don't think they'd say that if they saw me sitting upstairs some nights.'

'That's to be expected.'

Rosie brought the teas over. 'No cakes, I'm afraid – first delivery isn't coming until tomorrow.'

'That's OK – probably a good thing anyway. I certainly don't need the extra calories.'

Nicole was being modest. As Rosie had told her, she did have an amazing figure – curvy, but in all the right places. And she looked incredible for her forty years – great skin, sleek hair... like someone half her age. Some days Rosie looked in the mirror and felt Nicole seemed the younger of the two of them, even though she herself had only just turned thirty.

'Who's minding the shop?' she asked.

'No one – it's dead today. I'm wondering whether Sundays are worth it, to be honest. I decided to lock up for half an hour. If anyone comes by desperately wanting a key ring or a fridge magnet, there's a note on the door telling them to ask at the farm shop. Layla or Tom will ring me if I'm needed.'

'It's good you have each other to lean on.'

'*You* have us to lean on too – don't keep forgetting that. Whatever you need, you can just ask any of us – especially being on your own here.'

'Actually, I won't be. I have a lady starting tomorrow.'

'Brilliant! What's she like? Do I know her?'

'Letitia Grove? I think she's fairly local but doesn't live on the marina.'

Nicole shook her head slightly. 'Nope, don't think I know her. But she's good?'

'Seems it. She gave a good first impression anyway. She's quite a bit older than me, which I think I need – head screwed on, lots of experience. I'm hoping she'll show me the ropes rather than the other way around, seeing as she's worked in catering and this is my first time.'

'No regrets about leaving your old job and your old life behind?'

'God, every day! But Fergus and I made the decision together and I owe it to him to see it through.'

Nicole frowned. 'The only person you owe anything to is yourself. It's you who needs to be honoured – your needs, your happiness. Do what you want, not what you think others want of you. I'm amazed you're here at all – everyone expected you to head back to Tyneside after Fergus had gone. I must admit I thought you ought to, but here you are, stubbornly sticking it out. If you did that for Fergus, then I wonder if it was the right thing, but if you did it for yourself... well, I can't argue with that.'

'I wish I could be like that – just pleasing myself. It must be very liberating.'

'As we both know, life's too short, and even shorter and less fulfilling when you spend it doing things you don't want to do in order to please everyone else around you.'

'I know. I *do* want to do this – it's just scary, that's all. I went from sitting at a desk all day typing out letters at the council to business owner in the blink of an eye.'

'Not to mention moving halfway across the country and suffering a bereavement into the bargain. If you think of it that way, you're stronger than you give yourself credit for.'

'Hmm...' Rosie sipped her tea.

'You are!' Nicole insisted.

'Not like you are,' Rosie said. 'You seem to cope with anything, and if you're not happy with a situation, you say so, and if you want to do something, you don't waste time asking for permission – you just do it. I wish I could be like that.'

'Trust me, it comes with age.'

'You're not that old!'

'Ten years older than you – that counts for a lot. You're still a baby. They say life begins at forty. I'm not sure about life per se, but your tolerance to bullshit certainly takes a battering between the ages of thirty and forty – you'll soon find that out.'

Rosie smiled. 'I shall look forward to that development then.'

'You'll like it – finally seeing you're allowed to do what you want instead of what's expected of you.'

'Maybe. For now I'll have to knuckle down; I've put so much into this place that I have to make it work... and, if nothing else, that fact will keep me focused when I feel like quitting.'

'You won't feel like quitting. I have an inkling you're going to be just fine.'

'I hope so.' Rosie shrugged. 'Fergus had courage and ambition enough for both of us. I just followed where he led.'

'If he could see you now he'd say something quite different. You're doing it all by yourself now.'

'Only because I don't have a choice.'

'But you do. You just said as much yourself. You could have quit any time but you didn't.'

'I felt like it plenty of times.'

'We've all felt like quitting at one time or another.'

'Even you?'

Nicole pursed her lips. 'Me? I've felt like checking out many times over the years.'

Rosie sipped her tea again. She didn't know what Nicole meant, exactly, by checking out, but she didn't like the sound of it. She also felt it was a line of conversation best left unpursued... at least just then. Nicole didn't elaborate either, which only reinforced Rosie's belief that there was no more she wished to say on the matter.

But if it meant what Rosie thought it meant, then it wasn't something she would have expected from Nicole. They'd only known each other a short time, but Rosie's marina neighbour always seemed strong, resourceful and confident – not that Rosie had any hard evidence of this, just a feeling from the way Nicole held herself and spoke. But she supposed everyone had secrets, impulses that weren't apparent to others, darker sides they kept hidden, private moments of despair... Lord knew Rosie herself had faced enough of those, especially since Fergus's death. Nicole had been through a loss too – her ex, Ralph, was still very much alive, but by all accounts the divorce had been difficult and trying and hardly amicable.

In its own way, it must have been as tough as what Rosie had gone through losing Fergus. It was no wonder Nicole had experienced darker moments that not everyone had seen. It might have been much worse, of course, had Ralph put up a fight for the gift shop. But he'd taken off with his new woman and now lived in Sussex – a nice safe distance away, Nicole said, and had left Nicole with the shop as part of their divorce settlement. That distance meant Nicole didn't have to face him and could move past the pain of their split – at least, that's what she always told Rosie.

Nicole drained her cup and gave Rosie a vague smile. 'I should let you get on. I expect you have a lot to do for tomorrow and I have a product order to put through – those things take hours.'

'Of course,' Rosie said. 'Thanks so much for popping over.'

'I'll call in tomorrow, see how the grand opening is going. In the meantime, don't forget what I said. Shout if you need anything – and I mean anything at all.'

'I will,' Rosie said. 'Thank you.'

Nicole got up and Rosie followed her to the door to see her out.

Nicole turned and waved before heading back to her own shop. It was easy to see, sitting on a gentle bend in the river, which meant Nicole's front door was in full view of Rosie's own.

She liked Nicole. At first, she'd found it hard to warm to her, but she quickly realised that was her failing and not Nicole's, because Fergus had liked her straight away, and he was a good judge of character. Because he'd persevered, they'd all become pally quickly, though it had been a vague acquaintance more than anything meaningful. It wasn't until after his death that Nicole had really stepped into the breach to be a true friend to Rosie. But then, Rosie supposed that might have had a lot to do with the fact that Fergus had been in Nicole's shop when his heart attack had struck. Nicole had gone into the stock room to fetch some packing tape he'd asked to borrow, and she'd returned a moment later to find him on the floor. She'd called the ambulance and tried her best to revive him, but he was already dead and no amount of CPR was going to bring him back. Nicole had been forced to deal with the immediate aftermath alone. Rosie had been visiting her parents out of town, and it had taken a while for anyone to get hold of her on her mobile to let her know.

For a long time, Rosie had blamed herself for not being there, and Nicole had blamed herself for not being able to save him, and it wasn't until the coroner had ruled that his heart defect was an undetected genetic fault and that nobody could have saved him that Nicole, at least, seemed better. Rosie, however, not so much, because she hadn't been with her husband at the end.

In fact, there had been more than physical distance keeping them apart, and for that, Rosie didn't think she'd ever be able to forgive herself. People had told her she couldn't beat herself up over what had happened, and as nobody could ever see anything like that coming, to live in constant fear of the possibility of such an event was silly. Nobody could live like that, and if they did, they'd never leave home. Rosie had tried her best to be comforted by their words, but it had been hard. Instead, she'd focused on helping Nicole come to terms with the circumstances of Fergus's death and the part she'd played in it, and from that a new and closer friendship had been forged. It would never replace having her husband by her side of course, but Rosie liked to think he'd be happy to know something good had come from the tragedy, and that Rosie had someone like Nicole looking out for her.

After locking the door again she went back to the table full of menus, picked one up, and started to read. There was a lot to do before the morning.

CHAPTER FOUR

Rosie couldn't settle. At this rate she'd be a zombie for the opening day of Marigold Cafe – if she was going to sleep at all later on, she needed to do something to soothe her nerves and help her to relax. Right now, she felt like a rubber band wound round a top and ready to let rip. After Nicole's visit, she'd worked herself into a frenzy checking and rechecking every little detail and now she couldn't switch off. She'd tried camomile tea, a relaxing bath and a viewing of her favourite film. She'd found it impossible to concentrate on the film, had found herself leaping out of the bath before she'd had ten minutes in it, and her tea had gone cold as she'd stared out of the window running every conceivable disastrous scenario for the following day through her head.

As everything else had failed, and even though twilight cloaked the marina, Rosie decided on a long walk. It was quite safe there – at least it always felt it. The community looked out for each other, and outsiders were rarely wandering around after the businesses had packed up for the day. If she was lucky, Rosie would see an owl on the wing; or the first of the night's bats slipping out from the boat shed where Grant's narrowboats for hire were kept at night; or the fox and her cubs that lived at the end of the access lane to the marina behind the bins, feeding quite happily on the food everyone left for them. There would be moths circling the lamps that lit the paths, delicate and feathery, bumping into the globes over and over.

Rosie had taken only a passing interest in wildlife before – the odd documentary on TV, delight at seeing a deer on country walks – but she'd never appreciated it until she'd come to live at Marigold Marina, and she'd never been in such close proximity to so much. It never failed to make her happy to see a rabbit emerge from a burrow or a tiny stoat or weasel dart out of the hedgerow, or so many new species of birds she had no name for most of them.

She recalled now the first time she'd seen a badger cross her path. She and Fergus had been at the marina for a week – a week in which the stress of the move and living in a building site had begun to bite. Rosie was tetchy and sometimes teary, and so that evening they'd had a Chinese takeaway from their new favourite place, which they'd eaten on blankets in the tiny back yard by a patio heater. It was winter, but Fergus had insisted they needed to be outside. It had been fun for a while, and they'd soon warmed up with the whisky coffees they'd followed the meal with. Then Fergus had suggested a stroll to take a proper look around the marina and to help Rosie sleep because, despite the exhaustion she was suffering from, a bout of stress-induced insomnia had been keeping her awake for some nights.

They'd wandered from the path that followed the line of the river and towards a copse of trees shading a large Georgian house when the badger had waddled sedately across the grass in front of them.

'Oh!'

Rosie had grabbed Fergus's arm and he'd burst out laughing.

'Look at him,' he said. 'Doesn't give a rat's arse that we're here, does he?'

As if the badger had heard him, it turned and looked, before sniffing the air and then going on its way.

'I've never seen a badger that close up before!' Rosie squeaked. 'It's so cute!'

'Cute until it goes for your ankles,' Fergus countered with a lazy grin as they started to walk again and the badger disappeared into the undergrowth.

'Still.' Rosie smiled. 'I feel as if I'm properly in the sticks now. The most we'd have got at home was a fox going through the bins.'

'At home?' Fergus raised his eyebrows and looked down at her. 'Isn't this home now?'

Rosie had given him a coy smile, cheered by the good food and booze and excited by her recent encounter. 'I suppose it could be,' she said.

He'd squeezed her hand. 'Didn't I tell you? Didn't I say you'd learn to love it? Sometimes, Rosie, I think I know what you want better than you do.'

'I think you might be right,' Rosie said. 'I know I can be hard work, but thank you for sticking with me.'

'Well, maybe you could try to remember this conversation next time you want to get hysterical about missing your mum or not being able to have a shower, eh?'

The memories still circled around her head as she grabbed her shawl and went out. The night was warm, but she took it in case she was out for a while and it cooled. Fergus used to laugh at her shawl; he said she looked like a character from a period drama. She'd been persuaded to buy it from a street vendor in Valletta on their five-year anniversary trip, a sweet old woman who'd wrapped it across her shoulders as she'd stopped to peruse the stall and told her the money would buy her grand-kids some shoes. Rosie knew that probably wasn't true, but she'd liked the old lady's tanned, crinkled smile and she'd liked the shawl and so she had bought it. When she wore it now, it reminded her of that holiday and brought Fergus a little closer again.

As she walked the towpath she could see that some of the boats moored alongside had lights on in the windows. There were all kinds: old, renovated narrowboats that would have once traversed canals carrying goods; newer ones built especially for holidays; longer, broader barges; pleasure cruisers and even rowing boats. Most of them were for hire, some housed permanent or long-time residents, and some were home to businesses that operated out of them during the day. Of these there was Angel's Cocktail Barge, which Angel took out along the river into Stratford or Warwick to make the most of tourists on days out; there was Hal's River Trips, Luca's Gelato boat, and the sandwich place owned by Juliet.

Rosie had expected hostility from Juliet when she and Fergus had first arrived to turn the old, very run-down and unfrequented cafe on the marina into what they hoped would be a welcoming, successful and popular one. Fergus had worked his charm, however, assuring her that as she often took her trade out and about like Angel did, and that his and Rosie's cafe was very landbound indeed, there was probably room at the marina for both of them. Since then, though they were hardly bosom buddies, Juliet had been friendly enough, and even quite sweet after Fergus had died.

As she passed Juliet's boat, she noticed the one moored outside Nicole's shop which had, up until this point, been empty, now had a light on inside. So this was the bookshop Nicole had told her about? And someone was clearly in there – perhaps getting ready to open like she was? Rosie had been so busy of late she'd barely walked this way and hadn't noticed any activity until now, but could see even in the lamplight that the hull and cabin had been freshly painted and the deck was strewn with flowerpots. As she drew closer she could see a man inside arranging books on a shelf. He looked busy, absorbed in his task, but should Rosie knock and introduce herself? It seemed rude not to, as he was about to become one of her neighbours, and they would probably end up drumming up trade for each other too, after all. Coffee and books went together like... well, coffee and books.

She hesitated. She *could* knock, but he did look very busy.

Rosie had just decided she would leave it for now rather than disturb his work – he must have a lot to be toiling at such a late hour – when he turned and caught sight of her.

She froze. Now she looked like some passing nutter standing by his boat and staring in at him. But his vague look of query turned into a smile and he held a finger up to indicate, she presumed, that she should stay where she was.

A moment later he was on the deck, leaning over, his smile warmer still. 'It's Rosie, isn't it?'

'Yes. How did you...?'

'My sister described you perfectly. She said you had big blue eyes and violet hair... That was the clincher – not many people with violet hair around here.'

'Your sister?'

'She came for a job interview with you.'

'She did?'

'Yes. I don't know if you remember her. She didn't get it – of course, you know that.'

'What was her name?'

'Tabitha.'

'Tabitha! Of course!' Rosie suddenly felt quite guilty that she hadn't given Tabitha the job after all. If she'd known she'd have her brother for a neighbour... 'She was very good,' she said. 'Lovely, in fact. It was just... I needed someone a bit more...'

'Experienced. I get it. She's had a bit of that so she wasn't surprised to hear it from you. Don't worry, there's no hard feelings. Business is business. I'd give her a job, but I can't afford her – not yet anyway. Doubt I'll ever be able to. Not much money in second-hand books.'

'Why did you open a bookshop then?' Rosie asked without thinking, then blushed at her bluntness.

But he just looked puzzled by her question. 'Because I like them. You have to love something if you're going to put all your savings into it, don't you?'

Rosie nodded. She wasn't about to tell him that she had never really wanted to run a cafe and was only doing it now for a man who was no longer with her. Did that make her sound mad? To say it out loud might sound a bit mad, now that she thought about it.

'So we're going to be neighbours,' he continued.

'Looks like it. When do you open?'

'Tomorrow if I can get all this done on time. How about you? Are you already open?'

'Tomorrow too,' Rosie said. 'There won't be a lot of fanfare, no opening party or anything. I mean, I've put posts out on Facebook and a few posters up around the town, but that's about it. Not much of a budget for proper paid advertising. I'll be giving away free cake though, if you buy a coffee – a sort of opening offer. If you get time, drop by and you can have free coffee too. Just a neighbourly thing, of course.'

'Sounds good. No fanfare for me either. I'll just open the doors and hope people come in.'

He leant further over and stuck out his hand. Rosie inched closer to the water's edge to shake it but kept one eye on the bank. She couldn't swim – another reason she had given against moving to a riverside location, and another thing Fergus had persuaded her didn't matter. The way he'd put it had made sense at the time – she had no reason to venture out onto the water if she didn't want to and was quite safe in the cafe – but he wasn't there now, and sometimes she forgot why it had made so much sense. Anyway, the last thing she needed that night was to end up in the river, whether she could swim to shore or not.

'I'm Kit. Pleased to meet you, neighbour.'

'I'm Rosie,' she said. 'I mean, I know you know that already. Pleased to meet you too.'

It felt as if his hand had rested in hers for hours, but it must only have been seconds. There was something oddly comfortable about it. In fact, she didn't want to let go. She suddenly realised how inappropriate that was and stepped back.

'I should let you...' she said finally, her face burning, glad it was too dark for him to see it.

'Yeah,' he said, straightening up. 'I should get on – I'll be here all night otherwise.'

'I could lend a hand if you like. I'd probably be more hindrance than help, but I could try if you tell me what you need.'

'I couldn't. You've got plenty to do at your place, I'm sure.'

'It's no bother. To be honest, I could do with something to take my mind off tomorrow.'

He regarded her frankly for a moment. 'I couldn't ask you to get involved in my terrible stock system, but maybe it'd be nice to take a break. I don't know many people on the marina yet... If you fancy a brew, I'm sure I can find two mugs in my mess below deck.'

'Oh, I...' Rosie hesitated. She didn't know this man at all, and having a drink with him meant going aboard his boat, but for some reason, she was tempted. But then she shook her head. 'Perhaps I should get back after all... things to do for opening tomorrow...'

'Yeah.' He smiled. 'Another time, maybe?'

'Another time sounds nice. So... well... it was good to meet you.'

'Good to finally meet you too, and good to see Tabitha doesn't exaggerate like me.'

Rosie gave a slight frown at his strange comment, but before she was able to ask what he meant by it, he was already bidding her goodnight and heading below deck.

It was such an odd thing to say, Rosie thought as she continued her walk, slower now, more pensive and no longer quite as interested in the boats quietly bobbing on the calm river, the moon hanging low in the sky, or the rabbits emerging from their burrows.

They'd only shared the briefest conversation, but her new neighbour had made quite an impression, and she couldn't decide how she felt about that.

Rosie woke at dawn. The sun was pouring in through a crack in the bedroom curtains. It was probably what woke her, but she quickly decided it was an auspicious sign, despite wishing she could have had ten extra minutes in bed.

The sun was shining on her venture. It felt like a good day to open a cafe.

She turned to the empty pillow beside her and stroked a hand over it. 'Well,' she said. 'Here it is – the big day at last. I wish you could have been here to share it with me. I'll do my best to make you proud.'

She was sick with nerves, too nauseous to make breakfast, even though she realised she'd regret not eating in a few hours as she tried to navigate her first day in what was effectively a new job for her, as well as Letitia, on an empty stomach. At least she had her new waitress coming in, for backup. If Rosie desperately needed a break and a bite to eat mid-morning, she was certain Letitia would be able to take up the slack. So she made black coffee – though she probably didn't need the extra stimulation of a caffeine kick – and drank it standing at the window of her still-closed cafe, watching as the other buildings of the marina came to life.

Grant arrived first in his vintage Aston Martin. Fergus used to joke that Grant thought he was Sean Connery in *Goldfinger*. Strangely, Rosie did see a resemblance. Sometimes she got the impression that Grant was about the only man on the marina who'd intimidated Fergus a little, which was strange because Grant was about the friendliest man Rosie had ever met. To her, he didn't appear to have a hostile bone in his body. Fergus had never said anything concrete to her; it was just a vague feeling she'd had. They'd never even really had a proper conversation, as far as she could tell. She supposed it was one of those things – not everyone got along with everyone, even people who were nice to everyone else.

Grant parked and Rosie watched as he pulled open the vast doors of the boathouse. One of his sons arrived a minute later – she must learn their names – and hailed his dad before they both went into the little office that stood next to the boathouse.

Luca arrived next, dragging an impossibly large trailer emblazoned with a large, colourful graphic of an ice cream and the name of his business, Luca's Gelato, behind a push bike. It suggested next-level strength. He stopped it beside his boat and opened up the trailer, taking boxes of supplies out and taking them aboard. He was quickly followed by Angel, whose barge was moored close to his. They shared a brief chat and some laughter before she went aboard her own barge and disappeared below deck.

The lights in the farm shop across the bridge went on next. It would be Layla or her husband Tom. It was a farm shop in name, but it wasn't connected to a farm that they owned. Instead, they were supplied by local growers and lived on site as Rosie did; though, she supposed, given that Nicole had said they planned to open a pick-your-own site, they'd decided to put some of the land they had at the back of the shop to use growing some produce themselves. Since Nicole had mentioned it, she'd noticed plastic sheeting stretched over large frames, like those huge greenhouses you sometimes saw in fields. She wondered what was growing in there.

Nicole arrived next. Instead of going into her own shop, however, she knocked on the side of Kit's barge.

Something about the familiarity of it piqued Rosie's interest, though she hardly knew why. Had Kit spent the night aboard his boat? – that was her first question. And if he had, how did Nicole know? Did they know each other better than Nicole would have Rosie believe? If that was the case, why cover it up? Were they having a fling, despite what Nicole had said about the age gap? Rosie couldn't imagine why Nicole would hide it, or why she'd feel that Rosie would judge her if she'd taken Rosie into her confidence. There was no bigger difference in their age than there had been for Fergus and Rosie, and that had never been a problem – why would Nicole and Kit be any different?

Despite what Nicole had said to Rosie about him being younger, if they wanted to have a fling, good luck to them, Rosie thought, and she didn't see why it had to be a secret. If Rosie had been in Nicole's position and had battled through a painful divorce like she had, she'd be looking for a bit of light relief wherever she could too. And Kit would definitely be that, if not more, with his dark eyes and dishevelled curls that needed a cut but were cuter for it, his warm smile and obvious intelligence and charm. He seemed like a genuinely nice guy, and what was even more compelling than his obvious attractiveness was that he seemed completely unaware of how handsome he was. If ever there was a turn-on – in Rosie's eyes, at least – it was that.

Of course, Rosie was about as far from Nicole's situation as it was possible to get. Nicole had been on her own for a while now and was probably more than ready to let her hair down – she might even be ready for a new relationship that proved to be something more. Rosie, on the other hand, was still reeling from the loss of Fergus, even nine months on. The way she felt right then, nine decades could pass and she still wouldn't be ready to try again.

All this ran through Rosie's thoughts as she watched Nicole wait, feeling a little stalkerish but unable to stop looking. A moment later, Kit emerged from below deck, hair looking even wilder and more unruly than it had the night before when she'd talked to him. He was pulling on a sweater as Nicole greeted him. Perhaps he'd only just woken up; though for someone about to open his business for the first time, as Rosie herself was, it was awesomely relaxed. Rosie could only envy that as the butterflies did circuits of her tummy. Another moment later, Nicole climbed on board and they both disappeared below deck.

Rosie waited for them to come back up, but they didn't. Then she was surprised by a rogue yawn. She eyed the coffee cup in her hand. 'Fat lot of good you are.'

If only she hadn't woken quite so early – at this rate she'd have to ask Letitia to mind the cafe for more than a quick bite to eat: she'd have to ask her to take over so she could head back to bed.

Still, she had work to do, yawning or not. With a last look along the riverbank towards Kit's boat, she downed her now lukewarm coffee and took the cup to the sink to wash. Then she turned her attention back to the real issue of the day.

Luckily – or perhaps because she'd obsessed over being prepared for this day – the cafe itself was ready to open: clinically clean, tablecloths meticulously ironed and draped with precision over the tables, vases of flowers placed with methodical care, prints hung on walls with mathematical precision, glass shelves gleaming, and all cooking surfaces so clean someone could... well, eat their dinners from them. All that remained to do was to prepare the food.

She'd done what she could in advance, but some food would

have spoilt if done too early. Even then, there were choices on the menu that couldn't be prepared until they had been ordered, but things like grating carrots and slicing onions... that she could happily do now. There was also the water heater to fire up, hotplates and griddles to heat and the coffee machine to fill.

Rosie glanced up at the clock. There was still ten minutes until opening time but she would have expected Letitia to be there by now. On starting a new job, Rosie would always arrive early. Perhaps that was just her – maybe other people were more relaxed about these things. And as Rosie had never been a boss before, she wasn't quite sure if she ought to be annoyed about the lax arrival or not. Fergus would have told her to chill, that everything would be fine, and it would have been, almost as if he'd manifested it. That seemingly supernatural ability to make his confidence real, his optimism and faith, the ability to think a positive result into existence was the reason she'd been persuaded to follow him down the path that had led to Marigold Marina and her new life hundreds of miles away from all she'd ever known.

She loved it here now, of course, but given the choice in the beginning, she would have stayed put in the safe, pedestrian life they'd had before. It was a pity his endless optimism had failed him in the end – no amount of positive thinking had been able to fend off his heart attack.

By 8.30 a.m., there was still no Letitia. Rosie opened the front doors to nobody and declared herself quietly open. She hadn't expected hordes of waiting customers, but perhaps one might have been nice. Even nicer – certainly more encouraging – would have been the arrival of her new waitress. Where was Letitia? If this tardiness was going to be a regular feature, Rosie was going to be in trouble. Funny, though, as Letitia really hadn't struck Rosie as the unreliable type, and Rosie usually had a good instinct for that sort of thing.

. . .

At 9 a.m. Rosie decided to phone Letitia but got no reply. She didn't plan to shout but was seriously worried now that something had gone very wrong for her. At 9.15 a.m. the first customer of the day arrived. Just Grant, who'd decided to fetch a coffee. Rosie was sure he had plenty of coffee at the boatyard but had just wanted to show some neighbourly support. She thanked him, grateful for the sound of coins dropping into the till drawer as he left with his takeout.

She passed a good portion of the morning in a similar vein. She tried Letitia a couple more times, to no avail. Then she decided not to call again, trusting that Letitia would return her calls eventually and that if there was some kind of emergency, the last thing her waitress needed was hassle from her new boss.

Customers were thin on the ground – a tea here, a slice of cake or a bag of crisps there. Some took up the free cake with a hot drink offer. Rosie had assumed there would be enough passing trade in the marina to keep her busy but was beginning to question her assumptions now. Perhaps she should have taken out ads or something. The one saving grace was that at least trade had been manageable, considering she was currently running the place alone.

That changed at midday, however, when a party of twelve, freshly moored after a week on one of Grant's boats, decided to grab lunch before heading home from their trip.

Rosie's breath caught in her throat as they cheerfully filed in. She ought to have been pleased; this was the kind of custom she'd been geared up for, the kind of custom she would come to rely on if the cafe was to stay open, and though she knew it was good news after a worryingly quiet morning, she was filled with dread.

How on earth was she going to cope on her own?

'Aunty... Uncle... Ted, Chad... you sit there...' A woman,

seemingly the head of the party, organised people over to the tables. 'I'll go and order drinks,' she continued. 'Tea? How many teas...? Five? So, coffee – oh, of course, Tracy wants a smoothie if they've got it. What kind, Trace?'

Rosie watched the exchange, glued to her spot behind the counter, a smile frozen in place. She looked the part of the welcoming, confident hostess but she certainly didn't feel it.

The woman came to the counter. 'Five teas please. Six coffees. Do you have any smoothies?'

'Just the premade ones – the bottles are in the fridge,' Rosie said, hoping drinks were all they'd want. That wouldn't be too difficult, would it?

'Trace!' the woman shouted. 'Have a look in the fridge there to see if any of those bottles are any good.'

Tracy got up, the scraping of the chair on Rosie's tiled floor echoing around the room. 'Oh, I don't like any of these,' she said, staring at the shelf of the open fridge. 'Haven't you got any that are just fruit?'

'That's all I have, I'm afraid,' Rosie said.

'You can't make one up?'

'I don't have the facilities.'

'Hmm... I suppose I'll have to have a glass of water then,' she replied sullenly. 'I hate tea and coffee and I can't drink anything fizzy.'

'I have chilled peach tea.'

'I hate tea and coffee,' the woman repeated very deliberately.

'Right, sorry...' Rosie went to the sink to run the tap for her water.

'Are we getting food?' the first woman shouted across to her companions.

There was a chorus of agreement and Rosie held in a groan. She couldn't afford to be ungrateful for their business but the next hour or so was going to be a nightmare.

As the woman was collecting orders, every one of them deviating from the usual (no cress in the egg sandwich, extra cheese on the tuna toastie, gluten-free bread on one ham sandwich but not the other, two children's portions with revised children's prices, and so on) the cafe door opened and Rosie looked up to see Kit walk in.

He smiled warmly at her, taking up a station at a respectful distance while Rosie dealt with her current customers. Or, rather, listened to them debate how many portions of chips they wanted between them.

Then the louder woman, suddenly noticing Kit waiting, stepped back. 'We're not quite decided yet, love,' she said to him. 'Jump ahead while this lot makes up their mind; we're in no rush.'

'Thanks,' Kit said, moving to the counter as she stood aside. 'How's it going?' he asked Rosie.

'Good,' Rosie said.

He raised his eyebrows slightly. 'Good? Is that why you have cheese in your hair?'

'What?'

Kit grinned and reached over with an unnerving familiarity to fish it out and show her. 'There you go – cheese!'

'Oh, I must look a mess! There's no more, is there?' she asked, putting a hand in her hair to shake it out.

'No, the rest of it looks just perfect. So, how's it really going? I think we can agree we shared a moment with the cheese, so you can be honest with me now.'

'I'm just not used to doing this yet,' she said, abandoning the pretence and lowering her voice to add: 'I never knew people could make a ham sandwich so difficult. I suppose I'm finding out the hard way. What can I get for you?'

'Well, I was going to ask for a ham sandwich but now I'm scared to.'

Rosie couldn't help but relax into a smile. 'Sorry, ignore me.

I'm being ungrateful; I should be glad of the custom. It's just that I'm on my own.'

'Oh? I thought you'd taken someone on.'

'I did, but she hasn't showed up for work. I don't mind admitting I'm worried, and that's hardly helping my mood.'

'No contact from her?'

'Not a dickie bird, and I've tried calling a number of times. I can only assume something bad has happened, but at the same time I really hope not.'

'Is it a big problem for you?'

'I suppose I can manage – I don't have any choice. Enough of that anyway – how's your first day going?'

'A lot calmer than yours, I suspect. Made a few sales, nothing earth shattering, but then I hardly imagined people beating down my door for old books.'

'It's OK though?' Rosie asked.

'Sure. As long as I can pay my rent, I'm not after big bucks. If I was, I've certainly gone into the wrong line of work.'

'Me too.' Rosie smiled, and if she'd been tempted to follow up with how this life hadn't been her idea at all, she kept it in check. 'Just ham on your sandwich?'

'Ham and pickle,' he said.

'Nice and simple – I like it.'

'That's been said many times,' he replied cheerfully. 'Mostly by ex-girlfriends.'

Rosie's mind went back to early that morning as she buttered bread. She wanted to ask whether her hunch was right, whether he and Nicole were an item, even though Nicole had denied any interest, but she couldn't figure out how without sounding impertinent or nosy, and she couldn't work out why it should matter to her anyway.

'Does the farm shop across the bridge sell smoothies?'

Rosie and Kit both looked round to see the second woman, holding her glass of water, standing at the counter.

'I don't know,' Rosie said.

Would it be very rude to add that it wasn't her job to memorise the stock of someone else's shop?

'I don't think so,' Kit chipped in. 'It's mostly local produce – eggs and bread, that kind of thing.'

'What about that other sandwich place? The boat?'

'Juliet? I think she just left,' Kit said. 'She mostly caters in town anyway, rather than on the marina, but I saw her cast off a few minutes ago either way.'

'Oh.'

Kit glanced at the fridge. 'There are smoothies in there.'

'I don't like those.'

'Right... they look pretty good to me.'

'Too much weird stuff in them.'

'So, what's not weird to you?'

'I don't know – regular fruit, I suppose.'

'Strawberries?'

'Yeah. Maybe banana or grape or something.'

'So you'd be happy to have something made up for you?' he asked.

'I don't have a smoothie maker,' Rosie cut in. 'Sorry.'

'But you have a normal blender?' Kit asked.

'In the kitchen, but...'

'You have any fruit?'

'Yes, some—'

'Crushed ice?'

'Yes, but...'

Kit was thoughtful for a moment. 'I could whip something up in your blender. I made smoothies all the time for my sister when she was home. We used to use up old fruit that way.'

Rosie tried not to frown. She wasn't sure if she ought to be grateful for his offer or frustrated that it made her look a bit useless in front of a customer.

'It wouldn't take me a minute,' he said.

'Could you?' the woman asked. 'It'd be far better than water.'

Kit looked at Rosie, who nodded towards the kitchen, looking as receptive as she could. She was sure he was only trying to help but it was still slightly annoying. However, common sense had to prevail, and at this point she'd take help however it came.

'It's on the worktop,' she said. 'And there's fruit in the fridge.'

Twenty minutes later, the party was sitting with their orders and things had quietened down. Apart from the smoothie debacle, Rosie had managed, and she wondered now why she'd panicked at all.

Kit picked up the sandwich she'd just packed for him.

'I've just realised,' Rosie said suddenly, 'your book barge... who's looking after it?'

'I put up a closed sign,' he said. 'And Nicole's keeping an eye out.'

'Oh, of course... she can probably see from her window.'

'Yes. It's handy, I can tell you. How much do I owe you?'

'God, nothing! You helped me, so the least I can do is a free sandwich!'

'It only took me a minute.'

'Still, it made for a far happier customer. You'll have to write down the recipe for me.'

'As long as you remember half a cup of fruit to a full cup of liquid you can't really go wrong,' he said, grinning. 'Will you be OK?'

'I think so. I'm going to try Letitia again, but it's not looking good, is it?'

'No. I don't want to overstep the mark here, but Tabitha is

still free if you need her help. She'd be glad of the money and, of course, wouldn't expect to stay if Letitia turns up.'

'I'd feel terrible taking advantage of her like that.'

'Honestly, you wouldn't be. She's bored at home with Mum, so she'd be glad of something to do. I could phone her – it'd be no problem.'

'The thing is, I don't know how busy things will get. The rest of the day might be dead and then I've got her over here for nothing.'

'It might also be frantic.'

'True. But I think I'll take my chances. I'd hate for Letitia to walk in and see someone else in her place already too, especially if something awful has happened to her this morning.'

'As you like, but let me know if you change your mind.'

It was tempting to change her mind almost as soon as she'd refused his offer – in the immediate term it would make her life a lot easier. But she stuck to her guns and steeled herself to continue the day under her own steam. If the afternoon – the post-lunchtime rush, if she was lucky enough to experience one of those on a regular basis and she could call it that – proved to be as quiet as the morning had been, then she'd be glad she hadn't put Kit to the trouble of fetching his sister to work for her. She suspected he was only being kind and that Tabitha might not have been so keen to race over to help the woman who'd over-looked her for the very job she was being asked at short notice to cover. It was a bit 'insult to injury' – probably not a good plan.

'I'll be fine,' she said. 'I've got to get used to days like this, I suppose.'

'Well, if you're sure...'

'I'm sure.'

'OK. Thanks for the sandwich. I'll see you around.'

'I'm sure you will,' Rosie said. 'Good luck for the rest of the day.'

'You too,' he replied, already making his way out with his lunch.

As the door closed behind him, there was a crash on one of the occupied tables. Rosie spun round to see a broken teacup on the floor and a pool of tea spreading around it. She held in a sigh. She was going to need more than luck to get through this day – she was going to need some serious patience.

Rosie was exhausted as she locked the cafe door; so tired, she wasn't even thinking about how lonely she was going to be as she settled down for the evening in her little flat, as she had done almost every night since Fergus's death. But she was happy. No, not so much happy... maybe it was more relief she was experiencing. She had survived the first day – a day that had gone to a plan barely recognisable from the ones she'd made for it – and she realised that maybe she did have the strength to do it after all. There had been months of doubt, second-guessing and angst; so many times she'd wanted to throw in the towel and hide under the wings of her parents at her childhood home, but she hadn't, and the sense of achievement she enjoyed now was her reward.

She'd thought about trying Letitia's phone again during quiet spells in the afternoon, but in the end had decided to trust that Letitia would contact her to explain or at least to let her know if she was planning to begin her job another day. It wasn't ideal, not for Rosie at least, but it seemed the kindest and most respectful course of action.

There was leftover chicken pie. Rosie was so tired that she took it from the cafe to her flat, ate it cold without accompaniment and then promptly fell asleep on the sofa.

. . .

Rosie was woken by the sound of her phone ringing. She had no idea how long she'd been asleep, but outside the sky was lavender and there was a chill in the air. Shivering and groggy, Rosie reached to retrieve it from the coffee table.

'Hello?'

'Is that Rosie?' A man's voice on the line.

'Yes. Who is this?'

'I'm Letitia's husband. I'm so sorry we didn't phone before, but—'

'Oh! Hi! It's fine... is she alright?'

'Not really. She fell this morning – on the way out to work actually.'

'Fell?'

'Down the stairs. Loose carpet. My fault really... she's reminded me enough times to fix it. I've been at the hospital with her all day.'

'Oh God! What's happened to her?'

'She's broken her arm and fractured her collarbone.'

Rosie let out a gasp, fully awake now and horrified.

'She's sedated,' he continued. 'Lots of painkillers. It took me a while to find your number and I couldn't get down to the marina...'

'Of course – please don't worry about that. I'm just relieved to get the news now, though I wish it could have been better. Please tell her not to worry about the cafe. She should focus on getting well; nothing else is important right now.'

'That's just it.' Letitia's husband cleared his throat. 'She's going to be out of action for some time – months possibly. She says to tell you she completely understands if you want to give the job to someone else.'

'I don't want to do that,' Rosie said, though she'd already been forced to consider the possibility. Months without help? She didn't think she'd be able to survive a week running Marigold Cafe by herself, let alone months.

'But we understand that you might need to.'

Rosie was silent for a moment, eyes on the darkening windows. 'I'm sure I could keep her job open,' she said finally. 'Though I might need to get temporary help.'

'She said to tell you she's sorry to let you down on such an important day.'

'She shouldn't even think of such a thing. I was fine; I managed OK. I mean, I'd have loved her there of course, but I muddled through and I'm here to tell the tale.'

'Good, I'm glad. Thanks for being so understanding.'

'Just keep me posted on her progress, won't you?'

'Of course.'

'And thanks for letting me know.'

'Sorry it wasn't sooner.'

'It can't be helped.'

'I'm going back to the hospital now, so I'll...'

Rosie paused as he paused. What did she say now? Was she supposed to send love? She barely knew Letitia, but they were already significantly connected, so she felt like she ought to offer something. In the end, she decided a get-well message would suffice.

Letitia's husband apologised again, promised to phone regularly and then ended the call.

Rosie set the handset down on the table. All tiredness had been banished and her brain flew through her options. She had some clarity, at last, but that brought a whole new set of problems with very little time to sort any kind of solution. She needed a new assistant, and she needed one fast. There was an obvious answer right in front of her, though she wasn't happy about it. How insulting would it be to know you were a consolation prize for a job you'd wanted? It happened all the time of course, but it had never happened to Rosie during her working life, and she couldn't imagine how she'd feel. Perhaps she'd be far more practical about it if it was a choice between a wage or not?

One thing was for certain: if Rosie didn't want to go through the whole advertising a vacancy and interviewing process again – which would be made harder this time by having to state upfront that it would only be a temporary position – then she was going to have to approach someone she'd already seen, and the best candidate from those people after Letitia had been Kit's sister, Tabitha. She could go to an employment agency, she supposed, but she knew that would cost her more because the agency would want commission on top of any wage, and she was in no financial position to take that kind of hit.

Would Kit still be at the book barge? she wondered. Was it time to swallow her pride and take him up on the offer of contact with Tabitha? It didn't matter how many times she tried to tell herself it was no big deal, she still didn't like it. But if ever she needed the young girl's help, it was now. It was also the ideal opportunity to thank Kit for his help earlier that day. Now that she'd closed the cafe up and had time to mull things over, she could see that she oughtn't to have been irritated by him helping her to make smoothies but grateful. With that in mind, she foraged in the fridge and boxed up a couple of fresh cream cakes to take over, hoping he didn't have any allergies that would prevent him from eating them.

Grabbing her shawl and balancing the box on her arms, she headed out into the evening. Dusk had fallen properly now and the lamps were just coming on along the path. The scent of freshly cut grass filled the air, and Rosie noticed the verges had been trimmed. Kit's boat bobbed serenely on the water, its freshly painted hull gleaming. It looked as if he'd added to the plants that covered the deck, and there was also a small mosaic table with two chairs sitting next to a heater. It was beginning to look homely. She wondered if Kit was planning to live there as well as run his shop from there, but it seemed cramped if he was.

As she drew closer she could hear voices and laughter. Then she recognised one of them and realised that Nicole was there. The lights were on below deck but the curtains were closed. It sounded like the two of them were very relaxed and sharing a joke. Rosie could hear glasses clinking. Nicole was definitely flirting; Rosie might have been away from the dating game for a long time but she recognised a flirty voice when she heard one.

She hesitated. She wanted to speak to Kit, but if something intimate was happening there, she certainly didn't want to be the person to spoil it for them. Nicole had stated quite emphatically that she felt Kit was too young for her, but it looked as though she had changed her mind. Rosie didn't blame her. He was good-looking, smart and charming. If she'd been at a different point in her mourning for Fergus, or if there had been a divorce, like in Nicole's case, rather than a bereavement of the kind that still sucked the breath from her lungs every time she thought of it, maybe Rosie would have been interested in Kit romantically too.

After a moment of indecision, Rosie decided not to disturb him, and instead to take the cakes back with her and give him something else next time she saw him. She needed Tabitha's help, but not that badly. Perhaps she'd be able to catch Kit early in the morning to ask him for his sister's number and also to thank him for his help in the cafe then. Right now, more than anything, she was annoyed at herself for being stupid enough to throw Tabitha's details away after the interviews. She should have realised she'd need a contingency plan in case anything happened with Letitia. She certainly couldn't blame Kit for being unavailable, though the idea still irked her and she couldn't quite understand why.

She'd barely taken five steps back down the towpath when

she heard her name being called. She turned to see that Kit was now above deck with Nicole. They both had a beer bottle in their hand.

'Rosie! Wait!' Kit put his bottle down and leapt from the boat to chase after her, Nicole standing on deck watching them. 'I meant to catch you before you closed up but I got busy. How did the rest of the day go? Did Letitia turn up?'

'She's had an accident,' Rosie said. 'Nothing life-threatening,' she added hastily at the look of concern on both Kit's and Nicole's faces. 'Broken bones, but she'll be out of action for a good while. Actually' – she glanced between Nicole, who had now decided to walk down the path to join them, and Kit carefully; she hoped they didn't think she'd been spying on them – 'I wanted to pop over and ask you about Tabitha. But I didn't want to disturb you.'

'Oh!' Kit laughed lightly. 'You wouldn't have been disturbing me. Nicole was just about to leave.'

'I was returning a book he'd lent me,' Nicole added in a careless tone that suggested that, far from feeling careless about her motives for being there, she was feeling decidedly cagey.

'A book?' Rosie tried not to frown. He'd been at the marina for a matter of days and Nicole – who Rosie had never seen reading – was borrowing books from him? And, apparently, returning books also required a beer to help that process along. Now she knew Nicole was interested – and not just so Kit could recommend her a page-turner.

Sometimes she wondered why people didn't just say what they meant. Nicole had denied an interest in Kit, but clearly that wasn't the case. Why hide it? Rosie certainly wouldn't judge; she couldn't see the point in that and – even more importantly – it made her a little disappointed that Nicole had felt she had to hide it from her. Rosie was convinced they'd become good friends since Fergus's death, but perhaps they weren't really as close as she'd imagined.

'I can phone Tab if you like,' he said, breaking into her thoughts. 'I'm sure she'd be happy to step in for a few weeks.'

Rosie looked at Kit. 'I wouldn't be able to promise anything permanent, and I wouldn't want to stop her from finding another job. It's a bit of a bum deal if I'm honest, but I'm pretty stuck and you did say—'

'I don't think any of that will be a problem. Let's face it – she ought to be grateful to work down the road from her awesome brother so she gets to see him every day.'

Rosie smiled. 'Doesn't she see you every day anyway?'

He grinned. 'Not if she can help it.'

'Well, I can't deny that I'm desperate for the help,' Rosie replied, trying to ignore the intense stare she could feel coming from Nicole. There was no reason for it that she could think of but she sensed it just the same. 'I'd really appreciate her stepping in if she can. Do you want me to phone and ask? I don't have her number still but...'

'Don't worry. I'll do it now. I know she's home with Mum. You want her to come tomorrow morning?'

'I'd love that if she could.'

'Great. I'll let you know if otherwise, but expect to see her tomorrow, bright and early.'

'Thank you so much. I owe you one.' Then she remembered the box in her arms and held it out. 'And I thought you might like these... cream cakes... I hope you can eat them... no allergies or anything. I think about allergies a crazy amount since I started on the cafe!'

'God, no! I love any kind of cake!' Kit beamed, taking the box from her.

'Cream cakes, eh?' Nicole put in, her face a mask that Rosie suddenly couldn't read. 'I don't get cream cakes.'

Was she being sarcastic? Was she annoyed at Rosie? Had Rosie somehow crossed some line she hadn't even realised was there?

She decided to dismiss the comment.

'There's definitely a cream cake next time you come to visit,' she said as brightly as she could, though she hardly felt it at that moment.

They stood and looked at each other for a few seconds more. If Nicole hadn't been there, Rosie would have invited Kit over to the cafe for a drink as a getting-to-know-her-neighbour kind of thing, but she was aware of how that might look – not her intention at all – and she didn't want Nicole to think she was trying to ruin her chances with him, or that she might want a chance to get with him herself. Nicole already looked as if she thought that without Rosie making it worse.

But then Kit did it instead. 'Stay for a beer if you like.'

Rosie glanced at Nicole, who looked faintly annoyed but gave a stiff smile anyway. 'Yes, why don't you join us?'

Kit turned to her. 'I thought you were leaving?'

'Well, if Rosie's staying for a beer, I don't have to go just yet, do I? I'd quite like to know how her first day at the cafe went too.'

'No...' Kit looked flustered now as he glanced between the two of them. 'Of course you don't have to go... it'd be great to have you stick around.'

'I'm not sure...' Rosie began, feeling very much as if she was getting in the middle of something by staying. At least, it seemed Nicole felt that way, though Rosie understood she could hardly say so in front of Kit.

'Go on,' Kit said. 'I didn't get that brew with you last night either...'

Nicole threw Rosie a quizzical look now. 'You came by last night?'

'I was out walking and I saw the light was on,' Rosie said. 'Just being neighbourly, that's all.'

'Oh.'

'So, one beer?' Kit asked. 'And you do owe me for saving your arse with the smoothie incident...'

Rosie sighed. 'You're really not going to let me off the hook, are you?'

'Nope.'

'I would, but, well...'

'She doesn't want to get on the boat,' Nicole put in.

Rosie flushed. 'I'm just nervous around boats... I mean, they don't bother me as long as I don't have to have anything to do with them.'

'That's easy to fix,' Kit said cheerily. 'We can sit on the bank and have our beer there. No need for you to get on at all.'

Rosie shook her head. The subliminal message from Nicole was coming through loud and clear – Rosie wasn't welcome right now. It stung a little, but she'd never been one to stay where she wasn't wanted. Nicole must have had her reasons. 'Thanks, but I'm shattered and I've got another early start tomorrow.'

'Another time then?'

'Yeah.'

'I'm keeping track, you know. Because you said that last night as well.'

'I did, didn't I? I promise when things have settled at the cafe you can both come over for drinks with me there.'

'Right,' Kit said, giving Nicole an uncertain glance.

'Goodnight then,' Rosie added, smiling at him and Nicole in turn. 'Thanks again... you know, for talking to Tabitha for me.'

'No problem,' Kit said. 'Thanks for my cake! I'll be in for a butty tomorrow,' he added. 'I'll see you then.'

'It'll be on the house,' Rosie replied. 'Another favour I owe you in no way repaid, but it's the least I can do.'

'Hey,' Nicole put in. 'It's what we do around here – help each other out.'

'It is,' Rosie said. 'I guess I'm still not used to it. Goodnight. I'll see you both tomorrow.'

'Rosie...'

She turned back at the sound of Nicole's voice.

'I just... I'm sorry I didn't get over to see how you'd got on today. I know I said I would but I've been busy... you know how it is.'

Rosie looked between the two of them. It had probably been far too obvious, but she couldn't help it. Nicole's excuse didn't ring true, and Rosie was disappointed to hear it. She'd rather have heard the truth – Nicole had obviously decided her free time was better spent flirting with the new guy than going to see how her friend was at the end of one of the most important days of her life.

But she was tired, and perhaps she was overreacting. Nicole's world didn't have to revolve around Rosie – she didn't expect anyone's to. She only wished that Nicole would set her straight on what the deal was with her and Kit, and then she would know how to avoid putting her foot in it; and she'd also know not to expect as much attention from Nicole as she'd had in the past.

'Don't worry about it,' she said. 'I do know how it is.'

'I'll try and see you tomorrow.'

'That would be nice, but don't stress if you can't.'

'Goodnight, Rosie.'

'Goodnight.'

Rosie headed back to the cafe. One problem had been solved, but in the process, a million new questions had been posed.

CHAPTER FIVE

Tabitha was outside well before opening time.

'I got an SOS,' she said with a smile as Rosie let her in. 'I take it you do still need me? I'd have phoned ahead to warn you I was coming but I figured—'

'God, don't apologise!' Rosie ushered her inside before locking up again. She wasn't quite ready to go and didn't want customers wandering in before she was. 'Please don't worry about that. It's good of you to come. I guess Kit filled you in on what happened with the lady I hired.'

'He did. That's a horrible shame. I mean, I have to admit it's lucky for me but not so good for her. Is she alright?'

'I think she'll pull through. The question is how long it will take her. Here... let me show you where you can put your things...'

Rosie took Tabitha through the kitchen, through the storage area beyond, and into a little room that had once been an old coal house but had since been converted into a small conservatory. Rosie had earmarked it as somewhere to take breaks during the day, away from the cafe but still very separate from her home in the flat above, so she could keep a distinct divide between her work and private time. She'd kitted it out with rattan furniture, a second-hand sideboard and a small table and chairs.

A fresh June sun streamed in through the vast windows overlooking the garden beyond. It wasn't much of a garden really, but Rosie had filled it with pots and baskets of flowers and shrubs, and who needed a back garden when the beautiful River Avon was your front garden? Rosie was blessed with scenery that would be the envy of friends and family back home, there to enjoy whenever she looked out of her windows. And she barely had time to garden anyway, she reasoned, so a tiny back yard really wasn't such a problem. There was room for a chair or two and shade from an overhanging willow, and the lavender and honeysuckle that filled the space would bring enough bees for her to feel like she was sitting in a summer meadow.

'You can store your belongings in the sideboard when you're on the cafe floor,' Rosie said. 'And there's a coat stand for when you need to bring a jacket.'

'Don't have one today.' Tabitha went to the sideboard and opened a door to stick her rucksack in.

'Of course not. It looks as if it's going to be glorious,' Rosie said. 'About time this summer got started proper.'

'So...' Tabitha closed the cupboard and straightened up to face Rosie again. 'What do you want me to do first?'

'Well, there's not a huge amount to do right now. I wasn't sure if Kit would get hold of you in time, so I got the food prepped – most of it anyway. I guess you could do the bits I haven't managed. I still need the napkin dispensers filling, and the fridge could use a restock too.'

Rosie paused for inspiration. 'I'll show you where everything is and what I need, if you like. Later it will be a case of just feeding the masses as they arrive – at least now you're here I can hope for masses. Yesterday I had customers I sort of didn't want. Today I have help; it will be Sod's Law if they don't come in.'

'I hope I'm not your jinx,' Tabitha said. 'I'd rather be busy than standing around. Having nothing to do is so boring.'

'At least your brother is a few steps away. I won't mind you going over for a quick hello.'

'Kit won't want me over there cramping his style. I'll always be an annoying little pipsqueak to him.'

Rosie smiled. 'What's the age gap? If you don't mind me asking.'

'Ten years. Kit's almost thirty.'

'That's big for most siblings, isn't it? Not that I know all that much – I'm an only child.'

'We're half brother and sister actually. Same mum, different dad. I came along late for Mum after her second marriage. She already had Kit of course. And the age gap didn't stop him being an amazing brother. Always looked out for me, even though he was too old to play with me.'

'So he's *really* your big brother.'

'Yeah, really. Warning off bad boys when I was at school and everything...' Tabitha grimaced. 'He's still warning them off now.'

Rosie detected, for the first time, a tone that hinted at something a little less appreciative in Tabitha's statement. She didn't comment on it but guessed that perhaps Kit meddled where he wasn't wanted; still overprotective, maybe still covertly vetting Tabitha's boyfriends even now, when she was old enough to decide for herself.

At the interview, hadn't Tabitha told Rosie a bad boyfriend had sent her back to live with her mum? How had Kit dealt with that? she wondered. Perhaps he'd had something to do with the split. Or perhaps he was overprotective now because of it.

'In all honesty,' Tabitha continued as they walked back into the cafe, 'we look out for each other. If he dates someone I don't think is good for him, I'm not scared to tell him. He doesn't always want to be told of course, but what sort of sister would I be if I sat back and let him make a dick of himself?'

'Well, I wish I had a sibling who would look out for me like that.' Rosie handed Tabitha an apron.

'So you're an only child? At least you got all the treats.'

'Yes. I'm used to it now, but when I was little I was desperate for a brother or sister. I would have swapped all those treats and money for one any day of the week. You and Kit seem very lucky to me.'

'I suppose we are,' Tabitha said. 'It's hard to appreciate it when you argue and you have to share things, and when we were growing up it meant we didn't have so much money... Mum raised us alone. But we got by and he's not so bad. I could definitely have landed a worse brother.' She grinned. 'So where's that stuff you want me to do?'

Rosie raised her eyebrows. She'd never been this confident, this self-assured at Tabitha's age. Already she felt less than her boss, and by the end of the day it might well be Tabitha running the place and telling Rosie what to do. She couldn't help but admire that, as well as feeling vaguely threatened by it. During her marriage to Fergus she'd always let him lead. She'd never argued, even when she had doubts – she knew better than to try. She always followed anyway. She had a feeling that was something Tabitha would never do. Kit probably had his hands full with her as a sister to look out for, and she probably didn't take advice kindly from him either, despite his maturity.

Rosie opened the fridge and began taking out packs of fruit and vegetables. 'We'll chop together. While we work we can get to know each other a bit.'

'Sounds good to me.' Tabitha took a bag of carrots and tore it open. 'You know, I was actually excited when Kit phoned me last night.'

'You were?'

'Yes. I think helping out here is going to be a laugh. I was going mad spending my days at home.'

'Couldn't you have helped Kit out on the boat for something to do?'

'I offered – he said he couldn't afford me.'

Yes, Rosie remembered him saying that now.

'I would have done it for free, but... I get the feeling he'd rather run it alone.'

'Why?'

Tabitha shrugged. 'Not a clue. It's just a hunch; so I'm leaving him to it. I guess it's his business and he wants to prove he can do it or something... He worked in a warehouse before – we all told him he was way too smart for the job and got treated terribly by his boss, and it took him a while to believe us. I don't think he was even bothered back then; he just wanted the money to help with... well, never mind. The thing is, he believes now that he can make a go of it and I'm glad. I'm not going to interfere. If he needs me I'm sure he'll ask... Then again, he might not.'

Rosie nodded slowly. 'He's one of those stubborn types who can't accept help?'

Tabitha smiled as she washed the carrots but didn't reply.

'Oh?' Rosie cut open a bag of lettuce. 'I'm sure running his own place will cure him of that. I know he's already had Nicole watching the shop for him; yesterday, in fact, when he came over to get some lunch.'

'Who's Nicole?'

'She owns the gift shop that overlooks his mooring. Apparently, she sort of knows your brother already – friend of her sister's at school or something? I expect that's why he's comfortable asking for her help.'

'I don't know her,' Tabitha said, her forehead creasing. 'But I don't know much about Kit's old school friends – I was still so little when he was at high school. I wouldn't recognise a single one of them if they knocked on this door right now.'

'It's strange, isn't it? You two are brother and sister and yet you must have two separate little worlds that only intersect in the odd place here and there.'

'Oh, Kit knows all my school friends.' Tabitha laughed. 'He might have a secret world, but I don't. He kept a close eye on mine, and woe betide anyone who upset me.'

Rosie smiled as she ripped lettuce leaves from the stalk. 'Must have been nice, really, having someone look out for you like that.'

'You don't have anyone... I mean, like a partner or anything?'

Rosie took a breath and looked at her, forcing a smile. 'I never said at the interview... it didn't seem relevant... I actually bought this place with my husband. We were meant to run it together, but he died before we could finish the renovations.'

'God!'

Rosie nodded. 'I've been on my own for about nine months now. It was hard at first but I'm getting used to it. Don't worry, I won't be crying all the time.'

Tabitha cast a glance around the place, at the freshly plastered cream walls, exposed beams on the ceiling and vast windows opening out onto a paved patio dotted with plants, the river meandering by beyond the entrance gates. 'You did all this yourself?'

'Mostly.'

'Wow. Kudos to you. Go, queen!'

Rosie's smile was a little more genuine now. Tabitha hadn't offered empty condolences but had focused on Rosie's achievement alone since Fergus had gone, and she had to admit she quite liked it.

'I mean,' she added modestly, 'I got tradesmen in to do the things I couldn't, but most everything else was me. Probably bodged half of it... after a week things will start falling off walls, I'm sure.'

'Still, just to plan and execute – that's pretty awesome. Not sure I could do it, especially...'

After what you went through, Rosie thought, though she didn't say it and neither did Tabitha.

'Well,' Rosie said, deciding it was time to change the subject. She managed to stay fairly positive when she was in company, but there was only so much she could do to keep the maudlin thoughts at bay, and the more she talked about Fergus, the greater the danger was that her mood would darken. It wouldn't be a good way to start her working relationship with Tabitha, and she really needed to keep that on an even keel because she was going to be relying heavily on her over the next few weeks. 'The work doesn't stop because the cafe is ready for business. In fact, it's really only just begun.'

'Funny, that's what Kit said about his boat. Sort of. What he actually said was his *adventure* had only just begun. Though I'm not sure how sitting on a leaky barge surrounded by musty old books can be any kind of adventure.'

Rosie smiled. 'I hope you didn't say that to him.'

'Of course I did! What kind of sister do you take me for?'

'What did he say to that?'

'Said he'd put some jet engines on the back and whizz up and down the river firing copies of *Bleak House* from a cannon at passers-by just to make it more exciting for me.'

Rosie giggled. 'Every time I pass his boat now I won't be able to get that image out of my head.'

'I know, he's weird, right?'

'Hmm, well I wouldn't say weird... interesting, that's for sure.'

'You say that because you don't know him.'

'You don't really mean that.'

'Second-hand books? You've got to admit he's got some strange ideas about adventure.'

'I don't know... Look at my adventure. I'm running a cafe. Not exactly climbing Everest – though it's felt like it at times.'

Tabitha's reply was interrupted by a knock at the cafe's front door. Rosie shot a puzzled glance at Tabitha before drying her hands on a tea towel and going to answer. At the glass of the door she could see Kit – his back to her, gazing out across the marina as he waited.

He turned with a smile as she undid the lock. 'Good morning.'

'Kit? Did you want Tabitha?'

'She's here then? Good. You don't need to bother her if she's busy. I just wanted to check she'd come and that you were all set for today.'

'Yes, thank you. Are you sure you don't want to...?' Rosie hooked a thumb at the cafe to indicate he was welcome to step in if he wanted to speak to his sister, but he shook his head.

'I've got to open up myself in a minute. I'll grab her at lunch when I come to get my ham and pickle sandwich.'

'Ham? Again? You know I do other fillings?' she said wryly. 'I've got tuna, cheese, turkey—'

'What can I say? I like ham.'

Rosie smiled. 'In that case I'll have one ready for you.'

He tipped a finger to the flat cap he was wearing and started to walk back to his boat. 'Good luck with my sister,' he called as he went. 'You're going to need it!'

Rosie watched him go, a pensive look on her face. He was funny and charming and useful to have around and he'd be a good addition to the community at the marina. Already she looked forward to him coming to get his sandwich later.

She started to lock the door again but then glanced at the clock and decided it was near enough to opening time to leave it open. If anyone came in while she was in the kitchen, she'd hear the door go.

'Let me guess – Kit checking up on me?' Tabitha's tone was knowing as Rosie returned to her.

'Yes. I think he meant well – just being neighbourly, you know. Not really checking up on you as such; more checking I was OK.'

'Yeah, he was checking up on me – stop trying to stick up for him. Then again...' she added with a sudden sly look, 'if he just wanted to know that I'd managed to get up and get here on time, he could have just texted me instead of walking over to see you, couldn't he?'

'I suppose he could.'

'Funny that, isn't it?'

When Rosie looked up, her new waitress was wearing a slightly knowing smile. What was that about?

They got a good system going very quickly: Tabitha took the orders and Rosie dealt with the catering. Tabitha cleaned the tables and Rosie washed the dishes. Tabitha, who was as confident and charismatic as her brother, entertained and charmed the customers, while Rosie took care of the boring but necessary details of actually running the cafe. It worked well and they quickly settled into their groove.

Rosie loved having someone to do the schmoozing. It took the heat off her, leaving her relatively unnoticed in the background – which suited her just fine. It's how things would have worked with Fergus, how they'd agreed it between them. Fergus had loved being the host, the centre of attention, while Rosie had been happy to let him have his glory and support him from the sidelines.

'The couple on the table by the window said to tell you that that was the best French toast they'd ever had.' Tabitha dropped some money into the till, taking the change owed and dropping it into a newly created tip jar – something Rosie hadn't even thought about until Tabitha had been left so many tips that they needed somewhere to put the coins for safekeeping.

Rosie looked up from the hotplate to see them wave and leave. She looked back at Tabitha and gave a slight frown. 'Really?'

Tabitha laughed. 'Don't look so shocked. It looked pretty good to me as I took it over – I think I'll get some later, if you don't mind cooking it for me.'

'It's not hard to make.'

'Maybe not, but even things that are easy to make can be done badly. Take the compliment.'

'OK,' Rosie said, not knowing what else to say. She looked up at the clock. 'I think that ought to be the last of the breakfasts for today if I'm going to be ready for the lunch customers.'

'I've been thinking about that – I meant to mention it.'

'What?'

'It's none of my business of course, but I think you should put an all-day breakfast on the menu. You wouldn't have to do the whole lot – maybe just keep bacon and egg on or something.'

'Should I?'

'I mean, it's not like I'm telling you what to do, but people love an all-day breakfast. Well... Kit does.'

'It's a lot more work.'

'Yes, but I think it would be worth it. And you have me now, don't forget, so you can do more.'

'Not today. Maybe I'll work out how to do it for another day.'

'You definitely should. The cafe I worked at in Leeds used to get loads of customers asking for that.'

'Was it Leeds you came back from?'

'Yes. I thought I'd said.'

'You probably did.' Rosie grimaced apologetically. 'I spoke to a lot of people the day I interviewed you. What made you come back? You mentioned a break-up but... weren't you happy living there after that? It sounds like you gave up a lot to come home. Kit tells me you're back living with your mum.'

'I don't mind that. It just felt right to be here, and Mum is always better for the company. She struggles a bit on her own, to be honest. I missed this part of the world too – and I never thought I'd say that. I thought living in a big city like Leeds would be thrilling – and it was for a while. The nightlife is amazing, loads of bands, great pubs... But after Ian... well, I just craved the peace I used to feel living here. It's a bit sad, eh? Twenty years old and wanting peace and quiet like a granny.'

'And I suppose it helps that Kit is here too? You seem so close.'

'Yes. There's that too. I know I take the piss out of him but he's actually great. He has this magical way of cheering you up. I definitely needed a bit of that.'

'He certainly won over the people on the marina faster than I ever did. He's only been here a couple of days and it's like he's been here forever.'

'Honestly, I don't actually know how he's still single; everyone loves him straight away.'

Rosie thought that a strange remark to make. She hadn't asked if he was single and Tabitha didn't elaborate any further than that. Though it did suggest that if Kit and Nicole had a thing going on, Kit had yet to share that fact with his sister. But it was early days and perhaps that was why. Should she mention to Tabitha she suspected they were together? Or was Kit keeping it a secret for good reason?

Rosie decided it was none of her business. And just in case she'd been tempted anyway, at that moment more customers arrived and put the matter firmly out of her mind.

. . .

With Tabitha alongside her, Rosie started to enjoy her working day. Tabitha really was pleasant company and made her life so much easier, intuitively knowing what needed to be done, usually before even Rosie did. And while she was respectful, she wasn't afraid to tell Rosie those things, or to make good suggestions on how the general running of the cafe could be improved. She really was a natural: in a world where success was granted on merit alone, she'd probably have owned the cafe rather than Rosie, who, by her own admission, had never really been cut out for such a life. But Fergus would have been thrilled to see the cafe finally open and going well, and it was that thought spurring Rosie on and giving her the greatest pleasure of all.

Rosie had scaled things down when she'd got the place ready for business of course. Since she'd have to do it alone, there was no way she could have implemented his more elaborate plans, but she was proud she was doing it at all. Fergus had been far more ambitious – a humble riverside cafe by day turning into an intimate bistro at night. There was huge potential in that, he'd said, with touristy Warwick and Stratford nearby, and plenty of visitors from both on the river and off. It would be a goldmine, he was convinced. He'd even already planned the decor and menus before they'd signed the papers to take over. Eternally optimistic, impulsive and spontaneous, adventurous... he'd been so different to Rosie and was perhaps what she secretly aspired to be.

She'd been smitten from the day she'd met him, despite the age gap making him twelve years her senior. Her parents hadn't approved at first, but even they'd found it impossible not to warm to him eventually. He just had a way of dazzling people. Whenever she needed a bit of encouragement, his natural enthusiasm had always carried her along to whatever new destination they were headed. She'd missed that impetus perhaps more than anything as she'd refurbished the cafe alone. But she'd soldiered on, knowing it was what he would have wanted and that he'd approve. And though the road had been so much harder, she was glad she'd done it, especially today, as she stood next to Tabitha, both of them in matching aprons, and surveyed the fruits of her labour.

The huge windows filled the cafe with natural light and afforded gorgeous views of the nearby river. Rosie had chosen wrought-iron tables and chairs for the outside patio and had surrounded them with pots of roses, lavender and marguerites that were constantly visited by fluffy bees. Inside, the walls were painted a delicate cream with marigolds stencilled across them to remind customers of the flower that had given the marina and the cafe its name. The tablecloths were crisp and white, and every table had a slim white vase containing whatever flowers the farm shop had available that day. To some it was humble, but to Rosie it was beautiful... and it was home.

Her musings were interrupted by the door opening.

'Hello, Grant,' Rosie greeted the owner of the boat-hire business.

'Thought I'd come to pick up a bite,' he said. 'Don't suppose you've still got a breakfast to take out?'

Rosie caught sight of Tabitha, who gave her a tiny smile of triumph. *OK*, Rosie thought, *right again*. She was going to have to start listening more closely to what Tabitha had to say.

'I also came in to give you this...' Grant put a card down on the counter.

Rosie glanced across as she cut open a pack of bacon. 'What is it?'

'My mum is turning ninety. We're having a little do at the boathouse – nothing fancy, just a BBQ; might do some fireworks too. We were hoping you'd come.'

'Oh, I don't—'

'Bring a friend if you like. There's no pressure of course, but I'd like as many as we can to come. It would make Mum's year.'

Rosie washed her hands and took the invitation, skim-reading before putting it behind the counter next to the till. 'Thank you,' she said. 'I'd be happy to come.'

'That's great. Mum will be so pleased.'

By now, Tabitha was cleaning a recently vacated table.

'That's your new help?' Grant asked.

'Tabitha's just filling in for the lady I'd employed. She had an accident and she can't start yet.'

'Lucky you got someone at such short notice.'

'Actually, she's Kit's sister.'

Grant looked puzzled.

'The new book barge,' Rosie added.

'Oh, him!' Grant nodded slowly. 'I met him yesterday, only in passing. Seems like a good bloke. Actually, thanks for reminding me; I should do an invite to Mum's party for him too – wouldn't want to leave anyone out.'

Rosie smiled and was relieved she herself wasn't being invited just because Grant and his family felt sorry for her. While she valued the support and appreciated the considera-tion, she didn't want to be anyone's charity case. It was hard enough being a thirty-year-old widow without being constantly reminded of it.

'He seems like the sort who would jump at an excuse to socialise,' she said.

'A man after my own heart then. I'll go over to his boat when I've picked up my breakfast.'

'If you're doing that, could you drop in his lunch order? I've got a sandwich made up for him. I expect it'll do him a huge favour not to have to leave his shop unattended.'

'No problem.'

'Thanks, Grant. You're a star.'

He gave a theatrical sigh. 'I wish someone would tell my customers that. A few members of my family too, come to think of it.'

Rosie laughed lightly. 'Well, if they ever come calling, I'll be sure to mention it.'

The door opened again and this time Nicole came in.

'Hey, Rosie!' She was obviously in a rush. 'Just wondered if you could do me a quick salad.' Nicole glanced at Grant and nodded solemnly. 'Alright?'

'Don't you usually make your lunch at home?' Rosie asked, suddenly aware of a new frostiness in the room. It seemed to be coming from Nicole and Grant. She quickly dismissed it as her imagination. 'I thought you had all sorts of food requirements.'

'God, that makes me sound fussy! I'm not that bad! Yes, I would usually but I wasn't at home this morning.'

'Oh... sure. What do you want in your salad?'

'I don't know... maybe tuna. Eggs and tuna... I need the protein.'

Rosie checked on Grant's breakfast before turning her attention to Nicole's salad, which wouldn't take a second to whip up now that she and Tabitha had all the bits prepared. She couldn't help but wonder why Nicole hadn't been home that morning. Where had she been? With Kit? Had they spent the night together? But Rosie had seen Kit early that morning, so that couldn't have been the case. She supposed it was a conundrum she didn't really have time to solve. More to the point... why was she so keen to get to the bottom of it?

As she mused on this, she suddenly realised that she hadn't imagined it and there *was* an awkward silence between Nicole and Grant. He was staring out of the window now and she was looking at her phone. It was strange, because everyone at Marigold Marina was usually chatty when they met up. She'd never seen them together before, so she'd never noticed that relations seemed cool between them.

Pushing the thought from her head, she wrapped up the box containing Nicole's salad and handed it over.

'Four pounds, right, Rosie?' Nicole handed over the exact

change. 'Oh... before I go, I might as well take Kit his sandwiches. Are they paid for?'

'Actually, Grant was going to...' Rosie glanced between the two of them, realised that Kit had probably asked Nicole to get his sandwiches, and that as Grant was based further along the marina, he was probably going out of his way to deliver them, where Nicole was practically next door.

'Don't mind me,' Grant said carelessly.

Rosie went to the fridge to get them out, but as she returned to the cafe floor, the door opened and Kit himself came in.

'Oh, here he is!' Tabitha said, bustling past with a laden tray. 'Has half of the marina offering to take his sandwiches over and comes out to get them anyway – that's about right.'

'Alright, pipsqueak?' He grinned. 'Rosie got fed up with you yet?'

'I said I'd pick them up—' Nicole cut in, but Kit stopped her. 'Yeah, thanks, but I haven't had a customer for an hour and it was doing my head in sitting around, so I thought I'd run over myself, just for a change of scenery...' He gave Rosie a warm smile as she offered him the parcelled sandwiches. 'Now that's what I call service. What do I owe you?'

'There's nothing to pay – I told you, they're on the house.'

'Even so...'

'Please,' Rosie said, 'it's the least I can do.'

'Well... thanks. I appreciate that. If you happen to fancy a book to read, you can come and choose any you like on the house – it's only fair.'

Rosie laughed. 'God, I'd love the time to read a book right now. I'll probably be over in the next five years to take you up on that.'

'I'd better go.' Nicole looked faintly annoyed again as she interjected, as if Rosie was a flea she couldn't get rid of. 'Sorry, Rosie, I know I said I might come over later but I might be struggling after all. I'll do my best to catch up with you before the week's out. Hope that's OK.'

'Of course,' Rosie said, doing her best not to seem disappointed. 'I'll probably be tired anyway.'

'Right... well, if I can get over later in the week, I'll bring wine – how's that?'

'Sounds nice,' Rosie said.

'Great! Must dash!'

Nicole marched out of the cafe at the same purposeful pace as she'd come in.

When Rosie turned back to Grant, he wore a curious look on his face. He was still watching Nicole through the windows as she walked towards her own place. What was that look? Rosie wondered. Impatience? Annoyance? Maybe even disapproval? Rosie had never noticed anyone be less than friendly to Nicole, and she couldn't imagine what gripe good-natured Grant could have with her.

Still, Rosie supposed it was none of her business and it was silly to imagine that just because everyone on the marina was a neighbour of sorts, it automatically meant they got along.

'I'd better get back too,' Kit said.

'Oh...' Rosie looked at Grant. 'This is Kit... didn't you say you wanted to invite him to your party?'

Grant offered Kit his hand. 'I'm Grant. I've got the boat-hire place along the way.'

'Right!' Kit shook. 'Yes, I've seen you with that very cool car, haven't I?'

'My Aston,' Grant said, his chest visibly puffing with pride at the mention of his beloved car. 'It is pretty cool, isn't it?'

'So you're having a party?'

'Well, it's for my mum actually. It's probably not your scene, but I'm inviting everyone from the marina, so—'

'I'd love to come,' Kit said. 'Any excuse to get to know my

neighbours a bit better is fine by me.' He turned to Rosie. 'You're going, right?'

'Oh... yes... at least, I think so.'

'Great!'

At this point, Tabitha returned with some used plates to take through to the kitchens.

'And you're invited too,' Grant said to her. 'If you wanted to come of course.'

Tabitha smiled. 'Aww, thanks. Maybe I will swing by.'

'I mean, it's just an old lady's birthday party, but there will be free food and drink.'

'In that case, I'm definitely coming!' Tabitha laughed as she disappeared with the plates.

'That's so kind of you,' Rosie said.

'Well...' Grant shrugged. 'It wouldn't do to leave her out...' He turned to Kit. 'And she's your sister, isn't she?'

'She is.'

'Seems like a nice girl.'

'She has her moments,' Kit said with a smile.

Rosie watched the exchange. How different Grant was from just a moment ago when Nicole had been present. He was far more relaxed and open again – just as he'd always been whenever she'd had dealings with him before. What was the deal with him and Nicole? She was itching to ask one of them, but something told her she wouldn't get a straight reply from either of them. Whatever it was, it wasn't common knowledge on the marina, as far as she could tell anyway, which led Rosie to suspect it was something they'd both rather stay hidden. But realising that only made her want to know more.

'I think your bacon is done,' Tabitha whispered. Rosie jumped to find her standing so close. She'd been so wrapped up in her thoughts she hadn't even noticed her waitress's return from the dishwasher.

'Oh...' Rosie gave a self-conscious laugh. 'Thanks.'

'No worries. Can I get a mushroom omelette for the window table when you're done with Grant?'

'Yes... I'm on it.'

Rosie wrapped up Grant's breakfast and offered it to him. *Get your head in gear*, she told herself. 'There you go!'

'Thanks, Rosie. See you later.'

'Enjoy!'

'I'm sure I will.'

Rosie watched him go, but there was no time to dwell on any of what she'd just seen because the table by the window was waiting for a mushroom omelette. She looked at Kit. 'I'm so sorry, I need to...'

'God, yes, of course,' he said, waving his sandwich pack at her. 'I need to get back too... Thanks again for these.'

'Made with love,' Tabitha said from behind Rosie.

'Then I know you didn't make them.' Kit laughed as he headed for the door. 'Thanks, Rosie! I never knew you cared!'

Rosie smiled as she watched him leave. It wasn't until Tabitha cleared her throat and whispered, 'Omelette... table by the window...' that she realised she'd been watching his back with a stupid smile on her face for at least thirty seconds.

'Yes, right... Of course...'

Fergus would have told her to get her head out of the clouds and focus, and he'd have been right. She had a cafe full of customers and they weren't going to get fed if she didn't get her act together.

CHAPTER SIX

There was a chill in the air. Summer was not yet old enough for balmy evenings, though it was still pleasant to be out at the water's edge, sitting on a bench as the midges played above the river and the sun slipped down the sky. Rosie was there now. It was nights like these that made the stress of the move worthwhile. If only Fergus had been here to share it with her, life would have been about as perfect as it got.

The cafe had been closed for a couple of hours – later than Rosie had planned, but she hadn't been about to turn down a last-minute table of customers. It had been a good day – both for trade and for confidence; better than her opening day. Most of that was down to Tabitha, who'd been a marvel. Rosie was beginning to hope Letitia wouldn't come back when her collarbone mended and that she could keep Tabitha after all – though that didn't seem very fair on poor Letitia and made Rosie feel guilty for even entertaining the notion.

Before she'd left for the day, Rosie and Tabitha had had a brief chat about how things had gone and whether Tabitha was happy to continue working for Rosie. The answer to the first question was that she felt it had gone well – and Rosie agreed.

And the answer to the second question was a resounding yes, which made Rosie in equal parts relieved but also very happy, because she liked Tabitha a lot already.

'Take this for your mum,' she said, handing Tabitha a bag.

Tabitha peered inside and then looked up at Rosie with a silent question.

'I heard you tell a customer your mum loves sourdough bread,' Rosie clarified. 'I heard right, didn't I?'

'She can't get enough of the stuff,' Tabitha said with a smile. 'That's so sweet of you.'

'Well, not really. I ordered too much in anyway – didn't want it to go to waste.'

'It definitely won't go to waste where Mum is concerned – she'll be slicing this up as soon as I walk through the door. Thank you.'

'I hope you and Kit will get some too.'

'I expect Kit will, like the gannet he is.'

'Oh, and don't forget your tips from the jar.'

'They're your tips too.'

Rosie smiled and shook her head. 'They're mostly yours. Take them – I know waitressing money won't make you a millionaire any time soon and I feel kind of bad I can't pay you more, so knowing you have at least a little extra will make me happier.'

Tabitha gave a broad smile as she went to get the jar from the counter and emptied out the contents. 'You're sure?' she asked, looking up.

'Completely. In fact, I'll be annoyed if you don't take them.'

'In that case...' Tabitha scooped up the change and put it in her purse before retrieving the bread and her coat from a chair. 'So I'll see you tomorrow?'

'God, I hope so!' Rosie exclaimed. 'I'm up the creek without a paddle otherwise!'

Tabitha's grin spread further still. Bidding Rosie goodnight, she headed out, leaving Rosie to do the last of the tidying before she called it a day.

Once she'd finally locked the front door, Rosie had grabbed a quick bite in the conservatory and, seeing through the windows just how glorious the evening sky was, had decided to head out and enjoy it first-hand.

Now, she sat in silent contemplation of the marina as the last of the businesses that traded late packed up for the day. She watched as Luca's gelato boat moored up. The space next to him where Angel would usually be remained empty. Rosie figured there was good money to be had in town for someone selling cocktails and that later in the evening was probably her busiest time. Juliet's barge had already been locked up when Rosie arrived. Rosie knew, however, that Juliet's business could probably count as more of a hobby than a living, because her husband was some hotshot City trader, and they didn't exactly need the money – or so Nicole said. Juliet had probably decided to close up early, and if Nicole was right, she was easily able to please herself on that score.

Rosie's gaze wandered more than once to Kit's now silent barge. Was he living on it all the time or not? She couldn't tell. Maybe she'd ask Tabitha in the morning.

And then she remembered that it had been a few days since she'd called her parents. They wouldn't want to interfere in her life, but they would want to know how she was getting on now that the cafe was up and running. With one thing and another, Rosie hadn't had a chance to tell them about it. They'd been there in the early days after Fergus's death, helping her to gut the cafe even though they'd said many times it was against their better judgement to let her continue with the project alone. While she'd told them she was grateful for their concern and advice, she'd made it clear she wasn't about to give the cafe up and they'd backed off. Due to work commitments, they'd only been able to spare a couple of weeks before they'd had to go home and hadn't been able to get down again since. Rosie missed them, but their absence from her everyday life was just another thing she was getting used to.

She FaceTimed the number and her mum appeared on screen. 'Rosie! Hello, pet! We were just talking about you.'

'I thought my ears felt hot. Were you complaining that I hadn't called?'

'Well, no, but we were wondering how you'd got on.'

'I'm sure you were. I would have called yesterday but—'

'It's OK, you're here now. How are you? How did the opening go? Was it alright? Were *you* alright? Was it very upsetting?'

Her mum's face was taut with worry and Rosie knew why.

After Fergus's death, Rosie had been in the worst state she'd ever been in, and her poor mum had borne the brunt of that. Rosie had returned home to grieve with her family around her before heading back to Warwickshire. She'd debated whether to come back to the marina at all and very nearly hadn't, and she'd agonised over it for weeks. And before that too, her mum had been called on to deal with Rosie wanting to leave Fergus when they'd had the biggest argument of their marriage... that had been about the cafe, of course. It was the row that had taken Rosie away from him to sulk and lick her wounds the day before he'd died. And then his heart attack had happened. The last thoughts Fergus would have had were that their marriage was over, and that Rosie hated him.

Rosie would have given anything for the chance to go back and tell him that that was never true and that she was sorry for making him think it was, and how she hated the fact that he'd died thinking the worst. She'd only ever wanted to prove a point. She'd have sulked at home for a weekend – maybe not even that long – and she'd have come back a day or two later and everything would have been fine.

'It was great,' Rosie lied.

Her mum's features relaxed. She smiled, the blue eyes that were so like Rosie's own full of warmth. At least, everyone told her they were like her mum's. Her dad said looking at Rosie these days was like looking at her mum when they'd first met. Rosie couldn't really see it but assumed it must be true because he hadn't been the only person to say it over the years. She supposed her hair dye made her look different now and perhaps if she went back to her natural chestnut, she and her mum would look even more alike.

Her mum was wearing a favourite embroidered blouse, one she'd bought on holiday in Athens. Rosie had definitely inherited her mum's sense of style – that she couldn't deny. Whenever Glenda had come home with something new, Rosie had always loved it. Sometimes she'd even asked to borrow it.

'Your dad will be relieved,' Glenda said now.

'He's not there?'

'No – got called out. Some emergency over at the flats on Garrow Street.'

'Doesn't he ever slow down? He's been doing call-outs for years now; surely he's had enough.'

'They're good money and usually it's only a nail through a pipe or something easy that doesn't take too long.'

'Do you still need that extra money?'

'Not really, I suppose. But if you can earn it then it's hard to turn your nose up at that, isn't it?'

'True,' Rosie said. 'Not that I'll ever know. A rural cafe is hardly a lucrative business.'

'Oh, Rosie...'

Rosie could have kicked herself. 'I know what you're going to say, Mum. It's fine – a throwaway comment I shouldn't have made. I've told you I'm happy here now. I made the decision to stay and I'm sticking with it.'

'But you're so far away and all on your own.'

'I have loads of neighbours only too happy to help when I need it – don't worry about that.'

'Is that actually true?'

'Of course it is! You know how good people around here were after…'

'Yes, you did tell me that, but I still worry. I'm bound to.'

'You don't need to – I'm very happy.'

'If it's true then I'm glad. You'd tell me if that changed, wouldn't you? I still worry you're lonely there – having good neighbours isn't the same as having a husband and family around you.'

'I couldn't possibly get lonely on Marigold Marina,' Rosie said, looking around at the buildings, most of them shuttered up and in darkness now. One or two had upstairs lights on where there were flats above the premises – like Nicole's and like Rosie's too. Some of the inhabited boats were lit from within too. Rosie had been in Nicole's flat a few times but she'd yet to set foot in any of the other homes at the marina. But that was down to her choosing, not the fault of anyone who lived there, and her mum didn't need to know that her existence was more isolated than Rosie would have her believe. As far as Glenda was concerned, Rosie had a good, happy social life and was never alone.

'So, when can we visit?' Glenda asked.

'Not yet… Sorry, Mum. I need to get everything running like clockwork first.'

'But you have your lady helping? What was her name again…?'

'Letitia. Actually, she's unwell and hasn't been able to start with me yet. I've got someone else though and she's brilliant. Just until Letitia can start of course.'

'That's good. Lucky you managed to get a replacement.'

'Very, and such a good one too. Honestly, it's like she's a mind-reader. I don't ever have to ask her to do anything – I open my mouth to say it and it's already done!'

'How lovely. By the way, your dad said...'

But Rosie had stopped listening. Her attention was caught by Nicole's shop door opening. A moment later Kit walked out. He didn't go to his boat but walked along the marina to the access road that led away from it. Going to visit his mum, perhaps? Tabitha had said they were close after all. Or to hook up with friends? It was none of her business, but still Rosie couldn't help wondering.

The light went on upstairs in Nicole's flat – it hadn't been on a moment before. That meant Kit and Nicole hadn't been up there, right? They'd been downstairs in the shop, and so all perfectly respectable...

'... what do you think?' Glenda asked.

'What?' Rosie realised she hadn't heard a single word her mum had just said.

'End of July,' Glenda repeated. 'Me and your dad could visit at the end of July. He has a week off.'

'Right. Wouldn't you be missing your annual trip to Greece? Don't you normally go in July?'

'We'd rather see you.'

'Well, I am honoured! You never miss your week in Greece!'

'This year's a bit different, isn't it?' Her mum's expression was shrewd.

'I suppose it is but I don't want to make a thing out of it. I'd rather not be reminded that it's different – or rather, the reason why it's different.'

'You lost your husband, Rosie. I can't pretend to know how that feels, but you can't just ignore that it happened.'

Rosie paused. 'Trust me, I never ignore it. I think about it every minute of every day.'

'All the more reason for us to come and stay with you then.'

'The flat's really not ready for guests.'

'Then we can stay nearby. There must be plenty of hotels in Stratford. Or we could hire a boat. We've always wanted a boat holiday.'

Rosie laughed lightly. 'No, you haven't. You've never once said you wanted to go on a boat!'

'Yes we have!' Glenda said indignantly.

'Well, I don't recall it.'

'Even so, do we have to tell you everything we discuss between ourselves?'

'God, no – please don't start doing that!'

Glenda looked vaguely miffed and so Rosie shrugged. 'I can't promise I'll have loads of free time, but if you really want a week on a boat I can ask Grant at the hire place what he has available for you.'

'That's a good idea.' Glenda was smiling now. 'Just give me a minute – I've got something in the oven and it's just pinged.'

'Don't rush. I should hang up anyway. I need a shower and an early night. I'll ring off.'

'But you will phone again tomorrow?'

'I'll phone when I have a minute, I promise.'

'Alright then. I love you.'

'Love you too. Give kisses to Dad for me.'

'Of course. Speak soon.'

Rosie ended the call. A sudden gust raced down the river and sent the hairs on her neck to attention. Nicole's light went off. The marina was quiet and still. Rosie pulled her shawl more tightly around her and headed home.

Rosie was relieved to see Tabitha back the following day. Silly though she told herself it was, part of her was convinced her help wouldn't show and she'd be left to struggle again, as she had been on the first day of opening. She'd never used to be so obsessed with abandonment, but something had changed since Fergus's death. Now she felt like everyone would eventually leave her when she needed them most.

'Morning.' Tabitha slipped off her jacket and took it to the back room to hang up. 'How's it going?'

'Good, I think. It's still early so anything's possible.'

Tabitha grinned. 'Want me to start anything in particular or just go for food prep like yesterday?'

'Food prep would be perfect.'

Rosie finished wiping down the counter and was putting the antibacterial spray back in the cupboard when Tabitha came through to the kitchen area.

'Did Kit give you a sandwich order today?' Rosie asked.

Tabitha tied her apron and cocked an eyebrow. 'He's more likely to give it to you than me.'

'So you didn't see him last night or this morning?'

'Course I didn't. We're not joined at the hip, and he lives next to you, so...'

'I didn't realise he was living on the barge. I mean, I know he's there a lot but...' Rosie stopped suddenly. She didn't want to sound like she was stalking Kit, and was even slightly concerned that how interested she was in his movements sounded a bit unhealthy. She decided quickly not to mention that she'd seen him leave the marina the night before.

'Perhaps "living" isn't quite the way to describe it,' Tabitha said airily, 'but he does seem to be staying there a lot. He wasn't supposed to be living there officially, but he's definitely staying out somewhere because he's not coming home.'

'By home you mean your mum's? I didn't think he lived there either.'

'He had to give up his flat and come home because of money and... well... It's not important now. But don't worry, he's not a mummy's boy.'

'I never thought he was,' Rosie said, taken slightly aback by the comment. Whether he was or wasn't, why on earth did Tabitha think the idea would worry Rosie? 'So he's not living there now? I'm confused.'

Tabitha shrugged. 'He's supposed to live with us but he seems to be staying out a lot. Mum assumes it's on the boat. To be fair, he's probably still trying to get his stock sorted out so I think he works late a lot. Probably just beds down there afterwards rather than coming home. Rather him than me; I can't imagine it being very comfy. I wouldn't want to sleep in amongst those piles of dusty books.'

Perhaps he *isn't*, Rosie thought, recalling him coming out of Nicole's place the night before. But if he'd been staying with Nicole, that was quick work on her part. It was odd if he was though, because he really wasn't giving any sign that he was interested in Nicole. But then, what did Rosie know? Fergus had always said she wasn't very good at reading situations.

'Anyway,' Tabitha continued, 'he'd want to come in for sandwiches himself.'

'Wouldn't it be easier just to ask you?'

Tabitha turned to Rosie with a wry smile. 'No reason in particular. I think he just likes it here.'

'Well, I suppose I have to be glad about that,' Rosie said. 'If people feel the cafe is welcoming, I'm halfway to a decent success.'

'Yes, the cafe – it's so welcoming... that's exactly why he wants to get his own sandwiches.'

Rosie was about to ask what Tabitha meant by that when the door opened and Nicole came in.

'Can I grab a couple of milky coffees to take out?'

'Morning, Nicole.' Rosie put on the water heater. 'Can you hang on a tick? Nothing's hot yet.'

'We're not actually open,' Tabitha put in tersely.

Her tone shocked Rosie. She'd never seen Tabitha be

anything like that direct towards a customer – it even bordered on rudeness. She wondered if she was going to have to watch out for that in future – she couldn't have Tabitha insulting customers just because she happened to take a dislike to something they'd done.

Nicole didn't flinch though. 'The door was open,' she said blithely.

'My fault,' Rosie said. 'I forgot to lock it when I let Tabitha in. Don't worry – if you don't mind waiting, it's no trouble to serve you. But don't you have coffee in the shop?'

'Instant crap. I thought I'd get us something nicer this morning.'

Rosie wondered who 'us' was and could only assume it was Nicole and Kit. So he was having coffee with her this morning? It was hardly surprising as he was that kind of guy – she could tell he loved socialising. After all, how many times since his arrival had he tried to get Rosie to stay and chat on his barge?

Nicole took a seat while Rosie got on with preparing what she could as the milk heated up. Tabitha went to the kitchen. If Nicole thought she'd been rude, she didn't show it. Instead, she chatted to Rosie as she waited. 'How is trade?'

'It's early days but it seems to be good.'

'I'm glad to hear it. I know you always felt like it was a gamble. Does it feel worth it yet?'

'I'm not sure. I mean, I did, but I also felt I owed it to Fergus to see it through and at least I can say I've done that now.'

'But surely it goes further than that? Don't you want to carry on for you?'

'Yes, but also because it was the life we'd planned together.'

Nicole regarded her frankly. 'You really are loyal to the end, aren't you?' Her tone was almost contemptuous – at least it sounded that way. Where on earth had that suddenly come from?

Rosie couldn't help but stare at her. 'If you'd known Fergus like I did, you'd want to be too.'

'You loved him that much?'

'Yes. I like to think he loved me that much too. I mean, I know we'd had a tiff just before... but it was just a tiff. It didn't mean anything.'

'Hell of a way to say goodbye though.'

Rosie's eyes widened. That was a cruel thing to say. Why was Nicole suddenly being like this? What was going on?

'Nicole, you know what happened. And if I could take it back I would—'

Nicole shook her head and let out a sigh. 'Ignore me. It's one of those mornings.'

'Oh... right... Sorry to hear that.'

With the temperature right, Rosie went to make the coffees, still reeling from Nicole's statement. It must have been a very bad morning, but she couldn't imagine why. From what she could tell, it ought to have been a very good morning.

'There's nothing going on between you and Kit, is there?' Nicole asked into the silence, her tone deliberately casual.

Rosie looked up. 'Of course not! I barely see him, so I don't know why you would think that. I actually thought there was something going on between you two.'

'Just a sixth sense. Ignore me... And no, there's nothing going on with us – we're just friends... for now.'

'I can assure you there's nothing between us either – just friends here too. Besides, I thought you said he was too young for you.'

'I did, didn't I?' Nicole smiled slowly. 'That's before I saw his cute backside getting on and off that boat from my window every day.'

'So you *do* like him?'

'Have you seen the guy? What's not to like? I'm definitely

interested, but I get the feeling his attention is elsewhere.'
Nicole gave Rosie a significant look.

'Me?' Rosie gave a disbelieving smile and shook her head
forcefully. 'I seriously doubt that. Look at me – I wear a shawl!'

'Yes, like a Victorian urchin, and he has a boat full of classic
novels. A match made in heaven I'd say.'

Rosie's smile grew wider. '*You* deserve some happiness. I'm
not ready to think about that stuff, even if I thought he was
interested in me, which I don't. I'm not sure I'll be ready any
time in the next ten years... Fergus and... well, you know...'

'Right, of course, I understand... I just wanted to be sure.'

'So I take it one of these is for him?' Rosie asked, holding out
the two cups.

Nicole gave a sheepish smile and Rosie didn't know
whether to feel vindicated that she'd been proved right, or
vaguely disappointed for a reason she couldn't quite put her
finger on.

It was Sunday and Tabitha was off, but Rosie decided to open
the cafe. She didn't have anything else to do, and as the week
had improved and she'd started to find her feet, she felt she
could manage a few hours by herself. Instead of her usual early
opening, she allowed herself an extra hour in bed and decided
she'd shut at three, and she'd only offer cooked breakfasts,
which was all she'd imagined anyone would want. Most of the
other businesses on the marina were closed, so the owners
wouldn't be in for sandwiches or coffee, but holidaymakers or
the crews of newly arrived narrowboats might fancy treating
themselves to a bacon bap. The extra takings would come in
handy too – anything that bolstered the finances was worth
doing.

As she unlocked the door, she was rewarded with her first
customers – an older couple just off a boat and keen for break-

fast, exactly as she'd hoped. They both ordered a full English with a pot of tea and took a seat at a table.

While Rosie cooked at the hotplate behind the counter, she asked them about their trip.

'This is our last day,' the man said.

'We'll be sorry to give the boat back,' the woman said. 'I could happily carry on sailing along for another year. It's so relaxing, the calmest I think I've ever been.'

'Don't the locks and tunnels worry you?' Rosie asked.

'You soon get used to them,' the man said. 'They're no worse than traffic lights in the road.'

The woman laughed. 'Well it's a bit more physical than that. You don't have to crank a traffic light open.'

'It's a good job we've still got muscles,' her companion agreed. 'And there's usually help around somewhere if you get stuck.'

'I don't think I'd like locks,' Rosie said.

'It depends on which bit of the waterway you travel how many you get,' the woman said. 'On some parts you can go for miles without a single one, but on others there's one after the other – if you do your research, you can largely avoid them if you'd rather.'

'Where did you go?'

'We did the Avon Ring... some of it anyway.'

Rosie looked blank.

'It's all the connecting waterways in this part of the world. We did the Grand Union, took our time, joined the Avon and visited the Cotswolds but didn't go all the way to the Severn. Wanted to see where we were at. No point in racing through places, is there? And the Cotswolds alone are beautiful enough to spend a week in.'

'It sounds lovely. So this is where you finish?'

'Sadly yes.'

'So I suppose you're one of Grant's customers?' Rosie asked.

'Grant?'

'Across the way.' Rosie cracked an egg onto the griddle.

'Yes, he's checking the boat over now. We're going to eat this and then see about getting our deposit back. Then we'll be on our way. We might spend a bit of time in Warwick first, as it's so close.'

'You should,' Rosie said fervently. 'I've only been for the afternoon but Warwick is very pretty. And the castle is huge – it's amazing. Not sure about today, but they often have jousting displays by the river.'

'Have you lived here long?' the man asked. 'You don't sound local.'

'I moved here from Newcastle a few months ago.'

'North-east, eh?' he said. 'That's quite a trek.'

'I suppose it is.' Rosie plated up their breakfasts. 'We weren't set on this area as such, but the right place came on the market that fitted the bill perfectly, so we made the move here.'

'Lovely,' the woman said. 'Looks like it worked out well.'

Rosie put their plates on their table. 'Anything else I can get you?'

'No, that's grand,' the man said. 'Fit for a king. I bet your hubby's well fed, eh?'

Rosie's smile slipped as she noticed him glance at the wedding ring she still wore, but she managed to hold on to it. She supposed it was a natural assumption to make, considering she still wore one, and it wasn't the man's fault.

Besides, bursting into tears in front of a customer – Fergus wouldn't have approved at all.

An hour later, Kit walked in. 'Don't you ever close?'

Rosie smiled. 'I wasn't doing anything else – I figured I might as well be open. Anyway, as you're here, I could ask the same question. You must be working too.'

'Just messing around with the stock, but I'm done now. You weren't doing anything else? How about sleeping? That's what Sundays are for.'

'For you maybe. Some of us like to be up and about.'

'Weirdo. So you're planning to spend your precious day off here doing more of the same? Is my sister planning to join you?'

'God, no, I wouldn't ask her to give up a day off. She's already done six days this week and we'll have to agree another day off for her when she's back in. I'm sure she doesn't want to spend her life here.'

'No one should... spend their life at work, I mean,' Kit added quickly. 'I didn't mean no one should be here... Obviously, here is very nice...' He glanced around. There was a family of parents and two very bored-looking teenage boys sitting at a table, fishing equipment on the floor beside them as they ate toasted sandwiches. 'What time are you planning to close?'

'I thought about three.'

'So you'll have some of the afternoon left?'

'A bit.'

'Here's an idea – Nicole's suggested getting a drink at a pub near here. They have some live bands... come with us.'

'But...'

'Please – it should be fun.'

Rosie didn't imagine for one minute that Nicole would be happy if she turned up. Kit might not have seen it as a date, but she'd bet Nicole would be planning to do her best to turn it into one.

'I don't think so. I've got a million things to do after I close up here. I haven't put the washing machine on for a week.'

'Oh my God. Civilisation will crumble.'

Rosie smiled. 'I know. That's about as exciting as it gets for me these days. Thank you for asking, but you'll have way more fun without me.'

'I doubt that.' He studied her for a moment. 'There's nothing I can say to change your mind?'

'Afraid not.'

'And you know what they say about all work and no play?'

'I'm afraid it's already too late to save me from that particular fate. Run, get away from me and save yourself.'

'OK, I know when I'm beaten. I'll see you tomorrow for my sandwich.'

Rosie raised her eyebrows. 'Your sandwich? Let me guess, ham and pickle? Now who's dull? You've had that every day this week.'

'What can I say? You make a great ham and pickle sandwich!'

'I *can* make other types of sandwich.'

'Yeah, I've heard of these so-called other sandwiches. I don't trust them.'

Rosie couldn't help but giggle. 'Daft.'

'That's what Tabitha says.'

'Don't worry, I'll have it ready for you. I suppose I should just get one ready every day from now on.'

'It would save a lot of time. All these minutes explaining what I want every day add up.'

The door opened and both of them looked up to see Grant coming into the cafe. He wiped his feet on the welcome mat for a second before making his way to the counter. 'Afternoon! Someone said you were open today. You could have warned me there was bacon in the area.'

'Hey, Grant.' Rosie smiled. 'Does that mean you'd like a breakfast?'

'A bacon bap will do until I get home. The missus would kill me if I'd eaten a full English when she has a roast waiting.' He looked at Kit and nodded. 'Good to see you again. I know I haven't dropped that invite in for you yet, but I'm getting to it, I swear.'

'Seriously, don't stress about it,' Kit said. 'I know you must be busy across there.'

'Yeah, something like that. I'll drop it in to you tomorrow.'

Grant turned to Rosie, who was putting his bacon on the griddle. It settled with a hiss. 'Now that I know you're open on Sundays, I'll send folks over when they pass through and want a bite to eat. Clarice – she had this place before you – only opened a few hours a week and only when she felt like it. She did as little as she could get away with, to be honest – don't think she cared much for running a cafe. I couldn't send people over back then because I never knew if she'd be serving or not from one week to the next.'

'Today was a bit of a spur-of-the-moment thing actually,' Rosie said. 'I wasn't doing anything else so it made sense to open up. I'm glad I did; it's been steady.'

'I expect the river walkers and boaters will be happy to see you open. Nothing nicer than a cold drink on a hot day or a warm drink on a cold one when you've clocked up a few miles. I've always done seven-day weeks – got to, in this trade.'

'I'm beginning to see that.'

'You can do them when you have help of course,' Grant continued. 'I approve of your dedication, but I should just add that you can't do it week in, week out alone. Even I need a day off from time to time.'

'Yes... of course.'

'Just what I was about to say,' Kit agreed. 'And as for having nothing else to do... well, you know there's an open invite for you this afternoon if you want it.'

'And that's not to lecture,' Grant said, giving Kit a curious glance but clearly deciding not to ask about what the invite might be. 'Far be it for me to tell you how to run your business. I'm just passing on my experience. You don't want to burn out.'

'No, I know... I appreciate your concern, but I'm really fine.'

While Rosie did appreciate the advice – even more that

they cared enough to offer it – she really couldn't see what she'd do with days off. Once in a while there might be an invite to a pub that she would actually be able to take up, but she was sure they'd be few and far between once Kit settled in and the novelty of trying to make friends with everyone on the marina wore off. Home with her parents was too far away to visit in a day, and she didn't really have anyone else close by to spend time with. But she realised Grant and Kit meant well, so she wasn't about to say so.

Grant began to ask Kit how the book barge was taking off as Rosie made his sandwich. The conversation turned to how he was settling into life at the marina. Rosie was only half listening until she heard Nicole mentioned and her ears pricked up.

'Nicole's your nearest neighbour, isn't she?' Grant asked.

'Yes, she's great. Keeps an eye on things for me if I need to nip off from the boat.'

'That's what this community does,' Grant said. 'You have a lot to do with her?'

'A bit. We've had the odd cuppa together. I mean, I've only just arrived so I don't really know anyone well yet.'

Grant took his sandwich and paid Rosie. 'If you need anything from us, don't hesitate to walk over to the boathouse. Even if that's just a chat. You'll find me or one of my boys knocking about somewhere.'

'Thanks. I'll remember that.'

Grant gave them both a last nod of farewell and left.

Rosie turned to Kit. 'Was there anything you actually wanted?'

Suddenly he seemed awkward. 'No... I would order, but I'm supposed to be going to Mum's for lunch in an hour or so.'

'Oh God, I didn't mean you couldn't come in unless you were ordering!' Rosie added hastily, feeling awkward herself now. 'I just wondered...'

'I was just passing... saw you were open, thought I'd say

hello. And, you know, ask if you wanted to come out with us later. The invite stands, by the way. If you want to come, all you have to do is say and I can pick you up.'

'That's really kind of you but maybe another time.'

'Another time. I'm kind of getting déjà vu with that phrase.'

Rosie gave a tight smile. 'I'm sorry. What can I say? I'm a much duller person than you're giving me credit for.'

'I guess you're busy with the cafe being so new and all.'

'That too,' Rosie said, appreciating how he'd spared her feelings rather than agreeing that she was dull.

'I guess I'll see you tomorrow for my lunch order then.'

'I'll have it ready. And thanks for stopping by. I don't mind admitting I don't exactly have friends coming out of my ears around here. I appreciate you making the effort.'

'I suppose being new I'm in the same boat... quite literally, if you think about it.'

'We'll have to be each other's new best friends then.'

A warm, genuine smile spread across his face. 'Sounds good to me. I'd better get going. See you tomorrow.'

'You will.'

Rosie watched him go. Her new best friend? She liked the sound of that.

CHAPTER SEVEN

Tabitha was fast becoming a welcome sight; Rosie opened up on Monday morning and there she was, bang on time as always, ready to start work.

'I hear you were open yesterday,' she said as they got the salad stuff out of the fridge. 'I thought you weren't going to do Sundays.'

'I know, but I realised that I was probably missing one of the best days, trade-wise. And I was right.'

'I thought Sunday wasn't about trade but about you getting a rest day.'

'I didn't need one.'

'You will at some point. No one can do seven-day weeks forever... I take it from what you've just said that you're planning to open on Sunday as a regular thing now?'

'It's only for a few hours in the middle of the day.'

'It's still a whole day off you'll miss. Why don't you let me do Sundays for you so you can be off? I could manage.'

'I'd feel terrible asking it of you – it would make a very long week for you.'

'You could give me a day off midweek.'

Rosie paused, thinking this over. 'I could, but I'm not sure if that won't leave me back at square one. It's still a day I'd have to work alone.'

'But you'd get a day off in return. You're working Sunday alone anyway – make my day off a quiet one. I'm not fussy right now when it is.'

'Really and truly I ought to be giving you two days off a week.' Rosie shook her head. 'I already ask too much of you.'

Tabitha shrugged. 'Well, I don't think it's smart to do seven days every week, but it's your cafe I suppose. Maybe I'd do the same if it was mine. But if you ever fancy the odd day off you can tell me. I'll help if I can.'

Rosie smiled at Tabitha. 'That's good to know, thank you. But as I have a distinct lack of social life and zero hobbies, I can't see me needing one often. I suppose I might take you up on your offer to visit family up north... but then I might just have to close for a few days because it's definitely not a day-trip kind of distance.'

'I bet you wouldn't like that. You could give me the keys to keep it open.'

'I suppose I could. It's good of you to offer. In all honesty, it won't be happening for the next few months, and I expect Letitia will be back by then so she'd be able to do it.'

Tabitha's face fell. 'You don't think I could manage?'

'I do! You know how to run this place better than I do! All I mean is... well, I promised I'd keep her job open, and I can't go back on that now. So as soon as she's better, she'll be here. You are still looking for something else, right?'

'Yes, but I sort of put it on hold.'

'Why? I never said—'

'I know – you made it clear it was temporary, but I didn't want to land something before she recovered and leave you in the lurch.'

Rosie gave a pained smile. 'That's so sweet of you, but you

have to think of yourself. If a job comes your way you fancy, you must take it. Don't worry about what's going on here.'

Tabitha gave an unconvincing nod.

Rosie couldn't tell if her reluctance was down to not wanting to leave her in the lurch as she'd said, or because she liked working at the Marigold Cafe and had secretly been hoping she'd be kept on. Rosie liked having her there too, but she'd made her promise to Letitia and had to keep it, no matter how much she also wanted to keep Tabitha. 'Promise me,' she said.

'Of course I will.' Tabitha grabbed a knife from the block and began topping and tailing the carrots.

'I'm not saying I wouldn't be really sorry to lose you,' Rosie continued. 'I'm thinking only of you when I say this.'

Tabitha turned to her with a forced smile. 'I know. I suppose... well, it's the first time I haven't felt totally useless since I got back home and the first time I've got up in the mornings and that pointless cretin of an ex isn't the first thing on my mind. When I started to work for you, I finally felt as if I was getting back on track. I know it's not forever but I'll miss it for those reasons.'

'I'm glad it's helped.' Rosie put a tentative hand on Tabitha's arm. 'Having you here has helped me too. But I'm older, and this has always been my ultimate destination. You're too smart and capable for it to be yours. You should aim higher – like this is a stop on the route for you to a better destination.'

Tabitha sniffed. 'I'm not bothered about any high-flying job – I like doing this.'

'You do now, but you might not in a couple of years. At your interview you said you might go to university.'

'I don't know what I'd study there.'

'There must be something you'd be interested in.'

'Maybe law... oh, I don't know. I don't think I'm clever enough.'

'Good God – you're joking! You'd wipe the floor with everyone on that course!' Rosie stared at Tabitha, eyes wide.

'You're just being kind.'

'And truthful. What does Kit think?'

Tabitha shrugged. 'He thinks I should apply too.'

'Well, there's your answer.'

'Kit is one to talk. He didn't go either.'

'Really? I imagined him studying literature or something.'

'Because of the book thing? He loves reading and I think he would have gone... it just wasn't that simple.'

Had some life circumstance, some cruel luck kept Kit away from university? Rosie wanted to know more but wasn't sure this was the time to ask. She liked both Kit and Tabitha but in reality had only known them for a week. Was that too soon to ask such personal questions about their pasts? Tabitha was open about hers, but maybe Kit's wasn't for anyone else to share but Kit himself?

'Time's getting on,' Tabitha said into the ensuing silence. 'Want me to finish up here while you open the doors?'

'Blimey, I hadn't realised. I'm glad you're keeping an eye on the time.'

'It's what I'm here for,' Tabitha said, and she seemed brighter again.

Rosie was glad to see it. She'd felt somehow responsible for the change in mood. She'd said the wrong thing or pushed topics of conversation that should have been left alone. She was worried she'd somehow offended Tabitha.

Silly, she thought. Fergus had always said she was hyper-sensitive and that she worried too much about what people thought of her. He never cared. Said it came with age and experience, but Rosie didn't think she'd ever develop that thick skin no matter how old she got. Sometimes she almost felt her sensitivity amused Fergus, as if he saw her as a broken watch he had to fix. But then sometimes, when she did try to be better, he seemed unhappy and it was like he wanted the status quo back. Sometimes she'd felt nothing she did pleased him...

'What the fuck have you done to my sweater?' Fergus had waved his new lambswool jumper at Rosie, who looked up from the hob she was cleaning with a frown.

'Why? What's wrong with it?'

'Look! It's shrunk!'

'Well I washed it at the right temperature so I don't know how—'

'I know how – you're an idiot!'

'But I put it in at thirty, just like it said on the label!'

'You're quite sure about that? Because when you have one of your gormless days, anything can happen.'

'Yes, I'm sure!'

'Well, the evidence here would suggest otherwise...'

'It probably just needs reshaping a bit... here, let me...'

Fergus snatched the jumper from her grasp. 'Don't touch it – you'll only make it worse! It's what you do with everything after all.'

'Fergus, I didn't mean to...' Rosie's eyes filled with tears. 'I was careful because I knew it was your new sweater, I swear.'

'Well someone's ruined it, and as you washed it, it has to be you who ruined it.'

'I'll buy another one.'

'It's not the point – the point is that you have to be more careful. You're absolutely useless... I don't even know how you survived all those years before you met me, because you can't do anything without screwing it up... and now here come the waterworks. For fuck's sake, Rosie... if you're not messing something up, you're crying about something.'

'I can't help it when you're shouting at me.'

'So I'm the bad guy now? Of course I bloody am – I'm

always the villain, aren't I? Well here's a newsflash – I'm helping you! I'm trying to show you what a waste of space you are so you'll get better. You're lucky to have me looking out for you because nobody else would. Nobody else would put up with all this bullshit – they'd have left you long ago. If not for me, you'd be alone in this world, Rosie. So if I were you, I'd buck up and stop the waterworks and try to get things right once in a while.'

At that moment, Rosie had hated him with every fibre of her being but at the same time was terrified that he might be right. Was she really so unworthy? If she didn't have Fergus, would she ever find anyone else who would put up with her? She supposed she did keep messing up, even though she tried so hard. He had more patience than most other men and let her get away with more than most other men too – didn't he always say that?

'Here.' Fergus had shoved the jumper at her. 'You'd better throw it away.'

'But I can fix it—'

'Can you, Rosie?' He'd asked it with such contempt, it had almost reduced her to tears again. 'Can you really? I wouldn't bother trying because we both know how that would end. Throw it away... if you can find the bin, that is... And I'm taking the cost of a new one from the housekeeping, so we won't be able to go out this weekend either; another thing you've ruined...'

Rosie shook herself, forcing herself away from the bitter memories and back into the present.

'I'll open up,' she said to Tabitha now, wondering what on earth had just happened. Perhaps it was one of those stages of grief everyone kept talking about. Hopefully it wouldn't last, and if she was moving through them finally, it was a good thing.

Determined not to let it distract her, she grabbed the keys from a hook on the wall and went to open the front door.

The lunchtime rush had hardly been a rush at all, more of a light flurry. *It's Monday*, Rosie reminded herself, so there were fewer day-trippers and more of her passing trade was at work, away from idle hours they might spend by the river. There had been a boat party who'd stopped off for something light, a few elderly walkers, and, of course, Kit had called for his now infamous ham and pickle sandwich.

Rosie was clearing the outside tables while it was quiet – Tabitha was taking a quick break – when she noticed a large van pull up alongside the boathouse. Grant came out looking very pleased. He shook the driver's hand and then they went round the back to open the van doors.

Annoyingly, Rosie was at the wrong vantage point, and would have been too far away to see properly anyway, so couldn't tell what was inside, but she got her first clue two minutes later when Grant wheeled out a bicycle and propped it up against the side of the boat shed. He and the driver stood and inspected it for a few moments, seemed to agree on something, and then more bikes followed. This time Grant took them straight inside a smaller outbuilding that was attached to his main shed, the driver helping him. At a guess, Rosie would have said there were around a dozen bikes of varying sizes. Grant and the driver had another chat, shook hands, and then the driver got into his van and left.

'What are you looking at?'

Rosie turned to see Tabitha standing behind her. 'Nothing in particular – I'm just being nosy.'

'Share what you've been nosying at then.'

'Grant, taking delivery of lots of bikes apparently.'

'Hmm. They won't be much good on the water. You'd think he'd know that. Will you tell him or shall I?'

Rosie laughed and continued collecting the rest of the used cups from the table she'd been clearing. 'Looks like he's trying something new. Either that or he just really likes bikes.'

'Why don't you go and ask him?'

'What, whether he has a bike fetish?'

'No, silly, what he's up to.'

'I can't do that. It would also give away how nosy I am.'

'That much is true. I'll ask him then.'

'No, you can't!'

'Alright, I'll get Kit to wander over there. The minute he sees the bikes he'll ask anyway.'

Rosie was tempted. 'How will you get him to go over?'

'I'll tell him you want to know what's going on but you're too chicken to ask.'

'Tabitha!'

Tabitha started to laugh and went back inside. Rosie hoped she was joking about getting Kit to go over and see Grant. As she was beginning to learn, however, with Tabitha you could never be sure.

An hour later, Rosie was thinking about closing up. Even if the doors weren't locked, it was so quiet now she could at least start the cleaning, and if it continued to be quiet she could let Tabitha leave early.

Just as she was putting this to her waitress, Grant came in. Tabitha shot a knowing glance at Rosie, who held her metaphorical breath and hoped very much she'd keep her mouth shut about Rosie's earlier curiosity. But she needn't have worried – the first thing Grant did was volunteer to solve the mystery of his bike delivery himself.

'I've bought some bikes,' he announced as he walked in.

'We noticed a van,' Tabitha said – hiding a smirk, Rosie was sure.

'I'm going to start bike hire,' he continued.

Not so much of a mystery then, and a bit obvious now that Rosie thought of it.

'What made you think of that?' she asked.

'There's definitely a niche for it on the marina. Star Marina has one and it does well. Sometimes people on passing boats stop off for the day – they want things to do with their time other than mooch around Stratford. It's a nice spot to cycle around here after all. Didn't think it would hurt to try.'

'And I suppose it fits with your boat hire, in that the systems for running it must be a bit similar. Damage deposits and that sort of thing?' Rosie was quite pleased with her business analysis.

'Exactly – I already have all that in place. I've got to figure out a few things and then I'll be up and running. I hope to be renting them out in a week or so. The bikes are grand – got them for a good price too. Come over and have a look if you like.'

'I'm not much of a cyclist – haven't been on one for years.'

'You can still look.'

'OK,' Rosie said, wondering what about her said 'bike enthusiast' to Grant. But it wouldn't hurt to be neighbourly, she supposed, and he did seem quite excited about the whole thing.

'In fact,' Grant continued, 'I was hoping to rope you in for a trial run.'

'Me?' Rosie glanced briefly at Tabitha before turning back to Grant. 'I'm not really best friends with exercise. Hate the gym.'

'It's hardly exercise at all – you can take it nice and leisurely. It wouldn't be just you either – it'd be you and a few others,' he said. 'I'm not sure who yet; I'm going to ask around. Could do with a little exploration party.'

'You should ask Kit,' Tabitha said. 'I bet he'd be up for it.'

'You think?' Grant asked. 'I will then.' He turned back to Rosie. 'So how about it? Come on – it'll be a grand evening out.'

'I don't know... maybe,' Rosie said slowly. If it would be just a leisurely ride – well, perhaps that might even be quite nice. It felt like ages since she'd done something just for fun.

'Brilliant!' Grant beamed, seeming to take her noncommittal interest as firm agreement. 'I want to be able to recommend cycling routes to customers; something they can do in one hour, two, three... that sort of thing. I obviously need to run them first myself, see how easy or how hard they are, and whether the timings I give out are realistic. That's where you come in. I could do with people of different abilities having a go at them. Then I can tailor my advice to whoever is hiring, as I'd have a better idea of what bikes and routes suit different people.'

'I'm just not sure... I don't know the area well enough yet. I'm bound to get lost.'

'Not if everyone sticks together. I wouldn't leave you out in the wilderness.'

'Who else has agreed to it?'

'Me and my boys will be going. My goddaughter, Marcie... Tabitha here seems to think Kit will come too.'

'He definitely will if you do,' Tabitha said to Rosie, who held back a frown. She and Kit had become friends since his arrival at the marina to a point, but what made Tabitha so sure?

'Have you asked Layla and Tom?' she asked, turning back to Grant.

'They don't have time – busy with the farm shop extension, more's the pity. That's fair enough though. Angel said she would ordinarily but summer evenings and weekends are her busiest time and she doesn't want to lose the trade – fair enough too. Luca straight out laughed at me when I asked him...' Grant grinned. 'So I'm guessing that means no.' He glanced at Tabitha. 'Would you fancy it?'

'I'd love to if you have enough bikes!' she said. 'It sounds like a laugh.'

'Did you ask Nicole?' Rosie nodded in the direction of the gift shop. 'Only they're...'

She stopped herself. She didn't actually know if Nicole and Kit were anything yet; she was only guessing.

'She'll be too busy,' Grant said shortly.

Rosie couldn't see how that would be true and, even more importantly, how Grant could know that without talking to her first. She got the feeling Grant had reasons he didn't want to share – and she also suddenly recalled how frosty they'd been with each other that time they'd crossed paths in the cafe – and so she said nothing more about it.

'When are you going?' Tabitha asked.

'The weather looks promising tomorrow and most people aren't too busy on a week night. I was thinking about seven. It should be light for a couple of hours, and everyone will have had a chance to down tools and lock up for the day.'

Tabitha narrowed her eyes. 'I think you just want an excuse to go on a big jolly with loads of mates on bikes like you did when you were twelve.'

Grant grinned again. 'How did you guess? But it will be research too – Scout's honour!'

'I went to Brownies at the same church as the Scouts – let me tell you, they weren't very honourable.'

Grant laughed loudly. 'So you'll both come?'

'Of course we will! I can't wait – it's been years since I went out on a bike!' Tabitha grinned broadly.

'Not as many years as it's been for me, I'll bet,' Rosie said. 'I'm bound to fall off before I'm even on it. Probably end up in the bed next to Letitia in the fracture unit.'

'You never forget how to ride a bike,' Tabitha said. 'Isn't that supposed to be a thing?'

'I bet I could disprove that theory,' Rosie replied.

'We'll look after you,' Grant said cheerfully. 'You'll be alright. And the whole point is to have cyclists of different abilities to see how my routes fare. It'll help me see which bikes are good for less confident riders too.'

'Alright...' Rosie said finally, wondering what on earth she was letting herself in for. 'I suppose I could do it just to help you out.'

'Brilliant! I'll let you know for sure what the arrangements are tomorrow morning when I've been able to speak to everyone else, but seven would be OK as far as you're concerned?'

'It's good enough for me,' Tabitha said. 'I could kick around Kit's boat for a while after we close here – it would save me going home and then coming straight back.

'Or' – Rosie was struck by a sudden bolt of inspiration – 'maybe you and Kit could have tea here after we close? I mean, I'd need some time to get showered and changed, but there'll be plenty of food left from the day that we might as well eat... and I'd like the company.'

'That sounds good!' Tabitha said. 'Kit will definitely be up for that!'

Rosie looked at Grant with a bright smile. 'In that case, seven should be fine.'

'Great.' Grant made for the door, practically bouncing.

Anyone would think he's excited about something, Rosie thought.

'I'll see you both tomorrow!'

CHAPTER EIGHT

'I couldn't bring food obviously, and I couldn't come empty-handed, so I brought you a book.' Kit smiled broadly at Rosie and held out his gift as she let him into the now closed cafe. 'I don't know how right I've got your taste,' he said, an apologetic tone in his voice now, 'but if I'm way off, then feel free to come and browse what I have to swap it.'

'*My Family and Other Animals*...' Rosie turned the book over to read the back cover.

'You haven't already read it, have you?' he asked.

'No. I've heard of it but, no, I haven't read it. But if it's your recommendation then...'

'I just thought it might resonate with you, to be honest. As it's about a family relocating and building a new life – kind of like you are. I mean, obviously you're not in Corfu or anything, but...'

'I'm sure I'll enjoy it.' Rosie smiled up at him. 'I love Greece – I've been there a couple of times – and you're right, it's definitely a bit like my situation here. Thank you – that's so thoughtful of you.'

He gave an awkward shrug but seemed pleased that he'd got

it right. Rosie wasn't sure when she'd get time to read it, but she wasn't about to insult him by saying so. Instead, she went to put it on the table in the little conservatory, so that maybe she'd be able to pick it up during breaks at work.

'Take a seat,' she told him before she went. 'I'll just put this somewhere safe and then we'll eat.'

Tabitha met Rosie on the way through, casting a glance at the book. She raised a questioning eyebrow. 'Kit?'

'Yes.' Rosie held the book up. 'He said he thought it might resonate with me so he brought it over.'

'Of course he did,' Tabitha said with a light laugh, as she continued on her way. 'Probably spent all day choosing it too.'

Rosie put the book down and then went back out to the cafe to join them. When she got there, Tabitha was already putting leftover sausage rolls, sandwiches and salads out on a table, while Kit was behind the counter wrestling with a monstrous rubbish bag he'd just taken from the bin.

'I'll sort that!' Rosie said, dashing over to him. 'You're a guest – you can't be putting our rubbish out!'

'Yes he can,' Tabitha said. 'I told him to make himself useful.'

'I'd have done it anyway,' Kit fired back. 'I don't mind helping if I'm being fed.' He looked at Rosie. 'It's really good of you to invite us over – helping you to finish the cleaning is the least I can do.'

'But, Kit...' As Rosie tried to take the bag from him, his hand closed over hers, and when she looked up, he smiled. For a moment, she could do nothing but stare into eyes that she suddenly realised were the colour of midnight. She'd never really taken that much notice before...

'Let me do it,' he said, bringing her back to the room. 'Please.'

'I only meant, you've done a full day's work at your place... you shouldn't be over here working at mine.'

'Well,' he said, deftly tying up the bag before hoisting it up, 'I'd hardly call what I do "work". Most of the day I spend actually reading the stock while I wait for customers. I might dust a shelf or two – but I'm sure it's nowhere near as physical as what you do here.'

'He wants to be useful – I say let him,' Tabitha called over. 'What do you want to drink, Rosie? We might as well make a start while Kit takes the rubbish.'

'But I just needed to clean the grill and—'

'Come and eat,' Tabitha said. 'It can wait. In fact, I'll do it after we've eaten while you freshen up and get changed.'

'I can lend a hand with anything else that needs doing,' Kit put in amiably.

Rosie went to the door and unlocked it for him to go out with the rubbish bag. Once he'd gone, she turned to Tabitha. 'I ought to do it.'

'Why? Why do you need to do everything? Kit wants to help – we both do. Let us. You do almost everything by yourself all of the time – it wouldn't kill you to accept a hand when people want to offer it.'

Rosie wanted to argue, but she got the impression it wouldn't be much use, so she relaxed into a smile. And the truth was, a helping hand was actually pretty welcome. She muddled through – better than she'd ever thought she could and certainly better than Fergus would have expected had he been there to see it – but muddling through felt like a constant battle. 'I suppose you're right.'

'So come and sit down.'

Rosie went to the table and took a seat. A moment later, Kit returned. He took the keys from her, locked the door, went to wash his hands and then joined them.

'This is my favourite kind of tea,' he said, giving the table an approving once-over. 'It reminds me of when you used to go to family gatherings as a kid and there'd be a buffet and you got to take the leftovers home with you so you could eat them the next day and pretend you were at the buffet all over again.'

Tabitha laughed. 'Only you'd get excited about dried-up old sausages. Not that these are like that,' she added quickly, shooting Rosie an apologetic look.

'Don't worry – I'm not offended.' Rosie smiled. 'I've been to enough family dos to know what you mean.'

'And we are talking about the man whose idea of culinary excellence is a ham and pickle sandwich,' Tabitha added.

'I'm not arguing with that,' Kit said, reaching for a sausage roll and cramming it into his mouth. 'Sorry,' he mumbled through it. 'Starving.'

'Doesn't it feel weird too?' Tabitha said, helping herself to some rice salad. 'Remember when you were a kid and you imagined that, like, stores and cafes had a secret life after they locked up for the night and you always wanted to get locked in so you could see it?'

'No.' Rosie laughed softly. 'Not really.'

'Really you didn't?' Tabitha asked. 'I thought everyone did.'

'You always had a very active imagination,' Kit said. 'I'm sorry to break it to you, but I think that might just be you.'

'But, you know,' Tabitha continued, undaunted, 'like that film where the exhibits come to life in the museum after it closes?'

'I'm really lost now,' Rosie said.

Tabitha shrugged. 'I was just going to say, being in the cafe and eating here after closing feels a bit naughty and a bit special, like that. We have the whole place to ourselves like we're VIPs.'

'We are VIPs,' Rosie said. 'There'd be no cafe if not for us.'

'Well, if not for you two,' Kit said. 'You two are the power-houses behind the business. I'm afraid I don't bring much to the table apart from my massive appetite.'

'You bring charm and humour.' Rosie offered him a bowl of

tuna pasta and he spooned some onto his plate with a beaming smile.

'I'll take that,' he said.

'Oh God.' Tabitha rolled her eyes. 'Please don't flatter his ego, Rosie; his head's big enough as it is.'

'And you also bring books and helping hands,' Rosie continued with a grin. 'You can bring those any time you like. In fact, I think we should do this more often. We're using up the leftover food and we're enjoying ourselves into the bargain. I could almost convince myself I'm eating out somewhere fancy instead of just having tea in my own home. This is way nicer than just eating upstairs in front of the telly.'

'I have to agree with that,' Kit said. 'Honestly, my idea of cooking for myself is pretty much beans on toast. I might stretch to a crisp sandwich if I'm feeling extra fancy.'

'You're the only person I know who eats student food without actually being a student,' Tabitha said.

He gave a vague shrug. 'I can cook if I need to. I just don't see the point in cooking when it's just me... seems like a lot of effort for not a lot of reward.'

'I've never been a great cook either,' Rosie said. 'Every time Fergus sat down to a dinner, there was something either over-done or underdone on the plate. He used to say he'd sack me and hire a proper maid.'

Tabitha stared at her. 'What?'

'He was only joking of course,' Rosie replied hastily, flushing. She'd never considered what Fergus had meant by that, even though he'd said it a lot during their marriage, but repeating it out loud now to Tabitha and Kit, she was suddenly aware of how bad it sounded.

'I'd have told him to cook his own food if he didn't like it,' Tabitha muttered.

'Tab...' Kit said in a warning voice, and then turned to Rosie and forced a smile. 'Well, I can't speak for what your food was like before, but it's definitely good whenever I come here to eat.'

'Well...' Rosie turned her face to her plate, cheeks still burning and feeling as if an awkwardness had suddenly descended over the table. 'It's quite hard to mess up a ham and pickle sandwich.'

'This is all pretty good too,' Kit replied, gesturing to the spread in front of them.

'Well... I...' Rosie shot from her chair. 'How about we put the radio on? Sitting here in silence... feels like we're in the school dinner hall.'

'I don't know about your dinner hall but mine was bedlam,' Kit said. 'Certainly never silent.'

'Catholic school...' Rosie said, going to the shelf behind the counter and twiddling the knob of the retro radio to find a decent station. 'Very strict...'

'Oh, leave it there!' Tabitha called. 'I love this song!'

As Rosie came back to the table, Tabitha began to jiggle around in her chair, humming through a mouthful of tuna.

'One D?' Kit asked scornfully.

'Who doesn't love One D?' Tabitha replied airily. 'Don't pretend you're too cool – even you've been known to sing along from time to time.'

'Only because I heard them coming from your room so bloody often the songs were programmed into my brain. I was brainwashed into singing along.'

'What about you, Rosie?' Tabitha asked. 'Where do you stand on this debate?'

'Well... I guess they're OK. I mean, I like some of their stuff.'

'See!' Tabitha turned to her brother with a look of triumph. 'Rosie likes them too – anyone with taste likes them!'

The song came to an end. It was followed by a moment of chit-chat from the presenter and then 'Mr Brightside' started to play.

'Oh, now this is more like it!' Kit said. He looked at Rosie. 'I bet this is more your thing, right?'

She cast an apologetic glance at Tabitha. 'Sorry...'

Tabitha shrugged. 'It's not your fault you have no taste.'

Rosie started to laugh but was then distracted by Kit staring up at something. She followed his gaze to see a scarlet butterfly trapped inside with them. The top windows were open, but it seemed to be struggling to locate its exit.

'Oh, poor thing,' Rosie said, watching it circle but not finding the gap. 'I'd better open the doors so it can leave that way.'

'They're so dim,' Tabitha said. 'You could have every window and door open and it still wouldn't be able to get out.'

Rosie went to unlock the door anyway and propped it open. They watched it circle at the windows for a couple of minutes more, tucking into their food as they did, and it seemed Tabitha was right – it didn't go anywhere near the wide open door.

'Maybe I could catch it,' Rosie said, standing on her chair to reach.

'I'm pretty sure you're not supposed to touch their wings or it can hurt them,' Kit said. 'Let me get something...'

Going to the counter, he began to rummage around on the shelves of containers for something suitable, returning a moment later with a lidded bowl.

'He's not going to like this,' Kit said, pouncing as the butterfly rested for a moment on the glass, wings idling. 'But it's for his own good.' Trapping it, he slid the lid over the bowl and then dashed for the doorway before releasing it again. They watched as the butterfly lifted on a light breeze and then flew away.

'Softy,' Tabitha said with a knowing smirk as he joined them at the table again.

Rosie smiled at him. She was still smiling at him when he

glanced across and caught her eye, returning it with one of his own.

How long had she been staring? It couldn't have been more than seconds but despite that, she suddenly felt awkward, as if she'd been caught doing something she shouldn't be.

'Drinks!' she exclaimed. 'Who needs another drink? Tabitha... want something out of the fridge?'

'I'd love a lemonade.'

'One for you, Kit?'

'You've done all this,' he said, getting up. 'I'll fetch them. What do you want?'

'Sparkling water please.'

'Coming right up.'

When he returned a moment later he had three bottles. He placed one in front of Tabitha, and then went to put Rosie's down. She reached to take it at the same time, so that their hands collided somewhere in between, ending with a self-conscious laugh.

'Sorry...' Rosie said. 'My clumsy genes strike again.'

'There's nothing to be sorry about,' Kit said, handing the bottle over. 'It was just a thing that happened, no big deal.'

Tabitha coughed loudly into the gap that followed before doing the comedy-mumble thing that people did when they were hinting very obviously at something. Rosie didn't catch it, but Kit glared at his sister before turning back to his plate.

If it bothered him that much, perhaps it was just as well Rosie hadn't been able to tell what Tabitha had said.

'Come on – we'd better make a dent in this food,' she said in a bid to distract them from a sibling tiff. 'We've got a ton of cake to get through.'

Tabitha winked at her brother. 'Sausage rolls, cake and the best company you could ask for – beats lonely crisp sandwiches on your barge, eh?'

Whatever bad mood had affected Kit momentarily cleared just as quickly and he grinned. 'You can say that again.'

Tabitha had been bang on the money about Grant's outing: it was definitely an excuse for a jolly on bikes with a gang of mates. Rosie felt conspicuous and a bit stupid in her cycling helmet, but Grant had insisted everyone wear one. She could think of a million jobs she could be doing at the cafe instead of this and knew she'd regret not doing them come the morning.

As the trip got underway, as well as trialling Grant's new business venture, it became apparent that it was also an excuse to visit the very many pubs that lay along the route. In fact, it seemed more than just a very happy accident that there were pubs along the way, Rosie thought. There were so many in fact, that she suspected the route had been designed around them and that their regular appearance was no accident at all.

Apart from having to wear the ugliest helmet she'd ever seen, the evening started off better than Rosie could have hoped for. Not only had things settled at tea with Tabitha and Kit, meaning that by the end of it they were all getting on famously – so much so that she was sorry to have to leave them to get cleaned up and changed and did everything at top speed in order to rejoin the fun – but her clumsy genes were nowhere to be seen. She didn't fall off the bike as soon as she mounted it as she had feared, and not even as they all began to pedal. In fact, she was genuinely shocked at how quickly she became proficient again. There had been a wobble and a few close shaves, but once she got going it was like she'd never stopped riding a bike.

The evening was perfect too. Bright but cool, with a fresh breeze and the last of spring's blossom on the air. Hedgerows and towpaths were bursting with bright foliage, and wildlife bustled about within the bushes and trees. The sun mellowed as the evening wore on and the landscape turned from gold to bronze, the light catching midges and dragonflies and butterflies of all colours. Grasshoppers trilled in the verges, out of sight but undoubtedly there, and the river, whose path they followed for a while, was silver-blue and serene. Even Rosie couldn't get stressed about cycling so close to the water when the scene was so enchanting.

Grant and his two sons were way out ahead as they cycled. Kit and Tabitha kept time with Rosie. She suspected they'd made a pact to keep an eye on her and that they were riding more slowly than they might have ordinarily. Luca from the gelato boat, despite laughing at Grant when he'd mentioned it, had joined them on the excursion. Grant's goddaughter, Marcie, was a pencil-thin twenty-something who looked as if she cycled for miles every day and whizzed along without breaking a sweat. The rest of the party was made up of people who worked with Grant from time to time, but who Rosie didn't know well at all.

Half an hour had taken them down the river for a while and then off onto a track towards a Tudor-era building that became recognisable as their first pub.

Grant stopped and got off his bike, his boys following with Marcie. 'Time to wet our whistle,' he announced as everyone caught up with him and came to a halt beside him. 'Come on...' He opened the gate onto a beer garden still bright with late sunlight.

'"The Poet's Ruin",' Kit said, gazing up at the pub's sign as he took off his helmet to reveal perfect curls.

Rosie was sure her hair wasn't going to be quite so unaffected and considered for a moment leaving her helmet on. It was a toss-up which look was going to be worse. It didn't help that Tabitha's hair looked pretty good too when she removed her helmet. Rosie decided they must have hat-hair-resistant genes.

'I wonder how many poets did get ruined here,' Kit continued as they found a group of tables close together and everyone secured their bikes and sat down.

'Maybe Shaky himself drank here,' Tabitha said.

'Clearly it didn't do him any harm if he did,' Kit said with a chuckle. He turned to Rosie. 'I'd hardly say his career was ruined. I'll go to the bar, save us all trekking in.'

'I'll have a lager,' Tabitha said. 'Make it a pint.'

'Bloody hell – a pint?'

'Yeah, cheapskate.'

Kit grinned and turned to Rosie.

'I'd better have a Coke,' she said.

'Don't be daft – have one drink,' Tabitha said. 'You've worked hard today.'

Rosie thought about arguing but then decided that Tabitha was right – she *had* worked hard and maybe she did deserve a proper drink.

'Alright, I'll have half a cider. Thank you.'

'So that's a pint for Rosie too,' Tabitha said to Kit with a wink.

Kit didn't give Rosie the chance to complain, marching off to the bar.

'Everything alright, ladies?' Grant came over to their table. 'Can I get you a drink?'

'Kit's getting ours thanks,' Tabitha said.

'In that case I'll owe you one,' he said. 'I'm just off to get the rest.'

Rosie watched as everyone got comfortable at their tables and began to compare aches and injuries. The mild summer air was filled with good-natured ribbing and laughter.

'Kit will be gutted when he realises Grant would have bought a round.' Tabitha remarked with a laugh.

Rosie turned back to her with a vague smile. Despite all her initial uncertainties, she hadn't felt this free and untroubled in a long time. There was nothing to worry about right then other than the scenery flying past as she cycled, and where the next pub was. She closed her eyes for a moment, felt the evening sun warm her face and was at peace in a way she hadn't been since…

Rosie paused. When had life become so fraught? When she stopped to consider it, she couldn't actually remember, but she also couldn't recall a time when it wasn't. Even during quiet moments there had been a strange undercurrent, a vague background hum of menace, some hidden and unspoken anxiety waiting to drag her down whenever she felt as if she might just find contentment.

But not this evening. This evening, for the first time in a long time, Rosie was happy.

Ten minutes later, Kit was back with two pints of lager and a pint of cider.

'Look at us… we should have had cider too – then we could have said we were having cider with Rosie.'

'Trust you to think of that lame joke, book boy,' Tabitha said, but she was smiling anyway.

'But we are!' he said.

Tabitha took her drink from him. 'I don't know about that, but I could do this a lot more often.'

'Me too.' Rosie took the other glass from Kit. 'Thank you.'

'I wasn't sure which one to get,' he said. 'I hope it's alright. The landlady said most people like that one.'

Rosie took a sip. 'It's lovely.'

'That's a relief.'

'What was she going to do if she didn't like it?' Tabitha asked wryly. 'Punch you in the face? Let's be honest, she'd tell you she liked it even if she hated it.'

Rosie took another sip of her cider. 'I wouldn't.'

'Yes, you would. You're too nice to do anything else.'

Rosie gave a sheepish grin. 'Honestly, I do like it.'

'See...' Kit gave Tabitha a triumphant smile. 'I'm good at this sort of thing.'

'Yeah, right...' Tabitha snorted.

'OK, let's see if you do any better – you can choose Rosie's drink next time.'

'Um... maybe Rosie wants to choose her own drink next time!' Rosie cut in.

Kit and Tabitha burst out laughing.

'As if!' Tabitha said. 'Trust me – I'll pick a nice one and it'll be better than lame-brain's here.'

'Oi!' Kit shot back.

'You know nothing about drink.'

'Oh, just because you went to every bar in Leeds means you know more about booze than I do? I've had ten years more experience than you.'

'So you were drinking when you were ten? Does Mum know?'

Rosie grinned as she watched their banter. It was nice. They could say anything to each other and nothing changed between them – the love was obvious. Rosie envied it.

Grant returned shortly afterwards with everyone else's drinks. The party shuffled the tables and chairs around so they were all facing each other and could chat more easily. They were getting rowdy already, only one pub in. Rosie glanced around the beer garden more than once, but none of the other patrons seemed bothered by them.

Grant called for their attention and started a slightly more serious conversation about what people thought of the route so far and how they were finding the bikes. At least he tried to, but it soon descended into a free-for-all where Grant and his family and those who knew them all better than Rosie started to tease him about completely unconnected things. Most of them were about habits he had or silly things he'd done while under the influence of alcohol at various events. There was at least twenty minutes of this, which concluded as his oldest son, Chris, put on a pair of sunglasses.

'What's that about?' Grant said as Chris turned to him, pretending to shield his eyes.

'It's... so... bright!' Chris replied with a laugh. 'My eyes...'

'What are you on about?' Grant demanded.

'Your head... the sun bouncing off...it's blinding!'

'You cheeky beggar!' Grant exclaimed to much laughter from everyone else. Rosie felt a bit sorry for the owner of the boat shed, but once the laughter had died down, he didn't seem too offended and so she guessed he was either used to such ribbing or really didn't care all that much.

'Come on, you daft git,' Grant said, giving his son a playful nudge. 'Drink up... we've got plenty more pubs to get to before last orders. Time to move on.'

The next bit of their route took them across farmland this time, and then back onto a minor road. They'd been pedalling for less than twenty minutes when another pub appeared on the horizon. Grant announced he was thirsty and that they ought to stop again.

'"The Cross",' Kit said as they stopped. 'Disappointing. They could have tried a bit harder with the name.'

'Perhaps they lost some of the sign,' Tabitha said. 'Maybe it should have been the Cross Badger or something.'

'Right, yeah, twinned with its sister pub the Pissed-Off Squirrel?'

Tabitha giggled and Grant led them all to another beer garden – this one partly shaded by a canopy that was dressed in lights. It was too early for them to be on yet, but Rosie would bet it looked lovely when they were. The stone building looked newer than that of the Poet's Ruin – Georgian maybe. Fergus would have known.

Grant found them a cluster of tables in the corner of the beer garden in the shadow of a clematis-gowned wall and ushered them over. There was a momentary fuss as everyone found places to stand their bikes, and then they settled on seats.

Grant insisted on buying all the drinks this time and persuaded Rosie to have another cider. Kit made the joke again – apparently delighted that Rosie's order hadn't changed from last time so that he could make it a second time.

Tabitha rolled her eyes. 'Please don't do that again. It's not funny; it's just sad.' She looked up at Grant. 'I'll come in with you. I've got to pick a good one for Rosie.'

'Can't she choose her own?' Grant asked, throwing a puzzled glance at Rosie, who just laughed.

'Apparently not. Go on, Tabitha – impress me.'

'Oh, I will!' she said, following Grant into the pub.

'I'm going to miss her when Letitia comes back,' Rosie said as she watched them go.

'I think she's going to miss you too,' Kit said.

'Well, I expect she'll still be coming over to the marina to see you. She can call to say hello at the cafe any time she likes. She could make herself useful and fetch your sandwich order for you.'

'Then I'd have no excuse to come over, would I?'

'Oh...' Rosie said vaguely, her attention caught by a group of children playing hide-and-seek around a huge oak tree as their parents sipped drinks at a nearby table. 'I suppose so.'

When she looked back, Kit quickly turned away, as if he'd been staring at her while she'd been distracted. Rosie tried to hold back a frown. Was there something he needed to say?

'Raspberry Revenge!' The moment passed as Tabitha returned and set a glass in front of Rosie with a look of satisfaction. 'Now – drink that and tell me it's not better than what Kit got you last time!'

There were two more pubs on the outgoing part of the circular route – the Old Post Office and Falstaff's. Rosie couldn't remember asking for them, but another pint of cider appeared in front of her at each one. There was another raspberry cider (Tabitha's doing again, Rosie presumed) and then a good, old-style scrumpy. Rosie didn't actually know whose idea that one was, but it was definitely the strongest drink of the night and she giggled, feeling a little unsteady as she clambered back on her bike outside the pub.

'Are you sure you're going to be alright?' Kit asked warily. 'Maybe you should walk a bit till it wears off.'

'Paha! Probably not! You'll catch me if I fall, won't you? I could do with a pee though... probably should have had one at the pub... Tabitha... if I need a nature wee, you'll have to cover me.'

Tabitha burst out laughing. 'You're slaughtered.'

'I'm not. I'm a bit merry, that's all.'

'Well,' Kit said wryly, 'we're certainly seeing a side to you that we didn't realise you had.'

'Are you saying I'm boring?' Rosie squeaked.

'No,' Tabitha said. 'We just thought you were the sensible one.'

'Pah!' Rosie said again as she began to pedal. That was all she'd ever heard during her marriage to Fergus – he was the fun one; she was the sensible sidekick. Well, Fergus was gone, so what did that make her now?

They were almost back at the marina and close to the centre of Stratford when Grant suggested the last pub. The sun had almost set and Rosie couldn't deny now that she was a little drunk. More than once, she'd almost come off her bike, and then she'd had to stop for the pee she'd been afraid she wouldn't be able to hold, Tabitha laughing as she kept guard at the bush Rosie had been forced to use as the others went ahead, fortunately oblivious to the emergency pit stop behind them.

'There's no bonding like a girl looking out for another girl while she pees in a bush, right?' Rosie had said as she emerged.

'Damn right!' Tabitha had grinned.

One more drink at this final pub might just send Rosie over the edge, but they were nearly home and so... why not? What was the worst that could happen this close to the end of the ride?

She asked Luca for another of those raspberry thingies and emptied her purse out on the table for someone to take the change. Luca clarified with Tabitha what a raspberry thingy was and then went to join Grant as he walked inside, leaving Rosie's money on the table. Tabitha scooped it silently up and put it back into Rosie's purse and tucked it into her shoulder bag.

Everyone was saying what a great night it had been and how their heads would ache in the morning but how it was worth it and that they ought to make this a monthly event.

When Grant and Luca came back with trays of booze for them all, Grant said, 'I just realised, we're having cider with Rosie!'

'I'm not!' Marcie shouted. 'I'm having a lager top!'

Everyone laughed, Kit the hardest of all, who'd made the joke twice already that night and yet still seemed to find it hilarious.

Some of their party had started to get cold, so they'd gone inside. This pub, being closer to town, was a lot rowdier, even for a Tuesday night. Rosie could hear different accents too. Tourists and visitors she supposed. The pub was as pretty as the more rural ones they'd visited, perhaps even prettier, blessed with a view of the river, but also more commercialised. The decor felt more brash and bawdy than the interiors of the country pubs they'd visited, with posters advertising branded beers and spirits and upcoming events, and a television showing a golf tournament at a volume that was just on the wrong side of loud.

While they were in there, one more pint of cider appeared in front of Rosie. She had no idea who'd bought this one, and it wasn't a raspberry; it was a well-known apple variety. This time Rosie sipped at it – she didn't really want it. Even she knew she was just about to cross the line from fun drunk and into horrible drunk territory; she was sure if she drank the whole lot she'd be sick.

Tabitha and Kit seemed to be faring much better.

Rosie watched their playful banter and was struck once again by their obvious closeness. She didn't have anyone who knew her well enough to say the sorts of things they said to one another and for it to be OK – at least, it often felt that way.

School friends had envied Rosie for being an only child, but Rosie had often found it lonely. Her dad had worked too many hours to spend a huge amount of time with her, and while her mum tried hard to make up for that, she didn't always have the energy or the time to give Rosie as much attention as she'd have liked. It was no wonder then that meeting an incredibly attentive Fergus had had an instant effect on her. From the first date he'd been keen, messaging her daily, showering her with flowers and other gifts and complimenting her at every opportunity. He'd been unable to keep his hands off her when they'd been alone; it had made her feel desired and noticed and like she finally had the one important person to share her life with that she'd always felt was missing. Not in the form of a sibling of course but perhaps better, because while all siblings grew up and went their own ways, Fergus would always be there. With such an assault, it was inevitable she'd fall for him.

After the wedding she'd told him just that.

'I know,' he'd said with a sly smile. 'That was the plan.'

His cryptic response didn't worry her, because she had him and that was the main thing. She could even deal with the comments that had been less admiring as time went on and more critical, because they came from that same place of love – she was certain – and she still had that constant companionship she'd so craved. She'd folded his shirt wrong – it was OK for him to tell her so she didn't do it again. If she had to organise visits to her mum and dad, she ought to do it when he had other plans too – that way, she'd always be home for him. Her hair needed to be longer – he was only saying so because she'd look so much prettier... whatever might have sounded like criticism to anyone else Rosie knew was for her benefit, so she could be the best version of herself, so that she could keep him by her side.

Until she didn't of course.

Nobody had told Rosie that even if she gave so much of herself to keep Fergus, she might still lose him in circumstances that she had no control over, no matter how far she went to please him...

'Penny for them.' Kit had turned to face her. She hadn't realised she'd been staring.

Tabitha noticed her now too. 'You're absolutely leathered!' She laughed. 'God help us in the cafe tomorrow.'

'Do you think God is free to do a shift?' Rosie asked with a grin. 'Because neither of us will be fit.'

'I'll be alright – I'm not a lightweight.'

'I wasn't actually thinking of hangovers – my legs are seizing up already. I don't think I've done this much exercise for about twenty years.'

'Let's hope for a quiet day then.'

'I wish. It'll be Sod's Law we'll be heaving – and I can't really complain about that.'

'Cherry juice.' Tabitha drank down half of her beer in one go. At least it looked that way to Rosie.

'What?'

'I read somewhere if you drink cherry juice after exercise, you won't ache.'

'Where am I going to get cherry juice at this hour?'

'Buggered if I know.'

'If you've got cherries, I could stamp on them for you,' Kit said.

'I don't.'

'Let's do a raid on the farm shop,' Tabitha said. 'They're bound to have some.'

'I'm sure that'll go down well when they catch us on their CCTV carting all their cherries away,' Kit said.

'Nobody mentioned us all going in,' Tabitha said carelessly. 'We're going to send you and then you can go to prison if you get caught.'

'Wow, thanks.'

'So you're saying we're not worth the sacrifice?'

'You're not. I'd do it for Rosie, but you can ache.'

'Well, we all know you'd do anything for Rosie, don't we?'

Kit flushed and shot his sister a warning look, and then a weird and awkward beat of silence descended over the table.

Just as Rosie felt she was going to have to say something to break it – and she had no idea what – Grant stood up, suggesting they all took the bikes back to his shed and returned on foot to continue drinking, unburdened by the worry of getting his precious new equipment back in one piece.

Everyone cheered in agreement, they all drank what they had left – except Rosie, who hoped nobody would notice she'd abandoned her drink – and then they went to get their bikes from the rack at the front of the pub.

. . .

The going was slower on the way back. Some walked, pushing their bikes along the towpath, while others meandered lazily, riding them as slow as gravity would allow. The sun had disappeared behind the horizon but the last of the daylight hadn't yet gone. The sky was that strange, ethereal indigo where it was dark but the stars hadn't yet fully appeared. If she hadn't been so drunk, Rosie might have noticed the chill in the air and she might have wished she had her lovely woollen shawl with her. She would also have given far more thought to the strange moment in the pub between Kit and Tabitha, just before Grant had moved them all out.

But Rosie didn't think about any of that. She was happy to concentrate on staying on her bike. Her helmet wasn't fastened properly and had slipped to one side and her bike wobbled as she pedalled. She felt barely able to coordinate her limbs. She was aware of Kit and Tabitha both shooting her cautious glances every now and again. She thought about telling them that she wasn't *that* drunk, but she couldn't get her mouth and her legs to work at the same time. She decided it was probably better to put her legs first, as they were the things getting her home.

She'd had a brilliant night. Right then, as they rode along a riverside path, she wasn't even bothered that they were so close to the water, which was remarkable in itself and definitely said a lot about her state of mind. She hadn't wanted to come but, as so often happened, she was glad she had. Often, it was the activities one didn't expect to enjoy that were the biggest surprise. Rosie would never have imagined for a single minute that a cycling country-pub crawl would be so much fun. She wanted to do it all over again.

But maybe not right then. Maybe some sleep would be good first...

She wondered, in a drunken haze, what Fergus would think

if he could see her now. He'd probably just be pissed off that he hadn't been invited.

Like Nicole.

Oh. Nicole hadn't been invited! Rosie hadn't given it a thought all night, but she should have done. What kind of awful friend did that make her? Would she hate Rosie when she found out what a good night they'd had, especially when she discovered that Rosie had spent most of it in the company of Kit? Rosie decided she would have to go over first thing and try to explain. She had to make it right – she couldn't bear the thought of Nicole being upset about that. She couldn't actually believe now that she hadn't thought of it before, but she'd been so wrapped up beforehand, not knowing what to expect and whether she'd be able to stay on the bike that she hadn't thought about it. And she hadn't expected to stay out this long either. She wasn't to know there would be all these pubs and so much cider. She'd expected to wobble up and down a couple of lanes and be home in time for the ten o'clock news.

While these thoughts occupied her, she realised Kit was watching her. He was walking, pushing his bike along.

'Are you alright?' he asked. 'Not going to pass out on me?'

Rosie was just about to reply when her bike veered from the path and hit a tuft of grass on the verge. The next thing she knew she was falling off it. She thudded into something soft, heard a splash, and then realised she'd accidentally pushed Kit into the river.

A cheer went up from the party.

'Oh God!' Rosie raced up and down the bank, her face a picture of shock and horror. She was suddenly very sober. 'Help him!'

'He's alright,' Grant said, and when Rosie looked again, Kit was happily swimming towards them.

'That's sorted me out,' he said as he clambered back onto dry land.

'Enjoy your dip?' Grant called over.

'I'm so sorry!' Rosie gasped, but Kit just grinned at her, hair dripping onto his face. Rosie bunched up the sleeve of her cardigan and tried to wipe him down, but he just ducked out of her way with a laugh.

'Don't stress – there's no harm done. Thank God the bike didn't go in with me; I don't think Grant would have found it quite so funny then.'

Tabitha cocked an eyebrow at him. She didn't look particularly concerned about the fact that her brother was sopping wet and had bits of algae in his hair. 'We can't take you anywhere.'

'It was my fault,' Rosie said. 'I fell into him.'

Tabitha nodded at Rosie but spoke to Kit. 'Want me to push her in to even things up?'

'I can't swim!' Rosie squeaked and Tabitha looked suitably repentant.

'I didn't mean it,' she said. 'I'm sorry, I—'

'Don't worry,' Rosie said. 'I know.'

'God, for a moment there I thought you were going to fire me.'

'I can hardly fire you when your poor brother is standing there dripping because of me,' Rosie replied. She looked at him again and suddenly – though she still felt bad – started to laugh. 'I'm sorry, you just look so...'

'Wet?' he asked with a mock frown.

'And I can't believe you just swam back to shore all cool as you like.'

'It wasn't that far and the only alternative was not to swim back. I like swimming but there's a limit, even for me.' He started to wring out one of his sleeves. 'I wasn't lying about it sobering me up either. I could start that pub crawl again.'

'Come back into town with us,' Marcie called over.

'It's tempting,' Kit replied, 'but the state of me now... I probably ought to get showered and call it a night.'

'You've just had a bath!' Marcie fired back.

'I'll bet it wasn't the cleanest bath water ever.' Kit grinned. He retrieved his bike from the undergrowth where it had fallen and began to walk with it as the party set off again, clothes dripping and shoes squeaking as he went. Rosie didn't know whether to be absolutely mortified or start laughing again.

Rosie woke with a start, heart hammering. It wasn't yet dawn – she could just make out the glow of the moon behind the curtains.

She'd had the dream before. They were at the house they'd shared when she'd first married Fergus. She was downstairs in the kitchen cooking breakfast in a nightgown she no longer owned. She'd turn at the sound of a creaking stair, and Fergus – always Fergus – would come smiling into the kitchen to kiss her.

She'd had the dream before – a few times since his death – but never like this. This time, when she turned at the sound of the creaking stair, it wasn't Fergus standing there.

It was Kit.

She pushed herself up to sit. Her mouth tasted like old socks. It was a good thing she'd thought to bring a glass of water to bed. Already, her muscles had started to stiffen from her bike ride. When she'd joked with Tabitha that they'd need God to help out at the cafe, now she was seriously wondering if He would actually be free to do a shift because she was going to be fit for nothing come opening time. And if Tabitha felt half as bad as Rosie did then she'd be fit for nothing too.

She reached for the water and took a sip. The dream that had woken her was already fading, but the shock of it lingered. It was curious, but more than that, it had left her feeling uncomfortable and guilty that Fergus could have been replaced in her subconscious by a man she'd only just met.

Rosie reached for her phone. She'd tossed it onto her

bedside table before bed and, falling asleep almost instantly, hadn't noticed that Tabitha had sent her some photos she'd taken during their night out. Rosie scrolled through them now as she lay in the darkness. Most of them were group snaps of the gang at the various pubs they'd visited. Some were more candid shots of people cycling, the evening sun painting them with a golden hue. There were others of people pulling silly faces or looking drunker and drunker as the night went on. She reached one of her and Kit, caught unawares and laughing together. Kit's eyes were crinkled in such mirth Rosie could barely see them now, and her own mouth was a vast expanse of teeth. Not the most flattering photo of either of them, but Rosie liked the honesty in it. Whatever had been said, they'd both found it genuinely funny.

Rosie didn't have any photos like that, and as she realised it, it was like a punch to the stomach. It was a strange feeling, as if she'd suddenly realised she'd never really lived, which was silly because she'd been living a whole full life with Fergus.

Rosie scrolled further back to remind herself of her time with him. There were a ton of photos of her and Fergus, but they were very different. They were perfectly good photographs taken at parties or meals out; some at the marina in front of Marigold Cafe as it had looked when they'd first arrived. Always perfectly posed, always Fergus dominant, broad shouldered and confident, and Rosie... it was almost as if she was fading into the background, porcelain-faced, a forced smile on her lips...

What did these pictures say about their relationship? She'd looked at them so many times since Fergus's death, but she'd never seen in them what she saw just then. There wasn't a single one where she felt she looked genuinely happy, where she could recall the moment and honestly say she'd been having fun.

Scrolling back to the ones Tabitha had sent her, she took

another look before locking her phone and putting it to one side. They were silly thoughts caused by tiredness: of course she'd been just as happy in the ones with Fergus as those with her cycling buddies – it was simply a different kind of happiness.

She tried to put her thoughts out of her mind – she needed to get some sleep if she was going to have any chance of functioning at work in the morning. The problem was, now that she'd woken, she didn't feel tired at all. Despite this, she closed her eyes and did her best to settle down.

She just hoped there'd be no more strange dreams.

CHAPTER NINE

The hangover she could deal with – a cup of tea, some toast and an aspirin and she'd be sorted. The aching muscles weren't so easy to cure. Rosie suspected it was too late for cherry juice – even if she had the time to get some, and even if she was convinced it would work – and so she resigned herself to a tough day. The night before she might have said the pain was worth it, but today, faced with a day of lifting, bending, stretching and hurrying about, and all the while keeping a pleasant smile for the customers, she wasn't so sure.

She handed Tabitha a cup of tea and a breakfast sandwich as soon as her assistant walked in.

'Wow. I could get used to this,' Tabitha said. 'Thanks.'

'I decided the cafe could wait ten minutes while we self-medicate. We're no good to anyone with hangovers.'

'I don't have a hangover,' Tabitha said. 'But I'll take the sandwich anyway. It looks damn good.'

They sat at a table together.

'How's Kit?' Rosie asked. 'I hope he doesn't catch a cold.'

'Why would he do that?' Tabitha bit into her sandwich and gave a look of supreme contentment.

'For a start he had to walk home sopping wet. I'm sure that's enough to get a chill.'

'Does anyone even get chills these days? You're as bad as Kit, always using words he's read in a Dickens novel. Anyway, he's hard as nails – he'll be fine; he never gets ill.'

'He's lucky then.'

'That's what Mum says. It was funny though. Your face when he went in – like you'd killed him.'

'I thought I had!'

'He's a strong swimmer. Goes wild swimming – at least he used to.'

'You could have told me that – I was terrified,' Rosie said ruefully.

'I didn't think I needed to. It's not something you generally lead with, is it? Hello, this is my brother. He's a Libra and a really good swimmer so feel free to push him in a river any time.'

'Very funny.'

'Can you really not swim?'

'Me? Not a stroke.'

'God, I can't imagine not being able to swim. I wouldn't be able to paddleboard for a start.'

'You paddleboard?'

Tabitha laughed. 'I live near a river – of course I do! I love it.'

'I could never do that,' Rosie said with a shudder.

'You're scared of the water?'

'I'm quite happy to look at it, just don't ask me to get in.'

'Kit could teach you how to swim; he taught me when I was little. It's really not as hard or scary as you think and he's so patient you'd pick it up in no time. You could even come paddleboarding with me then – you'd love it, I promise.'

'Oh, no... I think I'm too old to learn now.'

'Of course you're not. What are you, like, forty?'

'I'm thirty!'

Tabitha grinned.

'Oh, ha ha again,' Rosie grumbled. 'It's not fair; I'm not well enough to defend myself today.'

'Go back to bed – I can manage here for a couple of hours.'

Rosie shook her head. 'I wouldn't be able to sleep knowing you were here alone running the place. Not that I don't think you could; I know you'd cope. I'd just feel too guilty for leaving you to it.'

'Fair enough.' Tabitha took another bite of her sandwich and an immediate mouthful of tea to follow. 'But the offer's still there if you change your mind.'

'You are good to me.'

'I know. So you really can't swim at all?'

'I really can't swim; it's not that shocking. And why are you so interested in my swimming anyway?'

'You mean lack of it. I just can't imagine how someone got through thirty years of life without being able to swim.'

'It's not that unusual,' Rosie said defensively.

'It is to me. Didn't you ever want to go to the pool with your mates as a kid?'

'Well, yes, but... I was too scared of the water so I always made an excuse.'

'What happened?'

'What do you mean?'

'Why were you scared? Most people aren't just scared for no reason.'

Rosie shrugged. Saying it was probably going to sound stupid to Tabitha, but she said it anyway. 'I fell out of a rowing boat at Whitley Bay when I was five. My granddad couldn't reach me. Somehow I managed to doggy-paddle close enough for him to grab my sweater but... well, it finished me and water off. Mum and Dad wanted me to have lessons after that but I'd freak out whenever they tried to make me go.'

'Oh, that's awful.' Tabitha put down her sandwich and looked at Rosie. 'Didn't you feel as if you missed out on loads of fun growing up?'

'It didn't bother me not to go to the pool with friends; there were plenty of other things to do.'

'And then you thought you'd go and live by a river?' Tabitha raised her eyebrows.

'It's not the same; I can't explain it. The river's OK because I know I'm not going to get in.'

'That's what Kit thought yesterday but he still ended up in the drink. If I was living here, I'd want to be able to swim. You never know when it might save your life.'

'I'll just be careful not to get too close then.'

'I'm being serious now. I bet Kit could teach you in a heartbeat. I bet he'd have you swimming in a week.'

'I don't have time for lessons.'

'Of course you do. What do you do when we close up?'

'More work – apart from days where I foolishly agree to go on drunken bike rides.'

'You must be able to spare an hour.'

'I'd need more than an hour.'

'Care to bet on that?'

Rosie stared at her. 'You think I can learn to swim in an hour?'

'I bet Kit could do it.'

'While I admire your faith in him, I think he'd have a shock if he tried. I know for a fact I'd be utterly useless. I have no coordination at all.'

'You rode a bike.'

'And look what happened! I pushed your brother into the river because I came off said bike!'

Tabitha grinned. 'That's still funny every time I think about it. I don't think it'll ever get old.'

Rosie crammed the last of her sandwich into her mouth and looked up at the clock. 'We'd better get weaving I suppose.'

'Right...' Tabitha began to chew rapidly.

'Don't worry,' Rosie said, 'eat at your own pace – I can start the food prep and you can come and chip in when you're finished. The state I'm in today, if people have to wait an extra minute then they have to wait.'

'That's fighting talk. I had no idea you had a rebellious streak.' Tabitha grinned at her boss.

'I don't – I just have aching muscles and a sore head. It's amazing how little you care when you can barely put one foot in front of the other.'

'You know what would ease that?'

'Cherry juice? I know – I don't have time to get any.'

'No, a nice swim,' Tabitha said.

Rosie rolled her eyes. 'Honestly, I'm hyperventilating just thinking about that.'

'That's why you shouldn't overthink it – you should just take the plunge, if you'll excuse the pun.'

Rosie got up. 'You won't persuade me. I'm going to get the stuff out of the fridge, otherwise I'll still be chopping at lunchtime.'

Just after eleven, Grant came in. On his arm, being gently guided to a seat, was an elderly lady. She wore a calf-length cotton sundress and sensible brogues and looked as if her white hair had been freshly tinted with a lavender dye and set in rollers that morning. He sat her down and then walked to the counter as she gazed dreamily around.

'How are you both this morning?' he asked Rosie and Tabitha, who were standing at the counter having just encoun-tered a lull in what had been fairly steady trade since opening.

Not too quiet but not too much to handle either, which Rosie had been thankful for.

'Better now than first thing,' she said. 'My legs are still killing me though.'

'Mine too,' he said, which made Rosie feel a bit less like a total weakling. 'It was a laugh though, wasn't it? I might organise another one.'

Rosie raised her eyebrows. 'I thought those bikes were for public hire, not pub crawls.'

Grant laughed. 'True, but they can do both.'

'I'd be up for it,' Tabitha said.

Grant eyed her with some amusement. 'You'd come out with the old fogies again? Don't you have a cool club to be at?'

'Yeah, loads. But being out with you is like doing my community service, isn't it?'

Grant began to laugh. 'Fair enough. There's definitely a bike for you if you want to go again. Mum and I are going to grab some elevenses. She wanted to see the cafe now it's finished.'

'That's lovely,' Rosie said. 'If you go and take a seat with her I'll come over to say hello and take your order. I'd like to meet her – anyone who's still getting around at ninety is a bit of a legend in my book. I'm thirty and today I can barely get around.'

'She's a legend alright,' Grant said wryly.

Rosie followed him back to the table where he'd left his mum. The old lady smiled up at her.

'Mum, this is Rosie. Rosie, this is my mum – known as Edith to everyone else.'

'Pleased to meet you,' Rosie said. 'I've heard so much about you.'

'Oh.' Edith turned to her son. 'She's pretty, isn't she?' She turned back to Rosie. 'Aren't you pretty?'

Rosie blushed. 'Thank you.'

'Your cafe is lovely,' Edith added, giving the room an

approving once-over. She was old, quite frail really, but still sharp and alert. 'We should have had my party here,' she told Grant.

'It's not big enough, Mum. You've got too many friends.'

'That's a nice problem to have,' Rosie said. 'Grant tells me you're ninety this time.'

'Yes. You do collect a lot of friends when you've lived as long as me. You lose a lot too of course. That's very sad.'

'It is,' Rosie agreed.

Edith turned to Grant. 'The fella who had this place died.'

'It wasn't a fella,' Grant said. 'It was Clarice before Rosie, remember.'

'No, not Clarice. That fella who wasn't here long. He came after Clarice.'

Grant looked faintly mortified.

Rosie gave a tight smile. She guessed that Edith was referring to Fergus. 'I think you mean my husband.'

'Oh dear...' Edith reached to pat Rosie's hand. 'I'm sorry – I didn't realise he had a wife.'

'But you must have seen Rosie when they both moved in,' Grant said to his mum.

'No, can't say I did. Saw him enough though, up and down at that place.' Edith nodded vaguely towards the windows.

Rosie couldn't tell what she was nodding at or what 'that place' was. Perhaps she was easily confused after all. Then again, Rosie herself wasn't exactly firing on all cylinders that morning. She was tired, aching, still not completely hangover-free, and the priorities for her energy and attention were strictly reserved for the cafe. She didn't have the time or attention to spare to worry about vague gossip.

'We'll have two teas,' Grant said very deliberately, suddenly looking as if he'd rather be anywhere than there. 'What cake do you have?'

'I like a nice bread pudding,' Edith said.

'I can do that,' Rosie replied. 'I've also got carrot cake, red velvet cupcakes, chocolate, vanilla sponge, lemon drizzle, and... oh, shortbread.'

'I'll have the shortbread,' Edith said.

Grant rolled his eyes. 'Bring us a slice of bread pudding and two shortbreads please. Mum is bound to decide she wants the bread pudding after all.'

'No problem. I'll be right back.'

Rosie left them to get their orders. As she walked away, she could hear Edith still chatting.

'I like her... very pretty. I don't like that earring in her nose. I don't know why people want earrings in their nose – they're called earrings for a reason. What happens when you have a cold? I'm not that keen on her hair either. She'd look much nicer if it was normal...'

Rosie grabbed two cups for their tea. It was a good thing she was too much of a wet lettuce to call anyone out, even if they had just insulted her hair colour and her nose piercing. She supposed it was a generational thing. Styles changed and what was acceptable to wear had changed too, probably a lot since Edith was a girl. Thank God Grant's mum couldn't see the little tattoo she had on her back.

'Talk about gangster granny,' Tabitha said in a low voice as Rosie poured hot water into a teapot.

'She seems sweet enough.'

'Yeah, apart from throwing shade at everyone.'

'I don't think she's realised people can hear.'

'God, imagine if she didn't like you,' Tabitha added with a grin. 'Nobody needs to overhear that kind of insulting.'

'She's old – probably reckons she's earned the right to speak her mind, I guess. Perhaps we'll all be like that if we get to ninety.'

'You're too nice, you know.'

'So you keep telling me. I'm afraid it's too late to change now.'

'Wouldn't want it to.'

Rosie set the cups and teapot on a tray and was plating up Grant's cake order when the cafe door swung open and Nicole marched in.

Normally she'd be smiling. Today she wasn't.

'Oh, it's her!' Edith said in a whisper loud enough to fill the cafe. Grant shushed her.

As Nicole realised they were there, she turned and gave them a curt nod of acknowledgement. 'Grant... Edith... Alright?'

'Fair to middling,' Grant said. 'You?'

'Same.'

Nicole turned back to the counter. If Rosie had needed crushed ice she could have scooped it from the air between Nicole, Grant and his mother right then. She recalled they'd been coldly civil before. What was their deal? And she also remembered now, with a sudden lurch of her stomach, that Grant hadn't wanted to invite Nicole to their bike ride when Rosie had suggested it. But Rosie had gone anyway, and so had Kit and Tabitha. Rosie hadn't imagined it would cause a problem at the time – they were all grown-ups after all – but now... surely that wasn't the reason Nicole looked so irked as she approached the counter?

'Tabitha...' Rosie angled her head at the tray, loaded with Grant's order. 'Could you take this over and say hello to Edith?'

'Sure,' Tabitha said, regarding Nicole carefully as she picked it up.

Rosie turned to Nicole, trying not to look as concerned as she felt. 'What can I get you?' she asked with forced brightness.

'You were out with Kit last night,' she hissed. 'He told me.'

'Yes,' Rosie said evenly. 'There was a whole bunch of us.'

'Who?'

'Some people from the marina and some of Grant's family. I'm sure if Kit told you we were out, he told you that too?'

'Where did you go?'

'Just out for a ride. To test Grant's new bikes.'

'As if they needed testing,' Nicole scoffed. 'I didn't have you down as a cyclist.'

'I'm not,' Rosie said, feeling flustered by the sudden and unexpected interrogation. 'I just decided it might be fun to give it a go.' She'd felt guilty about the fact Nicole hadn't been invited, but the way Nicole was being with her now, while she still harboured a little of that guilt, she was also starting to feel as if she wanted to remind Nicole that it was none of her business where Rosie went and who she saw and that she shouldn't have to explain herself, never mind feel bad about it. But the cafe during opening hours wasn't the place to cause an argument or make a scene.

'You went to the pub.'

'Yes, we went to a few pubs.'

'Which ones?'

'I really don't remember.'

'You must do.'

'Nicole...' Rosie paused, collecting her thoughts before she opened her mouth again. 'If I'd known you'd be this upset I wouldn't have gone, but I didn't see the harm in it. Grant asked and I said yes. Lots of us were there. I'm not trying to get with Kit, if that's what you think.'

'I don't...' Nicole let out a breath and looked repentant now. 'I just felt left out. Everyone from the marina went but me. Even Kit's sister went.'

'Not everyone,' Rosie said gently. 'And the only reason Grant didn't ask you was because he assumed you had something on.'

'I'll bet he did.'

Rosie lowered her voice further still, so it was barely more than a whisper now. 'Is there something I ought to know about you and him? Some history?'

Nicole's face closed. 'Absolutely not. We just don't gel, that's all. Some people don't, do they?'

Rosie had certainly never noticed any animosity when she'd first arrived at Marigold Marina with Fergus, but perhaps she'd simply been too busy to look.

'I'm sorry,' Nicole said. 'I should have realised you wouldn't have gone behind my back like that.'

'I'm sorry you felt left out.'

'Forget it. It's not your fault... I'd better get back to the shop.'

'Want me to pop over later so we can talk properly? Seems like you could use a friendly ear today.'

'I'll probably be out,' Nicole said. 'With a bit of luck anyway. I'll see you tomorrow maybe.'

Rosie nodded, but she wasn't going to hold her breath. Nicole kept saying she'd make time for Rosie, but lately she never actually did.

As Nicole strode out, Rosie heard Edith's voice: 'I don't like her...'

Tabitha was grinning as she came back to the counter. 'No filter with Grant's mum, is there?' she said in a low voice.

'I just hope Nicole didn't take too much offence.'

'Why would she do that?'

'I don't know... she didn't seem happy today.'

Tabitha was thoughtful for a moment. 'I don't know about her...' she said finally.

'Nicole?'

Tabitha nodded.

'But she's lovely... usually anyway.'

'Is she? So she just tore a strip off you because that's what lovely people do?'

'She didn't tear a strip off me,' Rosie lied.

'It sure looked that way to me. I think it looked that way to Grant too.'

Rosie shook her head slowly. 'No, Nicole's not like that.'

'Maybe,' Tabitha said. 'But I'm reserving my judgement until she does something to change my mind.'

'I'll take Kit's sandwich over. I'm going to take my break on his barge if that's OK.'

'Of course.' Rosie went to the fridge to get it. She would have liked to have seen Kit herself and had been hoping he'd come in, if only so she could see first-hand that he was OK after his dip in the river. But after her run-in with Nicole perhaps Tabitha's plan was a better idea. 'You want to go now?'

'If you don't mind – I'm starving. Can I grab a salad to take over for my lunch?'

'You don't have to ask,' Rosie said. 'You should know that by now. Take what you want; there aren't many perks to this job, but a free lunch is one I can give you.'

'I wouldn't say there are no perks.' Tabitha smiled. 'I get to work here with you for a start.'

Rosie flushed. Did Tabitha really think that?

Tabitha slapped some salad and tuna into a takeout box and closed the lid.

'I'll see you in thirty,' she called behind over her shoulder as she left the cafe.

As soon as she'd walked through the front door, Grant came back in, this time alone.

'Can't stay away?' Rosie asked with a smile. 'Want a coffee?'

'Actually, I wanted to apologise.'

'What on earth for?'

'Mum. She can be a bit... direct. She doesn't mean anything by it.'

'I don't know what you mean; I certainly didn't notice anything like that.'

'I just wanted to check, and if she said anything to offend you, I'm sorry.'

'Oh, God, no!' Rosie said fervently. 'Not at all! She's lovely.'

Grant relaxed.

'There was one thing, though,' Rosie continued, making a spontaneous decision to put something right that had bothered her since Nicole's visit earlier that day.

Grant regarded her with a silent question.

'It's just...' Rosie continued, 'well, I felt a bit bad... I think Nicole felt kind of left out yesterday.'

'Is that what she said to you?'

'Not in so many words, but yes.'

'I honestly thought she wouldn't want to come. I'm sorry if it put you in an awkward position.'

'It didn't. Please don't think I've mentioned it on my own account. I just felt... there was a bit of an atmosphere this morning and I felt like I ought to say something.'

'Nicole could have spoken to me if she had a problem,' Grant said, and his tone was suddenly less sympathetic. 'There was no need to take it out on you.'

'She wasn't taking it out on me.'

'If I was the culprit, she should have told me.'

'I think it was because...' Rosie paused. She couldn't very well say to Grant that Nicole was upset because she thought Rosie was trying to sneak Kit from under her nose. It wasn't her place to tell people that Nicole had a thing for him or that she intended to do something about it. 'Perhaps she just wanted to get it off her chest but thought that if she told you she might offend you.'

Grant studied her for a moment before he spoke again. 'I don't want to meddle where I'm not wanted, and this is the last you'll hear me say on the subject, but... be careful with her.'

Rosie stared at him. 'What do you mean?'

'Just... keep your guard up.'

'Grant, I don't—'

Before Rosie could finish, the cafe door opened and a woman with two toddlers walked in.

'I'll let you get on,' Grant said pleasantly, as if the previous conversation had never happened. 'I'll see you tomorrow.'

Rosie went over to greet the customer who was settling her children at a table. There was no time to dwell on what Grant had just said, but when she thought about it later, perhaps that had been a good thing.

The front door was finally locked. Everywhere had been cleaned and Rosie was ready for a bath and an early night when there was a knock at the door that she'd just closed. Through the windows she could see Kit waiting, a rucksack on his back. If it had been anyone else she might have been tempted to hide until they'd gone – it had been that kind of day.

'Hi,' she said as she opened the door. 'Everything alright?'

'Sure. Are you ready?'

'Ready for what?'

'Swimming.'

Rosie blinked. 'We didn't have an arrangement...' She frowned. 'Is this Tabitha's doing?'

'She said you wanted me to teach you how to swim. Said you'd be up for tonight...' He paused and then grinned. 'Little cow! I knew I should have asked you rather than take her word for it.'

Rosie smiled. 'She said I needed to learn how to swim and that you'd be the person to teach me, but I never agreed to go.'

'Well, now I feel like an idiot.'

'It's not that I don't appreciate the offer, but I'm not really into swimming, and if I was, quite honestly, I'm exhausted right now.'

'We could easily make it another night. It's really no bother to me at all.'

Rosie shook her head. 'I really don't think swimming is me.'

'So you don't want me to take you swimming?'

'I'm sure we'd have fun but—'

'You really hate the water.'

'Tabitha told you that much?'

'Yes, and it's actually why she thought I should take you. I thought she told you that she'd ask me and that it was all sorted.'

'She didn't say a word – because she guessed I'd turn the offer down if she did. Probably thought I wouldn't refuse you if you were standing on the doorstep ready to go.'

'She's sneaky like that. Well, as I've got my stuff together, I guess I'll just go alone.'

'Oh! Now I feel bad...'

'Don't. It won't bother me. I've found this great little spot on the river, lovely and calm... Actually' – he grinned – 'I think you found that for me last night by accident.'

Rosie laughed. 'Stop it! I already feel bad enough about that!'

'So you should.'

'If I could make it up to you I would.'

'You can.'

'If you say by swimming with you tonight, I'm going to clobber you, guilty or not.'

'OK, it was worth a try.'

'It was a valiant effort,' Rosie agreed.

As she looked at him now, smiling, relaxed – her friend – she was tempted to change her mind. Not because she wanted to learn to swim, but because he'd gone to the effort to come by and was willing to make the time for her, and because she would have enjoyed his company. But if Nicole got to hear about it, well... things were sticky enough in that regard without making them worse.

Rosie understood just what was going on – at least as far as Tabitha was concerned. For some reason she'd decided Rosie and Kit ought to be together, and for more than swimming lessons. But it wasn't going to happen, no matter what Tabitha did to engineer it. Even if Nicole hadn't been interested in Kit and even if Rosie hadn't known it, she simply wasn't ready. She didn't know if she'd ever be ready and she was in no hurry to find out. Kit was becoming a good friend and Rosie liked it that way.

It would be a difficult conversation, but she'd have to talk to Tabitha about it in the morning.

'Enjoy your swim,' she said. 'If you are actually going after all.'

'Nah... I suppose it's getting a bit late now for wild swimming.'

It wasn't, at least Rosie didn't think so, but she didn't argue.

'If you really want to go wild swimming, I bet Nicole would love to join you.'

'Nicole?' He suddenly looked doubtful. 'Really? Nicole?'

'Why not?'

'I mean, we're mates but... um... maybe I'll just head home and call it a night.'

But then he looked so disappointed and the idea of spending time with him was so tempting... and perhaps, as she was trying to get her life sorted in so many other areas, perhaps swimming was a thing she ought to tackle, even if it did terrify her.

'Is there a pool nearby?'

His forehead crinkled slightly. 'I thought you didn't want to go?'

'I don't, but...'

'Listen,' he said. 'We don't have to swim right off the bat.

Come with me – there's a lido a few miles down the road. We could go one night before sunset and you could just sit on the side and dangle your feet in for a while, maybe just stand in it and splash about a bit at the shallow end. Don't worry about swimming until you're ready, when you're a bit more confident. We have all the time in the world.'

'I couldn't keep asking you to go with me.'

'I love swimming so it would be no kind of hardship at all. We could go now if you wanted; I think they're still open for an hour or so.'

'Not now, if you don't mind.'

'Don't overthink it,' he said with a warm smile. 'If you leave it too long you'll talk yourself out of it again.'

'I know... I think I might be doing that in my brain already.'

'Like I said, there's no need to swim straight away. We could go a ton of times before you even do a stroke – no rush, take it at your own pace.'

Rosie gave a pained smile. She'd been at this point before – ready to try – many years ago. It had been Fergus offering to teach her – on their honeymoon in Greece, in fact – but he'd lost patience quickly and she couldn't help but feel that Kit would do the same.

Fergus had wanted to book a trip on a yacht to tour the islands, complete with a sea swim in a quiet cove. Just turned twenty, newly married Rosie couldn't think of a more terrifying experience, but she could see how much he wanted to do it and she wanted to be that mature, sophisticated, confident wife for him, the woman he deserved.

'I'll teach you to swim,' he'd said on their first day, as he'd booked the trip.

'In the hotel pool first?' she'd asked nervously.

'Yeah, of course.'

The following morning they'd made their way early to the glittering azure pool, the sun hot and high already, and Fergus had done his best to encourage her in. She'd stood on the ladder – in the water at least – too nervous to go any further. So he'd taken her hand and tried to lead her deeper into the water.

'I don't want to go too far.'

'But you'll float better in deeper water.'

Rosie had shaken her head and wrenched herself free from his grip.

'Seriously?' He'd looked so annoyed, the memory of it was as clear to her now as it had been all those years ago. They'd only just got married and already she was disappointing him, letting him down. 'You're not even going to try?'

'I just need a minute – it's not as easy as just getting in and going... Sorry.'

She took a breath.

'Ready to try now?' he asked.

'I will be, just... I don't know... now that I'm here it's all rushing back... you know, on the boat with my granddad...'

'Forget about that. It was years ago. You're not at sea now – you're safe with me in a pool.'

'Yes, but we will be at sea later in the week, won't we? I think that might be what's freaking me out.'

'So you're saying you don't want to go on the boat?'

'I do want to go, it's just... I'm scared.'

He'd scowled. 'I wish you'd told me all this before I'd booked it.'

'I didn't want to be the reason you couldn't go... you seemed so excited about it.'

'If that's the case then we need to nail this now. You're just going to have to swallow your fear and get on with it – it's the only way to learn. When I was a kid my dad just chucked me in and let me get on with it.'

'Oh!' Rosie squeaked, half afraid Fergus might try to do that with her.

She'd pulled herself together, got in and tried again, letting him lead her this time to slightly deeper water. But just as she'd trusted him and lifted her feet from the bottom of the pool, he'd let go of her. She'd panicked, thrashing about, certain she was going to drown as she grabbed blindly for him. It had seemed like an eternity, and then, finally, she'd felt his arms around her, lifting her to the surface.

'This is ridiculous,' he'd said, guiding her to the side but then leaving her there. She watched, close to tears, as he swam to the ladder and got out – heading over to the bar.

She was frustrated and angry at herself and wished she could be braver for him.

Taking a deep breath, she called over to where he'd found a seat poolside. 'I'll try harder,' she'd said, though her limbs were still shaking from her ordeal.

'What's the point? I know a lost cause when I see one.'

'What about the yacht?'

'I'll find someone else to take your spot.'

And that was exactly what he'd done. He'd made friends with a couple from Dagenham later that day and he'd taken the husband on the trip with him, leaving Rosie to make small talk with the wife for most of the day – a woman she had absolutely nothing in common with, and an excruciating experience for someone as naturally shy as Rosie was. She'd felt rejected and like a desperate failure, and hadn't blamed him for giving up on her. Already she was holding him back.

She'd resolved to try harder to be the wife he wanted. It was too late for the boat trip, but that didn't mean she couldn't fix the other things that annoyed him.

'We'll work something out when I see you tomorrow, maybe?' Kit asked then, his voice breaking into her thoughts. 'When you've had a chance to look at your diary to see when you're free?'

'Absolutely,' she replied with forced brightness. 'Totally.'

'You're sure you're up for it?'

Rosie nodded. 'Like you said, if I get there and freak out, I can just sit on the side and put my feet in. At least that will be nice... and I haven't seen the lido yet, so it's another new thing I'll know in the area, isn't it?'

While Kit looked faintly unconvinced, he did seem pleased at the turn of events. 'That's great. So I'll see you tomorrow for my sandwich and we'll make arrangements then? Now, I know it's fiendishly complicated, but can you remember what the order is?'

Rosie laughed. 'One day you'll shock me with something else.'

'Never going to happen.'

'Goodnight, Kit.'

Giving her a good-natured nod, he turned to go back to his boat.

As Rosie locked the door on another eventful day, already the nerves were kicking in. *What the hell have I just agreed to?*

CHAPTER TEN

Rosie stood next to the bollards that marked the end of the access road to the marina, the point where motor vehicles could go no further, and watched as the pink-roofed Citroen approached. A moment later it stopped alongside her.

'Nice car...' She grinned as she got into the passenger seat.

Kit turned to her with a grin of his own. 'I know, right? I'm not afraid to embrace my feminine side.'

'Be honest... it's your mum's, isn't it?'

'How did you...? Ah, Tabitha told you I'd be borrowing Mum's car? She's got a gob on her, that girl!'

'She did mention it... only to warn me astronauts in space would be able to see it from up there – with the naked eye.'

'Well...' Kit said, letting off the handbrake and turning the car to go the way he'd come, 'beggars can't be choosers. As I had to sell my car to buy the boat, it's either Shanks's pony or driving this.'

'We could have walked to the lido.'

'It's further out than you think – didn't want you exhausted before you'd even got in the pool.'

'That might not have been such a bad thing,' Rosie said darkly, causing him to grin again.

'Not getting cold feet, are you?'

'Too bloody right! I don't think you realise just what a terrible water-phobe I am.'

'You can't be that bad. You're here now – that's the first step, so you can't be totally beyond saving. I bet once you've been in the pool half an hour, you'll forget how scared you were.'

'I hope you're right but I wouldn't count on it.'

Kit raised a disbelieving eyebrow but said no more as the car emerged onto the main road. The sun was still high, despite the fact it was almost seven in the evening, which had been the deciding factor on choosing that day as a good day to swim outdoors. It did, however, also mean that there was a strong chance the lido would be busy. Rosie had worried about that – along with just about everything else – but as Kit had informed her that he really didn't expect her to do much actual swimming the first time they went and it was more about getting used to the water, she'd decided that perhaps it wouldn't be the huge issue she imagined it to be.

As the hedgerow-flanked lanes passed by, Rosie gazed out of the car window, her stomach churning, wondering why she was even doing this. What did she have to prove? Did it really matter if she couldn't swim? She'd got through thirty years without having it trouble her too much – and the few opportunities she'd sought to rectify the situation had ended up as pretty humiliating experiences. So why not leave things as they were? As long as she didn't get herself into situations that required her to swim, it wasn't a skill she necessarily needed, was it? And it wasn't like Kit had pressured her into coming. In fact, he'd been quite chilled about it – he'd expressed a keenness to help her but he certainly hadn't pushed her into it.

Now that she thought about it, she decided she must have

been victim to a temporary bout of insanity when she'd agreed to accompany Kit to the lido.

'You've gone very quiet,' Kit said after a couple of minutes of silence. 'I have to admit it's starting to worry me. You're not really scared, are you? You know I'll take care of you – I won't let anything happen to you.'

Wasn't that what Fergus had promised when he'd tried to teach her to swim on their honeymoon? Rosie tried to shake off the memories of that disaster and forced a smile as she turned to Kit. 'I'm always quiet.'

'I realise we've only known each other a couple of weeks, but I find that hard to believe.'

'It's true – I hate attention.'

'But you do like a chat.' He smiled. 'And you're good to chat to – I know that much. Unless you put on a very good act at the cafe.'

'Fergus used to say that – running a restaurant was all about acting. He said convince everyone you're good and they'll believe it, even if you don't have a clue what you're doing.'

'I have to say, I like his style, though I've never been able to pull that off. Fergus was your—?'

There was an awkward pause. Rosie could guess that Tabitha would have told Kit about her husband. Perhaps Kit hadn't been sure he ought to bring it up, but as Rosie had, he now thought that he ought to acknowledge the fact, even if it did seem difficult to talk about.

'Yes, Fergus was my husband,' Rosie said, deciding to try and put any awkwardness to one side. 'It's OK, you can mention him without reducing me to a sobbing wreck.'

'I can't imagine what it must be like to lose someone like that. I mean, I've been through some intense break-ups, like everyone, but to lose someone so suddenly like that...' Kit glanced at Rosie with such a look of tender sympathy that she wondered if she might become a sobbing wreck after all, just at the sight of it.

'It happens, doesn't it?' she said quickly. 'It's life – you never know what's round the corner and half the time there'd be nothing we could do to stop it, even if we did know what was waiting for us.'

'That's true,' Kit said thoughtfully. 'I still think it's brave, the way you've kept going. I'm not sure I would have been able to.'

'You never know what you're capable of until you're forced to try.' Rosie turned her face to the window to hide the tears welling in her eyes. Much as she appreciated Kit's sympathy, she wanted this conversation to end. But she was worried that to tell him so might offend him when he was clearly making an effort to be the understanding friend he must have imagined she needed.

'I'm sorry,' he said. 'I didn't mean to start a conversation that would upset you.'

'You didn't,' she said, eyes still fixed on the landscape rushing by.

'I don't think that's quite true, but I'll shut up for a minute if it helps. I'm always saying the wrong bloody thing.'

Rosie sniffed hard and turned to him. 'Please don't think that. I appreciate... well, it's just hard, that's all, being reminded of him, but that doesn't mean you can't ask. In fact, I suppose it would be weird if you didn't, right?' She gave a watery smile. 'I think we're starting to know each other well enough that something so huge couldn't just be ignored and, besides, it's not like I haven't talked to Tabitha about it, so I realise she would have told you things anyway.'

'She has a little,' Kit admitted. 'She said you were hardcore for carrying on with the cafe on your own.'

'Did she?' Rosie asked with a teary laugh. 'I've never been called "hardcore" before!'

'Well, now you have. I don't often agree with that pipsqueak but I do on this – I think it's pretty bloody hardcore too.'

'It's not like I set out to achieve some great thing,' Rosie said. 'It's more a case of not knowing what else to do. I had no other plan – so, might as well carry on with the plans we'd made together. It's not so hardcore when you look at it like that, is it?'

'That you kept going at all is hardcore,' Kit said gently. 'Give yourself that if nothing else. And' – he continued in a brighter tone – 'you'll shortly be able to add overcoming your fear of the water to that list of achievements. And that one will definitely be all yours.'

'I wouldn't be so sure of that...'

'Don't keep selling yourself short... Ah! Here we are!'

Rosie had been so engrossed in their conversation she hadn't noticed the signpost for the lido looming ahead. Now, Kit was pulling into the car park.

As the unmistakable swimming-pool smell of chlorine wafted in through the open car windows, Rosie's stomach went from churning to full-blown whirlpool status.

Rosie had put on an old swimming costume she'd owned since her honeymoon with Fergus but rarely had occasion to wear at home. It was a tad old-fashioned now, but she hadn't seen the point in buying a new one when she never swam. She'd slipped her clothes over the top so that she wouldn't have to mess around changing – which might have given her too much time to make a run for it. She was glad she had. The changing cubicles were right at the edge of the pool, in full view of other swimmers. Even with the door closed, Rosie felt exposed. Perhaps that was more to do with her nerves than the fact that people might see anything at all beyond the screen (logically they couldn't, but the nagging doubt remained), but as she peeled off her dress she was glad she didn't have to peel off anything else.

She and Kit met back at the pool, having both secured their belongings in their respective changing areas. He had a surprisingly good tan for a man who spent a lot of his time sitting on a barge below deck reading books. A surprisingly good physique too, Rosie couldn't help but notice, and she had to make a very deliberate effort not to stare. She had her towel wrapped around her as he made his way over. Her fears about the pool being busy had been realised – the air was filled with splashing and squealing as groups of teenagers, families and couples messed around in the water. It didn't bode well, and perhaps Kit could see the doubt in her face.

'We don't have to stay if you don't want to,' he said.

'We've paid now,' Rosie replied, giving herself a reason to stay more than she was giving him one. 'It's daft to pay and then leave without even getting in the water.'

'The money isn't important—'

'It is,' Rosie insisted, taking her towel off and leaving it on a bench. 'I could say it's not but I'm just giving myself excuses to back out and it's pathetic.'

'Don't say that. Nobody's fears should ever be thought of as pathetic. If it's real to you then it's real.'

'I know, but I'm sick of being afraid.'

He took her hands in his. For a second she stared up at him, wondering what to make of it. But then she realised it was his way of calming her and, to her mild surprise, it was working. With his hands wrapped around hers, she felt suddenly grounded, totally safe and supported.

'Whatever you need,' he said, holding her in his steady gaze. 'You've got this, I know you have, and I'm here to help you.'

She tried to smile but couldn't make her mouth form the shape. She could only nod mutely and allow him to lead her to the water's edge.

Kit shook his head as she glanced at the ladder into the pool. 'Let's sit on the side first and dangle our feet for a while.'

'People will wonder what we're doing—'

'No, they won't, and if they do, they should be minding their own business. Come on...'

He sat on the side of the pool and patted the tiles for her to join him. Rosie carefully lowered herself down and let her feet go into the water. He smiled across at her as he did the same, kicking his playfully in the water so that the spray created tiny little rainbows in the sunlight.

'No rush,' he said.

This is OK, Rosie thought as she moved her feet back and forth through the water. This was OK... perhaps she could do this after all.

Her gaze went to the gangs of friends, swimming back and forth, doing handstands on the bottom of the pool to emerge a second later laughing and dripping wet; to children no older than four or five happily swimming alongside their parents; to flexing teenage boys checking out giggling teenage girls before jumping into the water as close to them as they dared... they were all having so much fun.

When she'd told Tabitha she hadn't missed days like this with her friends as a child, she'd lied. She'd always wanted to be included in their trips to the swimming pool or the nearest lake on a scorching summer's day, but her fear had always got the better of her. It had mastered her so that her fear of the water was greater than her fear of missing out. And now that she really thought about it, that was some fear. She didn't want to be scared like that anymore.

'I think I could get in,' she said.

'You're sure?'

She nodded.

Kit slid into the water before holding out his arms for her to join him. 'I'll catch you,' he said.

She smiled, getting up and walking along the side. 'I'm sure you would, but this time maybe I'll use the ladder.'

'Fair enough,' he said with a smile of his own as he waded to meet her. She took a breath, the water cresting and glittering in the sunlight as the crowd of swimmers stirred up the surface, and she froze.

'You've got this,' Kit said earnestly. 'And you've got me. I won't let anything bad happen.'

'OK...'

With shaking limbs, Rosie took the steps carefully. The water was cold as it hit her ankles – far colder than she'd expected. She caught her breath.

'It's fine...' Kit reached for her, wrapping her hands in his again. 'Breathe...'

'Anyone would think I was having a baby, not getting into a swimming pool,' she said with a shaky laugh.

'Hey, remember what I said. If it's a big deal to you then nobody has the right to tell you it's not a big deal. Everyone has the thing that scares them, and no one has the right to judge you for yours.'

Rosie looked up at him – more for fear of looking at the water than anything else. 'Even you?'

'Of course me.'

'What scares you?'

A troubled shadow crossed his face, and he shook his head slightly. 'Doesn't matter right now. Today is about you, not me.'

'But if you're talking to me I can forget I'm standing in a swimming pool.'

'I hate to say it, but the reason you're standing in a swimming pool is sort of to acknowledge you're in a swimming pool,' he said with a wry smile. 'You're not going to stop being scared of swimming pools if you deny their very existence.'

'What book did you read that in?'

He laughed. 'Stop trying to distract from the issue. Look down... see, you're completely in the water now and it's fine.'

'I'm standing in the shallowest bit.'

'Yes, and you're OK. So how about we move down the pool? Try where it's a little bit deeper?'

'I don't know...'

'Yes, you do. Come on...' He started to move backwards, her hands still gripped in his so that she was forced to move with him.

The water was soon at her chest and she pulled back. 'No!'

'OK, that's fine. That's far enough for now.'

She was aware of eyes on her and looked over to see a group of teenage girls watching her and Kit.

'Ignore them,' he said quietly, following her gaze.

'I look stupid.'

'You don't – you look brave.'

'I don't.'

'You do to me, and if anyone wants to argue, I'll tell them so. You and I know how much guts it's taken for you to be doing this – that's all that should matter. Be proud you've come this far and stop worrying about what everyone else is thinking.'

Rosie took a breath and tried to ignore the girls. *Maybe they aren't even looking at me*, she told herself. *Maybe they're staring at Kit.* It wasn't such a stretch to imagine – he did look very good in his swim shorts.

'A bit further?' he asked.

She wanted nothing less but nodded anyway. He began to move backwards again, and she could feel the water creeping up towards her neck. 'Enough!'

He stopped. 'How's this?'

'Terrifying!'

'Want to go back?'

'No... yes... I want to but I'm not going to.'

'Hardcore – I told you!' He smiled. 'Think maybe you could take your feet off the bottom for a second?'

'I'd sink!'

'You wouldn't sink – I'm here, and you can still stand up anyway. Just a second – try it.'

She shook her head and he looked directly into her eyes. 'I'm going to hold you beneath your arms – will that be OK?'

'I... Don't let go!'

'I won't. I'm going to keep hold of you and you're going to take your feet from the bottom and kick your legs to tread water. You won't go anywhere because I'll have you, I promise... Ready?' Before she could reply he'd moved closer and had his hands beneath her armpits, holding her steady. 'One second, that's all I'm asking for, and then we'll take a break if you like.'

She nodded uncertainly, paused for a second, and after another second, lifted one foot and then the other.

Kit kept his promise and held her firm. 'You're OK?'

'Yes.'

'So you start kicking and I'll just loosen my hold a bit—'

'What!'

'I won't let go, I promise. I'll just let go a little. Trust me, you won't sink.'

'No, please, Kit, don't let go. I—'

Her words were stolen by an almighty splash and a wave that crashed over them both. Rosie felt Kit's hands leave her side, and she was thrown into a panic as the breath left her lungs. A second later he had her again. Spluttering, she opened her eyes to see he was glaring at a teenager who'd just cannon-balled into the water nearby.

'What the hell!' Kit snarled. 'Can't you see the signs telling you not to do that? Moron!'

'Sorry...' the boy said sullenly before swimming off.

'It doesn't matter,' Rosie told him.

Kit turned to her. 'Of course it does! I'm going to have a

word with the lifeguard; he ought to be stopping things like that—'

'Don't, please.'

Rosie already felt enough attention on her – the last thing she needed was for Kit to make a scene on her behalf. Besides, the damage was already done. Any tiny speck of confidence that had started to burn in her was well and truly out, drowned in the wave that had soaked her and Kit.

'Right... it's just... well, people can see we're trying to do something here... It's just a dick move, that's all...'

'He probably didn't realise that something's going on here,' Rosie said. Glancing at Kit's arms, she realised she was gripping them so tightly she was making marks on his skin. 'I'm sorry...' she said, trying to loosen her hold, but she was so uptight now that she wasn't physically able to.

'Let's take a break,' he said. 'Can you walk to the side?'

'Yes.' Still holding on to him, she followed him to the ladder. 'You must think I'm pathetic.'

'Ah! What did we say about using that word?'

'I know but you must. Even I think I'm pathetic.'

'I don't. I'm just annoyed that we were making progress and some little dick ruined it.'

'Don't be annoyed. I don't like seeing you annoyed because you're always so cheerful. It's like it's not you.'

'Right... sorry.'

'No – I didn't mean it like that. You don't have to be sorry – I just feel bad that I'm the reason you're annoyed.'

'You're not – that little Tom Daley wannabe is the reason I'm annoyed.'

She gave him a bleak smile as they reached the steps. Her limbs were shakier getting out of the pool than they had been when she'd climbed in half an hour earlier. She could have taken some pride in the fact she'd got in at all, she supposed, but it was hard to feel it because Kit looked so cross still, and despite what he'd said, she felt like it was because she'd somehow repaid all his efforts by letting him down.

They both grabbed their towels from where they'd left them and sat down on a nearby bench. Even though it was still sunny, Rosie was cold, and she pulled hers tight around her shoulders, staring mournfully at the busy pool.

'It probably wasn't the best time to come,' Kit said. 'My fault – I should have realised it would be heaving.'

'You weren't to know it would be this busy,' Rosie said. 'I didn't think of it either.'

She had thought of it, of course, but she wasn't about to make him feel worse by saying so.

He looked at her as he towelled his hair. 'I suppose it's too busy to try again?'

'Um... It kind of is... Sorry.'

'Don't be. We'll come back another time; hopefully it'll be quieter.'

'I'm sorry I made you drive all this way and we only stayed in for half an hour.'

'Stop saying you're sorry – it's not your fault. It's not like you didn't tell me how nervous you were in the water either.'

And there it was. Once again, Rosie had tried and once again she'd proved how useless she was. 'A lost cause' Fergus had called her when he'd attempted to teach her how to swim all those years ago, and nothing had changed.

Frustration ate at her. Why couldn't she simply pull herself together like a normal person would? She looked at the pool again. It was full of people, surrounded by lifeguards, mostly shallow enough to stand in; the safest she could possibly be, and yet she was still scared of it, and that fact vexed her more than anything. It was no wonder Fergus had lost patience with her so quickly that day in Greece, and now – even though he wouldn't say it – she'd managed to piss off Kit too.

'Shall we head back then?' he said into her thoughts, the question confirming every miserable one of them.

'Sure,' she said, feeling utterly defeated. 'Let's head back.'

A week had passed since Kit had taken Rosie on the swimming trip that had ended so disastrously. He'd put on a brave face during the drive back to the marina, had even started to crack jokes and become a little more like his normal self by the time they'd arrived there, but Rosie could tell he was disappointed that they hadn't made more progress. She was too. In between the attempts at humour, they'd both apologised far too often, Kit seeming to feel the failure had been as much his fault as anyone else's, while Rosie knew it was all down to her stupid brain that wouldn't let her get past her stupid fears.

She'd hoped and wondered at first whether he'd ask her to go again, but perhaps she really was a lost cause, because he hadn't mentioned it since, and things had gone back to friendly but casual whenever she bumped into him or when he called for his sandwiches. Besides all that, perhaps it was better not to tempt Nicole's disapproval either. While Rosie could have argued that it was a free country and two people could go swimming together if they liked, Nicole wouldn't have been pleased if she'd found out, and that was a complication Rosie could do without. So far she was happily in the dark, but if swimming with Kit became a regular thing she was bound to find out. There was only so much room in Rosie's life for that sort of stress.

Privately, although Rosie was disappointed by this turn of events, she couldn't help but feel that perhaps it was for the best. In the days since the swimming lesson, as well as the sense of failure and pointlessness, she had also started to realise that she'd felt things she oughtn't. In hindsight, it was probably best she didn't spend any more time alone with Kit. In fact, she made an effort to put any thoughts of him as an attractive man out of her mind, making herself think back to when he was just a good friend living on the marina. She resolved to keep it that way for everyone's sakes.

So why had she dreamt of him again?

Twice that week in fact, and Tabitha had even featured in one of them. Rosie had found herself on a paddleboard on the river, desperately trying to stay afloat while Tabitha and Kit simply waved and laughed from the bank. Rosie had woken from that one stressed and almost convinced that she was still on the paddleboard.

The side effect of keeping her distance from Kit was that her evenings were dull again. Grant's cycles were now in use by actual paying customers, so no more boozy bike rides, for the summer months at least. No Kit, no Tabitha beyond their regular work hours when they were mostly too busy to chat for long... and even Nicole was largely absent. Rosie wondered if this might be a good time to invite her parents to stay, before deciding that she still didn't think she could juggle them and her commitments in the cafe just yet.

She'd had regular updates from Letitia too, who was confident she'd be ready to start her job in the following three or four weeks, depending on how happy the doctors were with her progress. Rosie tried to be pleased, but in reality, she desperately wanted to keep Tabitha instead. Tabitha was funny, smart and capable, and she was fast becoming a valued friend. But Rosie had made a promise to Letitia, and she had to keep it.

On one of her boring nights, Rosie was out walking the riverbank, as she often did, when she noticed a flurry of activity at the boat shed. Grant and his sons were dashing about putting up lights, setting up tables and gazebos. Grant's mum was in a chair, directing them like Cleopatra from her throne.

Rosie walked over to see what was happening. 'You look

busy,' she shouted up at Grant, who was balanced on a ladder fixing a string of lights to a post.

'Oh, Rosie...!' Grant came down. 'We're just getting ready for the big day.'

'The big—oh! Your mum's party!'

'You forgot, didn't you?' he said, with a wry smile.

'No, of course— OK, maybe a bit.'

'But you'll still be here?'

'I wouldn't miss it for anything.'

'Who's that?' Edith shouted over from her throne.

Rosie turned to her. 'Hello!'

Edith peered at her for a moment. 'Oh! It's you! Come to help?'

Rosie glanced uncertainly at Grant. 'I suppose I could... I mean, I've got time on my hands.'

'You know what would really help?' Grant said. He lowered his voice. 'If you could distract my mother while we get on. Anything that stops her shouting at us is a win at this point.'

Rosie smiled. How could she refuse when he'd put it like that? 'I'm sure I could. I'll go and have a chat with her.'

'You're an angel, you know that?'

'It's no big deal.'

She spotted a folding chair leaning against a wall and pulled it over to sit next to Edith. 'How are you?' she asked. 'Excited for tomorrow?'

'If I wake up tomorrow,' Edith said flatly. 'At my age there are no guarantees.'

'The party should be good, though.'

'Noisy. I don't know why we need fireworks and nonsense. I'd have had a nice dinner dance.'

'I think Grant wants to make a splash – show everyone how much you mean to him.'

'I expect so. Still' – Edith sniffed – 'I think it's more for him than me.'

Rosie gave a knowing smile. 'I think you might be a little bit right about that.'

'Oh, he was terrible when he was young – you couldn't keep him away from a party. And the girls he used to pick up at them...' She shook her head. 'Never seen anything like them.'

'Bit of a lad in his day then?'

'I'll say!'

'But you must be proud of the way he turned out,' Rosie said. 'His own business, two strapping sons, well respected...'

Edith looked fondly to where Grant was trying to untangle another chain of lights, the pride in her face evident. 'I suppose he has,' she said. She turned to Rosie. 'Do you have children?'

'No.'

'Not one of these who doesn't want them, are you? I don't understand it – in my day you got married and got on with it. The human race will die out if everyone decides it's too much bother.'

'It's not that at all; it just hasn't happened for me yet.'

'Doesn't your husband want any?'

'My husband...' Rosie took a breath. It never got any easier to say the words, but she was getting used to the fact that she had to. 'He died.'

Edith studied her for a moment. 'Oh,' she said slowly. 'Now I know who you are.'

'I'm Rosie... you met me at the cafe – remember?'

'Yes. I remember him now, up and down all the time.'

Rosie frowned. There was that phrase again. What did Edith mean? 'We had a lot to do when we first took over the cafe,' she said shortly. 'I expect he was running a lot of errands – we both were.'

'I never saw you. I saw him, up and down, in and out. Errands... hmm...'

'There was a lot to do,' Rosie said again. 'The cafe was quite run-down.'

Edith nodded sagely. 'I expect it was – it was empty for a long while.'

'I bet you've seen a lot of changes on the marina in your time,' Rosie said, deciding to steer the conversation to something less jarring.

'I have.'

'Did Grant always have the boat-hire business?'

'My husband set it up and passed it down. It wasn't hire back then of course – it was a proper business with hard workers, taking goods all over the place. We had steel contracts and everything.'

'So you were eco-friendly before your time, eh?'

'Ec— What?'

'You know, using the water to move things rather than roads.'

'Oh, I see.' Edith looked more closely at Rosie. 'You're not one of those protestors, are you? Hanging from trees so no one can chop them down?'

'It depends on the tree,' Rosie said cheerfully. 'But not usually.'

'Good. I thought with your hair you might be. You're not a punk rocker, are you?'

'No – nothing like that.'

'Oh. Because they have all sorts going on up top, don't they?'

Rosie hadn't seen a proper punk for years. There were all kinds of tribes who liked to stand out, of course, but the people she suspected Edith was referring to probably hadn't walked the streets of respectable Stratford-upon-Avon since the late seventies.

'Grant brought one of those home once,' Edith said. 'Bright green her hair was, a big chunk missing on one side – I thought she'd had an accident with her dad's razor.' Edith folded her arms. 'I didn't like her.'

Rosie was starting to wonder if Edith's default setting was: 'I don't like her.' In which case, she was doing well just being allowed to sit and talk to her at all.

'I don't like that other one either,' Edith continued.

'Don't you?'

By now, Rosie was learning that it was better not to try and make sense of what Edith was talking about, so she simply smiled patiently.

'You know who I mean!' Edith said with slightly less patience. She pointed across the marina, though it was hard to tell exactly what she was pointing at. 'Tried it with our Chris, she did. Jezebel. He's young enough to be her son! Oh... she's not fussy at all!'

'Chris... you mean Grant's son?' Rosie asked, though she still had no idea where exactly Edith was pointing at or who she was calling a jezebel.

'Yes!' Edith shook her head forcefully. 'In my day we'd have a name for her and I won't repeat it here because it's not nice at all.'

'What happened?'

'Chris reminded her he was married. He's ever so fond of his Talia, you know. I can take or leave her, but *she* doesn't care if they're spoken for or not. Terrible business.'

Rosie's head was spinning. She was struggling to keep up with the conversation – she'd lost it pretty much from the beginning, she realised now.

'Perhaps I should go and see if I can help with the decorations,' she said.

Edith looked disappointed but with some degree of resignation that suggested she was used to people making excuses to get out of conversations with her. 'Blasted decorations. Everyone's forgotten about me.'

'They're just trying to make it fabulous for you. It shows how much they care.'

'I'd have had a nice dinner dance. I used to be a lovely dancer, you know.'

'I bet. I can see you have good posture.'

'Not like young girls now. They're up and down hunched over, more than old ladies like me.'

Rosie found herself unconsciously straightening up, just in case Edith decided to inspect her posture. Anything was possible.

'I really should...' she began in a bid to try another escape.

'Do you dance?'

'I'm not much of a mover, I'm afraid. You're more likely to find me curled up with a book than in the gym.'

'He sells books,' Edith said.

Rosie frowned slightly. 'You mean Kit?'

'What's a Kit?'

'I mean, Kit sells books – on the barge over there.' Rosie pointed.

'Does he? Her new boyfriend sells books too. I don't think he cares much for her, though.'

Rosie had thought she might be getting the hang of Edith's peculiar language but now she wasn't so sure. Was she talking about Nicole and Kit? And if she was, how did Edith know so much about it?

'Do you visit the marina a lot?' she asked.

'Yes. I sit at the boathouse. They're all too busy to do much with me, but it's nicer than sitting in my room at the home.'

'So Grant does his best to spend time with you? That's nice.'

'He's a good boy.'

'He is,' Rosie agreed. 'A lovely man.'

'I want to go to the toilet,' Edith announced.

'Right...' Rosie cast around for help. What was she supposed to do about it? Was Edith telling her because she expected assistance? Everyone was busy apart from her, but she'd only just met Edith and barely knew her; it didn't seem appropriate for her to accompany her to the toilet, especially if she had to do more than just accompany her when they got there.

As she panicked about her dilemma, Edith got slowly up from her chair and, before Rosie could do anything else, began to shuffle towards the doors of the tiny office that stood next to the boats.

'Toilet!' she shouted to no one in particular.

'Alright, Grandma!' Chris, Grant's oldest son, shouted back.

He didn't seem too concerned and didn't ask Rosie to do anything, so she figured she'd just wait where she was.

As she watched Grant and his boys work, she thought again about offering her services in a more practical way, and was about to get up and speak to one of them when Kit walked up.

'Didn't expect to see you here,' he said. 'Come down to help too?'

'I hadn't intended to but I was passing and I've sort of ended up Edith-sitting.'

Kit laughed. 'Don't envy you that job.'

'You've met her?'

'Not yet, but I've heard plenty.'

From Nicole? Rosie wondered. In which case, she was quite sure any account Kit had heard would be biased, but then, she could hardly blame Nicole for that. They weren't exactly best friends as far as Rosie could tell.

'She's not so bad,' she said. 'Just a bit outspoken. It goes from brain to mouth and there's nothing in between... half an hour with her and you know exactly what she thinks about everything. At least, you would if you could understand half of it. I've read less cryptic crossword clues.'

'That's something to look forward to then.'

'I'm sure you'll be one of the ones who gets a good review,' Rosie said.

Kit dug his hands into his pockets. 'I'd better go and catch Grant. I said I'd lend a hand after work, so... here I am.'

'Grant asked you?'

'A bit of extra muscle, he said, so I hope I don't disappoint. It's not often I'm referred to as muscle.' Kit's attention was caught by something beyond Rosie, and she turned to see the tiny shuffling figure of Edith coming back from the office. 'Looks like your charge is back.'

Here we go again, she told herself quietly.

They both watched in silence as Grant's mother made her way towards them slowly, hands reaching for posts and fences and any other support along the way. Rosie wondered if she ought to go and offer help but didn't want to offend her by implying she wasn't capable of walking. But then Kit did it anyway, darting over and offering his arm with a dazzling smile.

'You must be Edith,' he said. 'I'm Kit. Care to take my arm for the rest of the way?'

Edith peered into his face. 'Oh... you. I've seen you.'

'I'm sure you have. I run the book barge across the way. Do you read? I'd be happy to bring some books over if you'd like to borrow some.'

'I don't read – waste of time. I do crosswords. I like *Countdown*.'

'What about sudoku?'

'Sometimes,' she said.

'I have some sudoku books in; I'll drop them off at the office for you and you can get them the next time you're here.'

Edith nodded shortly. As they reached her seat she eased herself down, until at the final moment she gave up trying to control her descent and plopped into it.

'Are you looking forward to your party tomorrow?' he asked.

'I wanted a nice dinner dance,' she said. 'Do you dance?'

'Not really. I've been known to go for a drunken boogie but it's not pretty.'

'No one dances these days,' Edith said ruefully.

'I'd learn just for you if you wanted someone to dance with.'

'You can't just learn it.'

'I'd give it a go.'

She shook her head slowly. 'No one dances properly now.'

'Kit!' Grant waved him over from the top of a stepladder. 'Got a job for you!'

Kit nodded shortly to show he'd heard and then turned back to Edith with a look of apology. 'Duty calls. It was nice to meet you.'

Edith folded her hands over one another on her lap, and gave a look that suggested it would be mad to be anything other than pleased to meet her. After a last smile at Rosie, Kit walked away to see Grant.

'I don't like him,' Edith said in a carrying whisper. At least, Rosie had to presume that Edith thought it was a whisper. She only hoped the wind was blowing in a direction that would take her comment away from Kit's ears.

'Why not?' she asked, unable to help her curiosity even though it was giving Edith's gossip far too much encouragement.

'He's too handsome.'

Rosie laughed lightly. 'Is that all? He can't help that. It shouldn't be a reason to dislike him – he's always lovely.'

'The handsome ones are trouble, even when they don't mean to be.'

'I can't imagine Kit being trouble.'

'We'll see,' Edith said in a tone filled with a sense of impending doom. 'We'll see.'

Rosie sighed. She was beginning to wish she'd taken a different route on her walk that evening. She'd have been home by now, watching television instead of fending off Edith's muddled opinions on just about everything and everyone.

CHAPTER ELEVEN

The dress code was a mystery, if, indeed, there was one at all. Rosie had never been to a party/barbecue/fireworks event on a marina before, and she'd certainly never been to a birthday celebration for someone so old. Should she wear reasonably sensible (but stylish) outdoor clothes, or something smart-casual, like the sort of thing she might wear going out for a meal? Or was it a full-on glitter event where people were expected to make a real effort?

She'd asked Tabitha two or three times what she planned to wear, only to get the vague responses of 'Something nice' or 'I don't really know yet'. Not helpful at all. She also discovered that Nicole was going. This came as quite a surprise, all things considered, but Rosie could only assume that as practically everyone on the marina had been invited, Grant had decided that to leave Nicole out, regardless of any animosity between them, would be downright cruel. Rosie was glad to hear her friend was coming after all. And she had a new respect for Grant for his kindness – that he had enough of a conscience to know when a mistake he'd made (like leaving Nicole out of the bike ride) had hurt someone and wanted to put it right.

In a bid to mend relations and get things back on an even keel, Rosie had phoned Nicole to ask what she planned to wear as an excuse for a chat. But Nicole had just said, 'Something slutty enough,' and Rosie hadn't needed to ask any more to know that was a road she herself was definitely not going down.

As she stared into her drab wardrobe – at least, it felt drab these days – she could hear the party already getting underway: there was music and raised voices. She'd have to get a move on. Her hair was still wet from her shower, and since she'd messed around doing one thing or another, she was nowhere even close to ready.

She could probably get away with very little work on her hair. She often dried it straight to keep it tidy for the cafe, but if she left it to air-dry with a bit of product smoothed through, it would retain its natural wave and might even look cute. Make-up was tried and tested – nothing to worry about there and nothing out of the ordinary – and she could do it in minutes without thinking about it. The outfit... that was the thing that would make her late because she just couldn't decide.

She stood at the full-length mirror in her oversized and faded Hard Rock Cafe T-shirt. It was years old, stretched at the neck and some of the lettering had been rubbed away. Maybe she should just wear that and have done with it – after all, it wasn't like anyone was going to be looking at her anyway.

Going back to the wardrobe she looked again and eventually pulled out a black maxi dress. She'd had it for a couple of years, having bought it on a shopping trip with Fergus in a closing-down sale. It had only cost £10 and she'd been thrilled. It was her go-to colour, empire line in style and with tiny pink roses on it. She'd worn it to go out to dinner shortly afterwards and Fergus had said it made her look like a Jane Austen heroine, which pleased her because it was pretty much what she'd been aiming for.

She hadn't worn it since Fergus's death, however, and

though she felt it fitted the bill for the party, was she brave enough to put it on, knowing its history?

She rifled through the wardrobe again, but nothing else jumped out at her.

Taking a deep breath, she reached for the dress. Fergus wouldn't want this for her, would he? People always said that, didn't they? She was surrounded by museum pieces dedicated to her time with him, and if she attached that much significance to every one, she'd never move on.

It already felt as if she was in a limbo she'd never be able to leave, and that had been fine for a while but, as the sounds of the party reached her, the voices of new friends from her new life here, she realised that maybe she was ready to try now.

She put on the dress and went to the mirror again. It was just the ticket – even better when she'd done her make-up and pulled on her old Doc Martens. 'Let's do this!' she told herself, nerves jangling, stomach doing somersaults, and went to get her keys.

The weather couldn't have been more perfect. The evening was balmy, ribbons of cloud drifting across a shell-pink sky as the barbecue coals heated up, sending the delicious anticipation of good food to come into the air.

A small crowd was gathered at the water's edge as Rosie arrived; some she recognised and some she didn't.

The decorations Grant and his sons had put up were certainly impressive – rows and rows of lights shining out across the water, bowls of flowers dotted about the place and so much bunting there was probably not a scrap more to be had anywhere in Warwickshire. There were long trestle tables dressed in crockery, silverware and napkins, underneath starched white canopies. There were also smaller tables with seats, though it didn't look as if there was enough for everyone, so Rosie didn't think there was meant to be a formal sit-down with the food, rather that anyone who needed a temporary place to rest – perhaps the older guests – would have somewhere to do that.

Grant's sons were standing with women who Rosie assumed were their wives, and five small children, all under the age of ten, who raced up and down a bit too close to the river for her liking, though it was none of her business to say so.

Edith was sitting close by on a chair, and Grant was sitting next to her. Edith looked about as pleased to be the guest of honour at this function as she'd been about the prospect of the function in general.

She's probably wishing she was at a dinner dance, Rosie thought, though she did seem to brighten as Rosie went over to her with the potted plant she'd brought as a gift. Not knowing Edith well, and knowing even less about the kinds of things the average ninety-year-old might want, she had decided everyone had space for a plant in their lives, and so had gone for a beautiful chrysanthemum from the farm shop.

'Happy birthday,' she said, holding it out to Edith.

Edith looked up at the pot. 'Is that for me, Grant?'

'I expect so,' he said patiently. 'Aren't you going to take them?'

Edith looked at the plant again, and then at Rosie. 'Where did you get it?'

Rosie blinked, slightly taken aback by the question, though she ought to have been used to Edith's bluntness by now. 'I got it at the farm shop.'

Edith sniffed. 'Thought as much. I had one from there last year. It died.'

'That's because you didn't water it, Mum,' Grant said.

Edith turned to him, looking deeply offended. 'I did!'

'Then how come it looked like it had been on a collision course with the sun when I threw it away?'

'It didn't,' Edith huffed.

Grant gave Rosie an apologetic look. 'I'll make sure this one survives. Thank you so much.'

He took the plant from her and went to put it with a pile of other gifts that was now building up nicely in the corner of one of the gazebos.

Suddenly, there was a squeal from the water's edge. Two of the children were slapping each other. It was soon quelled by Grant's son.

'They're so noisy,' Edith said. 'They ought to be in bed by now. It's too late for them to be up. Makes them all unreasonable the next day.'

'It's very exciting for them to be allowed here though,' Rosie said. 'I'm sure they wouldn't have wanted to miss out on your birthday celebrations.'

'I don't like the big one,' Edith said. 'Always wants something. Children don't learn to go without these days, do they? They click their fingers and it's there. Not like in my day. We knew the value of things.'

'I wouldn't know,' Rosie said neutrally.

'You're not one of those who doesn't want babies, are you? I don't understand it.'

'No,' Rosie said patiently, though it took a lot not to point out that they'd had the exact same conversation the day before. 'It just hasn't happened for me yet. I'm not going to let it worry me – if it does, it does, and if not... well, that's just the way of things, isn't it?'

Grant came back and sat down next to his mum again. Just as Layla and Tom from the farm shop sauntered over.

'Hi!' Layla said, smiling at them all. She gave Edith a basket of food – biscuits, chocolates, fruit, crackers, cheese and sweets; all artisan or organic. Rosie's gift seemed paltry in comparison, and she'd have been thrilled to receive something like that. She'd bet it all cost more than it would appear to as well.

Edith looked pointedly at her son. 'Would you take that?'

Grant stood up. 'Thank you, this looks great. We're glad you could come.'

'We wouldn't have missed it,' Tom said. 'It's a big day.'

'Let's hope I last through it,' Edith said tartly. 'This party might kill me off.'

'Aww, I bet you'll have a great time really,' Layla said.

Edith sniffed at the hamper that Grant had set down on his chair for a moment. 'At least I won't have to do any shopping for the next year – though I won't be able to eat some of those things... don't even know what they are. I've had so much food given to me today it'll probably outlast me.'

'No, you haven't,' Grant said. 'You've had Layla and Tom's grand-looking hamper, a box of chocolates from Kerry and a tin of biscuits. Unless you're planning a hunger strike that's not going to last – stop exaggerating.'

He turned to Rosie, Layla and Tom. 'Help yourselves to drinks,' he said. 'We'll be starting the barbecue in half an hour or so too, but there are nibbles out until then.'

'Sounds good,' Layla said.

She and Tom started towards the bar tent, where Rosie could now see Grant had hired actual bar staff dressed in starched white shirts, dickie bows and waistcoats. He really had pushed the boat out (pun unintended but still occurring to Rosie) for this celebration. She followed them to get a drink, grateful for the opportunity to escape Edith for a while.

'How's it going at the cafe?' Layla asked as they walked. 'It's funny, I know we see you around practically every day but I never seem to get a chance to ask you properly.'

'It's like that for us all, I think. We're so busy with the day-to-day stuff...' Rosie looked at Layla and smiled. 'It's ticking over thanks, and to be honest, that suits me. I don't deal well with stress so if it was too busy that would almost be worse than not being busy at all. Perhaps when I've got into a rhythm I'll be glad of a few more customers, but until then I'm fine as I am.'

'Things are always changing too – at least, they seem to be for us. That takes as much getting used to as anything else.'

'That's true,' Rosie agreed. 'I'll just get used to working with Tabitha but then I'll get Letitia back.' She had told Layla already about her original waitress.

'Have you heard how she is?'

'Getting there, I think. I don't have a date for her to start yet, but Tabitha seems happy to stay with me until she's back, so I'm not too worried.'

'Tabitha seems great,' Layla said as she reached for a pre-poured white wine standing on the table serving as a bar.

'She is. I was so lucky to have her step in the way she did.'

'What does she plan to do after she leaves you? Has she got another job to go to?'

'I know she doesn't have another job yet, but I don't know what she wants to do – I don't think she knows actually.'

'She's not going to be working for her brother then?' Tom asked.

Rosie shook her head. 'She says not.'

'If things go well for us with the expansion, we might need another pair of hands, right, Layla?' Tom said.

Layla nodded.

'We might poach her from you.'

'Well, please don't do it just yet,' Rosie said with a grimace that made Layla laugh. 'I'm not quite ready for my nervous breakdown.'

'We wouldn't dream of it,' Layla said. 'But you might want to mention the possibility to her – that she could carry on working at the marina if she wanted to.'

'She does love it here, so she tells me. I'm sure she'll be interested.'

Leaving the bar tent, they saw that Nicole had arrived. In

the end, it seemed she'd abandoned her intention to be 'slutty enough' – or had at least toned it down – and she'd opted to wear a shimmery vest that showed off her toned arms and some leather trousers.

Layla and Tom looked mildly surprised to see her. It seemed most people had an inkling that all was not rosy between Nicole and Grant's family. Perhaps it was none of her business, but Rosie still resolved to ask Layla or Tom later – if she could get a minute alone with them – as it might be something she needed to know about.

'Hi...' Layla said uncertainly. 'How are you?'

Rosie guessed that Nicole would expect almost everyone who knew the marina well would have been surprised to see her there. Rosie was glad Nicole had chosen to ignore that and come anyway; at least she'd have someone to talk to where she could be a little more herself.

'Hi, Nicole,' she said warmly. 'You look great!'

Nicole gave them all a gracious smile. She was already clutching a glass with a bright blue drink in it. 'The cocktails are great!' she said. 'Highly recommended! Who needs to go into town when you can get them here for free? Cheers!' She clinked her cocktail glass with Rosie's.

Rosie hadn't known what to order, so she had let the bartender recommend a cocktail and make it for her. She'd chosen vanilla and strawberry flavours and vodka. Rosie would never have ordered that herself in a pub, but it was very nice.

As Nicole started to talk to her, Layla and Tom drifted off to chat to Luca. Rosie caught snatches of their conversation. She raised quizzical eyebrows at Nicole. 'Do Layla and Tom speak Italian?'

'God, yes,' Nicole said. 'Every time they see Luca they start – it's such a bore. Alright, we know, you spent two years living in Tuscany, there's no need to keep going on about it. It's totally unnecessary too; Luca speaks better English than most English people I know.'

'I suppose they think he likes it.'

'I suppose it lets them show off. Stuck-up pair.'

Rosie sipped her drink. 'I like them.'

'You would.'

Rosie frowned. What was that supposed to mean? She put it down to Nicole seeming to be drinking a cocktail that wasn't her first, and maybe not even her second or third. 'I speak as I find,' was all she said in reply. 'They're always nice to me.'

'Everyone is nice to you because they feel sorry for you.'

Rosie's eyes widened in shock. 'I don't ask them to!'

'You don't have to – they know about Fergus after all. I found him, you know, but nobody cares how I'm doing.'

'I'm sure that's not true – I care!'

'Yeah, I know.'

'Ah... Rosie!' Grant came up to them. He gave Nicole a brief nod before turning back to Rosie. 'There's someone I'd like you to meet.'

'But I...'

Nicole waved a careless hand. 'Go – don't mind me. I've got plenty to occupy me here.'

'Who is it?' Rosie asked as she followed Grant back outside.

'My friend, Cal... Actually, he's more Chris's friend than mine. More your age too.'

'Oh,' Rosie said with a horrible sinking feeling. Random male guest, just her age? What was coming next...? Newly divorced, just out of a relationship, great guy, et cetera, et cetera?

'He's a great guy,' Grant said. 'I think you'll really like him.'

'Grant, I should...' Rosie began, but suddenly found herself placed in front of a man who'd clearly been told to wait by the guest seating.

'Cal,' Grant said, 'this is my good friend, Rosie. Rosie, this is my good friend, Cal.'

Rosie smiled awkwardly. She didn't want to go through with this charade, and it would be a charade because she wasn't remotely interested in being set up with a man, but she didn't want to offend Grant either – he'd been so lovely to her and clearly cared about her welfare. Rosie had felt ready to rejoin society as she'd got dressed that evening, but it had to be baby steps. This wasn't baby steps – this was running, and it was too fast for her.

'Hello, Cal,' she said.

'Hi,' he said. 'You look lovely.'

Oh God. This was exactly what Rosie had feared and, what was worse, Cal seemed very much clued-up on the plan.

'This old dress? I just threw it on, but thanks.'

'I like your boots. Used to have a pair myself in my student days.'

Please stop... she thought. Cal was sweet and was even quite easy on the eye – tall, ash-blond hair to his shoulders, blue-eyed... but this was excruciating.

'I've never been a student,' she said. 'Apparently I just like the clothes and not the studying.'

'Ha ha, yes, good one.' Grant clapped his hands once. 'So, if you'll both excuse me, I can see I'm needed... the band has arrived.'

'Band?' Rosie watched Grant dash off. 'I had no idea there was going to be a band.'

'Some swing nonsense I think.'

'You don't like swing?'

'Well, it's old, isn't it?' Cal looked her up and down. 'Let me guess – you like The Smiths? Fall Out Boy? Something a bit emo?'

'It's the black, huh?'

'Well...'

'It's a common mistake. Actually, I quite like a bit of swing. I like all sorts of music – old and new.'

'Like what?'

Rosie shrugged. 'When I hear it I'll know if I like it.' Her eyes skimmed the swelling crowd of guests. Where was Tabitha? She said she'd come, and if ever Rosie needed her, it was now.

'So... do you get out to clubs much?' Cal asked.

'Not really – I'm pretty busy with work.'

'Oh yeah, you have a cafe, right? Grant says you own it. You run it by yourself.'

'Not entirely, but it keeps me very busy.'

'But you must have some time for a social life.'

'See me standing here tonight? This is pretty much my social-life allocation for this year.'

He laughed. 'No way! You've got to go out for a drink occasionally – you'd go mad!'

'Not me. I'm very dull like that.'

'So you have no time off at all?'

'Not a lot.'

'Ah! Then you have *some*!'

'Well, I have to sleep.'

'Yeah, of course. But if you were to get the odd night off... what would you do with it?'

'More sleep.'

'It's that bad? I'm almost envious your time is so full. Since my divorce I don't know what to do with myself. It's hard, going from having your evenings with someone else to spending them alone, you know?'

'Yes,' Rosie said. 'I do know, which is why I'm glad to have something to do with mine. Honestly, it sounds dull but when I'm not working in the cafe, I'm doing admin for the cafe or getting things ready for the next day... I open seven days a week, and I work all of them.'

'Jesus!' He downed the last of his pint. 'That's insane!' He nodded at her glass. 'Can I get you another one?'

The drink she had was barely touched, and she was about to refuse his offer when she saw Nicole walk by. Or rather, wobble.

'Could you excuse me for just a few minutes? My friend is here alone and I want to see if she's OK. I think she's hit the free bar a bit hard and a bit fast.'

'An easy trap to fall into,' Cal said, grinning. 'Of course.'

Grateful for a reason to leave him, Rosie dashed after her friend, although as soon as she'd caught up with her, she wondered whether she'd simply leapt from the frying pan into the fire. It was obvious by now that Nicole was steaming drunk and in a strange mood.

Nicole turned around as Rosie touched her on the shoulder. 'Oh, it's you. I thought Grant wanted you.'

'He did... He introduced me to this guy.' Rosie lowered her voice. 'I think he was trying to get us... you know... *together*.'

'Oh God.' Nicole let out a loud giggle. 'What a loser!'

'No...!' Rosie blushed and wondered how to persuade Nicole to lower her voice without actually saying so. 'I didn't say that.... He's sweet and everything but not really my type, and even if he was, I'd rather do my own... well, you know what I mean.'

'I thought you were never going to have another man again?'

'I'm not. I mean, I never said never again, I just meant it's going to be a long time till I'm ready to entertain the idea again.'

'That's not what you said.'

'Yes, but that was ages ago – months ago. Things change.'

'Things have changed?'

'Things *might* change – there's a difference.'

'You confuse me.'

Rosie suspected breathing confused Nicole right then. How

long had she been propping up the bar for? Had she arrived that much earlier than Rosie?

'Want to dance?' Nicole slurred.

'Not really—'

Nicole grabbed Rosie's hand and pulled her to the dance floor. The band was only just getting instruments from cases on the makeshift stage and in the meantime music was being piped in from someone's Spotify playlist; Rosie wasn't sure, but there was no DJ talking over any of it. Apart from the two of them, the dance floor was empty.

Rosie could feel eyes on them and she didn't like it. 'It's a bit early to start dancing,' she said. 'Nobody else is on here yet.'

'So? More space for us.' Nicole began to throw her arms and legs about as Rosie inched back to the edge of the wooden flooring.

'Rosie!' Nicole scolded. 'Come on!'

'Can't you just hang on? I might... I need to get another drink,' she said, a sudden light-bulb-moment striking. 'I bet you want one too – come on, come with me.'

'Great idea,' Nicole said and began to shuffle her way over. But then her attention was suddenly elsewhere. 'Oh!' she cried. 'Hang on...'

Rosie could only watch as she raced off. Then she realised why – Kit had arrived. No Tabitha as yet, it seemed – at least she wasn't with him now. Nicole flung her arms around him. Rosie tore her gaze away – she wasn't going to be accused of poking her nose in where it wasn't wanted and Nicole seemed too volatile right then to annoy.

She moved further away but in a direction that would also take her away from the dance floor and out of Cal's sights. She had no desire to get stuck in another conversation with him. She hoped fervently that Tabitha would arrive soon. Perhaps she'd decided not to come after all. It was hardly the coolest spot in town, and Rosie wouldn't blame her if she'd found somewhere better to go. In fact, she was surprised Tabitha had wanted to come at all.

Her gaze swept the crowd. Layla and Tom were still speaking to Luca. Grant and his mum were talking to a man Rosie could have sworn she'd seen photos of in the local paper in mayoral chains. She chanced a peep in Cal's direction, and even he was deep in conversation with Chris and his wife. Everyone seemed to be in a conversation with someone, and none of them looked like ones she wanted to crash. She longed for the band to start – at least then she'd have something to watch and it wouldn't matter if she was standing alone or not.

When she dared glance over again, Nicole was leading Kit towards the bar. Her gaze briefly connected with Rosie's, and though she smiled and waved, she didn't make an effort to come over. Rosie didn't want to come across as needy, but it hurt. Hadn't Rosie just told Nicole she wanted another drink? It had been a ruse to get her off the dance floor of course, but Nicole didn't know that. And if Rosie had seen Nicole standing alone – or anyone else for that matter – she'd have invited them to join her. But Nicole was firmly fixed on Kit, and it was like nobody else mattered.

Then Kit happened to look back and he spotted Rosie. He said something to Nicole, pointed to her, and they came over.

'Hey.' He smiled warmly. 'My sister not here yet?'

'Not yet.'

'She said she was coming – had to go somewhere first... God knows where she is. Well, why don't you come to the bar with us?' Kit said.

'Good idea,' Nicole said, but Rosie couldn't help feeling she didn't mean it.

Despite the warnings in her head, Rosie went with them back to the bar. The barbecue had been lit and now the scent of cooking meat was on the air.

'Man, that smells good,' Kit said. 'I'm going to have to get something.'

'What about our drink?' Nicole pouted.

'I can do that afterwards... I tell you what, grab me something and I'll come back to you. Want me to get you some food?'

He glanced between Nicole and Rosie.

'I'd like something,' Rosie said. 'I'm not sure what there is so I'm probably best coming to look.'

'I'd better come too then,' Nicole said, swinging so violently to change direction that Rosie thought for a moment she might fall over.

'Alright,' Kit said. 'Come on.'

And suddenly, so naturally that she hardly noticed it for a moment, Kit's hand was over Rosie's, leading her over to the barbecue pit.

Her heart raced. Without understanding why, she didn't want to pull away, but she also needed Kit to realise that this was not OK. But it had been so innocently done, almost without conscious thought from him, that she also realised it was a simple, tactile gesture of friendship on his part.

Of course it was.

The biggest fear – even worse than figuring out how to deal with this – was what would happen if Nicole saw it.

But then someone got in the way as they walked. Kit was forced to let go of her, and the moment passed. Rosie could breathe again, and Nicole hadn't seen anything.

It looked as if Grant had hired staff for the food too. There were three young men in chef's whites and hats cooking over the coals.

'Wow,' Kit said. 'This is the real deal.'

'Everything looks so nice,' Rosie said.

She turned to Nicole. 'What are you going to have?'

'Well, it's burgers or burgers, isn't it? Not hard to decide.'

'Actually, madam,' one of the chefs cut in, 'we've got venison burger, beef, chicken, tofu, pork sausages, bratwurst, trout fillets and shrimps. If we don't have it cooking right now, just give us a minute and we can cook to order for you. My colleague has pulled pork over there if you'd prefer that – served in sourdough rolls with salad.'

'God, I could eat all that!' Rosie said. 'Everything sounds amazing!'

'I'm not hungry,' Nicole said.

Kit gave a vague frown. 'You should probably eat something.'

Rosie was inclined to agree. Nicole needed something to sober her up – Kit had only just arrived and even he could see that.

'Oh, alright... I'll have a big sausage then,' she said and began to snigger.

'I think I'll try the trout,' Rosie said, giving the chef an apologetic smile. 'Maybe I'll have some shrimp too.'

'I'll need to cook those from fresh, madam,' the chef said. 'Will you be alright to wait?'

'Of course.'

The cook turned to Kit. 'And for you, sir?'

Kit grinned. 'Sir? I'm going to come here again! I'll take a venison burger please – I've never tried venison before.'

'It's a good flavour, sir – very strong and earthy.'

'I can't wait to try it then.'

'If you could wait for that too?' the chef said.

He laid Rosie and Kit's food onto the coals, then took an already cooked sausage from elsewhere on the rack and looked up at Nicole. 'Will you be having this with bread, madam? We have hotdog rolls or we can put it on sliced sourdough for you.'

She waved a hand. 'Whatever.'

By now, the chef was clearly holding back a frown. After a

pause that seemed to suggest an internal shrug, he cut open a hotdog roll. 'Any condiments, madam?'

'Sauce.'

'Any particular sauce?'

'I'm not really bothered – surprise me.'

He reached for the ketchup, wrapped her hotdog in some greaseproof paper and handed it to her.

'Thanks.'

'You're welcome.'

Nicole looked at Kit and Rosie. 'Do we have to wait for yours now? How long is it going to be? I want to get a round in before the bar gets busy.'

'I'm sure it won't be long,' Kit said. 'If you're that desperate to go to the bar, you don't have to wait for us.'

For the first time, Rosie detected a hint of impatience in Kit's tone.

'But I waited all night for you to get here,' she whined.

'I'm pretty sure you didn't,' he said shortly.

Nicole bit into her hotdog and looked sullen as she began to chew.

Had she always been this difficult? Rosie wondered. She'd never noticed it before in quite the way she had tonight. Then again, there hadn't ever been this much drink involved. Sure, Nicole could be a bit spiky at times, and there were moments when Rosie felt she had to watch what she said or did lest she offend her or send her into a sulk, but usually it was manageable. She didn't usually feel like throttling her, and she didn't usually regret that they had a friendship at all. She was certainly beginning to feel that now, and she didn't like it.

Rosie had a sort of innate loyalty. It was baked into her DNA, and once she was loyal to someone, it was until the end. The idea of forsaking that – even when someone behaved as badly as Nicole was behaving tonight – upset her in a way she couldn't explain; it went against every instinct she had. It would have been easy to tell Nicole to get a grip and to walk away, but she couldn't do that.

One thing was clear to her as she noticed Kit regard Nicole with some wariness – he wasn't into her. Rosie wondered now why she'd ever imagined it was a possibility – it was so obvious they weren't suited at all. He'd probably never been into her, but if Nicole was seeking to change that, she was hardly going about it the right way. If anything, tonight had probably made things worse.

'What's she doing here?'

All three of them whipped around to see Chris and his wife approaching the barbecue. His wife glared at Nicole.

Then the penny dropped for Rosie. The woman who'd tried to seduce Chris – it was Nicole.

How could she have not worked it out? It was obvious now that she thought about it, and it explained so much about the animosity between the families and Edith's intense dislike of her. Even if Edith pretty much disliked everyone.

'I was invited!' Nicole said, biting into her hotdog. 'Doesn't that husband of yours tell you anything?'

'Chris?' His wife's expression demanded answers as she turned to him.

'Look, I meant to tell you she'd been invited but I honestly didn't think I'd need to because I didn't think she'd be stupid enough to come.'

'Oops!' Nicole said. She looked at Chris's wife. 'Talia, right? Don't worry, Talia, I'm not interested in your man.'

'You'd better watch your step anyway,' Talia growled.

'Are you going to throw me out? Grant invited me.'

Talia turned to Chris. 'What the hell...?'

Chris fired a look at Rosie that made her cheeks burn. It was her – she was the reason Grant had invited Nicole, because she'd had that chat with him when Nicole had been left out of the bike ride. But if she'd known how much trouble it would cause, if he'd only explained it to her, she would never have made a fuss. Chris must have known about the conversation Rosie had had with his dad and that Rosie was the reason he was in trouble with his wife now.

'Ignore her,' he said to Talia. 'She's not worth your time.'

With an imperious look that said she agreed with her husband, Talia swept past all three of them, barely even giving Rosie or Kit a passing glance either. Chris followed, looking a bit more sheepish.

Nicole stuck her tongue out at Talia's back. 'Stupid cow,' she muttered.

'I think you should get out of the way for a bit,' Kit said to her quietly. 'Keep a low profile.'

'Why should I keep a low profile? I haven't done anything wrong.'

'Look,' Kit said, 'I don't know what's going on, but clearly that woman would disagree. Think about it – this is a party for a ninety-year-old woman, not a booze-up at a working men's club. The last thing anyone needs here tonight is aggro. If you can't do it for any other reason, do it for that one. Please.'

'Sir... madam! Your food is ready!'

Kit turned to the barbecue pit where the chef was waiting with their orders. Rosie followed and they collected their food. When they turned back, Nicole was nowhere to be seen.

'Shit,' Kit said. 'That got a bit intense, didn't it? What's going on with her?'

Rosie looked sadly at him. 'Oh, Kit... can't you see what's going on?'

'No.'

'She's crazy about you.'

He stared at her. 'Me?'

'Don't tell me you haven't noticed. She couldn't have sent bigger signals if she'd tied a message to the back of a plane and flown over the marina with it.'

Kit's venison burger stopped halfway to his mouth. He didn't speak. And then he bit into it and chewed, deep in thought. 'I don't understand,' he said finally.

'Well, there's nothing really to understand. Do you like her, that's the question?'

'No. I mean, she's a laugh and everything, but I don't like her in that way at all.'

'Then you need to tell her.'

'Shit.'

Rosie looked at him, at his confusion. 'If you don't mind a bit of unasked-for advice, it's always best to be open and honest and transparent about these things. When we hide the details, that's when confusion sets in and people get hurt. If you feel something, best to say it.'

'Is that what you think about everything? Is that true in every case?'

'Yes,' Rosie said, slightly puzzled by his response. 'Of course it is.'

'So I must always say how I feel, no matter what the circumstances or consequences? Even if I'm scared that the person I feel it for might not want to hear it? In fact, I'm fairly sure they won't want to hear it.'

'Yes! Put her out of her misery, for God's sake!'

'Right...' He took a deep breath. Rosie waited for him to go and find Nicole, but he didn't move. Instead, he looked right into her eyes and it was like he was staring into her soul. 'I'm in love with you, Rosie.'

Rosie stared at him. Had she just heard correctly? Things had been fraught and overwhelming enough tonight, perhaps she was just confused. 'What?'

'I love you,' he repeated patiently. 'I know it's not what you want to hear and, believe me, I've tried to fight it, but I can't. And you've just said I should be honest. So this is me, being honest.'

'I don't understand...'

'Don't tell me you haven't seen the signs,' he said, echoing the words she'd just spoken to him about Nicole.

'No...' she said, but even as she did, she knew that wasn't true. She'd seen them, loud and clear. She'd seen them every time he'd called for his stupid ham and pickle sandwich, or when he'd shout a greeting on the way to his boat, or when he offered to run some little errand for her, or take out her rubbish. Or that time he'd swept the front step of her cafe before she locked up because he'd said he was doing it while he waited for Tabitha so they could go home together, which, of course, wasn't true at all. He had never been waiting for Tabitha. He'd only wanted to be near Rosie.

How had she not seen that?

Or perhaps she had seen it and had chosen to ignore it because she'd been terrified of what it might mean if she acknowledged it?

'So,' he said. 'What now?'

Rosie clung to her plate of food. It was hot in her hands and smelt smoky and sweet, but even though she'd been hungry, she couldn't think about it. 'I'm sorry,' she said and turned to push her way through the crowd.

She needed to be at home. She needed to be anywhere but there.

CHAPTER TWELVE

From her bedroom, Rosie could hear the band had started to play 'Happy Birthday' for Edith.

Ten minutes after she'd locked the door and retreated into her safe place, there was hammering down below. Rosie knew who it was even before he called up.

'Rosie, I'm sorry. I didn't mean to upset you. Please come back to the party and I promise I won't say another thing about it!'

She sat on the edge of the bed. She wanted him to leave, but at the same time she wanted to let him in. She wanted to shout at him because he'd ruined everything, but at the same time she wanted to be in his arms. There were emotions, all jumbled up inside her, so many she was overwhelmed. She couldn't pick out a single one and feel it.

It was too soon for this. Why did it have to be now? Why couldn't Kit have waited? She wasn't ready for love with someone else yet... was she?

She didn't move. She sat in silence in the darkened bedroom and waited. Eventually she heard footsteps that told her he'd left.

In the bathroom she washed off her mascara and stared into the mirror at her bare, pale face. Kit loved her? How could anyone love the mess that looked back at her right now? She was a mess physically, mentally, emotionally... Hadn't Fergus always told her she was useless? Hadn't he always said nobody else would have her if not for him? She wanted to believe that wasn't true, but right then, she didn't know what to think.

After putting on her pyjamas she went downstairs to get a coffee. She was hardly drunk but she needed something to clear her head. On the table of her own tiny private kitchen was the parcel of barbecued fish she'd run home with. It had gone cold, and she threw it away before putting the kettle on.

While she waited for it to boil, there was another knock at the front of the cafe. Rosie stood next to the interconnecting door but took care that whoever was outside couldn't see her. Then she heard Tabitha's voice calling through the letterbox.

'I know you're in there!'

Tabitha she might be able to deal with, she supposed, as long as she could be sure Kit hadn't come with her. She wondered if Kit might have asked her to come on his behalf, but she could probably deal with that too – it would be easier to be frank with Tabitha about it all than him.

The fact was, she didn't hate Kit for what he'd told her at all; she was just sad that it could never happen. What she did hate was that she had to tell him so. So perhaps she hated him a little for making her do such a cruel thing, but it wasn't his fault.

As if her question had floated on the air and out into the night, Tabitha answered it. 'Kit's not here,' she called. 'If that's why you're not answering.'

So he'd told his sister. Of course he had.

Rosie pulled her shawl over her pyjamas and went to unlock the door.

Tabitha stepped in. 'Kit told me what happened. He's an idiot – I told him to be patient.'

'It's my fault. I gave him this stupid speech about being honest with people.' Rosie gave a small, rueful smile. 'Should be careful what advice I give out in future. I never imagined he'd use what I'd said in quite that way.'

'Come on, Rosie... you must have known.'

Rosie let out a short sigh and sat at a table. Tabitha joined her.

'Perhaps I did. A bit.'

'And you still didn't see this coming?'

'I'd hoped it wouldn't if I kept my distance.'

'You didn't really keep your distance, though.' Tabitha looked at her.

'I didn't encourage him. You were doing your best to push us together, if you remember rightly, and I asked you to stop.'

'I did stop when you asked me, even though I felt as if it wasn't just one-sided and that you liked Kit too, but you didn't stop... well, you hardly discouraged him. You were still spending time with him, letting him do little favours for you and all that other stuff, and you must have seen where it was going.'

Rosie stared at her. 'So it's my fault now?'

'That's not what I'm saying. Can you really put your hand on your heart and say you don't feel for him even a tiny bit of what he feels for you?'

'Of course I can't, but it's not that simple.'

'You're not ready...' Tabitha blew out a breath. 'He's an idiot. I told him you wouldn't be. I told him to give it six months.'

'Six months, twelve months, ten years... you can't put a time limit on these things. If you'd ever lost someone you'd know.'

'I lost my dad,' Tabitha said. 'So I do know. Don't patronise me. Just because I'm only twenty doesn't mean I haven't experienced loss.'

'Kit's dad?'

'No, we have different dads, remember? But Kit got me and

Mum through it. He's that kind of a bloke, good through and through, and yet he never gets a break.'

'I'm sorry. I wish I could feel differently about it, but—'

'I think you're doing it on purpose.'

'I don't understand what you mean, Tabitha. Pretend I'm thick and spell it out for me.'

'I think you want to stay like this, miserable – in mourning. I think you're punishing yourself because you're here having the life your husband wanted and he's not. I think secretly you like living here and you feel guilty about it so you can't allow yourself to be totally happy. I think that's why you can't admit you like Kit and why you feel you're not allowed to be happy with someone new.'

'None of that's true!' Rosie shrugged miserably. 'I loved Fergus... I'm still in love with Fergus, and I'm sorry, but I don't see how that will ever change. And if I'm still in love with Fergus...'

'Fergus isn't here and Kit is. You're allowed to still love Fergus, but why does that mean you're not allowed to also love someone who can actually be with you?'

'Love's a bit strong,' Rosie said, and Tabitha frowned at her.

'Tabitha,' Rosie continued, 'I get why you want to look out for Kit and you want to see him happy, but please don't push this.'

'Alright,' Tabitha said. 'I won't if that's what you want.'

'It is.'

'Right.' She stood up. 'I came over for that but also to tell you Grant has been looking for you – haven't you seen the missed calls on your phone?'

Rosie groaned. 'I guess he's still trying to fix me up with his friend, Cal.'

'Hmm, someone is popular tonight,' Tabitha said sarcastically. 'I don't know why he wants you,' she continued. 'What do you want me to tell him? I take it you're not coming back to the party?'

'If I say no, you're going to tell me I'm a chicken and I can't hide here forever, aren't you?'

'I'm not going to say anything of the sort – it's none of my business.'

'I don't really feel like being there now.'

'So I'll tell Grant and Edith that you can't be bothered to celebrate her ninetieth with her because someone made you feel bad.'

'That's not fair!'

'No, it's not. It's also not fair that Kit told you how he felt and you just blew him off!'

'I didn't ask him to tell me!'

'Yes, you did! That's exactly what you did!'

Rosie sighed. 'I look like crap.'

'You can get dressed again, surely?'

'I've got no make-up on.'

'Everyone will be too drunk to notice by now.'

'Would you go back looking this rough?'

'It's not about you, though, is it? It's about Edith's birthday. You're there to celebrate with her.'

Rosie narrowed her eyes. 'So where were you earlier?'

'With my mum,' Tabitha replied. 'Trying to stop her having a total meltdown. Is that good enough for you?'

'But Kit said—'

'Kit didn't know. Mum called me crying and I went over. I didn't tell Kit because he does enough for her already and he needed a break. For one night, I thought, he deserves to have fun and not have to worry about Mum, so I made up a lie and told him to go to the party without me and I'd catch up. You think you know him but you don't. You don't know either of us.'

Tabitha looked defiant now. 'We're both funny, couldn't give a shit, not a care in the world – that's how it looks, isn't it?

Everyone has a story they keep private. When my dad died, Mum went into shock, and I don't mean she cried a bit. She went off the rails. Kit gave up everything to look after her and to protect me from all the pain that trying to look after her would have caused me, coz I was, like, ten.' Tabitha scrubbed her sleeve over her eyes. 'He gave up a place at university, his friends, his job... he even lost his long-term girlfriend because he put Mum first. And when I was a totally selfish bitch and took off to Leeds to be with my cretin ex, Kit carried on looking after Mum. He had practically no social life. It wasn't until she started to get better that he even thought about doing something for himself and he got the barge, but even now she has relapses and we have to be there for her.' Tabitha drew a breath. 'I know you say you're not ready to move on, but I promise you'll never understand just what you've thrown away tonight.'

It was the first time Rosie had really understood what a complex life Tabitha and Kit had, and it wasn't just because Tabitha had told her. To hear her speak now, it was like listening to a woman far more mature and experienced than Tabitha's twenty years. It was like she'd lived a dozen lifetimes and understood all the complexities of existence in a way that Rosie never could even if she lived to be as old as Edith. It explained their uniquely close bond. It made Rosie feel pathetic, spineless, stupid. She'd been trotting out Fergus as an excuse for all these months, as a reason to close herself off and drop out of life, thinking that she'd been especially cursed and that no one else could possibly feel pain like she did. But, of course, that wasn't true and it had been an immature and selfish attitude.

The memory of Fergus wasn't holding her back; she was holding herself back.

But all that didn't change what was happening here and now. She couldn't love Kit, not like he wanted her to, because

Fergus was still in her past and in her thoughts. He was the reason she was there at all.

'Are you coming or not?' Tabitha said.

'I don't think I can.'

'Fine.'

Tabitha got up and went to the door. Her hand was on the latch when Rosie spoke again.

'You're going to leave, aren't you? I won't see you here again.'

'No, but only because Kit will kick my arse if I do that.'

'I'm sure he'd understand.'

'Yes, but he also understands a promise is a promise and friends stick by you, no matter what.'

'We're still friends then?'

'I expect we could be. It might take a while to be like it was again, though.'

'What about Kit? Do you think we'll be able to get back to how it was? Me and him?'

'I don't know,' Tabitha said as she opened the door. 'You'd better ask Kit that.'

CHAPTER THIRTEEN

After Tabitha had left, Rosie relocked the front door and went to make her coffee. She sat in the empty cafe, hands cradled around her mug, looking at the walls, the floor, the tables and chairs, the lamp-lit paths beyond her windows, thinking about what it had taken to be there and wondering whether it had been worth it after all. As far as she could tell, far from creating a legacy, a new life, a memoriam to Fergus... whatever this crazy project had become, all she'd created was a mess. She'd upset just about everyone who'd meant anything to her on Marigold Marina, and she had a feeling it wasn't over yet.

She could still hear the music playing out over the river, only now it wasn't pop music but the soundtrack of big-band dancehalls and wartime tea dances. The live music must have kicked in. It would have been fun to watch them play.

Rosie listened for a while. It was all songs about dimple-cheeked sweethearts and secret meetings under apple trees; sweet and romantic reminders of more innocent times. Then, just before midnight, the fireworks began. Rosie went to the window and watched them light up the sky above the river, silent tears spilling into her mug.

She went to her room long before the guests started to drift away. She didn't want anyone passing by to know she was in the cafe and, even though the lights were off, they might still be able to see her shadow moving around. And by anyone, she really meant Kit and Tabitha.

When it had gone silent outside she went to bed and lay there, looking up at the ceiling. Since she'd lost Fergus, whenever she'd felt unsure of herself she'd looked at the empty pillow beside her and imagined the essence of him was still somehow there, looking out for her, lending his support. She didn't feel that tonight. She couldn't even bring herself to look at that damned pillow and, after a while, she took it off the bed and put it in the wardrobe.

Now it was just her. She had only herself to rely on and she had to step up to the plate.

At some point she must have fallen asleep, though she couldn't remember it. Nor could Rosie remember if she'd dreamt or not, but perhaps that was a blessing. And though it seemed somehow pointless, she woke with her alarm – feeling like she'd never slept in her life and that she might never be happy again – and got ready for her working day.

She fully expected Tabitha not to show up, or at least to have a still-raging waitress coming over to get further things off her chest that she'd thought of since their heart-to-heart the night before, and so it was with trepidation that she answered the knock – earlier than usual – to find her outside waiting.

Tabitha was quiet, and she looked grave. Rosie's heart almost stopped on seeing the look on her face. Had something happened to Kit?

'We need to talk,' Tabitha said.

'Sure.' Rosie closed the door after Tabitha had walked in and locked it again. She was aware they had limited time before opening, but she could also see this wasn't going to wait, and it was probably going to take as long as it took. For once, if the cafe was going to open late, then it was going to open late.

'You've changed your mind, haven't you? You're giving me notice?'

'I thought about it, but no, it's not that. I have something to tell you. I thought hard about not telling you because I sort of know you're not going to want to hear it. I also know you won't believe it. But then I figured it was on me if I didn't say anything and you found out later from someone else, and I don't want to carry that kind of guilt around.'

'OK...' Rosie gestured for Tabitha to take a seat at a table and then joined her.

'Promise you'll hear me out.'

'Depends what it is you're going to say.'

'Promise. Otherwise there's no point in me starting.'

'OK, I'll hear you out.'

Tabitha gave a short nod. Her gaze flitted momentarily towards the spot on the marina where the river curved gently and where Kit's boat bobbed up and down in front of Nicole's shop. Then she turned back to Rosie. 'I went back to the party last night after I'd left you.'

'Right. And Kit...?'

'He's fine.' She paused. 'Well, obviously he's not fine, but that's not what I want to tell you, as you probably already guessed that. It's not important right now.'

'Sorry,' Rosie said. She waited for Tabitha to continue.

'I had an interesting chat with Edith.'

'Oh.'

'I know you think she's bonkers and she talks out of her arse, but that doesn't mean she doesn't see things that go on.'

'She sees everything, or so she says.' Rosie nodded. 'That's the problem – you don't know what bits are real and what's in her head.'

'She's not senile and she doesn't lie,' Tabitha said testily. 'She just gets a bit muddled trying to explain it.'

'Sorry, I didn't mean... Carry on.'

Tabitha paused. 'I wish it wasn't me having to tell you this.'

'Tell me what?'

'Edith told me that Fergus was having an affair.'

'She... what?' Rosie's eyes widened. Was she dreaming? Was this some horrible nightmare she was about to wake from? 'I don't understand...'

'Fergus was having an affair,' Tabitha repeated evenly, 'with someone on the marina.'

Rosie stared at her. 'That's insane! Edith doesn't know what day it is half the time – how can you take anything she says seriously?'

'I think he was too.'

'I don't believe I'm hearing this! You didn't even know us then!'

Tabitha folded her arms, her lips pressed together in a hard line. 'I knew you'd react like this. Edith saw him going in and out of Nicole's shop all the time.'

'Nicole! That's who Edith thinks this affair was with? She would say that – she hates Nicole!'

'For a good reason. Because Nicole is a homewrecker, and if Fergus hadn't died before she'd had the chance, she'd have wrecked yours.'

'Fergus went into her shop because he was just going into someone's shop! It doesn't mean anything. I go to the supermarket every week but I'm not sleeping with the guy who puts the trolleys away!'

'Look, do you want to hear the rest of this or not?'

'No! It's rubbish!'

'Right then.' Tabitha drew in a deep breath. 'So you won't want to hear the clincher?'

Rosie's eyes were wide. It was like a car crash that she couldn't look away from, even though it was horrifying. She didn't want to hear this at all. It was an insult to every memory she had of Fergus – it made a mockery of her grief, of her commitment to him, of every effort she'd made to honour his hopes and dreams for their life on the marina. How could she let such idle gossip sully all that?

But a small voice was telling her to listen, to hear the rest. Why was that? Was it because some of it was starting to make sense? Her mind went back to long absences, where he'd popped out for an errand that should have taken minutes but took hours, where she'd go out herself and return to the flat to notice something out of place – crumpled bedsheets that she'd been certain she'd tidied, damp towels, Fergus strangely evasive around any questions she'd asked...

At the time she'd dismissed it all, not thinking anything of it. Clearly she had been wrong.

Tabitha took her silence as permission to continue. There was no triumph in her face, only sadness and sympathy. 'One of the paramedics who attended the scene when the call went in about Fergus's heart attack is good friends with a nurse who visits the home where Edith lives. She told Edith about this call out to the marina because she knew Edith had connections there.' Tabitha paused. 'Where did you say Nicole found Fergus after he'd collapsed?'

'On the floor of her shop,' Rosie said quietly.

'I thought so. This nurse told Edith he wasn't on the shop floor when they got there. He was in the bedroom.'

Rosie shot out of her seat. 'No! She's lying!'

'Why would she lie? Think about it!'

'She shouldn't be saying anything at all – they're supposed to keep these things confidential!'

'People gossip – it's human nature. You've never told someone something you shouldn't?'

Tears burned Rosie's eyes. 'It's not true! Nicole must have moved him up there to make him comfortable or something!'

'How can that be true? Why would she do that? I'm so sorry,' Tabitha said. 'I had to tell you; you had the right to know.'

'No you didn't! You've ruined everything! I loved Fergus and you've ruined that! You've ruined my life! Why tell me this?'

'Because I had to. Your so-called friend is making you look like an idiot. She's the one who's ruined your life.' Tabitha was so calm, it was almost more infuriating than if she'd been angry.

'Fergus would never do that to me! You didn't know him – you know nothing about it!' Rosie felt the sudden urge to take Tabitha by the arm and throw her out.

As if she somehow sensed it, Tabitha spoke again. 'I'll leave if you want me to.'

'I do want you to! You can go now! Don't come back.'

'Fine.' Tabitha got up from her chair and waited at the door for Rosie to unlock it. 'I really am sorry.'

'So am I,' Rosie said.

Tabitha left and Rosie locked the door again. With shaking hands, she fetched sheets from the bedroom and nails and a hammer from the shed, and set about covering all the windows of the cafe. How could she serve anyone in this state? She could barely understand what was going on in her own head, let alone a customer's order. She needed time and space and to hell with the cafe or the customers or the takings or Marigold Marina. To hell with it all. She'd never wanted to go there in the first place; she'd only gone for Fergus, and Tabitha had made it all a lie.

Had it been her fault? Had she caused it by going home after they'd had their bust-up? Sometimes she'd worried she wasn't enough for him and sometimes she'd felt she couldn't quite trust him, but he'd loved her, hadn't he? He wouldn't have betrayed her like that... would he?

No, Rosie told herself, because it wasn't true. Nicole had

been so good to her after his death. She'd been a friend: she'd sat with Rosie as she'd cried, she'd listened as Rosie had poured out her heart. Whatever Nicole had done on the marina, however unpredictable she could be, surely that wasn't an act? Surely that had been genuine friendship? How could she have offered that if she'd been guilty of such a betrayal in the first place? And how could she have lied so blatantly to Rosie about the circumstances of Fergus's death? Rosie hadn't been at the marina when it had happened and she'd been punishing herself for that ever since. Nicole had helped her navigate that guilt. Why would she do that if she had something so awful to hide?

Did Kit know any of this? Did Nicole herself know what people were saying about her? Should Rosie tell her? But how could she tell her something so awful?

There was a knock on the door. Rosie looked up at the clock – just gone nine. She'd have been open half an hour ago usually. Luckily, she'd just put the last of the sheets up so she didn't have to run and hide. Instead, she flopped onto a chair and waited for the inevitable shout.

But nobody shouted. She heard two people talking quietly, confused about her being closed, but she didn't recognise their voices.

Perhaps none of her friends would come to see what was happening. Perhaps none of them actually cared. Perhaps that was for the best – it would certainly make leaving Marigold Marina easier when the time came. Because even if none of it was true, even if Fergus had been faithful to the end, she couldn't stay now. Too much had happened and too many friendships had been ruined and too much trust had now been broken. What was the point in soldiering on? Fergus didn't give a shit: he was dead. It didn't matter to him whether she ran a cafe here or a brothel in Outer Mongolia.

There was a second knock. 'Rosie, it's Grant. Everyone's

worried and you're not answering your phone – we just want to know you're OK.'

Rosie looked at the door, but she didn't move.

'Rosie!' Grant called again.

There was a long pause, and then the sounds of him walking away. Good. She didn't want to talk to anyone. She wanted to be alone. Wallowing in self-pity seemed very appealing right now.

CHAPTER FOURTEEN

The arrival of a text from Nicole lit up the screen of Rosie's phone. She opened it and stared at the message for what felt like hours.

Are you OK? What the hell is going on with the cafe?

Where did she even begin? It was a genuine message of concern – at least, it seemed so. But if Nicole was guilty of half of what Edith had accused her of, how could she dare pretend to be Rosie's friend? Not to mention how vile she'd been to Rosie the night before. She didn't get to just wipe that slate clean, even if the other things weren't true.

Rosie put her phone down and went to tip her cold coffee away. She could hear the sounds of the marina going about its day: boat engines, people calling to one another, birds singing. Through the sheets at her windows she could see it was sunny.

Going back to retrieve her phone from the table, she opened a web search and typed in 'Estate agents for commercial property'. She didn't know what to think and was just too tired to care anymore. She knew one thing for certain – she couldn't stay in a place where every memory was tainted, where she'd look and only see betrayal where she'd once seen trust. Every time she climbed into the bed she'd shared with Fergus, every time she used the towels in the bathroom, every time she walked by Nicole's shop and glanced up at the bedroom window she'd wonder – even if Nicole told her it wasn't true, she'd still wonder, and she didn't think she could stand it.

Marigold Marina hadn't ever been her dream, and it was over now.

Time to let go.

A couple of very keen-sounding agents responded to her enquiry within the hour. She made arrangements for them both to come and value the cafe the next day, which would give her time to pull herself together and for her puffy face to go down so she didn't look like a Premier League football.

Two more phoned in the afternoon and she booked them in as well. They all told her the market was buoyant and they'd have lots of buyers waiting.

Estate agents – they probably always say that, she thought, but she was hopeful for a fuss-free sale. Maybe she'd do alright out of it too. After everything, perhaps this would be Fergus's last real gift to her; not something he wanted that she'd been dragged along with, but something that might make her happy.

She thought about phoning her parents to see if she could go and stay with them, but she didn't trust her voice to hold, and she didn't want to worry them. If they thought for a second she was in any kind of distress they'd leap straight into their car and head down to the marina, and that was a complication she could do without. Besides all that, she really couldn't go home until she'd got the cafe on the market, and even then she might be required to return more than once to help the sale along.

Nicole sent another text while all this was happening and

she tried to call too – Rosie watched her mobile ring until it stopped. A few more people knocked on the door or called on the phone, but she didn't answer.

None of them were Kit. He'd have tried to contact her, wouldn't he? Especially if Tabitha had told him what she knew and that Rosie had fired her – if only just to complain about the last point.

Perhaps he felt too humiliated by her rejection. Perhaps he hated her now for leading him on. She didn't think she'd led him on, but on some level she must have done. The thought of that was almost as heart-breaking as the possibility that Fergus had been unfaithful. Kit and Tabitha had become so dear to her: they'd lit up her life so completely that she'd finally felt like Marigold Marina might be the place she belonged after all.

And then it had all collapsed with a few words.

I'm in love with you, Rosie.

She'd never forget the look on his face: forlorn hope but a reality that knew she would reject him. Yet he'd told her anyway, no matter that he knew what she'd say.

And the sad truth was, in a different time or a different place, she could have been happy with Kit. She could have loved him. Perhaps, given more time on the marina and without the shadow of her relationship with Fergus clouding everything she thought and felt, she and Kit could have had something. But she was beginning to see that Fergus had disappeared from her life and left her firmly in the lurch, and while she'd once believed his legacy was her own new life on the marina, she was now beginning to understand that wasn't it at all. The result of his constant undermining of her: of the drip, drip, dripped gaslighting that made her feel she wasn't good enough; that she'd never amount to anything without him; that nobody else would ever love her... Perhaps that was the real legacy. And she didn't think it was one she'd ever be able to get past.

CHAPTER FIFTEEN

'Rosie!' Nicole was hammering on the door. 'Rosie! I know you're in there! Open up!' More hammering. 'Look, I just want to know you're OK. I want to say I'm sorry about last night; I was drunk and I wasn't myself. Rosie, please!'

Rosie stared at the door. She'd been trying, in vain, to get her accounts up to date so she could show the agents who came to value the cafe that the business was viable as a going concern. The detritus of her efforts was spread over a table in front of her. If nothing else, it had given her something to think about other than how miserable she was. Not just miserable, but an all-consuming, soul-hollowing kind of wretchedness that she hadn't felt since Fergus's death. But at least then it had had a clear focus, a single recognisable cause. Today she felt miserable about so many things she hardly knew where to start.

'Rosie, come on! Just give me five minutes – I deserve that, don't I? Why are you sulking? Is it Kit? You can have Kit if that's what this is about. If that's what it takes, then I'll leave him alone.'

With a rush of sudden anger, Rosie leapt from her chair and flew to open the door.

Nicole was standing on the step, but she drew back uncertainly at the rage in Rosie's expression.

'You think this is some childish competition for the fittest boy in school?'

'What? No, I... Rosie, what the hell is going on? I thought this was about me and Kit last night... I only meant I know when I'm beaten.'

Rosie's anger left her like the air from a popped balloon. Did Nicole really not know what she'd done? It seemed so – or perhaps it was more a case that she didn't know that someone had spilt the beans.

'Can I come in?' Nicole asked.

Rosie wanted to say no. She didn't even want to look at Nicole right then, let alone have a conversation with her. But she set her impulses aside. If she was ever going to get answers, perhaps now was the moment to ask the questions.

She stepped back and Nicole crossed the threshold, closing the door behind her.

'Everyone is worried sick,' Nicole said. 'People are coming to me thinking I know the answers. I mean, how am I supposed to know? What's all this?' She waved a hand at the sheeting covering the windows.

'I'm closed. I didn't want anyone looking in.'

'Why?'

'What do you want, Nicole?'

Nicole suddenly seemed apprehensive. Was she hiding something after all? Was she afraid she'd been found out?

There was a heartbeat's pause. Then Rosie spoke again.

'Were you having an affair with Fergus?'

Nicole's eyes widened. 'Wow,' she said, after another pause in which the dust on the air seemed to pause too. 'Where has this come from?'

'Does it matter?'

'No.'

'No it doesn't matter or no you weren't?'

'We weren't.'

'Right...' Rosie paused, trying to hold it together, trying to be strong, trying not to sound hysterical, because that's what Fergus would have said. He'd have lied to her face and told her she was being hysterical about it, and this time Rosie knew she wasn't. This time she knew these were questions she had a right to ask. 'Then why did he die in your bedroom?'

The colour drained from Nicole's face, and in that instant Rosie knew the truth. 'Why?' she asked, struggling not to shake. 'Why Fergus? What had I ever done to you?'

'Nothing, we just... Rosie, I'm sorry... You have to understand, we didn't mean for it to happen... It was just one of those things you can't explain, an instant connection...'

'Too strong to resist for my sake? You both claimed to love me, and yet you did it still?'

'We never meant to hurt you; we did resist for a long time – when you first arrived, it was only friendship. We both knew there was a spark but...'

'So what changed?'

'Rosie, stop—'

'I need to know. What changed?'

'You left him.'

'I didn't leave him! I went home for a few days for some space because this bloody cafe project that he was so obsessed with was killing me!'

'He thought you'd left. He thought your marriage was over.'

'I never told him that!'

'It's what he told me the first time...'

'Oh God.' Rosie dropped into a chair. 'I can't believe this is happening. He told you that? But I never said to him it was over!' Then she looked over at Nicole, her gaze hardening. 'I don't believe you. I don't think he said that at all – I think you wanted him and you didn't care that he was married.' She paused, feeling sick. 'How? How could you do this? And after all that you pretended to be my friend!'

'I *was* your friend.'

'It's a bloody funny way of showing it!' Rosie exploded.

'If it's any consolation,' Nicole said quietly, 'he would never have left you for me.'

'It's not,' Rosie hissed. 'All that tells me is that not only did you go behind my back, but it was a pointless affair too! Maybe if you'd been in love I could understand it, but this...' She paused. Then: 'How many times?'

'Rosie, don't—'

'How many?' Rosie demanded.

'It was only a few times really, but it was enough—'

'How could you? You knew how much I loved him!'

'I loved him too!' Nicole cried but then paused, her voice more even again. 'I don't think he loved me, though... I was just comfort.'

'If he'd wanted comfort he could have got a stiff drink.' Rosie shook her head. 'And how could you talk about love? You can't have been together more than... we'd barely arrived at the marina! Unless you'd set your sights on him the moment we arrived... That's it, isn't it? You wanted him at the beginning. You led him on.'

'Yeah. Of course it was me,' Nicole returned savagely. 'Half the marina already thinks I'm a whore so why not join in the fun? I pinned him down and forced him – I must have done, mustn't I? It could never have been his fault. Because what man would go behind the back of perfect Rosie Ross?'

'That's low,' Rosie shot back. She was shaking now. She was furious, distressed, disgusted... she didn't know what she was. She was all those things and more; so many emotions that they almost cancelled each other out and made her numb, like a metal bar that's so hot you don't feel the pain when you first touch it.

'Not as low as you've just gone,' Nicole said. 'It takes two – don't forget that. I didn't force him to do anything.'

'You're lying.'

'Why would I lie? If anyone's lying it's you. You're lying to yourself if you think your marriage was as perfect as you keep telling everyone.'

Rosie's eyes filled with tears. 'All these months you've been lying to me! I trusted you; I told you everything. Why did you let me believe you were my friend?'

'I *am* your friend.'

'No you're not! How could you even think that? A friend wouldn't do something like that, and if it did happen, just suppose it happened by accident, a drunken fumbling mistake, they wouldn't continue to let me think Fergus had died faithful. They wouldn't have let me keep loving him; they wouldn't let me be eaten alive by guilt, thinking he'd died alone!'

'How could I have told you something like that when you were mourning?'

'How could you not?'

'Believe it or not,' Nicole said slowly, 'I care about you. I know my actions would say otherwise but I wanted to be a friend to you while you got through your loss. I felt like it might help me too. I felt in many ways we were the same, both mourning a man we had loved. The difference is all the time I had to keep mine hidden. You've no idea how hard—'

'Don't talk to me about hard!' Rosie cried. 'Don't you dare!'

'Of course, it's always worse for you, isn't it?' Nicole's voice had a sharper edge now. 'Poor Rosie. All that sympathy. All that fuss from everyone and still never happy. Even when I thought I'd try again with a man of my own, you had to go and spoil it.'

'What?'

'You knew how I felt about Kit but you couldn't leave him alone.'

'I did nothing wrong!'

'Is that why he's pining after you now and won't even look at me?'

'You *do not* get to make me the villain! This is not about Kit! You ruined my life!'

'No, you ruined mine. You could have stayed in Tyneside, you could have gone away for good after Fergus died, but no, you had to come back and martyr yourself to this stupid cafe. Bad enough I lost Fergus and I couldn't tell anyone how much that hurt, but I had to listen every day to everyone telling me what a hero you were for carrying on. Even without Fergus, you still had everything and I had nothing. I'm sick of it.' Nicole's voice rose to a shriek. 'I've had pain! I've had loss! I deserve a happy ending as much as you!'

'Well,' Rosie said coldly, 'I don't think either of us is getting one of those now. And I think it's time you left.'

'I haven't finished—'

'I have.' Rosie got up and went to the door. She opened it wide and waited. After an uncertain pause, Nicole walked through it and Rosie slammed it shut. On her way back upstairs, she passed the bin. Without another thought, she yanked off her wedding ring and threw it in.

CHAPTER SIXTEEN

The For Sale sign was up outside. People had stopped knocking. Perhaps word had got round – even worse, perhaps only fragments of the story had got round – and people had decided it was best to stay out of the way lest they get dragged into the drama. Rosie didn't know and she tried not to care, though she couldn't help but reflect on the fact that she'd been worth so little of their effort in the end.

The absence that hurt most of all was that of Kit and Tabitha. She'd peeled back the sheets at her windows from time to time and watched Kit go back and forth to and from his boat. Who was making his ham and pickle sandwiches now? It was the silly things that occurred to her. At least he was getting on with his life, she supposed; he was doing better than she was.

It had been three days since Tabitha's bombshell and Rosie hadn't set foot out of the door. She didn't want to have to explain to anyone what was going on, and she didn't want the pitying looks of those who might already know the truth. But she also realised that sooner or later she was going to have to venture out, if only to preserve what was left of her sanity. She couldn't hide forever, and hiding only added to her suffering.

No matter what anyone else thought, Rosie reckoned she'd suffered enough.

At least she'd stopped crying. It had been replaced with bitter thoughts for the way Fergus had treated her, for the injustice of the fact he'd never even had to face her and explain himself, that he'd never had to express regret for the hurt he'd caused her and others trying to defend him. He'd never had to do the one decent thing he could have done and told her he was sorry. And she was sick now of trying to defend him. This wasn't her mess, after all. It was his.

She'd been mourning Fergus for so long, mourning the life she'd had with him, but she was hit by a stark realisation now: that life had been a lie. And the knowledge had somehow made the way she'd been feeling since Fergus's death a lie. Her guilt around losing him had turned him into something he'd never been. Her flawed memory hadn't allowed him to be anything other than perfect, but that wasn't the truth.

The truth was their marriage wasn't what she'd pretended to herself at all. He hadn't been the wonderful, ideal husband who had dedicated his life to making her happy. The truth was that he'd bullied and gaslighted her and made Rosie totally reliant on him so that she would be forever his prisoner. If she'd ever shown signs of wanting to spread her wings, he'd clipped them so that she couldn't follow her own path, only his. And the biggest insult – while he'd been manipulating her, moulding her into the most precious, loyal little wife he could – he'd been having an affair with a woman who could not have been more different to that.

Which begged the question: what had Fergus really wanted of Rosie? What had he seen in her that had made him marry her?

Had he ever loved her like she'd loved him?

And the life she had now on the marina – was it really hers at all? It may not have been her choice to go there, but she'd settled and she'd been happy. Had that been an illusion too? Did the fact that she'd made her life at Marigold Marina simply prove that he could still control her, even from beyond the grave?

With that knowledge now guiding her, she could make a choice: she could bend to it, believe herself as weak and spineless as he had, or she could prove Fergus wrong: she could hold her head high and defy anyone to say it was her fault.

She could start living again. That wasn't going to be at the marina, but it didn't mean her new life couldn't start there.

But if she was going to move on, she had some old wounds to heal too. She had to start by putting things right that she had made wrong.

Rosie had thought hard about the text – she'd even written it out by hand first. It had to be right; it had to contain everything. It had to be enough for Tabitha to forgive her, because Rosie couldn't go and leave things as they were.

Tabitha,

I'm so sorry for the way I spoke to you when we were last together. Please forgive me. I'm leaving Marigold Marina soon but I'd hate to think we were parting on such bad terms. You were a true friend to me – perhaps the only genuine one I had here – and you deserve so much better than the way I treated you. I have no excuse other than that I was stupid and stubborn and didn't want to acknowledge the truth you were telling me. You were right about everything, of course. I shouldn't have doubted that. I should have listened, but I didn't want to because I was afraid to destroy all my own flawed truths, and I'd been clinging on to them for so long I couldn't let go.

I know my explanation isn't good enough and perhaps it doesn't make total sense, but I hope it helps you understand why I treated you so badly.

I will always think of you as a friend, and should you ever find yourself in Tyneside, maybe you'd even let me take you for a coffee to make up.

R x

Rosie put her phone to one side and went to run a bath. She doubted she'd get a reply but at least she felt as if she'd done what she could to rectify things by reaching out and admitting her culpability. It might ease her conscience a little. And when she'd had her bath and tidied herself, the next stop had to be Kit's barge.

What she needed to say to Kit was better said in person than in a text. Perhaps that was the very least she owed him. When she thought about what Tabitha had told her, what he'd been through, and how she'd only added to that, it squeezed Rosie's heart so that she felt she might never breathe again. He'd had pain and hardship enough for a man twice his age, and she'd simply piled on more. If nothing else, she had to make him see he'd never been the problem.

After her bath, Rosie felt calmer and clearer. Out of habit, she went to check her phone. To her surprise, there was a message from Tabitha.

I'm so glad you reached out. I'm not angry. I didn't contact you because I thought you needed space. Kit agreed. We knew you'd come round. I saw the cafe was up for sale. It's a shame but I get why. Don't worry about me. I've applied to univer-

sity. I want to go to Warwick so I won't be too far away from Mum and I'll be able to keep an eye on her.

I will always be your friend, Rosie, and I'll be sad to see you leave, but I get that too. I'm sorry it didn't work out for you here.

x

Rosie started to cry and she didn't know whether it was down to sorrow or relief. Either way, it was annoying. She'd done enough sobbing over the week and she'd just pulled herself together. How was she supposed to go out and face the world if every little thing set her off?

She sniffed hard and locked her phone. It was so good to know that Tabitha didn't hate her and even better to know she'd taken the opportunity to get her own life back on track too. It had been harder for her to come home after her disastrous relationship than she'd let on, Rosie was sure about that. It was good to see things working out for someone who deserved it, as Tabitha did.

Rosie quickly got dressed. As she slipped quietly out of the back door of the cafe, along the little alleyway that ran down the side of the building that was shaded by overhanging trees, she felt a bit ridiculous, like some fugitive from a cheesy movie. That was the sensible part of her brain working – at least it meant all wasn't totally lost in that regard. But she also wanted to avoid awkward encounters with anyone else: she wasn't ready to explain her actions to the likes of Grant yet. So she hurried along the riverbank anyway, hoping everyone would be too busy closing up to notice her.

Through the round windows of his boat, Rosie could see Kit reading a book. The barge was empty of customers, but it had never exactly been overrun anyway. She leant across, the gap between the bank and the boat slightly unnerving her, and tapped lightly on the window.

His head shot up. 'Rosie?' A second later he was on deck. 'I didn't expect... How are you? What's happening with the cafe? Tabitha messaged me; she said you were leaving.'

'Can I come in for a minute?' Rosie asked, fighting every instinct that wanted her to get away from his boat rather than get on it. This was bigger than her fear of the water and she needed to see it through. 'I'd rather not talk about it all out here.'

'God, yes! Of course!' He offered her a hand to help her climb aboard. The boat shifted beneath her, but he held her steady. His hand was warm and it made her feel oddly safe. Oddly at home too, just like it had done when he'd taken it so unconsciously at the party.

Below deck he cleared away the remains of a supermarket sandwich from a small table and beckoned her to sit on a long seat that ran along one of the walls.

'Cheese?' Rosie lifted an eyebrow.

He waved the packet at her. 'Afraid so. Nobody makes ham and pickle like you, so what's the use in trying?'

She gave a small smile.

'Listen...'

They both spoke at once.

'Please,' Rosie said. 'You first.'

'I just wanted to say I'm sorry for what I said to you at Edith's party.'

'You shouldn't be. It was my fault; I should have made myself clearer.'

'Right. The thing is, I think you did. I was just... I hoped...' He let out a sigh.

'I should be apologising,' she said. 'I shouldn't have left it the way I did.'

'You did nothing wrong. I made things awkward between us and now you're leaving.'

'Kit...' she said gently. 'You bear no blame whatsoever for my decision to go home. You're probably the only person who bears no blame at all. You've been nothing but good and kind and supportive. I'm lucky to' – she fought back tears and continued – 'I've been so lucky to know you.'

'But I've been useless,' he said helplessly. 'Tabitha told me what happened and I didn't know what to do for the best. I wanted to do or say something, but nothing seemed right. In the end, Tabitha and I talked it over and we decided to give you space, but I'm still not sure we did the right thing – we should have done something rather than nothing. If we had, you might not be leaving now.'

'Honestly, you would have had to put a grenade through my letterbox to get me out.'

He gave a small smile. 'So what changed?'

'I had a lot of time to think and I realised I was wrecking my life for a man who wasn't worth it.'

'I know you loved him, though.'

'I did, but I'm starting to see who he truly was. I think maybe in a few months I won't remember why I loved him at all.'

'You think maybe you'd be able to love someone else?'

'Kit—'

'Sorry – forget it. That was crass.'

'That was honest, which I'm beginning to see is more than Fergus ever was. Kit... I wish we'd met in different circumstances.'

'Circumstances don't change who we are.'

'Don't they?'

'I'm still me and you're still you and we'd still be good together, wherever that was.'

Rosie twisted her fingers together. 'Maybe circumstances don't change who we are, but maybe they change what we can give of ourselves.'

He nodded slowly. 'I suppose I get that. So the cafe's up for sale?'

'Yes.'

'And that's it? End of the line?'

'Looks like it. I know it's weak but I just can't stay there, not now I know what was going on under my nose and with Nicole living just across the way. You understand, don't you?'

He gave a brief nod. 'Well,' he said slowly, 'it's been good. Mostly. Sometimes.'

She smiled ruefully. 'It was always good when you were around.'

'Not good enough for you to change your mind though, and stay. And I'm not saying that just because Tabitha wants her job back.'

'She'll be off to university and she'll forget all about her days in the cafe.'

'She's going to need a job when she's home on holiday.'

'Actually, she ought to talk to Layla and Tom at the farm shop about that. I think they'd very much like to have her.'

'Right... I'll tell her.'

'Thanks.'

They were silent for a moment. Rosie looked down and realised her fingers were still knotted together, the knuckles white. She tried to steady her breathing. Though she hadn't expected this conversation to be easy, she had never seen it being so hard either. She'd wanted to set the record straight but now she almost wished she hadn't come. She wished she'd never seen this look on Kit's face, like a man facing the firing squad, stoically waiting for the inevitable and knowing that it was near. She wished she didn't have to be the cause of that.

'Do you want... I don't know, a drink or anything?' he asked. 'I'm in a mess but I have a kettle—'

'I'd better not. I just wanted to leave things in a better place, you know? I didn't want to take off and leave things as they were.'

'So you're going soon? What about the cafe?'

'It can stay closed for now. I'll be coming when I'm needed, but the estate agent says she can show buyers around for me so I don't really need to be here.'

'Where are you going?'

'I'll stay with my parents for a while and look for somewhere to live. Not exactly where I imagined I'd be at thirty but, hey, I didn't think I'd be a lot of things that I am now.'

'Will you come to say goodbye before you go?'

'Probably not. I'd rather just slip away while nobody is looking.'

He tried to smile, but Rosie could see right through it. 'People around here aren't very good at letting you do that. Don't let Grant get wind – he'll be trying to throw you a leaving party.'

'Which is why I'm just going to go. In all seriousness, it's not like anyone will notice I've gone.'

'I will.'

'Yeah, of course. You'll be back to supermarket sandwiches.'

'And I'll miss a face that lights up my world every time I see it.'

Rosie's eyes filled with tears again. 'Don't... Kit, please. Don't make this harder than it is.'

He leant across and grabbed her hand. 'If it's hard then you know in your heart you shouldn't be doing it. If it's hard, it's not what you want.'

'Of course it isn't,' she said, tears spilling out as she shrugged off his grip. 'But it's what I've got to do and I've made up my mind. I'm leaving.'

'We can do long distance...' he said hopefully.

'No, we can't. Kit, I just need time. And I can't honestly say I will ever want to come back to the marina, and would you want to move hundreds of miles to Newcastle?'

'I don't know, I have—'

'Responsibilities here, I know. People who need you. I'd

never ask you to put anything we might have ahead of those. It's best if we draw a line under things. Someone who is way better for you than me will come along, someone who wants to be part of your life here and won't ask you to move away from the business you've just got started and a family who need you.'

'What about the rest of your life? What are you going to do now?'

Rosie dragged a sleeve across her eyes and stood to leave. 'I really wish I knew. Goodbye, Kit. Take care of yourself.'

'I'm not saying it back,' he said defiantly. 'You're going to be back, I know it.'

'Fine, don't. It doesn't matter. It only takes one of us to say it to make it final.'

CHAPTER SEVENTEEN

The train was full and it was too warm. Rosie watched the Warwickshire countryside slip by as she settled down for the long journey home. She had two changes and a trek across central Birmingham from one station to another to contend with, but it was still better than driving because the way she felt these days, she didn't think her concentration would hold for endless stretches of motorway.

Leaning her head against the glass of the window she closed her eyes. She ought to have been feeling better with every mile that came between her and Marigold Marina, looking forward to letting her parents take care of her for a while, but she wasn't.

She hadn't told them everything when she'd called to warn them she was coming back. In fact, she'd told them very little. The details – some of them – would wait until she saw them face to face. Some details she might never be able to share with them. She hadn't told them the cafe was up for sale or that Fergus had, in fact, been a total shit and was still ruining her life even now. As far as they were concerned, she was home for a visit and Tabitha was looking after Marigold Cafe for her.

Rosie owed it to them to come clean at some point, she

knew that, but she had to get better first, so she could do it without making them suffer too.

The man in the seat across from her smiled pleasantly as she opened her eyes. 'Going far?'

'Birmingham,' she said.

'Oh, I'm going to Birmingham too.'

'It's not where I'm actually heading, though,' Rosie said.

'Right. Where's that then?' he asked cheerfully.

'Newcastle.'

'Oooh, that's a long way.'

'Yes.'

'How long will it take you?'

'About five hours with changes.'

'You'll be bored.'

'I expect so.'

'Might go a bit quicker with a chat, eh?'

Rosie wanted to say, *No, it wouldn't. It'll go quicker if you'd leave me alone and let me wallow.*

But he was old and seemed to be on his own and perhaps he didn't get much opportunity to talk. So she straightened up and tried to look interested. It was only an hour to Birmingham after all. Surely she could spare this man an hour of her time?

'I'm sure it would.' She smiled. 'Is Birmingham home for you?'

He nodded. 'I've been away for a long time, though.'

'You've been living somewhere else then?'

'Yes. I'm going back after thirty-three years and living in Stratford-upon-Avon all that time.'

'Wow! What's taking you back?'

'My wife passed recently. I'm going to stay with my eldest for a while. Until I can get sorted; she didn't want me to be alone.'

'I'm so sorry to hear that, but it's good your eldest is looking out for you. Were you married for a long time?'

'Sixty years.'

'That's definitely a long time!'

'It goes by in the blink of an eye. One minute you're a teenager, the next you look like this...' He gestured to himself and laughed. 'My Helen was the first girl I ever kissed and I never kissed another.'

'You must have had a lot of happy times together. That's something.'

'We fought like cat and dog,' he said with a chuckle. 'I wanted one thing and she wanted another and it was never the same thing. But we made it work somehow. Eventually we'd sit down and we'd work out a compromise; we wouldn't always get what we wanted, but we'd get something we could both be happy with.'

'That sounds a lot like a happy marriage to me.'

'Oh, I had a wonderful sixty years. Honestly, I was the luckiest man on earth. She was such a catch; I'd have probably given her whatever she wanted in the end. I think she knew that too, but she never forced it. She always stopped and listened, even when she thought I was wrong.'

'You must miss her a lot.'

The man nodded. 'I feel like half of my heart has been cut out. I can't describe the pain. We knew it was coming – she'd been ill for a long time – but that doesn't make it any easier, you know.'

'I'm sure it doesn't.'

'What about you? A sweetheart in Newcastle for you?'

'No, it's just me on my own.'

'Aw, a pretty girl like you – what a crying shame. Oh!' He put a hand over his mouth. 'I'm not supposed to say things like that nowadays, am I? It's not PC to tell a girl she's pretty. I am sorry.'

Rosie couldn't help but laugh gently: he looked genuinely mortified. 'It's alright, I don't mind at all.'

'Helen – my wife – she'd be giving me a slap to shut me up if she were here now.'

'I'm glad to hear she kept you in line.'

'She did. I'm lost without her, you know.'

Rosie could have told him about Fergus, how she'd been lost without him for a long time too, and perhaps a month ago she would have done. But a month ago she would have had no need to be on this train, leaving behind a life in tatters, and that was down to him.

'What's your name?' he asked. 'If that's not an impertinent question.'

'Of course not. I'm Rosie.'

'That's an old name. There used to be a Rosie at my Sunday school class. She was as big as a whale and she used to trap your fingers in the desk when she walked past. You didn't dare say anything about her taking up all the space on the pew during service.'

Rosie laughed again. 'She sounds like a legend.'

'She wasn't nice like you. I'm Wilf.'

'Pleased to meet you, Wilf.'

'So you've been visiting, have you?'

'Working actually. I've been running a little cafe by the river. Marigold Marina. Do you know it?'

He shook his head pensively, as if giving the matter a great deal of consideration. 'Can't say that I do.'

'Ah, well, I suppose you can't know everywhere. It's a lovely spot. If you ever get the chance to visit you should.'

'I will. So you've finished that now? Or are you just taking a holiday?'

'The cafe has closed down now. I'm off home like you.'

'So Newcastle is where you were born? I thought your accent was a bit Geordie.'

'Wye aye, man.'

He gave her a broad smile. 'Oh, that is funny. It makes you sound completely different.'

'Yes, I try to posh it up a bit when I'm away from home, otherwise no one can understand a word I'm saying.'

'Oh, I know, it's terrible. You know those two men off the telly... and that footballer...? They might as well be speaking Swahili for all I can understand them.'

'I think there must be a course somewhere to train as a Geordie interpreter,' she said, and he chuckled.

'There should be. That could be your new job.'

'It could be.'

'Have you got another job to go to, now that you've lost your job at the cafe?'

'Not yet.'

'I'm sure you'll find one soon; I bet there are loads of cafes up there in Geordieland.'

'I'm sure there are.'

And there would be – cafes on every street corner, but they wouldn't be her pretty little cafe on Marigold Marina with its primrose walls and wooden beams across the ceiling and picture-perfect views of the river. She'd left it behind for good reason, and her good memories were now tainted with bad ones and the knowledge of Fergus's betrayal there, but she'd still miss it and the community who lived there.

'Helen worked in a cafe when I first met her. She washed pots on a Saturday. Always smelt like frying oil when I went to pick her up at closing. I didn't mind – I used to sniff her coat and tell her it made me feel hungry. She used to bring me left-overs when they had them, wrapped up on a plate.'

'That's so sweet. What year would that have been?'

'Nineteen sixty-one.'

'Blimey – I don't think my mum and dad were born then! Actually, maybe my dad was, but he would have been little.'

'Oh, I know I'm an old man. I can't pretend I'm not. At my age, no amount of hair dye will hide it.'

'You're not a day over forty, right?'

'Ha ha, you're not fooling anyone, but good on you for trying. I'm an old fella and I've made my peace with it now. Not like you. I have to admit I envy you. You've got your whole life ahead of you. All those things to look forward to.'

'It must be nice to have them to look back on too.'

'I wouldn't change a single second of it. Wouldn't do any of it differently.'

'Even the bad times?'

'Even the bad times. It all fits together like a puzzle, doesn't it? Bad times can make good times and good times can turn into bad ones. But you can't have one without the other.'

'That's very true. And very wise.'

'That's the first time I've been called wise.'

Rosie smiled. 'Well, I'm surprised at that because I think you are. Is your daughter or son meeting you at the station?'

'My daughter Sarah is meeting me. Not sure if Charlie will be with her.'

'Who's Charlie?'

'My grandson. He's training to be a doctor, you know.'

'Wow, he must be clever.'

'He is.'

'Wise, like his granddad.'

Wilf grinned, and he was so obviously full of pride for his grandson it was a joy to see.

'Do you have just the one grandchild?' Rosie asked.

As he began to tell her about the others – their names, how old they were, what they did, who they took after – Rosie listened. She was totally engrossed in the little snapshot of his world he was creating for her. It was so strange how a complete stranger like that was making her feel lighter and happier than she had in months. Life didn't have to be all doom and gloom and the bad times didn't have to define you – Wilf was proof of that.

Forty minutes later, the train was pulling into Moor Street station. Rosie had barely noticed that it was approaching. The journey had flown by, and she and Wilf had hardly drawn breath as they'd chatted. She'd enjoyed every minute of their conversation.

The train halted, and after giving other passengers a moment to leave, Rosie helped Wilf with his suitcase before retrieving her own, and they walked down the platform together. At the barriers, a woman and a young man waved at Wilf.

'Sarah and Charlie?' Rosie asked.

'Yes, that's them. Right on time.'

He seemed excited to see them, and they seemed very pleased to see him, waving madly even though they were some distance away still. Rosie wasn't sure anyone had ever been that excited to see her – it must have been nice.

'Thank you,' he said, turning to Rosie.

'I didn't do anything.'

'You helped me with the suitcase.'

'Oh right. That was no big deal. Thanks for keeping me entertained. It could have been a dull journey, right?'

Wilf smiled. 'Right. You'll be alright for New Street, won't you? You know how to find it?'

'I don't think it's far, and my phone has maps so I should be OK.'

'Watch your step then, won't you? Have a safe journey to Newcastle.'

'I will. Bye, Wilf.'

'Bye, Rosie.' He waved once and then went to meet his daughter and grandson, who hugged and fussed over him.

Rosie left them to it and went to find the exit. Was that in her future somewhere? she wondered. This morning it had looked so bleak. It was funny how a random conversation with a stranger could give a whole new perspective. For the first time since she'd dashed away from Edith's party, Rosie had hope.

Perhaps everything was going to be alright after all.

Rosie had an open ticket, and she was in an unfamiliar city with no particular deadline to meet. Since her chat with Wilf, she'd felt cheerful, so she decided not to go straight to New Street station, but to spend an hour or two exploring Birmingham. Maybe she'd indulge in a little shopping. It had been a while since she'd treated herself to new clothes. She could catch a later train easily enough, and her parents wouldn't mind if she phoned ahead to warn them to expect her that evening instead of earlier in the day.

She discovered that it was far quicker to walk to the Bull-ring – the main shopping area – than to wait for a bus. As the weather was fine – a little overcast but warm – the walk was pleasant enough. She was used to big cities as her home city was large by most standards, but having spent the last few months mainly on the sleepy marina, the bustle was a shock to her system. She made the most of it though, losing herself in the sights and sounds.

The city centre was busy. There were families and groups of friends shopping and eating in pavement cafes. Rosie walked along, suitcase trundling behind her. It was a refreshing change to simply follow her natural curiosity to wherever that might lead. She walked the shopping streets for a while and went into one or two interesting stores, and then went to Centenary Square and sat eating a sandwich in the sunshine. In those few short hours away from Marigold Marina, it was like none of it had ever happened. Here, where nobody knew her, she was just a girl, sitting on a wall by the fountain, eating a sandwich. The ultimate clean slate. As she watched a couple kiss and cuddle on a nearby bench, she realised that for the first time she didn't feel the need to cry, wishing it was her and Fergus.

There would always be a place in her heart for Fergus and she couldn't deny that. She couldn't change it, no matter what she discovered he'd done, but did she still feel lost without him? She felt lost, but perhaps there were different reasons for that. She felt lost leaving Marigold Marina behind. It had become her life, though that would have to be another thing she left in her past, with Fergus.

But she had hope.

If she could feel like this, the way she felt cleansed of it all today, then maybe there was a light at the end of her tunnel.

The day was fading as the train pulled into Rosie's last stop. By now, she was excited to see her parents, despite the reasons she'd come.

Her dad was waiting for her at the end of the platform as she dragged her suitcase and shopping bags from the train. He looked as though he needed a haircut. Rosie could imagine her mum nagging him and him just ignoring her. He wouldn't get it done until he could barely see through his fringe, because he was fiercely proud of the fact he still had a decent mop and admitted he was a little vain about it too. He had his signature jeans and leather jacket on too, looking like James Dean might have done in his twilight years.

He broke into a broad smile as she walked towards him. 'Look at you!' he said. 'Have you left anything in Birmingham for anyone else to buy? We do have shops in Newcastle, you know.'

'I know – I got carried away.'

'Well, after the year you've had, pet, nobody is going to blame you for that.'

Rosie thought that he had no idea and also reminded herself that there were details he and her mum didn't need to know. At least not right away. When the time was right she'd tell them the rest.

'Let me take some of those,' he said, reaching for a cluster of bags.

'Thanks, Dad. I can manage the case.'

'Good journey?'

'It was nice actually. For some of it I had a chat with an old man.'

'Oh dear.'

'He was interesting. Just lost his wife and was moving in with one of his children. I felt a bit sorry for him.'

'That's not surprising, considering it's not so different from your own situation.'

'It's way different from mine.'

'Is it?' her dad said vaguely, but by the time she'd thought of a response, they'd reached the car. He popped the lock and helped her get the suitcase into the boot.

'Your mam's got shepherd's pie on,' he said.

'Oh, I hope me being home later hasn't ruined her plans,' Rosie said as she got into the passenger seat. 'I would have come home sooner if she'd told me that.'

'Don't worry about it, pet. A minute in the microwave will sort it out.' He got in beside her and fastened his seat belt before smiling warmly. 'It's good to see you; we've missed you.'

'I've missed you too, Dad,' Rosie said. 'It's good to be home.'

Home – or at least, home for her parents – was a tiny new-build on a small, new estate on the outskirts of Newcastle. It wasn't special or grand and had no discernible quirks or characteristics, but it was clean and warm and welcoming, and Rosie was glad to see it as her dad pulled onto the drive.

Her mum came to the front door as they were getting her stuff from the boot. 'You're here!' she cried, pulling Rosie into a hug. She could smell her mum's favourite Yves Saint Laurent perfume, one she'd been wearing since Rosie was a kid. 'Come in, come in... I bet you're shattered! It's a long day travelling, isn't it?'

Rosie went to take her suitcase, but her dad shook his head. 'Go in, pet. I'll see to this.'

'Thanks, Dad.'

'I hope you're hungry,' her mum said.

'For your shepherd's pie I'd make myself hungry.'

Her mum beamed at her. 'I'll have to warm it up.'

'That's OK. I can dump my stuff upstairs while you do that.'

'Spare room's all made up. I've aired the bedding and opened the windows to freshen it up, but you can close them again if it's starting to feel chilly in there.'

'I will.'

Her dad had already disappeared up the stairs with her case, leaving Rosie to collect her shopping bags and follow him.

The spare room had been her bedroom growing up, but when she'd moved out to marry Fergus, her parents had painted it in a biscuity colour and recarpeted in a soft peach, and now it looked more like a hotel suite than her old room. She sort of wished they hadn't been so keen to modernise it now, but she was hardly going to complain. Just to be in their house, in their company, where she felt safe and loved, was enough. If ever there was a place to heal, it was here. Nicole – the scheming, cheating, so-called friend – had been right about that much: it would have been better for everyone if Rosie had stayed there after Fergus's death rather than martyring herself to that damn cafe of his – Rosie most of all. She could have given herself time to grieve with the support of her family, to move on and start again with a life she wanted, not the one Fergus had cajoled her into.

'Got everything you need?' her dad asked as she dumped her bags onto the bed.

'Yep. I'll be down in a minute.'

'Righto, don't be too long. Your pie will get cold again.'

He left, and Rosie rummaged through her shopping. She'd bought her dad a T-shirt from a vintage store that she just knew he'd love, and her mum a bottle of the perfume she always wore. They were small, token gifts and could never express just how much Rosie appreciated them always being there for her, but she hoped they'd go some way towards it.

After her meal and a warm drink, Rosie felt content and sleepy. She was sitting on the sofa while her parents occupied the armchairs of their three-piece suite. Dad had his T-shirt on – Rosie had giggled at the fact he'd gone to get changed the minute she'd presented it to him, just like a toddler who'd been given a jumper with his favourite cartoon character on for Christmas. Mum had loved her gift too, though Rosie had apologised that it wasn't quite as inspired. Her mum had told her not to think of that at all, that she needed another bottle and it was a lovely thought.

Although she was about ready for bed, Rosie didn't want to leave their company. She hadn't been in a rush to get home during the day, but now she was there, she was glad to be, and she wished she'd come home earlier. There was so much she wanted to say, so much she needed to get off her chest – things her parents deserved to know. But it was late now and it would have to wait. She needed to choose a moment where they could take all the time they needed to discuss everything properly, where she could give the answers to their inevitable questions without having to rush.

She wasn't going to tell them about Fergus's affair – that hadn't changed; she'd never intended to tell them about that, because they'd somehow blame themselves that their attempts to warn her off hadn't been more successful, no matter what she said. But she did need to tell them about her decision to leave Marigold Marina for good. It wasn't that she worried they'd disapprove – on the contrary, they'd probably be thrilled to get her back – but they'd want to know why, and that was the tricky part. Tomorrow, she'd have to start looking for a job and somewhere to live too, and those things were going to take plenty of her time. At least there wouldn't be a spare moment to dwell on the recent months, and definitely no time to feel sorry for herself, and that was a good thing.

It was Glenda who broke the comfortable silence. 'I'm going to stack the dishwasher and then I'm afraid I'm going to have to go to bed – I'm dead on my feet here.'

'That's fine, Mum. I was thinking about it anyway as well.'

Glenda came over to kiss her on the forehead. 'It's lovely to see you. It seems a long time since my little girl was curled up on that couch. How long did you say you were staying? Not that I mind – I'm just asking so I know what to buy when I go shopping tomorrow.'

'Um... I'm not sure yet. Maybe a week.'

'Will that girl of yours at the cafe mind not knowing when you're due back?'

'The cafe's fine, Mum,' Rosie said carefully. 'You don't need to worry about it – I'm not.'

'Well,' Glenda said, straightening up, 'I'm sure you've got it all under control.'

If only, Rosie thought. But perhaps she was getting there.

CHAPTER EIGHTEEN

Rosie had unpacked her bags quickly, dumping her clothes into empty drawers with barely a thought for folding. And then, stuffed at the bottom of her suitcase, she'd found the copy of *My Family and Other Animals* that Kit had given to her the day they'd had their impromptu tea in the cafe after closing time.

Despite telling herself she was going to leave Marigold Marina behind her, Rosie hadn't quite been able to let go of everyone and everything that had been such a huge part of her life there. With a fond smile but melancholy heart, she ran a hand over the cover before snuggling into bed and starting to read.

She must have fallen asleep soon afterwards. The next thing she knew it was morning, and she'd been woken by a lorry outside sounding its horn. Looking at the clock, she saw it had just gone ten. She couldn't remember if she'd dreamt or not, but she'd woken with Kit on her mind.

Rosie supposed it was because she'd fallen asleep reading his book and decided not to try and make any more sense of it than that. It would take a while for the people of Marigold Marina to leave her thoughts, especially the ones who had meant so much to her. But that was her old life, a past version of Rosie Ross who had no place in the new world she was trying to create for herself.

She'd come back to Newcastle to get away from all that, and she intended to.

Rosie's dad had left early for work so it was just Rosie and her mum in the house having breakfast. Her mum's job at the local hospital had her doing shifts and she wasn't due in for another four hours. That was four hours for Rosie to try and offer some explanation for the upheaval in her life. Her dad wasn't there, but it was a decent window of time and Rosie decided to take advantage of it. Besides, perhaps it was better to deal with them one at a time. Her mum had always been the most practical, the most pragmatic of the two, and Rosie decided she might be a good ally when it came to telling her dad, who would find it more difficult to take in.

Her mum brought a plate of toast to the dining table and set it down. Rosie already had a mug of strong tea in front of her. Outside, a light rain troubled the windows. It was strange to be able to hear so much traffic noise from the house after living at the quiet marina for so long.

'I'm starving,' Rosie said, reaching for a piece.

'You look as if you've lost weight.'

'All that running up and down,' Rosie said neutrally. 'It's bound to drop off.'

'As long as that's all it is.'

'Of course. Running a cafe is hectic.'

'You've taken a lot on. How's your waitress getting on? Are you still happy with her? What about the first lady who couldn't start? Have you heard from her?'

Rosie paused, a slice of toast halfway to her mouth.

Letitia!

In all the drama she hadn't even thought to call her. She'd have to be told about the cafe closing and that her job wasn't going to be there after all. Rosie stifled a groan. That might possibly be the worst conversation she was going to have so far. Poor Letitia. She'd had absolutely nothing to do with any of the drama that had gone on since the cafe's opening, and yet she was probably going to come out of it worse than anyone. She hadn't even done one shift at the cafe and now had already lost the job, all on top of her current woes.

Rosie pushed the problem to one side. She would fill her mum in on developments now and speak to Letitia later to explain. It wasn't a call she was looking forward to, but it would be better to hear it from Rosie herself than for someone at the marina to tell her the cafe was on the market.

'Letitia hasn't had the all-clear from her doctor yet,' Rosie said. 'Tabitha has been brilliant. I'll be sad to lose her.'

'Couldn't you keep them both on?'

'Not really.'

'The cafe must be so much work for you. I'm sure it would help to have extra hands.'

'I know, but I can't.'

'I suppose it must be about money. Ignore me – I don't know the first thing about running a business... I'm sure you're doing what's right, it's just... well, we worry that you've taken so much on. It's a parent thing; I know you're doing brilliantly down there – of course you are.'

Rosie put down her toast. She couldn't put this off any longer. 'Mum... I've put the cafe on the market. I'm selling up.'

Glenda stared at her. 'Selling it? But you just...what's happened? Is it money trouble? What are you going to do instead? Have you got a job there?'

'It's not money trouble.' Rosie shrugged. 'I gave it a go and it wasn't for me. I thought I might come back home and get a job here instead. I feel like this is where I need to be now.'

'Not that I'm going to complain, but this is all very sudden. I thought you were determined to carry on with that business. You said it was—'

'For Fergus. I know. But there's no use in pretending that it was ever a good idea because it wasn't. If ever there was a stupid reason to do something, it was that. I mean, Mum, you said it to me yourself on more than one occasion. And you know Fergus and I weren't exactly in a good place at the end...'

Rosie had never admitted that to anyone at Marigold Marina. It was a secret between her and her mum. But when Rosie had come home all those months ago, desperately unhappy that fateful weekend when her world had turned upside down, she'd been having doubts about her marriage and the only person she'd felt able to share them with was her mum. They'd kept it between them, as Rosie had asked; as far as she knew, Glenda had never told her husband. And as Fergus had died soon after, it hadn't been a situation either Rosie or her mum had felt the need to address further, because doing so would only have caused more pain.

As far as Rosie knew, her dad was still blissfully unaware. Maybe it would prove to be impossible but, for now, that was the way Rosie wanted things to stay.

Perhaps she would have gone back and worked things out with Fergus and perhaps their marriage would have been successful. Or perhaps she would have left him after all and have been divorced by now. There was no way to know, because that same weekend he'd died and everything had changed. All the variables had changed too, and the outcomes that once seemed likely had become impossible. There was no marriage to save or discard, there was just Rosie, the thirty-year-old widow, stricken with guilt over the thoughts she'd been having as he'd been fighting for his life, hundreds of miles away.

'You tried to tell me, Mum. I know now that you were trying to tell me without looking as if you were interfering, out of respect for me as the adult and not the child I once was, but I made the stupid decision of a child. I shouldn't have gone back — No – don't blame yourself,' she added as Glenda opened her mouth to speak. 'I can't hold you responsible for my mistakes, but maybe it wouldn't have been so bad if you'd interfered after all.'

'You wouldn't have listened to me.'

'You're right, I wouldn't. I really don't want you to blame yourself, Mum. The mistake is already made and it's all mine. All I can do now is put it right.'

Her mum poured some fresh tea from the pot into her own cup and then refilled Rosie's. 'And this is the answer? Selling a business that took so much blood, sweat and tears to get going – not to mention the money?'

'I'm hopeful it will make more money than I spent on it. It'll have to, because it represents most of the money Fergus left me.'

Her mother nodded then opened her mouth before closing it again. But then she seemed to come to a decision and spoke: 'Rosie, you know that your dad and I would be thrilled to have you living close to us again, but are you sure this isn't a bit of a knee-jerk reaction? You've been so adamant that the cafe was what you wanted up until now. This seems so sudden. Even last week we spoke to you on the phone and you never even hinted at it. Has something happened to change your mind?'

'No.' Rosie swallowed the lie. 'I just changed it. I suppose I'm tired – I've got nothing left in me to give. It's harder than I imagined it would be; it's stressful, heavy work, and it never stops. I knew it would be hard, but I didn't appreciate how relentless it would be until it was open. There's just me, keeping it all afloat, and that's scary too. I don't think I'm cut out to be a boss. I think I'm better off as an employee rather than an employer.'

Her mum was silent as she sipped at her tea thoughtfully. Rosie wondered what was going through her mind. Did she buy Rosie's story? Partly it was true – she hadn't realised just how difficult the reality of her life running the cafe would be; how all-consuming the day to day would become.

But, of course, that was only half the tale.

'You know we'll support you any way we can, whatever you decide to do,' her mum said finally.

'Thanks, Mum.'

'Does this mean you might be staying with us longer than a week?'

Rosie gave a sheepish smile. 'Would that be OK?'

'You know it would. I'd better pick up some extra teabags.'

'You know me so well,' Rosie said, biting into her toast.

Glenda took a deep breath, turning her gaze to the window for a moment. 'What are your plans for today?' she asked finally.

'I suppose I'd better start looking for a job and a place to live – I know I can stay with you for a while longer, but I can't stay forever. I need to arrange to get all my stuff here from the cafe too. Actually, there's plenty to keep me busy over the next few weeks.'

'So no time for a trip out with your old mum? I booked tomorrow off because you were coming home – thought we might go out together for the day. But things have changed after what you told me and I understand if you'd rather not have the distraction—'

'No, I'd actually like the distraction!' Rosie smiled warmly at her mum. 'It sounds lovely. And I guess I don't have to start my job hunt right away. I mean, when you really think about it, I've got the rest of my life to sort all this out, haven't I?'

Her mum had suggested a few trips they could take, including taking the metro out to the seaside or heading into the city centre to shop. As neither had access to a car because Rosie's dad had taken the only car to work, it would have to be something they could reach by public transport.

Rosie woke that morning feeling more relaxed than she had in months and a little lazy too, and in the end, they decided they'd mooch around at the quayside in the shadow of the Tyne Bridge and take a leisurely lunch.

These were the sorts of days they'd put aside regularly to catch up on when Rosie had first married Fergus and they'd moved into their little house close to her mum and dad. Rosie would meet her mum somewhere pretty – often the quayside – and they'd eat and drink and generally enjoy each other's company. The conversations were meandering and silly and mostly idle chit-chat, but they meant the world to Rosie. Their days together became less and less frequent as the months and years went by, however – Rosie had worked long hours as a secretary, while renovations on her and Fergus's house had become more involved. Fergus had complained more and more about Rosie being missing when he wanted her, and then he'd started dragging her into hare-brained plans or schemes that never ended up working out: there was the dog kennels up on the Northumberland coast, the stables in Norfolk, the parcel of farmland in Scotland he was determined to buy... There had always been some crazy dream; their perfect life was always waiting around the corner.

He never saw any of them through, however. There would be some unforeseen problem, some skill or permit he hadn't realised he needed to have, some unexpected curveball. Often they wasted money on the journey to that abrupt end, but it never bothered Fergus. 'There's always more where that came from,' he'd say, and before Rosie had had time to take a breath, there'd be a new plan on the table.

Then, by some fluke, before she'd barely realised what was happening, they'd signed the papers for the cafe at Marigold Marina. Rosie was in shock for some time after that, because a large part of her had assumed it would never happen, just like his other plans.

All of which meant she'd missed spending this kind of time with her mum, and she was looking forward to it.

Today, they both took a well-earned lie-in and then headed out to the quay mid-morning. The day was cool, with a stiff breeze, but it was bright, and when the sun peeked from behind a cloud it felt like gold on Rosie's skin. The quayside was busy, but they managed to get a table at one of their old favourites: an Italian with great views of the broad expanse of the river as it swept a path to the sea and the bridge, which stood solid and dependable above it.

Rosie was gratified to see that little had changed there and that walking into the restaurant took her right back to the days when life had been no more complicated than whether they'd be able to beat the lunchtime rush to get seated.

A young man came to their table to take the drinks order. Rosie asked for a gin and her mum requested a glass of Prosecco before changing her mind and ordering half a bottle.

'Might as well take advantage of going home on the bus,' she said in answer to Rosie's grin.

The young man went away again, but not without a parting smile at Rosie that lasted just a bit too long.

'I think he's taken a fancy to you,' her mum whispered.

Rosie looked again. It was flattering and he was good-looking, but she felt nothing. 'It's too soon to think about that, Mum. And he's got to be, what, eighteen?'

'Oh, I know all that, but I thought it might bolster you a bit to know. After all, it's nice to be appreciated, isn't it?'

'I suppose it is.'

'And it has been... well, it'll soon be a year. And you said yourself that you and Fergus were—'

'Don't ruin our lunch, Mum. I know what I said about Fergus but that doesn't make his loss any easier. In fact, it almost makes it worse. I still loved him; we just... well, we were just in a sticky spot, that's all.'

Glenda poured some water from a carafe on the table. 'Rosie, I know you don't want to, but I really think we ought to talk about it.'

'What good will it do?'

'I think it will do a lot of good actually. Sometimes you need to say things out loud to force yourself to confront them.'

Rosie frowned slightly as she rubbed a water mark from a knife. Since running the cafe, she noticed things like that a lot more than she used to. 'You think I have things I need to confront?'

'I do.'

'Like what?'

'Like the reason you've suddenly decided to sell the cafe you worked for months to get going. And why you're so hung up on being faithful to Fergus when you said yourself your marriage was almost over.'

'It wasn't over; it was on the rocks – there's a difference.'

'That's not how I remember it.'

Rosie let out a sigh. 'I thought we'd come out to have a nice, relaxed lunch and a wander. Do we have to do this now?'

'No, but I think we have to do it at some point.'

'There's honestly nothing to talk about.'

Her mum looked unconvinced, but Rosie was spared any further comment by the return of the waiter with their drinks. He smiled right at Rosie again as he placed hers down in front of her.

'That's a nice gin,' he said. 'My favourite actually.'

'Oh... glad to hear it,' Rosie replied, wondering what she was supposed to say to that. Looking across the table, she caught a wry smile on her mum's face.

'Would you like a few more minutes with the menu or have

you decided what you'd like to eat?' he asked, his gaze mostly fixed on Rosie.

'I think we need a bit longer,' she said, glancing at her mum again. *We've been too busy trying to sort my life out to look at the menu.*

'Right... no problem. Grab me when you've decided. My name's Robbie, by the way... just in case you might need to know.'

'Thank you, Robbie,' Glenda said very deliberately.

Rosie tried not to roll her eyes. Now she knew she was getting old, because Robbie seemed like a schoolboy to her. He probably was.

Glenda gave Rosie a triumphant smile as he left them again.

'Mum, he's, like, twelve,' Rosie said with a light laugh.

'Surely you can appreciate a good-looking boy, even if you don't want to go out with him? Allow your ego to be flattered a little.'

'Yeah, but even allowing thoughts with someone that young is practically cradle-snatching.'

'OK. But you're telling me that in the whole time you've been away in Warwickshire you haven't even thought about... well, you haven't seen anyone who takes your fancy?'

'I was kind of busy being a widow.'

'Hmm. There's no need to be sharp; I was just wondering...'

Her mum poured some Prosecco into a glass and Rosie turned to her gin.

It wasn't true of course. There was Kit. Rosie had avoided thinking about him. When he'd popped into her mind she'd pushed him out. It had been easier the last couple of days because she hadn't had to see him every day, but her mum had managed to undo all the progress she'd made in a couple of minutes. Now she couldn't think about anything but him.

Kit was her wrong-place-wrong-time Mr Right. He was the one who might have got away had there ever been any danger of catching him. He was her nearly-was, her almost. And, lately, she was finding that she mourned what might have been with him more than she mourned Fergus – and then the guilt spiral that was keeping her from Kit in the first place would start up all over again.

Rosie was beginning to think there was no help for her.

'I fancy salmon,' her mum said.

Rosie turned her attention back to the menu to choose her lunch. At least here was something she might actually be able to get right.

Once they'd got the awkward interrogation out of the way and the conversation had turned to safer topics – a teacher from Rosie's old school who'd just been awarded an OBE, the new supermarket with no checkouts that Glenda was absolutely never going to set foot in, whether they'd be able to squeeze in some shopping after their lunch and whether they were going to be too squiffy to see straight in the changing rooms – Rosie had started to relax. It had been like old times again, just her and her mum chatting about nothing of consequence and yet every sentence containing hidden meaning and deep affection.

They'd arrived home giggling like schoolgirls, much to the bemusement of her dad, who was already cooking an evening meal that they were both still too full to eat. He made a pot of coffee to sober them up while they told him about their day, ate his dinner and put the rest in the fridge as leftovers, and then they all settled down to watch television together.

Rosie was curled up next to her dad on the sofa as they laughed at a panel show when her phone began to ring. She looked at it with a frown. 'Sorry...' she said vaguely as she got up and started to walk to the kitchen, 'I've got to take this.'

If she'd happened to look back, she'd have seen her parents

exchange a look of misgiving, but she was too preoccupied with the name on the phone screen to notice.

The smell of her dad's beef stew lingered in the kitchen, though the dishes had long since been washed and put away. She sat at the table with the hum of the fridge behind her and darkness beyond the windows and swiped to take the call.

'Tabitha? I didn't expect to hear from you... I mean so soon. Is everything OK? Kit, your mum...?'

'They're fine – we all are. I'm not sure I should be calling at all. I don't even know if you'd need to do anything about it.'

'About what?'

'Nicole's leaving Marigold Marina.'

'Leaving? As in moving away?'

'Looks that way.'

Rosie was silent for a moment. 'I don't understand,' she said finally. 'She has no need to go; I'm not there now. She can get on with her life as before – I thought that was what she wanted. How do you know all this? Have you spoken to her?'

'Apparently she stopped your estate agent after they'd shown someone around your place and asked them to come and value her shop too.'

'Who told you that?'

'The agent did after I...' Tabitha paused.

'After you what?'

'Asked her if anyone had bought Marigold Cafe yet. I suppose I was kind of hoping nobody would be interested and you'd—'

'Have to come back.'

'Sorry. It's just that I miss working there with you. I've got some shifts in a pub to keep me busy until I go to uni, but it's not the same.'

'Didn't you go and talk to Layla and Tom?'

'Yes, but they weren't quite ready to take me on yet. By the time they are I'll probably be gone.'

'Tabitha, I don't know what to say to you.'

'I shouldn't have called; I knew it was a bad idea.'

'No, I'm glad you did. It's good to hear from you.'

'Is it...? I don't know... Does it change anything for you? Are you happy up there now? I suppose you are. Silly question.'

'I'm content. I think that's the best I can hope for.' It was Rosie's turn to take a long pause. 'How's Kit?'

'Quiet,' Tabitha said bluntly. 'He doesn't say but he misses you. I think he'd like a phone call from you.'

'I don't think that's a very good idea. I feel as if I'd make things weird. We left on good terms, in agreement that our paths were just going in different directions now, and I wouldn't want to mess that up.'

But that wasn't the only reason Rosie wanted to continue to stay out of Kit's way. She still felt messed up herself, reeling from what she'd learned about Fergus and the way he'd betrayed her with someone she'd considered a friend, not to mention the epiphany she'd had about the true state of their marriage and just what sort of man he'd been. How could she be good for Kit if she didn't even know who she was or what she wanted? Kit didn't deserve that: he deserved stability, someone who'd be solid, dependable, there for him. Rosie wasn't sure that person was her at all. And it would mean returning to Marigold Marina, the place that held so many mixed memories for her – though the bad seemed to outweigh the good since she'd found out about Fergus and Nicole.

'You wouldn't. It would cheer him up – I know it would.'

'I seriously doubt that, not after everything...'

'He doesn't blame you for any of that. He's accepted it – wrong place, wrong time, that's what he says. Story of his life. Call him, Rosie. He still wants to be your friend.'

'OK,' Rosie said slowly, not convinced at all. 'Maybe... but I don't know when. I still need time to get right.'

'You've been gone for ages.'

'Two days – and it's taken me that long just to stop thinking about milk orders.'

'Are you looking for a house up there?'

'Sort of, but I could do with selling the cafe first really. I don't think that will take long.'

'So... what are you going to do about Nicole?'

Rosie tore the edge from a sharp fingernail and stared at it, her forehead creased into a vague frown. 'Nothing. It's none of my business if she wants to sell up too, is it?'

Tabitha paused. 'Do you still hate her?'

'I never hated her,' Rosie said. 'I felt betrayed and I was hurt, but I never hated Nicole.'

'I would have done.'

'I suppose most people would have. But she told me she loved him and I have no reason to doubt that, and, at the end of the day, she put her feelings aside to help me get through the weeks after Fergus's death. Not many people in her position would have done that. I realise, now I've had time to calm down, how hard that must have been for her.'

'I never thought about it like that. I didn't realise she'd been so crazy about him.'

'I think she must have been. She wouldn't say it if she didn't mean it, especially not to me.'

'I guess...' Tabitha sounded unconvinced.

'Is everything else alright there with you?'

'Everything is the same.'

'Right, so I'm... Say hello to Kit for me, won't you?'

'Yeah, I will. I think you ought to do it really, but...'

'God, please don't... I already feel like a cow. Don't make me feel any worse.'

'I'm not trying to; I'm just being honest. You have to be honest, right?'

Had Kit told Tabitha how Rosie had said those words to

him on the fateful night of Edith's party? Was Tabitha having a dig at her now, using her own words against her?

'I've got to go,' she said, deciding not to dwell on it. There was really no point, whatever Tabitha's intentions. 'Take care.'

'Yeah, I get it. Bye, Rosie.'

'Bye.'

Tabitha cut the call. Rosie watched as the phone screen went black. What was she supposed to do now? Had Tabitha given this information about Nicole thinking she ought to do something about it? Had she hoped it would bring her back to the marina, after all?

Rosie looked around her parents' safe, familiar kitchen. As next steps went, leaving this behind and throwing herself back into that situation might just be a little mad, but that didn't stop her from thinking about it.

CHAPTER NINETEEN

Rosie had to know for sure that what Tabitha had reported to her was what was actually happening, but would the task of finding out open up old wounds again?

While she was enjoying spending time with her parents and was looking forward to revisiting old haunts and seeing old friends over the weeks to come, something wouldn't allow her to feel quite right. She felt like a stranger to the city now, like a visitor, rather than feeling she belonged there. Newcastle was as vibrant and friendly as she'd always remembered it to be and she gazed on landmarks fondly as she made her way around, but something had changed.

It was the feeling of unfinished business still waiting to be resolved at Marigold Marina, she told herself – that was the reason she couldn't settle. Once the cafe had been sold and was no longer her responsibility, that would change.

If only she could actually believe that.

She'd registered with a couple of temping agencies anyway, but the list of jobs they had available did nothing to make her feel any better. Hours and hours of her life sitting in a dusty office somewhere surrounded by people who barely spoke to her – the prospect didn't fill her with joy. She could have changed careers – she had catering experience now, of course, and had run a cafe of her own. Perhaps she could wait tables, or even try for a job as a manager? But she felt that working somewhere like that would only make her think of Marigold Cafe, and that wasn't going to help her get over what she'd left there.

What had she left there? That was the one recurring question that kept bothering her. It was a building, bricks and mortar; it was nothing special. Sure, it was in a beautiful spot – and that was the other thing she was finding hard about being at home. Most of the houses she'd looked at to buy after the sale of the cafe were on residential streets or on estates where her view promised to be more houses just like her own. That beautiful riverbank, the trees, the boats going sedately up and down, the wildlife, the size of the moon as it rose over the river on a summer's evening... those were things that were hard to replace. But even then, she could get used to another street, and she'd learn to love what beauty there was to be had, she was sure. So that couldn't be it either. Could it?

She'd had to chase the idea that it was *someone* and not something from her mind more than once, but she was beginning to wonder why she kept doing that. Was it so wrong to admit that it might be a person making her want to return? Was it so wrong to imagine how that person might have made her happy? If not, why did she keep punishing herself for it?

Perhaps it was a ghost she needed to exorcise. Perhaps if she went back and saw Kit again she'd realise she'd built him up into something he wasn't, that he wasn't the answer to everything and that perhaps it wasn't him she needed – only the promise that her future could be one where she'd move on from Fergus and find love again. Kit represented that, but perhaps that was all he really was to Rosie.

· · ·

It was Rosie's third evening at home, and she was in the kitchen washing up after their evening meal. Just before dinner she'd had a long overdue, awkward conversation with Letitia, having now decided properly that she wasn't going back to Marigold Marina. Letitia had been very understanding and had said she'd appreciate Rosie approaching whoever bought the cafe to see if they could use her services, and they'd left it on amicable terms. That hardly left Rosie feeling good about it though, and as soon as she'd ended the call, she'd started to doubt all the decisions she'd made over the past few weeks concerning the cafe and her life there.

Her parents had both been to work while she'd scoured the job sites for anything that might vaguely appeal, determined to press on regardless now that the die had been cast, increasingly convinced she would have to settle for a job that paid enough to live on and not one that she necessarily liked. She'd put that task to one side to cook for her parents and was just cleaning the kitchen when the sudden impulse to phone Nicole seized her. She wasn't even sure why, but almost as soon as she'd asked herself the question, she decided against it. If it was closure she wanted, phoning Nicole might just reopen newly healing wounds and get her the opposite.

Throughout the day, the conversation she'd had with Tabitha had hummed in her brain, like a wasp stuck at a window that wouldn't fly out. Rosie decided to open the window wide. If she was going to get any peace, she needed to face this head-on.

She was just putting the place mats away when her dad came into the kitchen. 'Need any help, pet? We're sitting in there like lumps of lard – must be like a busman's holiday in here for you.'

Rosie smiled. 'Not for much longer.'

'Ah, yes, of course. Heard anything more from your estate agent?'

In the end, Rosie had also come clean with her dad, who'd seemed far more accepting and far less worried about her decision to sell the cafe than her mum. She'd been grateful for the lack of judgement from him but did wish he'd had more to offer in the way of advice when she'd asked him if he thought she was doing the right thing. 'Whatever you want is fine with me,' was all he'd had to say, and he wouldn't be drawn any further than that.

'Dad,' she said, slowly submitting to a decision that had been threatening to derail the plans she'd been pursuing so steadfastly over the last couple of days. 'I think I might have to go back to the marina for a while.'

'So soon?'

She nodded.

'Is there any reason why you've suddenly come to this conclusion? When we spoke, you said you never wanted to see it again.'

'Well, that was then. I know, I know...' she added in answer to his quizzical look. 'I don't make any sense to me either. I just feel as if I need to answer a question.'

'What question is that?'

'It's not one I can put into words; it's more abstract. Like a question my heart is asking.'

He shook his head. 'I can get your mam if you want to talk abstract; I'm no good at times like these.'

'You're perfect actually. I don't have to explain it to you, which is good because I'm having a hard time explaining it to myself. All I know is I won't truly settle until I've gone back and faced it and made myself face all that I'm giving up. I won't know until I do that I'm making the right choice. Does that make any sense at all? And I feel as if this is it, my one last chance to get it right. I want to do it properly.'

'I suppose it makes a kind of sense.'

'It's just... well, I think now that I was running away from my life there like it was on fire, and now I think it would have been more sensible to check how big the fire was before I did. And, you know, it might have gone out in no time, and I might have thrown the whole thing away when I didn't need to.'

He scratched his head. 'I really ought to get your mam for this.'

Rosie smiled. 'I'll come through with you and tell her myself.'

Rosie's mum had wanted to come with her, but Rosie had insisted that she'd be able to think more clearly on her own. Their support had been welcome, as had their respect for her decision. They'd told her, as they always did, that there was a place for her with them should she decide to return – that there would always be a place for her with them. Whatever she needed, no matter how many times she changed her mind, came and went, it didn't matter – they'd be waiting to support her.

Rosie suspected her mum approved of the choice she was making to go back. She'd be sorry to see Rosie go, she'd said, but she felt Rosie needed to be certain because it would be that much harder to go back once the cafe was sold.

So she now stood with the key in her hand at the door of Marigold Cafe. It was late, dusk was all around and the other businesses had closed up for the day. The usual lights were on – Nicole's upstairs, one or two of the boats, the lamps that lit the paths – but the cafe was in darkness. Rosie could just make out the lettering of the For Sale sign hanging above the door and the signage on the front of what had once been her pride and joy.

She'd stood like this more than a year before, only that time she and Fergus had driven down from Newcastle, picked up the keys from an agent and had let themselves into their new home. They'd walked into a shell of a building, cold and dank: dust-coated equipment, a smashed window and doors that creaked horribly when they were opened. Rosie had burst into tears. She'd been exhausted from the day of packing and the journey down, worked up, terrified of the future they were heading into, and standing in what looked like a hovel had confirmed the very worst of her fears.

Fergus had simply laughed and told her she was overreacting. He'd said she could go and check into a hotel if it bothered her so much but that he was staying put. So she'd made the best of it, slipped into the sleeping bags they'd brought to use until the bedroom was habitable, and had slept on the cafe floor with him, chinks of streetlight showing through the whitewash covering the windows and playing tricks with the shadows on the walls.

It had all seemed better in the morning, of course, and Rosie had rallied. Fergus had never looked so happy – how could she deny him that?

Over the next couple of weeks he seemed to have made friends with everyone, while Rosie watched shyly from the sidelines. It wasn't until after his death that she rediscovered those same people on her own terms, re-forged those relationships so that they meant something to her as an individual and not just as Fergus's wife. He'd always been too big a character, had always filled a room so completely that there'd never been space for her to be noticed.

She recalled now the day Nicole had come to her attention. She'd seen the owner of the gift shop going about her day from afar. Rosie had thought her glamorous and confident and everything she herself wasn't. She envied Nicole's independence. Fergus had told her she'd come out of a divorce with the shop in her name and a defiant attitude. Good for her, he'd said. He admired her strength. She made him laugh and she seemed to say whatever came into her head and didn't care what anyone thought of it. All three of them had started spending time together and so Rosie hadn't thought it strange at all when he'd started to 'pop across' to ask her about one thing or another, or to borrow something from her, and would be missing for hours. They'd be chewing the fat, Rosie had thought as she'd scrubbed a floor or stripped the varnish from a door frame. They had a lot in common and Fergus needed more intellectual stimulation than Rosie alone could give him.

God, she thought that version of herself stupid now. If nothing else, the events of the last few months had changed her, and she hoped for the better. She hoped she was a more mature, stronger Rosie now.

Strong enough to do this? she wondered as she unlocked the door to Marigold Cafe and stepped inside.

It wasn't dark and dank like it had been that first day, but it did have the faint mustiness of a room not used for a while. That would soon disappear once she'd opened some windows and aired the place. Being there felt strangely right, though, after it had felt so wrong. How could that be? Already she felt like ripping down the sheets from the glass and throwing the doors open. She felt like welcoming people in – a week ago she'd never imagined she could feel that way. It was funny what time away to clear one's head could do to change everything. Fergus would have rolled his eyes and told her she'd reacted like the teary, frightened little girl he always said she was.

Angry as she still felt when she thought about him, he would probably have been right.

The truth was her relationship with Fergus, months on from his death, was more complicated now than it ever had been while he was alive. She loved him and hated him, despised him and yet still craved his approval, felt wronged and yet done right by him all at the same time. He'd pushed her where she hadn't wanted to go – she felt both cursed and blessed by that. If he hadn't, she wouldn't have had her sliver of life on Marigold Marina, and whatever that meant, she'd always be grateful she'd had that.

CHAPTER TWENTY

A loud thud outside woke her. It was followed by the sound of scraping metal and Grant's voice: 'Reverse! Don't panic – paint can be put back on... steady now...'

The roar of a boat engine followed. Rosie pulled on a sweatshirt and went to the window. The light hurt her eyes for a moment and she squinted while they adjusted. Then she saw Grant standing at the waterside directing someone in one of his boats – or at least she assumed it was one of his. They were making a pig's ear of navigating it back into the mooring as far as she could tell. Rosie smiled – even she could do better. And maybe she'd even have a go one day. The river looked clean and beautiful in the morning sun. She hadn't noticed the night before as she'd arrived, but Rosie could see now that he'd painted the outside of his boathouse a pearl grey. She approved – it looked good.

Angel's cocktail barge chugged past the melee, Angel looking calm and completely unfazed by the shouting. Business would be good on the riverside in Stratford on a day like today and she probably wouldn't return until nightfall. She'd always done long days and it had never seemed to bother her.

Two couples crossed paths on the riverbank with dogs on leads. The dogs stopped to say hello and the couples exchanged pleasantries before they dragged their reluctant pooches apart and went their separate ways again. A family of four wheeled a bicycle each from Grant's shed and rode off, the kids squealing with delight.

Letting the curtain fall back across the window, Rosie went to find her slippers. Her shabby old bedroom, in desperate need of decoration, still looked shabby and in desperate need of decorating, but she didn't mind so much this morning. Besides, there would be time to worry about that later. There was something she needed to do first.

There was an identical For Sale sign to the one hanging over Rosie's cafe at Nicole's building as Rosie walked past. When Rosie had called them, the agent had sounded disappointed about Rosie coming off the market but said she would be over later that day to take her sign down.

Kit's boat was locked up. It was 10 a.m., so he would normally be open by now. Rosie tried to get a quick look in through the windows to see if there was any sign of life, but all looked quiet. Wherever he was, it wasn't at work. She was about to phone Tabitha to ask if she knew anything when she heard her name being called. She spun round to see Nicole standing at the door of her shop.

'What are you doing here?'

Rosie shrugged. 'Honestly, I'm not sure. I think I'm here to try again but... I'm still not sure.'

'You're opening up the cafe again?'

Rosie nodded.

'That's good,' Nicole said flatly. She pointed to her own For Sale sign. 'You won't have to worry about me for much longer, if that helps to make up your mind.'

'Nicole... whatever else happens, you don't have to leave the marina. I can stay out of your way if you can stay out of mine.'

'You think I'm leaving because of you?'

'Aren't you?'

'No. I've just had enough. This was Ralph's place after all – I've held on to it for far too long.'

Rosie didn't think that was completely true, though she could see the logic in it. Whatever the truth, she let the comment go without questioning it. She was silent for a moment. Her gaze went back to the For Sale sign. 'Just answer me one thing truthfully. Do you really want to do this, or is this because you don't feel you have a choice?'

'Both. But unlike you, when I make up my mind I don't change it. I'm leaving, and I don't want to talk about it again. Now, is there anything I can get you? A fridge magnet? Some fragrance sticks that smell like pine disinfectant layered over old sick? A tea towel with a print of Shakespeare that will wear off the first time you wash it perhaps?' Her bitterness was evident, and it made Rosie look away.

Rosie shook her head. 'No. That's it.'

Rosie turned, and her gaze fell on Kit's boat once more. She must have hesitated without realising, still puzzled by the mystery of where he was, because as she walked away, Nicole spoke again: 'And no, before you ask, I don't know where he is. Frankly, I don't care.'

Rosie looked back, tried to think of something final to say but couldn't and turned once more towards the cafe.

An hour had passed. Rosie kept checking from her window but there was no sign of life on the book barge. While she'd pondered the question, getting herself worked up and then telling herself not to be silly, she'd tried to call Tabitha, but to no avail. She wondered whether to call or text Kit but wasn't sure how she'd even begin a conversation with him, so she decided against it. Then she'd admitted defeat, for a while anyway, and started taking the sheets down from the cafe windows.

She was cleaning the floor when there was a tap at the door. She looked up to see a beaming Grant outside.

'You're back!' he said as she opened up to let him in. 'Are you staying or is this a flying visit?'

'Well...' Rosie leant on her mop. 'I'm being cautiously optimistic at this point, but I think I'm going to stay.'

'That's great news!' Grant said. 'Wait until I tell Mum. She's been so upset – she thought it was all her fault... you know, all that...' He paused and flushed slightly.

Poor Grant. Whoever's fault it might be, it was certainly not his, and Rosie hated to see him so embarrassed. 'There's no need to apologise,' she said. 'My dad always says truth will out – it was bound to come out one way or another, even if it hadn't been from your mum. How is she, by the way? I'm sorry I didn't stay that night—'

'I totally understand. She's absolutely fine – stroppier than ever, which is always a good sign I think.'

'I think so too. Please bring her over next time she's at the marina. She'll be able to see for herself I'm fine, and I'd like to explain what happened at her party. I feel terrible about leaving so early.'

At least Rosie would explain something, though maybe not the whole truth.

'No need,' he said. 'All water under the bridge now. You're here – that's the main thing. There'll be other parties.'

She was quite sure, knowing Grant, that he'd never spoken a truer word than that. She fully expected to be dragged into another pub crawl before the week was out.

'Are you really alright though?' he asked, looking more serious now.

Rosie nodded. 'Never been better. It's amazing what time off will do for you.'

'What's time off?'

Rosie laughed and he gave a smirk that said he knew he'd made headway with his joke.

'It's really good to see you,' Grant said. 'The place hasn't been the same without you and the cafe.'

'Thanks, Grant. It's good to be back.'

'Well' – he stuck his hands in his pockets and nodded at her mop – 'I expect you have a lot to do. I'll leave you to it.'

'There is quite a bit. I'm planning on being open again before the weekend.'

'Ooh, I'll look forward to my bacon bap then.' He turned to leave through the still open door.

'I don't suppose you know where Kit is today?' Rosie asked on impulse.

Grant turned back to her with a puzzled frown. 'I thought you'd know.'

'Know what?'

'Something's happened to his mum.'

'His mum?' Rosie repeated. 'What...? Is she OK?'

'I don't know much about it, only that he's with her at the hospital.'

'When did this happen?'

'Last night I think.'

'How did you...?'

'He phoned to ask if I'd put a sign up on the door of his shop. Didn't say much about it but it sounds bad – must be if he's closed up the barge.'

Rosie realised she hadn't got close enough to see the sign when she'd gone over to visit Nicole. 'Do you know which hospital it is? Do you know if they're still there?'

'I can only assume it's the main one, and I have no idea if they're there. Have you tried calling?'

'No... well, I have tried Tabitha but not Kit.'

'Want me to try him now?'

'Could you? I just want to know he's alright. I don't think they have much in the way of family support, and if this is serious... well, I don't want him struggling alone.'

Grant nodded shortly and dialled the number. 'Kit, it's Grant. I've got Rosie with me... Yes, she's back. I hope I didn't talk out of turn but I've told her about your mum and she wants to know you're alright. Are you still at the hospital? ... I'll tell her, but she won't like it. Keep us posted, eh? Bye.' He ended the call. 'They're still there but he says not to come. He'll see you when he's back at work. Says he's fine, and you don't need to worry.'

'Does he sound fine?'

With a wry smile, Grant shook his head. 'Not really. But what can you do? It's family business... he needs to deal with it and he'll tell everyone else if and when he's able to. All you can do is respect that.'

Rosie was just about to tell him she disagreed and that she knew Kit was just trying to avoid burdening anyone else, and that she had about as much intention of respecting that as she had running for prime minister, when her own mobile began to ring.

'Tabitha,' Rosie said briskly as she took the call. 'We've just spoken to Kit. Grant has anyway. What's going on?'

Tabitha sounded tired, her voice thick with emotion. 'It's Mum. Had one of her meltdowns again. I think... I think it's my fault. I'd just got notification of a place at uni through clearing but it's not at Warwick – it's at Sheffield. I should have waited for the right moment before I told her but I was excited... It's only two hours on the train and I thought... I realise now I should have asked her how she'd feel about it before I accepted the place. Things went downhill from there – I don't know what to do.' Her voice broke on the last few words and Rosie felt her own eyes well in sympathy.

'Are you at the hospital now?'

'I'm outside. Kit is in with her. He told me to get some air and then I saw your missed calls. Where are you? How did you know...?'

'I'm at the marina with Grant.'

'Oh,' Tabitha said, obviously too exhausted and distracted to question any further.

'I was going to come over. Thought you could do with the support.'

'I'd like that.'

'It's just that Kit said no—'

'Ignore him. He's just doing that brave man thing. It would do him good to see you – he's so down right now and this has made things a million times worse.'

'I'll get to you just as soon as I can. I'll call so you can meet me at the entrance – is that OK?'

'Yes.'

'See you shortly.' Rosie ended the call and turned to Grant. 'I'm going to the hospital. I don't know how to get there, though – can you tell me?'

'It'll be quicker if I drive you over. Hold on here and I'll go and get my car.'

They were there within the hour. Grant left at Rosie's insistence so he could get back to work. Chris was holding the fort but wouldn't be able to for long. Rosie told him she'd get a taxi back.

She didn't need to phone as Tabitha was already outside the hospital, sitting on a bench near the entrance when Rosie arrived. The early sun had disappeared and now there was a brisk wind sending granite clouds scudding across the sky. It felt like there was rain in the air, but Tabitha didn't seem bothered by the ominous skies or her hair whipping around her face. She'd obviously been crying. Rosie wondered how many hours she might have been crying for – quite possibly it had been the whole night. She hated to see her friend so distraught, and to feel so powerless to do anything about it.

When Tabitha looked up and saw Rosie, she flew from her seat and ran to hug her. 'It's so good to see you.'

'You too,' Rosie said. 'Want to fill me in before we go inside? What should I expect? How bad is it?'

'She took an overdose. We caught her in time thank goodness. She's been treated and she's recovering now.'

'So that's good news,' Rosie said in the most encouraging tone she could muster.

'Kit doesn't want to leave her; he doesn't want her to wake up alone. I feel so bad but I just couldn't...'

'Everyone deals with situations differently. And if you feel like the cause of it, that's even harder. Don't beat yourself up. You're here doing your best.'

'I should never have accepted that stupid place.' Tabitha sniffed.

'You shouldn't think like that. I'm sorry to say it, but this would probably have happened anyway.' Rosie gave her friend a kind smile. 'If not that, something else would have set it off. The root cause doesn't go away just because you try to stop life upsetting her, and you can't control everything that happens, no matter what you do.'

'That's what Kit says.'

'There you go then. We all know Kit's a smart Alec.'

Tabitha gave a watery smile. 'I'm glad you're here.'

'Let's hope Kit feels the same way,' Rosie said. 'Want to lead the way?'

'You might not be allowed into her room, but I'll bring him out to you if you're not. He needs a break anyway.'

'Will you be alright going back in?'

'I will now I know you're here.'

'I don't know what *I* can do, but if it helps in any way then...'

'You don't need to do anything. It'll cheer him up just to see you.'

Rosie wasn't so sure about that when she recalled how she'd left things with him, but she gave a stiff smile.

They didn't say much more as they walked the corridors to the ward where Tabitha's mum was being cared for. When they got there Tabitha spoke to a nurse, confirming what she'd suspected – that Rosie wouldn't be allowed in as she wasn't immediate family and they had a limit on outside visiting hours – and then she went into the room to fetch Kit.

She was gone for at least five minutes. Rosie waited at the nursing desk feeling conspicuous. More than once she was asked what she needed and had to explain that she was waiting for someone.

Just when she'd given up on him, Kit emerged from the room.

'Hey,' he said. 'You didn't have to come.'

'I know you said not to. I'm sorry, I just—'

'I might have guessed you'd come anyway,' he said flatly.

'You look shattered. Have you been here all night?'

'Pretty much.'

'Tabitha filled me in.'

'That's good.'

'Kit... I'm so sorry to hear about all this.'

He gave a vague shrug. 'Yeah...'

'Tabitha isn't coping well, is she?'

Kit dragged a hand through his hair. 'I keep telling her it's not her fault. She's going to blame herself whatever I say. I just hope this doesn't put her off going.'

'To university? Me too. I think she'd regret it.'

'Trust me, I know she would.'

Rosie recalled how he'd given up his own place when his mum had first become ill. She would have expected some bitterness in his tone when he spoke of it now, but there was none; there was only a weary resignation that broke her heart to hear. She'd only ever known her Kit – the carefree optimist, everyone else's crutch, not this broken and sad Kit. But she realised now that this Kit was the one Tabitha had told Rosie about, the one who kept trying and trying for his best life but never seemed to get a break. There was nothing Rosie could do to change that, but she dearly wished she could. She'd give anything to have her Kit back again.

'I think I saw a canteen down the hall,' she said. 'Want to get a coffee?'

'At this point I'll take anything that keeps me awake.'

'Maybe you should go home and get some rest.'

'I can't. I can't leave in case she wakes.'

'Tabitha says she's able to stay with her now for a while, and I can't go in but I can be outside for her if she needs some moral support. Everything would be fine for an hour or so if you wanted a break. I don't mind waiting for as long as I need to.'

'I can't ask you to do that, but coffee does sound good right now.'

They began to walk the corridor.

'Why are you here?' he asked after a few moments of silence.

'I was at the marina when—'

'No – *why are you here*? At the hospital, right now? It's not that I'm not pleased to see you, but this is tough enough for us. You shouldn't be putting yourself through it.'

'It's what friends do, isn't it?'

He said nothing more about it and they were silent once more. They found the canteen and Kit went to get some seats while Rosie bought two coffees. When she found him again he'd nodded off, his head resting on his folded arms on the table in front of him, his dark curls spilling over his face. Rosie was struck by the sudden urge to run her fingers over them. She hesitated for a second and then decided to wake him. She figured he'd be annoyed if she let him sleep.

'Kit...' she said gently. 'Your drink.'

He looked up, confused and bleary for a moment, and then broke into a smile, as if he'd forgotten where he was and why he was there. He continued to smile up at her while she placed his cup in front of him. 'I can't understand why you'd do this for us but I'm glad you're here,' he said.

She sat across from him. 'You'd have done it for me.'

He'd have done anything for Rosie – wasn't that what Tabitha had once said? It was only fair she had his back in return. And despite the stress and the circumstances, Rosie wouldn't be anywhere else right now, even if she thought she had a choice. To have someone let you in like Kit was letting her in right then was an honour, a gift not to be taken lightly.

And Rosie didn't take it lightly at all, especially after what had gone on between them.

Kit held his coffee in one hand while the other rested on the table. Rosie reached for it, wrapping her fingers around his. He didn't pull away and he didn't speak.

They stayed that way for the next ten minutes. One of them would sip their drink or notice someone come into the canteen or gaze out of the window at the darkening skies, but they didn't say a word.

Eventually Kit finished his coffee. He looked at Rosie. 'I should get back.'

'So soon?'

'I want to be there when Mum wakes up if I can. Listen, could you do me a favour and look after Tabitha for me? Get her to eat something, maybe even persuade her to go home?'

'She could stay with me if that helps.'

'At the cafe?'

Rosie gave a small smile. 'That's where I live now.'

He paused, a faint look of confusion on his face as his brain caught up with the information she was offering. 'Wait – you're back for good?'

'That's the plan.'

A tired smile spread across his face. 'I'll get Tabitha to come and find you.'

'Anything you like. Whatever you need, I'm here.'

He gave one last nod and turned to go. Rosie watched him leave the canteen with slow, weary steps.

Sometimes it took something like this, some monumental test, some terrifying adversity, to force a person to look inside and figure out what really mattered. During the ten or so minutes Rosie had sat silently with Kit, she'd done just that, and there was no hiding from the truth.

She loved him.

Of course she couldn't say so, not now, not in this situation.

Wasn't it just like her to find the worst possible time to make up her mind?

CHAPTER TWENTY-ONE

Kit's shop had been closed for a further two days. In that time, the For Sale sign had come down at Marigold Cafe and word had got round the marina that Rosie was back to stay. She'd never been so popular: almost everyone had been in to see her – it didn't matter that she wasn't officially open yet.

She'd wanted to wait until she'd had word that Kit and Tabitha's mum was home and recovering before she did that. She wanted to be on hand if they needed her again. She figured she'd be able to manage financially for a little longer on what was left of Fergus's money and didn't see the point in rushing. There were more important things than the cafe after all.

It was raining when Tabitha arrived at the cafe to catch up with how Rosie was getting on settling down at the marina again, and to fill her in on what was going on with her mum. Despite Rosie offering her a bed in her flat over the cafe, Tabitha had wanted to go home and get the house ready for her mum's return, and Rosie respected that – she'd have done the same. Tabitha shook out her umbrella at the door now before going to sit at a table Rosie had already prepared with cups and plates of sandwiches and cake.

Tabitha smiled. 'You can't help catering, even when the cafe is closed.'

Rosie locked the grey murk outside and came over to join her. Even though it was summer, the damp weather had made the air chilly and Rosie had put on a little fan heater. It chugged and whirred away in the background as Tabitha got up from her chair briefly to take off her coat and give Rosie a hug before sitting down again and helping herself to tea from the pot.

'So, how's everything?' Rosie asked, taking the pot from her to pour herself a drink.

'Well, Mum's out and she's got a referral now for help, so things are going in the right direction...' Tabitha spooned some sugar into her cup. 'We're being cautious but hopeful. Personally, I think this was the make or break one for Mum. It was bad this time and I think even she recognises it, which is half the battle, because it's the first time she's recognised that she really needs help. I think she'll stick with the sessions. Of course, Kit and I will have to keep a close eye on things, but I think it might be time for us all to try and get back to something a bit like normal.'

'What does that mean for you?' Rosie sipped at her tea.

'Well, Kit's going to reopen the barge.'

'He thinks she'll be OK while he's there?'

'He'll probably phone, like, every ten minutes, but he can't do a lot else. He's got to start earning again and she's going to have to fend for herself sooner or later. It sounds harsh but—'

'No, it doesn't. It sounds realistic. I'm sure your mum can see that.'

'I hope so. The good thing is, as I'm only working at the pub in the evenings I can be there for a large chunk of the day, unless...' Tabitha raised a cheeky eyebrow at Rosie, who smiled ruefully.

'You know I'd have you back if I could, but I checked with

Letitia and she's much better now and ready to start work. In fact, I kind of owe her for messing her around so much. Sorry.'

'Yeah, I know... it's probably for the best anyway. So I can be with Mum most days, and Kit can do most evenings, and we should be able to keep things on an even keel until, hopefully, Mum can keep things on an even keel by herself.'

'And your plans haven't changed? Still going to Sheffield?'

'Kit's adamant that I should. I feel a bit guilty leaving him with the responsibility but he said – and I quote – "I've failed you as a brother if I let you waste all that potential, so I'm going to bully you until you say you're going."'

Rosie smiled as she reached for a sandwich. 'He's absolutely convinced you're not going to miss out like he did.'

'So...' Tabitha said wryly, 'I take it he's also told you to talk me out of it if I look like I'm going to back out?'

'He might have done,' Rosie said.

'Typical Kit. Well, you don't need to worry. I can't say I'm massively happy about leaving things, but there's a couple of months to go before I have to move and for now, things seem calm again, so I haven't changed my plans as yet.'

'You're not to change them at all.'

'So Kit says.'

'So *I* say too.'

Tabitha grinned. 'Thanks, Rosie. But if I have to go, then you have to promise to stay this time. And if you and Kit don't—'

'Tabitha...' Rosie warned.

'Aw, come on! You two are made for each other! There's absolutely no reason now for you to stay apart! Make me believe in true love again!'

Rosie laughed lightly. 'I wouldn't go that far. I don't think it's fair to Kit to rush it, to be honest. I rejected him once and he was pretty hurt, and now there's all this... I don't want to add to it.'

'You won't be adding – you'll be making it better. He's still nuts about you.'

'He said that?'

'No, but he doesn't need to. I'm the person who knows him best, remember? I'm telling you – he won't ask you because he doesn't want to push you like before, but if you ask him he'll be there like a shot.'

'Maybe...' Rosie said thoughtfully. 'I'll think about it.'

Tabitha wasn't the only person to stick to her plans. Nicole's For Sale sign stayed firmly nailed to the front of her shop, and though Rosie felt a little bad for her, she understood that it probably needed to happen for all their sakes.

Rosie was strangely nervous as she unlocked the door of Marigold Cafe on her first morning of reopening. It was like opening for the first time all over again.

Letitia was in the kitchen prepping the day's food while Rosie went to the counter to line up cups and pots, ready for the first teas of the day.

The first customer was Kit. At least, he was the first person through the door – whether he'd come to buy something or just to say hello Rosie had no idea, but it was typical that it would be him.

'Come to order my sandwich,' he said cheerfully.

'Well!' Rosie looked at him and smiled. 'You look a thousand times better than when I last saw you.'

'Thank you... I think.'

'It's definitely a compliment.' Rosie leant on the counter and regarded him fondly. He looked rested, relaxed, more like his old self and – although he hadn't made any special effort – more handsome than she'd ever seen him look.

'So this sandwich?' she added. 'What do you want on it?'

'Guess.'

Rosie grinned. He grinned too. He reached the counter, still grinning as he rested his hands on it in front of hers. He was so close she could...

'Kit,' she said in a more serious tone, 'I want to ask you something.'

'OK,' he said uncertainly, his grin fading. 'Ask – you know you can say anything to me now.'

'OK.' Rosie paused and looked at him. 'Could we start again?'

Kit frowned. 'I don't know what you mean.'

'Go back to the beginning, you and me. Forget all the crap that happened in between and pretend we're brand new, meeting for the first time.'

'Like... totally back to the beginning? Forget everything? Because there are some bits I'd definitely want to keep.'

'Maybe we'd keep a few bits then. But would that work? Could we?'

'Hmm,' he said slowly. 'I'm not sure how it would work but I guess we could try. It's the least I can do after you stood by me and Tabitha.' He stuck out his hand with a smile. 'I'm Kit. I own the book barge across the way.'

'Pleased to meet you, Kit,' she said, shaking his hand. 'I'm Rosie. This is my cafe.'

'Nice cafe. I like it – makes good sandwiches.'

'Thank you.'

'You're welcome.'

'I like your hat.'

'Thanks, I quite like it too. I like your hair.'

'I like your jacket.'

'It's very nice of you to say so.' He peered behind the counter. 'Cool boots.'

'Thanks. I think so.' She grinned broadly. 'So, Kit...' She paused. Their game had been fun but there had been a point. It was time to get to it. 'I was wondering... I don't suppose you fancy a drink sometime?'

He frowned again. 'Wait... you and me?'

'No, you and Grant.'

He let out a soft chuckle. 'I could take my custom elsewhere if you're going to be sarky.'

'You could but you wouldn't.'

'True. A drink, huh?'

He held her gaze while her stomach turned itself inside out. Surely he wasn't going to turn her down? What if he was going to say no? She wasn't sure she'd ever be able to look him in the eye again, which was a shame, because he had very nice eyes.

And suddenly her thoughts were all over the place. It was too soon. He'd been rejected by her before, how could he know to trust her this time not to hurt him again? This had been a bad idea – what the hell was wrong with her?

'I'd like that,' he said softly. 'What are you doing later?'

Relief and now anticipation flooded through her. 'Tonight? But your mum—'

'It's Tab's night off; she'll sit with her if I tell her why. She spent long enough trying to make it happen after all. So...?' He waited for her answer, his eyes never leaving hers, sending her into a delicious tailspin as she plunged into their depths.

'It looks like I'm going for a drink later,' she said with a smile so wide she felt it would be stuck there forever.

CHAPTER TWENTY-TWO

'Seriously, are you even trying?'

'Of course I'm trying!' Rosie huffed, swallowing a mouthful of water as she did. She'd probably ingested about a million gnats, some algae and maybe some microscopic water creatures too, but she tried not to think about that.

'Kick harder!'

'I'll kick you in a minute!'

Kit chuckled as he pulled her gently along the surface of the water. Every muscle in Rosie's body ached already and they'd only been at it for fifteen minutes. How did Kit make it look so effortless? Even swimming backwards and supporting her he didn't break a sweat.

'That's it – come on! You're going now!'

'I'm... not... going!'

'You are! Watch – I'll let go and you'll be swimming.'

'No!' she squealed.

'Seriously, there's nothing to be scared of. I'm here; I've got you.'

'You were going to let go!'

'Because holding on to me is making you more scared. Just

let go and swim – there's nothing to worry about.'

'It's not the swimming that's worrying me; it's the not swimming that's freaking me out. What if I go under?'

'You won't.'

'I will!'

'I'm going to let go...'

'No, Kit, please!'

He tried to loosen his grip but Rosie clung on, wrapping her fingers around his in a white-knuckle grip.

'Come on,' he said with an encouraging smile, moving right into her eyeline. 'You trust me, right?'

'It's me I don't trust. More specifically, my weakling arms and legs.'

'Rosie – I would never ask you to let go if I didn't think you'd be alright, would I?'

'I suppose not.'

'Then...' He tried again to pull his fingers from her grip. For a few seconds she resisted, but then she took a huge breath as if she was getting ready to dive. Then she let go. She started to thrash about, a desperate doggy paddle towards him as he moved backwards.

There was no way it could have been a good look.

'Yes!' he shouted, clapping his hands. 'That's it!'

There was a moment of triumph, where Rosie thought she'd nailed it, but then it all went horribly wrong and her head disappeared beneath the water. His hands were round her waist in an instant, pulling her back up.

'I told you!' she spluttered.

He gently wiped water from her eyes and kissed her lightly. 'But you were swimming. You only stopped because you thought you weren't.'

Rosie coughed. 'That makes no sense at all.'

He held her at arm's length once more. 'Legs up, back straight – I've got you.'

'I'm worn out.'

'We've hardly started.'

'I want a pint.'

'Diversion tactics won't work – even if you're using my favourite thing against me.'

'I thought I was your favourite thing.'

'Alright, second favourite. Legs up, come on.'

'Kit...'

'You wanted me to teach you to swim; you can't change your mind when things get tough.'

'Fine.' She blew out a breath and began to kick towards him again.

'Let the water carry your weight... that's it, you're a natural.'

'Now... I... know... you're... lying,' she panted.

Then he stopped and pulled her across the water and into his arms. 'I'd never lie to you, Rosie. I will always be honest with you.'

She narrowed her eyes, a smile about her lips. 'Are you using my words against me again?'

'Not exactly. More like paraphrasing. That's alright, isn't it?'

Pulling her closer still, he kissed her again, more deeply this time. 'Even if I tried to lie to you, you'd see right through me. I wouldn't want to anyway – you know I have too much respect for you.'

'I *would* see through you,' she agreed. He kissed her a third time. 'And you'd do well to remember that.'

He smiled down at her. 'Ready to try again?'

'See, now you've ruined my flow by kissing me. I just want to kiss again.'

'Swim now, kisses later – if you're good.'

'Ugh! I've swallowed so much water. Couldn't we have done this in a proper pool?'

'You said you wanted to broaden your horizons and push

yourself to do new things.'

'I meant like trying a new flavour of crisp.'

'I picked a good spot, didn't I? It's nice and gentle and way less crowded than any public pool.'

'What about the fish? They don't have fish in public pools. Or bugs or pondweed.'

'Fish and bugs don't cannonball when you're trying to do a length in peace. They're far better pool buddies than a bus full of schoolchildren.'

'It's Saturday – they're not at school.'

'Funny. You have an answer for everything, don't you?'

'That's rich coming from you! You're the king of answers for everything!'

He grinned. 'Why, thank you.' And then he leant in and kissed her again, longer and harder this time, so that her insides fizzed.

'I knew I could make you kiss me again,' she whispered. 'And I didn't even have to try. Now, why don't we get out of the water so we can really do some damage?'

A voice came from the bank. 'Jesus! Do you have to do that in public?'

They looked around to see Tabitha settle on the grass at the riverside.

'How did you get all the way out here?' Kit asked with a grin. 'I've got the car.'

'Motorbike,' she replied airily. 'Had you forgotten about that?'

'I still can't believe Mum is letting you ride that. She'd never have let me have a motorbike at your age.'

'Maybe she just thinks I'm a better rider.'

'Yeah, you carry on believing that.'

'Anyway' – Tabitha yanked a blade of grass from the ground and twirled it round in her fingers – 'I'm an adult. She couldn't very well stop me.'

'If I'd been allowed a say, I would have stopped you.'

Tabitha grinned. 'You and whose army?'

Kit unconsciously pulled Rosie closer, though he continued to regard Tabitha. It was a protective gesture and she knew it stemmed from a desire to protect everyone who meant anything to him, so much so that he didn't often know he was doing it. 'I suppose it means you'll be able to get home more often if you have transport. Have you done all your paperwork then? Student loan, accommodation, new GP, dentist...?'

'Yes, Dad. It's all under control.' She looked at Rosie and rolled her eyes. 'Have you managed to get any swimming in or has he been sucking your face off since you got here?'

'God, you're annoying!' Kit fired at his sister.

'I have,' Rosie said, laughing. 'He's a very good teacher actually.'

Kit turned back to her. 'You said I was a terrible teacher!'

'I'm not going to let your head get any bigger, am I?' She nudged him playfully. 'I'm ready for a rest. I'm a bit cold now too.'

He swept her into his arms and began to wade to the bank.

'What? Was it that shallow all along?' Rosie asked, regarding the water with an accusatory look.

'Of course. You didn't think I'd take you to a deep bit, did you?'

'But I... I was panicking when I could stand up in it the whole time!'

'Ah, but if you'd known that you wouldn't have tried to swim.'

'You wouldn't have wanted to put your feet down if you knew what was beneath them anyway,' Tabitha said. 'Mud and all sorts. Better off keeping them out of it.'

'Easily washed off in the river,' Kit said. 'Keep your nose out, Tab.'

Tabitha grinned, and when Kit lifted Rosie up to the riverbank, his sister stretched out a hand to help her climb out. They'd left towels spread out on the grass ready, and Rosie flopped onto hers and gathered it around her shoulders. Kit followed, his curls dripping little rivers of their own onto his chest. He lay back on his towel with a contented sigh. 'Not a cloud up there.'

Tabitha lay back too. 'It's weird, I never realised how much I was going to miss this place. I want to go to uni, of course, but I'll miss having all this on my doorstep.'

'It's not forever,' Kit said. 'At least, you'd better be coming back.'

'What, leave you to fend for yourself?' Tabitha asked. 'Like I could do that.'

Rosie leant back and joined them on the ground to stare up into a clear blue August sky. 'I envy your big adventure,' she said.

'You could go,' Kit said.

Rosie laughed. 'To university?'

'Why not? What's stopping you?'

'Plenty. I'm way past it, I have a business to run and... oh yeah, I'm not brainy enough.'

'They are only things you choose to let stop you,' Kit said to her, mock-severely. 'I think we've established by now, Rosie Ross, that you can do anything you set your mind to.'

'Don't be daft.'

'Of course you can,' he said.

'Well, thank you for believing in me. I think you might be on your own, though.'

'I agree with Kit,' Tabitha said. 'Look at what you've done by yourself just this year. You must be a bit proud.'

'There were plenty of wobbles on the way.'

'But you did it.'

'I've always believed you could do anything,' Kit said gently.

'From the very first moment I met you. Give yourself some credit.'

A slow smile crept across Rosie's face. She could do anything? Kit really believed that? Was that as crazy as it seemed? The longer she was at Marigold Marina, the more she believed it herself. Going there had changed her life in so many ways. While Fergus had sought to hold her back and make her dependant on him, the irony was that by bringing her here, he'd given her freedom. Kit had helped her find that freedom – or at least see that she could have it. He'd never talked down to her, never tried to make her need him; he'd shown her she could be the best version of herself and she didn't need anyone else to make that happen. In his own quiet, humble way he'd shown her that she needn't accept boundaries and that nobody ought to dictate who she was – not even him, and she loved him for that. He'd given her a gift bigger than he could ever appreciate, more than his love, more than his need to protect her.

He'd given her self-belief.

Now she knew she could tackle anything, and if she had to do it alone then she could do that too. But there was another irony. Kit had taught her she could do it alone, only now she wouldn't want to. She'd always want Kit at her side.

She turned to look at him and their eyes met. Lying on the grass, side by side, they both smiled. Neither of them needed to say how much love they shared; all they needed to do was this. Rosie saw it in every fleck of brown in his midnight eyes; she saw it in every line as his face crinkled into a smile and she never had to question it, never had to doubt it.

'That's enough of that.' Tabitha sat up and looked down at them both. 'Pub?'

Kit leant up onto his elbows and grinned, then looked at Rosie. 'Pub?'

'Pub,' Rosie said, turning her face to the perfect sky with a deep, contented sigh. 'Sounds good to me.'

A LETTER FROM TILLY

I want to say a huge thank you for choosing to read *The Cafe at Marigold Marina*. If you did enjoy it and want to keep up to date with all my latest releases, just sign up at the following link. Your email address will never be shared and you can unsubscribe at any time.

www.bookouture.com/tilly-tennant

I'm so excited to share this book with you. I've wanted to write it for some time, especially as aspects of Rosie's journey feel very personal to me, but for one reason or another, it didn't happen – until now. I'm so glad I finally got to tell Rosie's story.

I hope you enjoyed *The Cafe at Marigold Marina* and if you did I would be very grateful if you could write a review. I'd love to hear what you think, and it makes such a difference helping new readers to discover one of my books for the first time.

I love hearing from my readers – you can get in touch on my Facebook page, through Twitter, Goodreads or my website.

Thanks,

Tilly

HEAR MORE FROM TILLY

https://tillytennant.com

 facebook.com/TillyTennant
twitter.com/TillyTenWriter

ACKNOWLEDGEMENTS

I say this every time I come to write acknowledgements for a new book, but it's true: the list of people who have offered help and encouragement on my writing journey so far really is endless and it would take a novel in itself to mention them all. I'd try to list everyone here regardless, but I know that I'd fail miserably and miss out someone who is really very important. I just want to say that my heartfelt gratitude goes out to each and every one of you, whose involvement, whether small or large, has been invaluable, and is appreciated more than I can express.

It goes without saying that my family bears the brunt of my authorly mood swings, but when the dust has settled, I'll always appreciate their love, patience and support. The coronavirus pandemic has meant it has continued to be a strange and difficult time for pretty much everyone on the planet, and though our everyday freedoms have been curtailed, I'm seriously thankful to have my writing to escape into. My family and friends understand better than anyone how much I need that space and they love me enough to enable it, even when it puts them out. I have no words to express fully how grateful and blessed that makes me feel.

I also want to mention the many good friends I have made – and since kept – at Staffordshire University. It's been ten years since I graduated with a degree in English and creative writing but hardly a day goes by when I don't think fondly of my time there. Nowadays, I have to thank the remarkable team at Book-outure for their continued support, patience and amazing publishing flair, particularly Lydia Vassar-Smith – my incredible and long-suffering editor – Kim Nash, Noelle Holten, Sarah Hardy, Peta Nightingale, Alexandra Holmes and Jessie Botterill. (I know I'll have forgotten someone else at Bookouture who I ought to be thanking, but I hope they'll forgive me.) Their belief, able assistance and encouragement mean the world to me. I truly believe I have the best team an author could ask for.

My friend, Kath Hickton, always gets an honourable mention for putting up with me since primary school, while Louise Coquio deserves a medal for getting me through university and suffering me ever since – likewise, her lovely family. I also have to thank Mel Sherratt, who is as generous with her time and advice as she is talented, and is someone who is always there to cheer on her fellow authors. She did so much to help me in the early days of my career that I don't think I'll ever be able to thank her as much as she deserves.

I'd also like to give a shout-out to Holly Martin, Tracy Bloom, Emma Davies, Jack Croxall, Carol Wyer, Angie Marsons, Sue Watson and Jaimie Admans: not only brilliant authors in their own right but hugely supportive of others. My Bookouture colleagues are all incredible of course, unfailing and generous in their support of fellow authors – life would be a lot duller without the gang! I have to thank all the brilliant and dedicated book bloggers (there are so many of you but you know who you are!) and readers, and anyone else who has championed my work, reviewed it, shared it or simply told me that they liked it. Every one of those actions is priceless and you are all very special people. Some of you I am even proud to call friends now – I'm looking at you in particular, Kerry Ann Parsons and Steph Lawrence!

Last but not least, I'd like to give a special mention to my lovely agent, Madeleine Milburn, and the team at the Madeleine Milburn Literary, TV & Film Agency, especially Liv Maidment and Rachel Yeoh, who always have my back.

CPSIA information can be obtained
at www.ICGtesting.com
Printed in the USA
BVHW042206050622
638987BV00012B/54